Still Water
Runs Deep

MARIANNE GUTTERIDGE

Seattle, Washington
Portland, Oregon
Denver, Colorado
Vancouver, B.C.

ISBN 0-89716-610-8
LOC 95-071986
13.0026
Cover design: David Marty
Editing & Production: Elizabeth Lake

First printing February 1996
10 9 8 7 6 5 4 3 2 1

Peanut Butter Publishing
226 2nd Avenue West • Seattle, WA 98119
Old Post Office Bldg. • 510 S.W. 3rd • Portland, OR 97201
Cherry Creek • 50 S. Steele • Suite 850 • Denver, CO 80209
e mail: P NUT PUB@aol.com
Printed in the United States of America

I dedicate this book to my mother
Anna Elvera Backstrom Brown
(called Vera)
who started her teaching career
in the country schools of Iowa
and who gave me the background
information which made
this book possible.

Chapter One

It was the last week of August 1922, in the state of Iowa. The weather was oppressively hot and humid. For six weeks there had been no let-up; the corn was growing splendidly; the people were wilting. Women dabbed at their faces with a handkerchief or the skirt of their apron, many of them standing over a hot cook stove canning the garden's produce. Men walked slowly from the fields, sweat running down their necks and faces, anxious to get in for a cool drink.

Anna Swenson waited with her mother and sister Elsa on the station platform in Fort Dodge. She was twenty years old and embarking on her first job as a school teacher. Though she was rather old to be starting as a teacher, circumstances had not been easy after her father died, leaving her mother with the two girls. They had managed to eke out a living, but just barely. Now that Elsa was through high school she could take Anna's place and help full time with her mother's dressmaking and alterations business. Anna always wanted to be a teacher, saving every penny to attend the Cedar Falls Normal College. This summer she was fortunate enough to be able to do it, and completed the twelve-week course. A week ago the news came that she had passed the state boards. Now the job in Grabney was hers.

Mrs. Swenson took a clean white handkerchief from her purse and patted the perspiration from her face. Anna fidgeted with the ruffles on the bodice of her dress as she looked anxiously around the platform.

"What's the matter Anna? Is something wrong?" her mother asked.

"I don't see my trunk. Do you think they forgot about it? It should be on the platform by this time. The train will be coming in a few minutes. Shall I go look for it?"

"No, you stay here. Elsa, hurry into the station and see if Anna's trunk is there."

As Elsa disappeared into the station, Mrs. Swenson looked with some degree of uneasiness at her daughter. "Anna, be sure to keep your valise with you. When the train pulls in, grab it, because the porters will want to help you up into the train and then you will have to pay them a tip. I don't know how much a tip is, but we can't afford to pay it. The valise is not so heavy."

"Oh, no. I can manage fine."

"And when you get into the car, you can put it beside you on the seat. There should be plenty of room."

"Yes, I think so. It doesn't look like many people are traveling in this weather. Oh, I see my trunk. A man is pushing it on a cart. Now where is Elsa?"

"Here she comes."

Elsa appeared to look rather worried. "I can't find her trunk anywhere. Oh, there it is, just in time too. Isn't that the train whistle?"

"I think so," replied Anna. "It seems to be coming from the east." She quickly checked her purse for her ticket, found it and kept it in her right hand, closing the purse.

"Put your ticket back, Anna," Mrs. Swenson advised. "You won't need it until the conductor comes by to check them after the train starts. Make sure he understands you are to get off at Grabney. It doesn't always stop there you know."

"Yes mother, and I hope that they remember to take my trunk off there too."

"You be sure to check when you get off, and if they don't have your trunk tell them to get it. I don't want your trunk to get lost."

Anna put her ticket back into her purse and carefully shut it. This was the moment of suspenseful waiting. It was only the second time she had left her family. The first was earlier in the year when she had taken the bus to Cedar Falls to stay with Mrs. Phipps who ran a rooming house for girls attending the normal school. She knew more or less what to ex-

2

pect at the college, but this time everything was unknown. The situation had come up at the last minute when the Grabney teacher had quit to get married, and Anna wouldn't have been offered the position if her Uncle Lars had not known the superintendent of the county schools.

"Oh, Anna, here comes the train," called Elsa. "I hope you have nice people to live with, and that they have nice children, and that you don't have to walk too far to school, and that..."

"Hush, hush Elsa," scolded her mother. "Now look Anna, if there are any problems you write and tell me, and Uncle Lars will do something about it I am sure. You have the two cent stamped envelopes I bought you?"

"Yes, they are in my purse."

"Don't look for them now. Grab your valise. We can't get on the train with you because it doesn't stop long enough."

With that remark the locomotive thundered past them, rendering conversation impossible. The train slowed and halted. It was a walk of about twenty paces to the door of the coach. The three women hurried with Mrs. Swenson in the lead, followed by Elsa, and last by Anna, lugging her valise which was slightly overweight with several books.

"Help you with that case ma'am," called the red cap.

"No thank you," replied Anna panting, "I can manage." She dragged it up the steps taking them slowly, resting the case on each one, and feeling quite uncomfortable as the porter eyed her every movement.

"Get a seat now Anna, in there," called her mother, pointing to the coach.

Anna trudged through the doorway and into the aisle. Fortunately the first seat was unoccupied, and it was also on the depot side, so she heaved her valise onto it. Her mother and sister were watching through the grimy window, which she now attempted to open by pulling up on the handles. It was stuck and wouldn't budge even though she exerted as much strength as she could muster.

"Hurry up," yelled Elsa. "The train will be leaving."

"I can't!" Anna called back frantically.

At that moment another voice was heard. "Here, let me help you with that ma'am." A young man pushed past her and with a mighty heave, forced open the window. "Hot weather does that, plus all this humidity," he nodded to her before returning to his seat on the other side of the aisle.

After Anna had recovered from her surprise at this assistance, she noticed Elsa giggling into her hand.

"Tell him thank you Anna," remonstrated her mother.

She turned to the stranger, "Thank you very much," which he acknowledged with another nod.

"Do you have a good seat?"

"Yes, mother. It is fine."

"Before you sit down check to see if it is dirty. You don't want to arrive with your new dress soiled. And before you get there, straighten your hair, and see that your hat is not crooked. Let me see your gloves. Are they still clean?"

"Yes," Anna replied as she held out her hands for her mother's inspection.

"When will you be coming back?" ventured Elsa.

"At Christmas. That's the first vacation."

"What about the fall harvesting vacation?" queried Elsa.

"I don't know if they have one."

"They all have one."

"But maybe they have young children who don't harvest," Anna nervously responded. "I don't know, probably not until Christmas."

"How long will that be?" Anna counted on her fingers, September, October, November, December. "Four months."

"Oh, Anna!" called Mrs. Swenson. "You must not count on your fingers. Teachers don't do that. Remember now! You are a teacher."

Slowly the train chugged away from the depot. Elsa ran along the platform until it ended. Anna could hear the goodbyes from both of them and continued waving and saying goodbye until they were out of sight. It was not until then that she remembered she had forgotten to give them a hug. In all the excitement there were no farewell embraces. How terrible! What a beginning to this new life. She had also neglected to thank her mother again for the beautiful new dress she had stitched for her, and all the help that Elsa had been in getting ready. But she also knew that if she had hugged them, she might have cried, and the last words of her mother were still ringing in her ears. "Remember now! You are a teacher." It would never do for a teacher to cry.

She turned to check the seat. It was clean so she sat down. Looking around she saw the young man across the aisle. He was probably about fifteen years old, and sat next to his bedroll. At this moment he was looking out of his window, so she turned to look out of her window and this way would avoid conversing with him. It was not that she wanted to ignore him, but she realized that she would be quite self-conscious if she had to talk to him.

For the first time in her life she was completely on her own. She had been reared in a small Iowa city, close enough to farms so that she was familiar with country life, but actually she was a city girl. Her father and Uncle Lars had owned a dry goods store, which sold clothing, notions, fabric and a multitude of other things. Her family lived above the store, so that when her father died ten years ago, Uncle Lars had continued to let them live there rent free. In exchange for this Mrs. Swenson assisted in the store, however her main source of income was dressmaking and alterations. The living quarters consisted of four rooms: a kitchen, two bedrooms and a parlor which was also used as a sewing room. After she graduated from high school Anna had worked in the store to let her mother concentrate on dressmaking so they could save enough money to send Anna to normal school. Also they had been somewhat in debt to her uncle and Mrs. Swenson finally was able to pay this off.

Continuing to look out the window, Anna thought of her mother and sister now living alone. She hoped that she could send them some money, or save enough to buy her mother a new sewing machine. What kind of farm would she live on? Grabney was a very small town, just a depot, post office, and general store, with a community church and parsonage across the bridge. The school was not in the town, but a couple of miles east. How many pupils would she have? How old and how big would they be? She understood there were to be twelve from grades one through eight, however she had heard tales from Mrs. Phipps of huge trouble-making boys who were still in school. The worst tales came from teachers who had quit mid-year. She didn't want to quit. She had to succeed. Did the other teacher get married because the school was too difficult? If so, it would not be the first time that had happened. She thought about the Rural School Problems class. "Get them outside playing volleyball to tire them out," the professor had said.

"Tickets, please! Tickets please!" came the call from the conductor as he marched through the door.

Anna opened her purse, getting the ticket. While handing it to him she said, "I'm to get off at Grabney. Will you make sure the train stops there?"

"I can read. I can read," came the surly answer. "We're already stopping at Grabney." He punched the ticket and gave it back without a glance in her direction. He looked at the young man across the aisle, gave a curt nod and passed on.

She wondered if all conductors were like this. He had made her feel foolish, even a little stupid. Did the fellow across the aisle hear the conversation? She hoped he had not. After this brief encounter she felt quite unnerved. She looked out the window, hoping to take her mind off the experience, and also hoping to avoid the conductor should he pass her way again.

Her seat was on the side opposite the river and she could see the farms which were beautiful, the corn was a gorgeous green, and the farmhouses looked so welcoming. Miles and miles of farms filled the flat landscape. She imagined what kind of people lived in the various houses; what were they doing and what dreams of the future did they have? Were there any families who had sent a daughter off to teach as her mother had? Occasionally she would see children playing, as some houses were close enough to the tracks to observe the activities of the occupants. Sometimes there would be men working even though the sun was scorching hot. She felt sorry for the horses, pulling loaded wagons. At least by harvest time it would be cooler.

The open window let in quite a hot, stiff breeze, but it was a welcome change from the stifling air of the station platform. Anna let the wind blow on her, enjoying its cooling effect. It was pleasant to sit with no work to do, thinking about the future, reflecting on the past, and indulging in daydreams.

She stole a glance at the boy across the aisle and was surprised to find that he was looking at her. With some embarrassment she managed a self-conscious smile, then quickly lowered her head and stared at her hands, which were folded in her lap. She soon realized how ridiculous the situation was for her to become so shy with a young boy, so she looked at him again to give him a more friendly smile, however he had turned and was staring out his window.

"Grabney! Grabney!" called the conductor as he marched back through the coach.

Anna was startled. The time had gone too quickly. Her hair was windblown, her dress was wrinkled and she felt sticky with perspiration. Quickly she tried to tidy herself, all the while listening for the clickety-click of the wheels to go more slowly. She inadvertently jumped at the sound of the whistle, which meant they were within visual distance of the town.

Peering out the window, she could barely see two small buildings; looking out the window on the other side of the train there was only the river, which they had been following for many miles. Gradually the train slowed and finally came to a stop next to the depot. They were in Grabney.

Chapter Two

Anna stood up feeling apprehensive. She tucked the loose ends of her hair under her hat, quickly grabbed her pocketbook and reached for her traveling bag.

Just as quickly a strong, tanned arm reached past her and took the valise. "Let me take that ma'am," came the voice of the passenger from across the aisle, and he and the bag disappeared out the door.

Following in his wake, she nearly stumbled down the steps in her anxiety to disembark, and had to catch herself to wait for the porter to put down the metal stool for that last long step to the platform. The young man, who had jumped the eighteen inches or so from train to platform without the stool, had put her valise down. She blurted out a hasty thanks; he smiled with a nod of acknowledgment and was off.

Her next concern was her trunk, but her fears seemed unfounded as she saw a train employee open up the baggage car.

"Hey Matt! Give us a hand!"

A middle-aged gentleman ambled out of the small country station, which also served as a post office, and made his way several cars down the line to where her trunk stood poised, ready to be hoisted out of the doorway. Together they tugged it out and lowered it onto the dirt.

"Holy Jehosophat! That is a heavy one!" exclaimed the man named Matt that Anna assumed was the stationmaster. Before she could consider what to do next, the conductor waved to the engineer, the doors were shut and with that tremendous rhythmical surge of power that only a steam engine can produce the engine pulled the train slowly down the track, leaving her trunk sitting in a heap of dust and dirt.

9

Where were the people who were to meet her? She glanced at the station to reassure herself that it did say Grabney. Looking toward her trunk, the old gentleman was seen shaking his head as he walked away from it.

"Jimmy! What're you doin' in these here parts?" someone shouted from the other side of the station. Looking in that direction she saw the young man who had been on the train, being greeted by one of the farmers. Other than those two and the stationmaster, there was no one in sight. She paid scant attention to the ensuing conversation and feeling somewhat frustrated and more than a little forlorn decided to wait near a bench located outside the station door. It was under the wide porch roof, thus she could escape the direct sun.

With more determination than strength, Anna picked up her heavy valise and lugged it to the bench, plopping it on the wooden floor of the porch. Seeing the dust laden surface of the seat, she vetoed the idea of sitting down, so stood next to her bag, trying to look properly calm and collected. Surely someone would arrive soon to greet her. Fragments of the discussion of the three men reached her as the stationmaster joined the other two.

"Well, Matt, Jimmy says he's goin' to be around a spell workin' at the Wheelers."

"Whatcha goin' to be doin'?"

"Oh, guess Charley 'n Bill need some help with those ol' sheds."

"Otta tear 'em down and start over again," Matt replied.

"Yeah, I know. But the ol' lady wants to keep 'em. Says it's a waste of money to tear 'em down. You otta know Floyd. Your place is across from hers."

"An' that woman has the first nickel that place ever took in. Why, when them boys was young and their ol' man died, she worked in the fields herself so as not to get a hired man."

"Them boys is now in their forties," laughed Matt.

"Say now, I was a thinkin'," You've been holdin' out on us boy. I saw you get off the train with that there young lady. She's dressed purty fancy to live in the ol' Wheeler bunk house. Or did you bring a bride for Charley or Bill?"

10

Jimmy gave a self-conscious laugh while his complexion took on a sunburned appearance.

Floyd continued with, "Now jus' own up boy. You kin tell Matt 'n me all about it. You sure knows how to pick 'em. A real good looker she is. Why I ain't seen the likes gettin' off at Grabney since Matt brought home his missus, 've you Matt?"

"Not me. And I'm here to do the watchin'."

"I tell you if she ain't the purtiest little lady I done seen in a long time. And don't tell the missus I said that, 'cause Inger jus' might take offense," continued Floyd.

Anna was feeling quite ill at ease. She knew she was being teased, because it was obvious she could hear their conversation. Is this the way teachers were welcomed at country schools? If so, the people at Cedar Falls had neglected to mention it. She didn't let herself glance at the men. More conversation started. She feigned indifference.

"What'r you doin' here this time o' day Floyd?" asked Jimmy. "Don't spose fer a minute you come down to git me."

"Naw, but yer welcome to have a ride. It seems I got a problem. Ya see I was sent down to meet someone comin' in on the 5:10, but I guess she never showed up."

"What's she look like?" asked Matt.

"Well, you know, old 'n ugly, and I ain't never seen nobody like that gettin' off the train. Jus' spose she heerd too many stories about the ruffians we have aroun' here and backed out. I guess everyone's talkin about the last one quittin'. It's amazin' how you try to keep somethin' quiet, but to no avail." Realizing that this farmer named Floyd had come to meet her, Anna decided she did not feel comfortable making any overtures to him. Let him come to her. If this banter had happened in the store at home she would willingly have joined in, however she didn't know these folks. She hoped desperately that she wouldn't have to stay with Floyd and his family.

"Well, I guess I better be moseyin' along," announced Floyd.

Anna felt a desperate sinking feeling. "Say Matt. I seen you got a trunk sittin' down the line. How about me and Jimmy helpin' you with that before we leave."

"Much obliged," answered Matt, and the three men walked toward the trunk.

11

"Howdy ma'am. Nice day," greeted Floyd tipping his hat to Anna as he passed her with a knowing grin on his face. The other two smiled their acknowledgment. She smiled shyly in return, keeping a close watch on them to determine what the next development would be in this charade.

Floyd's voice was the first to be heard. "Well, tarnation!" he exclaimed as he read the name tag on her trunk. "If this don't beat all. This here says Anna Swenson. Now that's the name of the teacher I'm sposed to meet. Do you boys think that this here lady could be Anna Swenson?"

"Guess so," Matt replied in a droll manner. "Since you aim to put this on your rig Floyd, I'll let you and Jimmy handle it and get me back to the post office. Besides I lifted that once today, and I jus' love to see other people work."

"You're thinkin' that Jimmy and I can't lift this little ol' trunk? Just a featherweight for two ol' hands like us." So saying he grabbed one handle, and Jimmy got hold of the other. Expecting it to be lighter than it was, both were jolted in their tracks at their attempt to lift it. "Now, Jimmy. That ain't fair. You're sposed to lift too. Get some muscle into it."

"It shore is heavy," came the amused comment.

Anna was amused too, so much so that she relaxed a little and started to laugh, quickly caught herself, and covered her mouth with her gloved right hand.

The men brought the trunk the thirty yards or so to where she was standing, letting it drop in the dirt next to the porch.

"You must be the new school teacher," began Floyd. "I'm right please tameecha. My name's Floyd Parker, and I guess you must be Miss Swenson."

"Yes. How do you do Mr. Parker?"

"I'm doin' jus' fine or was until I met up with that trunk a yours. I swear you musta packed it clean full a books. Now maybe you thought that here in the country we don't have books, since you're from the city an' all. But I know we got books, cuz I saw at least half a dozen there once. We only got twelve kids in the school, so twelve books should be enough. Can't read more'n one book at a time anyways. Heh! Heh! We'll shore have plenty a books this year."

"I did pack some books," said Anna with a giggle. "I guess it is pretty heavy."

"Well you jus' wait right here while I get the rig, then me'n Jimmy'll watch. Since we drug it this far, reckon we'll let you have your turn to put it up on the wagon," and he disappeared around the corner of the porch to get his horse and wagon.

The two of them stood there awkwardly. Jimmy was the first to break the silence. "Think you're gonna like it here?" "I'm sure I will," said she, not sure of anything. "Do you live here?"

"Naw, I jus' work here from time to time. My dad has a farm near Webster City and I was raised over that a way."

The horse and wagon came into view and pulled up alongside the porch. "Whoooaa Nellie! Take it easy now!" Floyd jumped down. "Well jus' this once Jimmy 'n I'll lift up your trunk. You can get it off at the other end of the line." They hoisted it up in the back next to a sack of sugar, and some other supplies. Last came her valise. "You help her up. Let her sit between us. Don't want her to fall out and hurt herself and be havin' the job of findin' another teacher."

Anna glanced quickly at Floyd's grimy overalls and the dusty seat, and thought of how she had struggled to stay clean. "Whatsa matter? You scared you'll fall off," commented Floyd, noticing her apprehension. "Jus' sit close to us and you'll be all right." He jumped up and seated himself on the wooden plank. Jimmy helped Anna up. There was no choice so she sat down as Jimmy climbed beside her and they were off.

Anna now had the opportunity to look around the town. Across from the station and post office was a general store. Several people had come out of the door. The arrival of a new teacher was probably the biggest event in a long time and had piqued their curiosity.

"Hi Floyd! How're ya doin'?" called a young man.

"Jus' fine and dandy Ed."

"I see you're still drivin' ol' Nellie. When're you goin' to get one of them fancy automobiles?"

13

"Well, I'll tell ya Ed. If God had wanted us to have automobiles, he'd never invented the horse. Giddap Nellie!" and they turned right to go over the bridge.

"We got about a coupla miles to go so hope you don't get jolted to pieces. This board ain't so soft for sittin' on. If you think you're gonna fall, grab ahold of Jimmy there. He won't mind a bit."

They crossed the bridge. "Look there to the right and you'll see a path. That's the way you take to town when you're walkin'. Much shorter. Now we're goin' past the parsonage and the church, and then we got a mile or so before we turn to the farm. You'll be stayin' with my sister-in-law an' her family. She's a Swede jus' like you, same as my wife. We call her Milly. Her name ain't even Mildred. Some Swede name, but anyway we call her Milly. Oh and is she a worker. She'll have you up before the rooster crows."

"Say Floyd! I heard they have another baby."

"That'd be Lucy. Lucy the screamer. I think that's why they wanted the teacher frankly, to sleep with Lucy and keep her quiet so's the folks could get some rest. But don't you worry none Miss Swenson. If things get too bad you walk a spell up the road to the Wheeler's. Jimmy'll let you sleep in his bedroll in the bunk house. Jus' shake out the bedbugs first and you'll be fine. As I always said, Jimmy Burns is a real gentleman."

"Las' time I was there and you tol' little Davey he could sleep with me in the bunkhouse, and Milly said no. I'll never forget how he carried on," laughed Jimmy.

The remainder of the short journey continued in much the same vein, until Jimmy asked to be let off at the corner at the Wheeler farm. They had gone two miles by this time, having turned right after the first mile, continuing on to the next crossroad, which led north to Parkers and Wheelers, and south to the Jensens, where she would be staying.

They turned right and headed south. Anna strained to look over the corn to see if she could locate a farm house. They went by two farms without stopping. Then to the right she made out a barn and a house which was badly in need of paint. It didn't look like the home of an ambitious Swedish woman, and she hoped it wasn't. To the left she spied a lovely white home, nestled in a sea of green corn. Behind it was a sturdy red barn. Surrounding the house was a garden of flowers.

"In you go Nellie!" came the reassuring call, and horse, wagon and occupants turned in at the attractive farm, which was to be her home for the next nine months.

Chapter Three

"My goodness! My goodness!" exclaimed a dumpling young woman as she wiped her hands on her apron, and bounced down the back steps. "So you are here so soon. Oh, Floyd, how could you let Miss Svenson ride on your hard old wagon seat. You didn't even bring a cushion for her. Oh, I am so sorry Miss Svenson."

"Now Milly, just calm down," came Floyd's slowly uttered admonition as he climbed down from the wagon. "Miss Swenson ain't made of china, and she ain't goin' to break."

"Here, let me help you down." Milly Jensen held up her hand to Anna. Her smile which blended through her rosy cheeks to her twinkling eyes made the newcomer feel very welcome. Her slight Swedish accent added to her charm.

"Now Milly! You jus' let me do that. It ain't often that I get to hold hands with a purty young lady, and helpin' her down out of the wagon is the best excuse that I can think of." He reached up and in an instant had lifted her to the ground.

"Oh Miss Svenson, I am so happy to meet you. Oi, yoi, yoi and so pretty too! What a beautiful dress. I think you made it yourself. Pink is such a pretty color. Oh, and with hat and gloves. How nice."

"Milly, are you gonna stand there all day and chatter? C'mon you can help by bringin' in her trunk, while I set a spell on the porch and wait until you get it down. An' by the way Miss Swenson, this is my sister-in-law, Mrs. Jensen, but I think you'll probably end up callin' her Milly." With that, Floyd plunked himself on the top step.

This happened so quickly that Anna was slightly bewildered.

"Floyd Parker! I will do no such thing as to try to take down that trunk," laughed Milly. "The next thing is that you

17

will want Inger to help me," and to Anna, "Inger is my sister and is Floyd's wife." She grinned and rolled her eyes skyward.

"I was about to suggest that, but seein' how I'm married to Inger, and she might not take too kindly to that idea, I thought that Miss Swenson could give you an assist. She packed it, and well . . . it just does me a whole heap a good to think of settin' here and watchin' you two wrestle with that trunk."

"I would be glad to help," offered Anna, knowing that this was all a game, "but I don't think that we could manage it."

"Never mind," replied Milly as she patted her hand. "Don't you pay any attention to this man here. Anyway Peter is coming in from the field. He couldn't let a new teacher arrive and not be here." Turning to her brother-in-law she said, "Yes, Floyd, I am sorry that you are not strong enough to do this job so you have to ask two women, but never mind, I have a strong, young husband coming in, so you sit and rest."

"Don't you go gettin' highfalutin on me, Milly Jensen, or I will take you over my knee and spank you."

Small giggles erupted from the kitchen door, and Anna looked up to see two little children, a boy and a girl. "You won't spank our mama," said the girl.

"Of course he won't Sarah," replied her mother. "He wouldn't dare."

At that moment the sound of a crying baby came from the house. "Oh, Davey, will you get Lucy?" asked Milly. "I forgot about her."

"I told Miss Swenson about Lucy," exclaimed Floyd. "Now don't you worry none about Lucy, Miss Swenson. In just two or three months I am sure that you will have her quieted down."

"Here comes daddy!" yelled Sarah as she jumped down the steps and ran into the field to meet him.

Peter Jensen was as tall and thin as his wife was short and plump. He introduced himself and before long he and Floyd had the trunk moved not only down from the wagon, but into the house, through the kitchen and dining area, up the steps and into Anna's bedroom on the second floor. Anna followed them up the half dozen weathered porch steps and into the house.

18

The entryway porch was first. It was a small but practical room, painted white, with the washing machine and washtub on one side, and on the other hooks heavy with winter coats, under which were boots.

Through the second door was the kitchen, the center of household activity, a large room which took up nearly half of the main floor. A quick glance showed her that a big black iron cook stove dominated one inside wall. She noticed that two rooms lead off the kitchen, one of which was a parlor. She passed a round, oak dining table on her way to the stairs, which she quickly climbed, finding her room at the head of the steps.

She entered the room. It was lovely with pink rose flowered wallpaper, a birds-eye maple dresser and a brass double bed covered with a golden wedding ring quilt. There was a closet built into the eaves, with a door about five feet high which touched the edge of the sloping ceiling. A window with organdy curtains faced east. She would see the sunrise.

Her reverie was interrupted by Davey who announced, "My room is next to yours. Do you want to see my room? And Sarah's is on the other side."

"Oh, Davey," called his mother. "Let Miss Svenson alone. There will be plenty of time to show her your room." To Anna she offered, "Now you make yourself at home, and when you are ready come downstairs and we will have some cake and a nice cold drink." With that the family left, and she was free to examine her new surroundings.

She walked to the bed and gingerly ran her fingers over the pattern of the quilt. It was so beautiful, and all handmade. Under the bed was the chamber pot, with a crocheted silencer for the cover. She looked at the dresser, walked slowly over to it and opened one of the top drawers, which slid out so easily. After glancing at the empty interior she carefully pushed it shut. In front of the beveled mirror on an embroidered cloth sat a porcelain pitcher full of water with a matching basin. A coal oil lamp was next to them. There was also a towel, and a bar of homemade soap on a washcloth. One glance in the mirror told her that she needed to freshen up, so she poured water into the basin and gratefully splashed some on her face and arms. She dried them quickly then tidied up her hair.

Her trunk had been put in front of the window , and there it probably would remain since the door to the closet was too small to accommodate it. She could cover it with a shawl she had brought and it would look like a piece of furniture. A chair stood next to the trunk. She continued glancing around the room wishing that her mother and Elsa could see it. How she wanted to sit down right at that moment and write to them about this room, about this family and then the spell was broken as she looked up and saw Sarah standing in the doorway.

"Oh! I didn't see you there. Is it time for me to come downstairs?" A shy nod followed her question.

"Your name is Sarah, isn't it?" The child nodded again. "How old are you?"

"Three," came the answer, "and Davey is six and he gets to go to school." At this remark she looked downcast.

Anna smiled and reached out to take Sarah's hand. "Even though you can't go to school, I am sure we will be good friends, and play games and read stories." Together they walked down the stairs to the kitchen.

Floyd and Peter were seated at the table deep in a discussion on farming, while Milly was getting glasses from the sideboard to be filled with cold tea from the heavy glass pitcher. She glanced up to see the two coming into the room. "Oh, Miss Svenson, please sit down."

Anna looked at the group and somewhat hesitatingly said, "Please call me Anna, if you don't mind."

A smile filled Milly's face. "Yes, that would be very nice. And you must call me Milly." She quickly put her hand on Anna's arm. "Oh, yes. I think we are going to be good friends. I can yust feel it. But the children, they must call you Miss Svenson. You are an adult, and you are going to be Davey's teacher, so children," and she looked directly at them, "remember that you must call her Miss Svenson, and don't forget."

"Mama," asked Davey. "Do I call her Miss Svenson or Miss Swenson?"

"Oh, Davey!" She laughed and her eyes crinkled up. "You rascal! Please call her Miss Swenson," and she struggled to get out the word. "Pull up a chair Miss Swenson, oh dear, I

20

mean Anna and everyone help yourselves to coffee cake and cold tea." She lifted little Lucy into the high chair.

During the subsequent conversation Anna learned that the cold tea was made from well water that remained quite cool during the summer. The well was located about twenty feet from the back steps. Another pump was in the kitchen which had water from the cistern, soft rain water that was collected from the roof runoff. The soft water was used for washing hair and bathing. She also noticed coal oil lamps, as they did not have electricity, and there was the usual battery telephone installed on one wall.

She heard the screen door to the entry porch bang, and looked up as a woman somewhat older than Milly walked into the room. "I heard the train come in, and saw Jimmy Burns walkin' up to the Wheelers so decided that you'd given him a ride Floyd."

"Now ain't that jus' like a woman. I can't be gone five minutes but what she's chasin' after me." Inger took a chair and sat down joining in the uproarious laughter.

Anna was introduced and was surprised that Milly's sister had hardly a trace of a Scandinavian accent. She also gave the impression of being pragmatic.

"Some people don't even guess that we are sisters," volunteered Milly, "but Inger was here in the United States about ten years before I came. She learned English so quickly and changed so much. I had to look twice before I recognized her when I got off the train."

"After Inger and I was married, she nagged and nagged to get her little sister over here. You know how them women folks are. Well, I don't know if you do or not, but anyways nothin' to do but to send for her. And then just as I was gettin' used to an extra hand doin' the chores, thinkin' that I could take life easy, Pete here up and marries her."

"Don't listen to him," countered Inger shaking her head and smiling.

By this time nine month old Lucy had slid down in the high chair and had started to cry.

"I nearly forgot," said Floyd as he jumped up. "I'll put Lucy's crib in Miss Swenson's room. I explained to her that she would be the one to take care of the baby."

"Oh, you did not!" came a strong voice from Milly, and her face blushed a bright red. "If you told her that it's a wonder she didn't ask to be taken straight back to the depot." She continued with hands waving, "Anna, don't believe this man. My goodness! My goodness! What a terrible thing to do."

"Calm down Milly. I think Anna can take care of herself," replied Inger, and everyone laughed while Milly took the baby into their bedroom which was on the main floor, off the kitchen and next to the parlor.

"It's time we were gettin' along home Floyd," said Inger as she rose from her chair. "And I am happy to meet you Miss Anna Swenson. School won't start until next week so you'll have a few days to get ready. Tomorrow bein' Wednesday, we might just take you up and let you have a look around. Then you will have a couple more days to get ready."

"I would like that," replied Anna.

They continued their conversation as they got up from the table, walked to the back steps and waved good-bye as Inger and Floyd drove off.

Anna spent the rest of the afternoon unpacking some of her things, then helped Milly set the table for supper, which was a pleasant family meal. Using cistern water heated in a large teakettle on the coal and wood burning kitchen range, they washed the dishes. It was uncomfortably hot in the house as the stove gave off excess heat, so Milly suggested that they sit on the screened front porch. This also gave her an opportunity to show Anna her fine parlor, a room seldom used but the pride of the house. It had an overstuffed sofa and matching chair and two straight-backed chairs, plus a small walnut side table on which were family pictures. As they walked through it to get to the porch Anna also noticed the braided rug which was large enough to cover most of the bare floor. Milly proudly told how she and Inger had made it the winter before she was married, carefully cutting up old coats and wool dresses, saving every scrap to make sure they had enough.

Out on the porch they sat and watched the fireflies. It was so pleasant to rest and chat with this family she had known for such a short time.

"I see a farm across the road," commented Anna. "Are there any children living there?"

"Joshua lives there. He's six, like me, but he never gets to come over and play," Davey volunteered.

"Will he start school?"

"Yes, his father informed the board that he would be attending," added Milly, "so I hope that he does because it would do him good to be with other children."

The strident sounds of the clock chimed eight. "My, my but it is getting late. I heard the clock strike eight and time for two children I know to be in bed. So run along and I will be up to tuck you in."

"I think I will go to my room also," added Anna.

"I am sure you are tired," responded Milly. "We go to bed fairly early ourselves, about nine or nine-thirty, because we get up about five-thirty, but don't you get up when you hear Peter and me. The children will sleep until seven. Peter will have finished the morning chores by then so when he comes in we have breakfast."

Anna thanked them again for everything they had done for her, bade them goodnight and followed the children upstairs. She was given a short tour of their rooms, which were neat and clean as expected. Each child had several homemade toys and stuffed dolls and animals making the areas cheerful.

After Anna had closed the door to her own room, she went to the open window where a slight breeze was coming through the screen. She could smell the fresh smell of the farm, the grass, the animals. She decided to go straight to bed, so did not need to light the coal oil lamp. Later as she lay nearly asleep she thought how lucky she was.

Thus was her first day in Grabney.

Chapter Four

The sun streaming through the window woke Anna the next morning. She looked at the gold wrist watch that Uncle Lars had given her as a high school graduation present. It was a few minutes before seven o'clock. She should have been up long ago. She could hear Milly in the kitchen below, and quickly jumped up to close the floor register which was directly above the stove, letting heat through and warming her room. This would be welcome in the winter, but not on a summer day.

She paused at the window to look out on a cloudless sky of beautiful pale blue which contrasted with the deep green color of the corn. Both seemed to stretch forever to the far horizon. The red barn in the left foreground and the unpainted silo behind it were a reminder of people and work to be done, so she ceased her daydreaming.

Remembering that she would be going to school, no doubt to clean, she put on a summer print dress, finished her toilet and made the bed. She looked at the trunk which was only partly unpacked and decided that she could finish this chore later in the day.

As she opened the door of her room the smell of freshly brewed coffee wafted up to her. Walking quickly down the stairs she found the children seated at the table and Peter coming up from the basement with the milk and cream pails, Milly following him with the separator disks.

"I had not intended to sleep so late Milly," apologized Anna who was quite embarrassed to see the household in full action and couldn't believe that she had not heard the children go downstairs.

"Don't you worry. We won't be ready for breakfast until I get this separator washed and scalded, but it will take only a couple of minutes." Looking at the children she exclaimed, "I think that they didn't want to miss out on anything because they are up a little earlier than usual. Isn't that right Peter?"

"Yes that's true," Peter replied with a wink, "especially considering someone wants to make a good impression on his teacher."

"He has made a very good impression on me," said Anna. "Since I seem to be the lazybones around here, perhaps he should wake me up in the morning."

The soft giggles from the children were interrupted by a long and short ring on the telephone. "That's ours," said Milly. "I am sure it's Inger probably ready to go to the schoolhouse."

Peter answered the phone, turning it over to Milly who had a conversation consisting mainly of "Yes," repeated many times. She hung up and cheerfully told them that Inger would meet them at the school at eight and Mabel, their fourteen year old daughter would come to take care of Lucy and Sarah.

At this moment tears began to well in Sarah's eyes, her lower lip quivered and she hung her head. "Did you want to come too," asked her mother. The small head nodded. "It's a mile to the school and we are going to be cleaning, not playing. If you really want to go, you may, but I hope you will be awake enough to walk home." A teary-eyed smile took the place of the former disappointed look.

"Help yourself to the fruit from the bowl. I have oatmeal on the stove when you are ready, and there's plenty of cream, milk and coffee." Milly sat for a minute with the others, then jumped up to serve the oatmeal and was continually getting up and down during the entire meal which took about fifteen minutes.

Water had been heated for the dishes. Going to the sink, Anna noticed that the drain led outside where she was told the water splashed on some tiles before it was diverted to go into the flower beds. It was obvious that efficiency was the watchword of this household.

Around 7:30 a young girl walked into the kitchen. "Mabel, I want you to meet Miss Swenson," said Milly, careful to pronounce the "w" correctly. Mabel was a pretty brunette with her father's coloring but resembling her mother more than her father.

"How do you do, Mabel. I am glad to meet you," replied Anna. "It's nice of you to take care of Lucy while we go to the school."

"Oh, Mother said I had to come, but I don't mind because I like children, and it's fun to come here."

"I get to go to the school," Sarah chimed in, "so you don't get to take care of me."

"Never mind! Never mind!" stated Milly. "Now I have all the things ready that we will need: buckets, soap and rags for scrubbing, wax for polishing and I think we should take the broom because I am not sure we will find one at the school. And I have two aprons Anna, one for you and one for me. There! Are we ready to go?"

"You were going to bring the old catalogs," said Davey, "for the privies."

"You get them. You know where they are," said his mother. The troops set off for the schoolhouse with the children running ahead. The dirt road was a narrow two ruts since it served only the two households. Milly and Anna preferred to walk on the stubble of grass growing between the ruts and at the edge of the road so as to stir up as little dust as possible.

This was the first time that Anna had been alone with Milly. As they walked Milly told her a little about their neighbors and explained the layout of the farms. "You noticed that the roads are so straight, did you? I was surprised at this. Where I come from in Sweden there are only crooked roads because we have too many hills. Here the land is flat and so the roads are one mile apart in each direction. I guess you knew that."

Anna acknowledged that she did. Indeed it had fascinated her when long ago she had stood on a high piece of ground and saw the square mile sections of roads.

"You see I came here in 1912, so I have been here ten years. Land was not so expensive then. When I first lived with Floyd and Inger they had only 320 acres, but Floyd was smart and he saved and soon he was able to buy the whole section, 640 acres, one square mile. He owns the land the school is on. He has a mortgage, but the interest he pays is not so high as it is now. Oi, yoi, yoi, during the war the interest rate went up so high and so did the price of land."

27

"You have more than the 160 acre homestead size, don't you?" asked Anna.

"Oh yes we do. Before the war Peter bought from an old couple who had homesteaded. They each got 160 acres, giving them 320. When their children grew up they moved to the city and wanted nothing to do with farming. Peter was lucky to get the place. Even with 320 acres it is difficult to make a good living when we have to keep paying on the mortgage, but we have enough work with this much land. And Peter has had his hands busy fixing up the house."

"You have a beautiful house," commented Anna.

"When Peter bought the place it was very run down, not the land nor the barn, but the house. We were lucky it had a basement. You notice how the land slopes toward the river. Well, the land where the house is, is high enough so that a basement can be dug and the water doesn't seep in. Our basement is very dry. We keep the separator there and also that's where I store the canned goods. Peter lived in the house just as it was until the winter before we were married. By that time he had the land in fairly good shape, so he could start on the house. Every winter since then we have worked on it, and there is still more to do."

"It looks like a wonderful home to me, but how does Floyd manage with so much land?" asked Anna.

"Walter is sixteen and quit school after the eighth grade. There was no use trying to get him to go to high school, he simply was not interested and Floyd has enough work for him. Walter is not stupid by any means. He will make a very intelligent farmer and he loves farming."

"Perhaps he will take over the farm when Floyd retires?"

"Don't talk to Floyd about retiring. He will not listen to any talk about that. If Walter stays here he will continue to work for his father, and I think that is probably what will happen. Land is too expensive for him to hope to buy a farm, and Floyd's place needs two men to work it even when times are slack. During harvest he has to hire a man or two."

"I have met Mabel. What about the other child?"

"That will be George. He is a very nice boy and so clever in school. I hope Davey grows up to be as nice as George."

Milly continued as they walked, "This is the Schmidt house, next to our place. Their children are grown, and across the road from them are the Larsens. All their children but Erica are out of school. She is Mabel's age and they are good friends. Look up the road before we turn and you can see where Inger's house is, and across from them are the Wheelers. You remember the young man who came out on the train with you, Jimmy Burns. He is working for the Wheelers."

"Yes, I remember him," remarked Anna, blushing again when she thought of how uncomfortably shy she had been when she had met him on the train. They turned the corner and she looked toward the schoolhouse, which was still a half mile away. "I don't see the children."

"Oh, Inger is there already and the children are with her. She may have brought George, since there is not much work for him to do now. In November there will be plenty though during the corn harvest. That's when we have the week for harvesting vacation, and I guess you know that we have another planting vacation in the spring."

"Yes, I had heard about that because students could be excused from schools in town to work on farms during harvesting and planting."

As they neared the schoolhouse Anna could see it was a well kept white frame building with the customary entryway built in front which faced the road to the south. The two privies were out back. After climbing the few steps to the small porch, Anna noticed that there was no lock on the door, and asked about that. Milly replied that it was a law that no schoolhouse should be locked because it might provide shelter for someone lost in a storm. A few people had found refuge there during the years and never had any harm come to either the building nor its contents.

After passing through the entryway, and the second door, Anna saw coat hooks were on the left front wall and a shelf and another set of hooks on the right. Milly explained that each child had his own hook for his cup and towel. Lunch pails were put on the shelf. Names were pasted above the hooks. There was a pail for fresh water and a dipper. The school had its own well as it had remained from the original homestead .

29

The air smelled of soap and sweeping compound as Inger was busy scrubbing desks while George swept the floor. Anna took a rag and soap, put some water in a bucket and walked up to the teacher's desk. She began to scrub. It took about three hours to complete the work which included washing windows and waxing and polishing desk tops.

"It looks like we are ready for business," commented Inger as she scanned the room with an appraising eye.

"I think it looks wonderful," said Anna.

"Let's you and me sit down and I will give you a list of students and maybe answer any questions you have," she continued. The two of them took chairs by the teacher's desk and proceeded to cover any information Anna would need before school began. Teacher manuals were available listing requirements and course content for each grade level, and there was an adequate supply of textbooks. Students supplied their own paper, pencils, penholders and penpoints. In the nearby cupboard was a large bottle of ink and writing supplies for the teacher. She knew that in most schools the students had to provide their own ink. Perhaps she would start them out early with pen and ink.

"We've got a pump organ for the school," Inger informed her. "I guess you know that most schools have pump organs." Anna nodded her head, suddenly realizing that she hadn't missed this important piece of furniture. "Well it needed a little work so Anders Anderson brought it home for the summer. You'll like him. His Lars and George are best friends. He's a real good carpenter, and I figure it'll be brought back in first class condition looking like new. Last I talked with him he said he wasn't quite finished with it, but he'll get it back pretty soon. Anyway they don't have an organ so this will give them a chance to try to play it." Seeing the apprehension on Anna's face she added, "And don't you worry, they'll take good care of it."

Her monthly check of $100.00 would be paid to her on the first of the month by Inger who was the treasurer of the school, and out of that she would pay Milly $20.00 for her room and board.

That afternoon at the farm she paid Milly the $20.00 for her first month's room and board and spent the rest of the time unpacking. She often thought of the $80.00 she would have each month. It was fortunate for her that in this county all the schools paid $100.00. Some girls she had met at Cedar Falls were paid less.

She would add to her checking account in the Fort Dodge bank, save as much money as she could and plan to attend Cedar Falls again next summer. There were many courses she wanted to take, and while she had done well in her classes this past summer, she realized that most of her teaching methods would come from what she had observed from her own elementary and high school teachers.

Tomorrow she would spend at school getting ready for the first day, Tuesday, September 5th, the day after Labor Day. She would have twelve pupils, and teach six grades. There were no second nor fifth grade pupils. George appeared to be a good student as he was barely eleven and in the sixth grade. Some of the others might have started school at seven years instead of six which could explain why Mabel was 14 and in the eighth grade. Luckily her oldest pupils were girls, and she had met Mabel whom she liked. So far, so good. It was an auspicious beginning.

Chapter Five

It was Thursday the last day of August and Anna was up bright and early, eager to get to school. At breakfast she mentioned that she would probably spend the morning at school, returning home for the noon meal, and in the afternoon wanted to walk to the post office so she could mail a letter to her mother and sister.

"I hope you didn't write on a penny post card," Milly commented. "Liza Crawford, who tends the post office, reads all the mail she possibly can, and she is a terrible gossip."

"However," mused Peter. "If you ever want to find out something Milly, she is the first one you run to."

Blushing, Milly replied, "Of course. She is the one who knows everything. I yust wanted Anna to understand the situation."

"I put my letter in a two cent stamped envelope," Anna added. "Mother sent several of them with me. Grabney is not the only place where people in the post office read all the mail," she laughed.

"If you are going to town, then Davey and I will walk with you and show you the way. Davey needs to buy some supplies for school."

Davey's eyes lit up at this announcement. "I'll bring my own money. I've saved fifteen cents," and he leapt from his chair, dashing up the stairs to his room to count his pennies.

"He didn't even ask to be excused," Milly smiled, shaking her head. "Peter could you stay with Lucy and Sarah?"

"I think I could manage that," he answered. "It's the end of the month and I need to go over the books."

By 7:30 Anna was on her way to school. The road was dusty and she could see that before long the sun would have things heated up. When she arrived it was still cool, however by noon she was glad to leave, bringing with her a few items to peruse later.

By 2 o'clock they were heading out the back door and out to the road, which became a path beyond the driveways to the two farms. Anna noticed that it was customary for rural families to use the back door unless there was special company, like the minister coming to call. He would arrive at the front door.

"You run along ahead Davey. We'll meet you at the store," said Milly, and turning to Anna she said, "I wanted to tell you some things about the Kloster family, yust across the road, and don't want Davey to hear. They are a very strange family. We have all tried to be friendly, but Roger Kloster is a very difficult man."

"Have they lived here long?" asked Anna.

"Old man Evans, Bill Evans his name is, moved here maybe thirty, forty years ago. He was getting older when he married a nice girl from around here and they had one daughter, Grace. Mrs. Evans was never able to have any more children, too many miscarriages, which was a big disappointment to the old man. She died in childbirth when Grace was fifteen. The baby was a boy and he didn't live but a few hours.

"Grace's mother had insisted that she go to high school, so for two years during the winter she lived in the county seat with her aunt, her mother's sister. It was summer when Mrs. Evans died and the old man refused to let Grace go back to school the next fall. Instead he kept her home doing all the drudgery that had been her mother's lot. He even insisted that she harvest the corn during the fall so he wouldn't have to hire an extra hand. They did have half a section, but years ago he made some money by selling a small part of his land next to the bridge, to the church so they could build a parsonage and church and give the town a picnic ground. He still has nearly a half section.

"Peter and I were married in 1914, and Mrs. Evans died in 1912, so I never really knew her. I would see her at church, but I could only nod to her because I didn't speak English that well. That was when I was living with Inger and Floyd and helping them with their children. Uncle John had brought Inger here about 1900, and after she married Floyd and lived on the farm she would occasionally go see Mrs. Evans. When the last baby came, Inger was the first person they called until the mid-wife arrived."

"What a sad story," commented Anna. "I guess the person I really feel sorry for is Grace. She must have had a terrible time. But she is married and with a family of her own, so perhaps things turned out all right."

"No, I don't think so," Milly replied. "Grace and Eddie Marson, the son of the people who run the store, had always been sweet on each other. They had grown up together, and both went to the county seat to high school. Everyone assumed that they would one day get married. But when Mrs. Evans died all that changed.

"In the spring of 1915 Roger Kloster shows up at the farm and the old man hires him to help with the planting. Where he came from, nobody knows. Some thought that he became a farm worker so he didn't have to go into the army, but 1915 was too early for that. He was strong on his Bible though, and kept talking about the Lord telling him to do this and that. Of course nobody believed him but old man Evans, who had hardly ever set foot inside the church. He began to abide by every word that Roger said. Suddenly we learned that Grace was to marry Roger Kloster. We have always thought that she was forced into it, but we really don't know. She was eighteen."

"What happened to Eddie Marson?" asked Anna.

"That is a sad story. Before Roger came to the farm Eddie would come to see Grace, but the old man was so against it that she had to sneak away from the house even to see him for a few minutes. It was the summer after Roger arrived that Eddie and Grace met in the cornfield one night. Roger found them and told the old man, who dragged Grace back to the house. Peter and I were outside and heard such a terrible commotion. Roger was shouting about how the Lord would punish her. The next thing we knew Roger and Grace were getting married. Roger has had such an influence over the family that we wonder if the old man has deeded the property over to him. He seems to control everything now."

"I have heard of other cases where fathers have deeded the family property over to the daughter's husband, so it wouldn't be the first time," Anna added.

"You are right. For this and other reasons I am sorry I did not get to know Grace. I did call on her a couple of times but the old man made me feel that he didn't want any visitors. We were married only a short time before Roger came. He frightened me so that I didn't care to go over there, and Grace wasn't allowed to go visiting, so of course she didn't come here."

They had now come to the river, its banks lined with willows and a few cottonwoods. A path had been cut through down to the water and Anna could see tracks in the dust. It was more humid here with the smell of damp vegetation. "Is this where everyone comes to fish?" asked Anna.

"Oh yes," replied Milly. "It is one of the best places to fish. You can see how dark the water is, that means it is deep. See how steep the bank on the other side is? Davey loves to come here and fish but I won't let him go without Peter. A little farther down the river where it is more shallow the young folks catch frogs, and roast the frog legs over bonfires," she added with a shudder. "They have great fun and Davey always wants to yoin them. I am sure he will when he is older."

They turned west toward town. The path continued on the edge of the Evans' property, following the river maintaining a distance of about thirty feet from it. In some places the fence posts had rotted out. It was not so well kept up as the Jensen farm.

Milly continued her story. "Yoshua was born nine months after Grace and Roger were married. In 1918 Grace had another baby, also a boy. She had not seen her aunt for several years and begged to go for a visit but both her father and Roger refused to let her leave. The baby was a few months old and quite healthy, so one day Grace took him in her arms, walked to the train and rode to the county seat. She returned a week later and shortly after that both she and the baby came down with the flu. Grace recovered, but the baby died. Roger let everyone know that it was God's punishment for disobeying her husband. After that Grace seldom left the place, not even to go to church.

"She has another child, a little girl, Elaine, who is two years old. They did have this baby baptized at church so I saw her at that time, but since then I have only gotten glimpses of her once in a while. She seldom leaves the house.

"Now you can see the church and the parsonage. It's a Presbyterian Church. Are you Presbyterian?"

"I am Lutheran," replied Anna.

"I hope you won't mind going to the Presbyterian Church. There isn't a Lutheran Church around here. In Sweden I was Lutheran."

"I am sure I will enjoy going to this church. I love going to church on Sunday so I guess we Lutherans will have to get used to being Sunday Presbyterians," laughed Anna.

"You will meet the minister and his wife this Sunday. Look over there," and Milly pointed to a vacant area surrounded by cottonwood and willow trees. "That is our picnic ground. We are going to have a big picnic on Labor Day. Everyone comes. We have such a good time." They turned south and crossed the wooden bridge. "Let's go to the post office first and you can mail your letter."

They entered this small bare building with its brass fronted mailboxes on one wall. The well-swept, well-worn bare boards of the floor led to the cage of the postmistress. Anna met the loquacious and gossipy Mrs. Crawford, who wanted to engage in a lengthy conversation. However after Anna had informed her that she would receive her mail in the Jensen's box, she was able to graciously maneuver her way out of the post office with Milly at her side.

They crossed the street to the store. The front consisted of two large, dusty windows on either side of the main door. A roofless porch ran the length of the building, with two steps in the center which led up to the entrance. A MARSON GENERAL STORE sign, showed plainly below two small windows on the second floor. It was indeed a general store with everything from feed to hardware to household items. Fresh bread came in every day for those who did not bake their own, and there was a large section of canned goods and produce. They also handled dry goods, some fabric, notions and almost anything a person might need. While the town of Grabney itself consisted of the three families, this store served a vast community of farmers' families who came from miles around.

"You'll find Davey behind those boxes of supplies that just came in," said Mr. Marson. "I can't believe he is ready for school."

"This is Anna Swenson, our new teacher," said Milly. "This is Mr. Marson who owns the store, and over there is his son Ed."

"Glad ta meetcha," came the warm reply. "Name's Elmer, Elmer Marson, been here since the world began," he guffawed. "C'mere Eddie! Meet the new schoolmarm. Mother, come downstairs," he yelled. "Milly's got someone here you otta meet."

"This is Ed," said Milly as Ed came from the back of the store. The young man politely acknowledged the introduction and then returned to sorting the contents of the boxes. Anna remembered him as the one who had commented to Floyd about buying a car.

A scurrying on the stairway at the back of the store brought Mrs. Marson down from the family living quarters. She beamed at them and greeted Anna warmly. "I understand Davey's ready for school," she volunteered.

"Yes he came to buy a tablet and a couple of pencils. Have you found them yet, Davey?" Milly called.

A smiling Davey came around the boxes holding tightly to a tablet with a red cover and two yellow pencils. He walked up to the counter, placed the three items on it and dug into his pockets for his fifteen pennies.

"We have one tablet for ten cents and two pencils at two cents each," said Mr. Marson. "How much do you think that will add up to young man?"

Putting the pennies on the counter, Davey asked, "Is that enough?"

"First if the tablet is ten cents, then count out ten pennies for me." Davey did this. "Now count out two pennies for each pencil." Davey counted out four more pennies.

"I guess you have one left over to save for next time."

"And here is a red all day sucker for a boy who is old enough to go to school," said Mrs. Marson giving one to Davey.

"Thank you," he answered, smiling. With a a puzzled look he put his last penny on the counter and asked, "Would this buy a sucker for Sarah?"

"Indeed it would," said Mr. Marson. "You are a nice brother to think of your sister."

"She's sad because she wants to go to school too," replied Davey, "but she can't go until she's six."

"She may think she wants to go to school but after a few days she would get plenty tired of it," Mr. Marson replied. "By the way Milly, is there something I can do for you?"

"No, not today Elmer. I walked down to show Anna the way to town and to make sure Davey got the right things, so I guess we'll be getting along home now."

The three left the store walking across the bridge and along the path. Davey tore off by himself to beat them home and show his father and Sarah his purchases.

"The Marsons are such a nice family. Her name is Violet, but everyone calls her Vi," said Milly.

"Ed seems very quiet," added Anna.

"Yes. He was never talkative, but we feel that he has never gotten over Grace's marriage. He left town when he heard about the wedding, yust ran away. No one heard from him for months, not even his folks. Later we learned that he got yobs on farms in Minnesota. He wrote his parents about Christmas time. When he finally came back he looked so dejected. In these seven years I don't think he has set eyes on Grace. I understand that when Roger comes into the store he goes into the back room."

"Is that a Model T Ford that I see at the minister's house?" exclaimed Anna.

"Oh, yes. They have a car because he has three churches to serve. On Sunday we get the first service at ten o'clock. He has his dinner, then drives to Brewster about ten miles from here for afternoon service, and finally has the evening service in Langton before returning home."

"Considering that Sunday is a day of rest, how busy does he keep the rest of the week," laughed Anna.

"It is his busiest day," and Milly smiled at the joke, "but he still has to visit all the families in the entire area and help with problems. During the flu epidemic he nearly wore himself out there was so much sickness. Luckily not many people died. You can't see the cemetery from here, as it's on the other side of the church."

As they walked home they continued chatting, with Anna eagerly receptive to all the information about the town and its people. She felt such a kinship with Milly, her cheerful laugh, her good sense of humor and her devotion to duty and her family. She knew they would become the best of friends.

Chapter Six

On Friday September 1st Anna returned to school to continue her preparation. The school's smell greeted her as she opened the door, the sweeping compound George had used on the floor, the wax on the desks and the stale air from being closed up the day before. She left the doors open and raised a window. The windows were on the left side of the room, faced the west and looked out on Floyd's corn fields. School windows were always on the left side of the room so that right handed students would have better light. This meant that they would not have the morning sun, but no doubt would have enough light. There were no lanterns in the room, daylight being the only source of illumination.

The pot belly stove was near the southeast corner. The blacking had burned off in most places, but it had a flat top so they could use it to heat water in the winter. Nearby was a coal scuttle and scoop and a box of dried corn cobs which were used as kindling. The various families would take turns starting the fire in the mornings.

Bookcases and cupboards were along the east wall, the one without the windows. She walked over to them, checking the number of books. Some were well worn with ragged edges that showed years of use, and the dates inside proved this to be true. However there were some fairly new books, and all were usable.

She wanted to be as well prepared as possible since she knew the first day would not be easy. She completed some last minute tasks which included pasting the names above the coat and cup hooks. Some cups remained from the previous year, as well as some rather dirty towels which she would have them take home to launder.

The first thing she would do on Tuesday would be to learn everyone's name and sit each at a desk which hopefully would fit the student. Next she would give them a short background about herself, learn the rules and procedures that they had previously used and discuss the rules and procedures she wished to establish. She decided to write a time schedule on the blackboard, and would have to remember Tuesday morning to wind and set the clock which hung in a conspicuous place above it in the front of the room. As she wrote on the blackboard she felt for the first time the thrill of being a teacher. She turned to look at the empty seats trying to picture the students who would occupy them. Davey and Joshua would sit in the first row, other than that she was not sure.

There were no records left from the previous year, so she was at a loss to determine each student's ability and thus decided that first she would have them write an essay on their summer vacation, and use this as the beginning of a journal they would keep, writing in it once a week, on Monday. She found some paper they could use for a cover for these, and while she was checking their compositions, they could plan a design for the cover. When the older students were writing she could work with Davey and Joshua, the two first graders.

She worked and planned, trying to anticipate any problem which might arise, but realizing that the unexpected was certain to occur. It wasn't until 1 o'clock that she realized she felt hungry. Satisfied that she had done all she could, and becoming a bit drowsy in the stuffy, hot room, she shut the windows and walked to the entry, taking one last look around before closing the door.

As she walked home, she clutched a tablet which she would use to jot down any last minute ideas before she forgot them. She also carried the grade book and an attendance sheet, as she planned to fill these out during the afternoon. As she made her way down the dusty road her thoughts ran to her mother and Elsa, and how proud they would be if they could see her now. The joy she felt at being a teacher at last totally consumed her.

On Saturday after breakfast they changed the bedding. This was a major undertaking in a household of six people.

Milly explained that the bottom sheet was removed and put in the laundry, the top sheet put on the bottom and the clean sheet used for a top sheet. Everyone got clean pillow cases. Dirty clothes and bedding were put in the wash tub which sat on a backless chair in the back entryway, next to the washing machine. Anna mentioned that since she had been there only a few days it was not necessary for her to change her bedding this week, and this met with Milly's approval. Milly also mentioned that she would be happy to do Anna's personal laundry, and while Anna thought this might be too much of a burden, it turned out that it was less of a bother than to have Anna do her laundry separately. When she wished she was welcome to use the washtub and washboard, or do hand washing in a bucket. On most days the clothes were hung on the clotheslines in the backyard, however in the winter they were hung in the basement.

This Saturday afternoon they needed to make butter. Milly took Anna to the well to show her how she kept the cream cool. The well was covered with wooden planks, which surrounded the pipe which was connected to the pump. One of the boards had a ring attached to it. Milly gave a hefty pull on the ring, lifting the board and exposing the inside of the well. Immediately a cool, damp waft of air with a rather dank odor floated out of the darkness. Setting the board to one side, she reached into the well and pulled on a rope which was attached to the underside of a plank, and up came a bucket. Inside the bucket was a large covered can full of cream, which she removed. She then lowered the empty bucket into the well, which went just deep enough to not touch the water, and raised a second bucket in the same fashion. Anna looked into the well, could see the water about ten feet down, and couldn't resist calling out to hear the echo of her voice. Then she helped put the plank back and was surprised at how heavy it was.

"It has to be heavy," replied Milly, "so the children can't lift it. They understand they may come and pump water but are never to pull up the plank."

There was a cupboard in the basement where food kept cool, but the well was cooler. The cupboard was used more in the winter. They also kept milk in the well, but there was seldom an oversupply of milk as they fed the excess to the pigs.

43

The churn was barrel shaped and stored in the base-ment when not in use. Peter carried it up and set it in the kitchen. The barrel fit into a stand, and there was a handle which when turned flipped the barrel end over end. Milly had at least a gallon of cream, and while some of it had soured it didn't mat-ter so she poured the thick, lumpy liquid into the churn and Anna volunteered to turn it. It seemed to take forever, the tir-ing, constant turning, but finally Anna could feel the thump, thump of the butter hitting the sides. Milly opened the spigot, drained the buttermilk into a large pan, and then opened the barrel and took out the butter which was a light yellow. Anna knew that in the summer when the cows ate fresh grass the butter was a yellow color, however in the winter when their main feed was hay it was a creamy white. Milly explained that in winter time it was colored yellow with dye made from grat-ing carrots into a pan and heating them in a little milk. This would be put into a muslin bag and the yellow dye squeezed onto the butter which would color it when it was kneaded. Milly worked fast kneading the butter with a paddle in a wooden bowl to get out the excess water, occasionally wiping the per-spiration from her face with her apron, then salted and kneaded some more and finally formed it into one pound bricks in a wooden mold. She sold her extra butter to the store, and Elmer Marson resold it to a dairy in town. Anna had never made but-ter before and hadn't realized it took so much work.

After Saturday night's dinner, Peter pumped two buck-ets of cistern water and put them on the stove, as Saturday night was bath night. This was all very well and good with only one family in the house, but with a guest it added another di-mension. The routine was that the children were bathed first in the big washtub which sat on the chair in the entryway, and at the moment held the laundry. The tub was placed on the kitchen floor, each child was scrubbed and rinsed, put into clean night wear and hustled off to bed. Before the parents retired they bathed. The problem was, when should Anna take her bath, and where.

"I could use my wash basin in my room and take a sponge bath," suggested Anna, but Milly wouldn't hear of it as she vehemently shook her head and hands at that idea.

"Peter and I could go into the parlor while you bathe," she suggested.

"If the phone rings, then I'll be in trouble," Anna laughed. "Why can't I put the washtub in the back entryway and take my bath there?"

"Someone may come in the back door," giggled Milly, "and they will have a surprise. The lock on that door doesn't work."

"Who would come at that time of night?" asked Peter. "It would be yust like Floyd. He sometimes drops over at the oddest times."

"Then I will push the washing machine against the door," replied Anna.

"What will you do in the winter? It will be freezing cold on the porch then."

"I will have to think about that," Anna answered. "But for now, may I use the porch?"

With hearty approval from Milly and Peter, she went upstairs to get her nightgown, robe, slippers, towel, washcloth and soap. By the time she returned Peter had pushed the washer against the outside door, and poured a sufficient amount of water into the tub. Milly put a coal oil lamp on the floor.

Anna shut the door and she was ready. She suddenly felt somewhat apprehensive about this idea now that she was actually doing it, however she disrobed, and stepped into the tub. Fortunately there were no windows in the room, but she kept her towel on the washer, ready to grab and cover herself with it in case the unexpected happened. She thought she heard sounds, perhaps someone walking outside coming to the door. She grabbed at her towel. Perhaps this was not such a good idea after all. How would she explain to someone who wanted in, what was going on. The sounds died away, hopefully it was an animal. She dropped the soap in the tub and couldn't find it, but finally located it and grabbed it. In what seemed like an eternity, but was actually only a few minutes she was bathed and dressed.

She opened the door to the kitchen, peeped in to see Milly and Peter, sitting in their chairs, peeping back at her. They all laughed.

"Did you have a good bath?" asked Milly.

45

"Oh, yes," answered Anna, "however for a moment I thought there was someone outside."

"If Floyd had been here, he would have sneaked out the front door, gone around to the back and knocked on the door yust to scare you," laughed Milly.

"I thought of doing something like that," mused Peter, "but I knew Anna would probably leap out, tip over the tub, and then I'd be in the doghouse." He rose from his chair. "Here, let me empty the tub," and he quickly did that as well as pushing the washer into its rightful corner.

"I'm going to take the lantern and make one last trip to the outhouse," said Anna laughing, "and after that I promise to stay in my room so you can bathe in the kitchen in privacy." When she returned to the kitchen, hot water was in the tub ready for the next bather. She said her goodnights and climbed the stairs to her room. Saturday nights in Fort Dodge were never like this.

Chapter Seven

Sunday morning breakfast was over by eight o'clock and the table cleared. While Anna washed the dishes, amid protestations from Milly, the children were dressed in their Sunday best. Sarah sat on a stool in the kitchen, being careful not to wrinkle her new cotton print dress, as her mother carefully braided her flaxen hair into two rather short pigtails. Davey came downstairs wearing a stiffly starched white shirt, his dress gray knickers and home knit stockings. This was the first day of Sunday School after the summer vacation and everyone wanted to look their best.

This was also the first year that three-year-old Sarah would be allowed to attend the primary class and since the community was always short of teachers, Milly had volunteered to help. In the past Peter had walked Davey to Sunday School which started at 9 o'clock, and then returned home to walk with Milly and Sarah to attend the 10 o'clock church service. There was a nursery during church run by the older girls, one of whom was Mabel Parker. The other was her inseparable friend Erica Larson. After Lucy was born, Milly, Sarah and the baby usually remained home. This fall, however, Lucy was nine months old, and everyone was planning to go to church.

It was decided that Anna, Milly and the children would leave about 8:30, and Peter would come an hour later with Lucy. They usually walked to church instead of taking the horse and buggy. Some day when they had a car they might drive, although they all enjoyed the fresh air and the walk along the river. Milly left strict directions for Peter about getting Lucy ready, and was more than a little apprehensive about this arrangement. Her nervousness made her face a blushing pink, with her hands continually waving instructions.

Anna wanted to leave with Milly and the children because Milly had mentioned that she might be able to assist in the teaching of Sunday School. Since it was the first day in the fall, a spare person would be welcome. She had taught Sunday School in Fort Dodge and enjoyed it.

Armed with their Bibles, Anna, dressed in the same outfit she had worn the day she arrived in Grabney, and Milly, also wearing her good frock, hat and gloves, and the children set out on the path. It was a nuisance to have to step so carefully to avoid the dust, however they managed to arrive in fairly good shape.

To get to the front of the church, a white wooden structure, they walked to the main road, passed the parsonage, and climbed the eight steps to the door. Upon entering Anna could see that the sanctuary seated about fifty people. It had wooden pews and a slightly raised platform on which stood a lectern, behind which was a wooden cross. A pump organ was off to one side and a big cast iron heating stove on the other. There were windows on both sides of the building, making it light and pleasant. It was undoubtedly similar in both construction and furnishings to most country churches.

They turned to the left to go downstairs where the Sunday School was held. At the bottom of the steps, warmly greeting everyone was Rev. Thomas Blakeley, a middle-aged man of medium height who gave every appearance of being well fed, but not to the point of being fat. He reminded Anna of a Santa Claus without the beard and with thinning gray hair instead of white. As Milly was introducing Anna to him, Anna realized that this was a man who not only loved his calling, but loved people. He seemed gentle and kind. She knew he was well organized, as after his service in Grabney, he had barely enough time for a bite of lunch before leaving for his next service in Brewster. He made a fuss over Anna, saying that he was delighted to meet her and would be proud to introduce her to the group.

In the back half of the room stood plain wooden tables, used for church suppers. The benches had been lined up at the front since the first half of the program would be a group service. The children took places on one of the forward benches while Anna and Milly sat toward the back with the few adults, all women. The room was well lit with windows on both sides, the bottom of the windows coming to ground level. A smaller room was at the far end which Milly explained was the kitchen and it could also be entered from a back door. The cook stove was placed so that it could be used to heat both rooms. It was cool in the room, a welcome change as the temperature outside was getting quite warm.

Inger was standing to one side of the room in front of the piano, busily writing in a notebook. It was obvious that she was one of the persons in charge. Anna found herself somewhat of a celebrity and was so busy meeting the half dozen or so women who had come that she didn't notice that Rev. Blakeley had walked to the front of the room. As he began to speak, she glanced at the three rows in front of her, counted twenty-two children, and suddenly had a sinking feeling, wondering if all of them were in her district. To her relief, she recalled Inger mentioning that there were two other schools several miles from Grabney, as the Grabney School was not within walking distance for these children. This no doubt explained why several horse and buggy rigs were in the grounds next to the church, and why several men were seen walking over to the store, probably to pass the time until church began, and perhaps to have a smoke, or to stay there until both services concluded. While the store was not open on Sunday, this was the Marson home, and it appeared that Mr. Marson had nothing against opening the door and letting the men folk in for a little conversation, which usually centered on farming and the weather. In warm weather as today, they gathered on the porch, sitting on an odd assortment of chairs or on the porch steps.

Rev. Blakeley started by again welcoming everyone. He noted that the Sunday School was much smaller than it had been when his children were young, and remarked that most of the local farm families' children had grown up as his own had, so he was especially happy to have the present group and knew that they would make up in spirit what they lacked in numbers. He next mentioned that Inger was assigning students to classes, and would give her report later. Then he introduced Anna, and every child's head swiveled back to inspect the new teacher. Most faces were very solemn although she noticed that a couple of them were stifling giggles. After she gave them her best smile the stern countenances began to relax.

The middle-aged woman who had recently seated herself at the piano began to play the *Doxology* and all rose and joined in the singing led by the strong baritone of their pastor. Next could be heard the rustle of pages as children and adults alike fumbled to turn to the 23rd Psalm for a unison reading. One Bible was dropped and the mortified owner became more embarrassed as the entire group waited for her to retrieve it and turn to the correct page. The giggling of friends did not help her situation. After they were seated Rev. Blakeley gave a small sermon appropriate to the beginning of the school year, concluding that everyone was now starting over again, old slates were wiped clean, and by attending today they were off to a good start, hoping that everyone would have a year of perfect attendance.

Inger was next on the program explaining that the children were divided into four groups: primary, ages three to five, elementary, grades one through three, intermediate, grades four through six, and upper, grades seven and eight. She efficiently assigned classes to tables and introduced the teachers. Some groans were heard, but they were minor. Milly was to be one of the teachers for the intermediate group. At that point Anna was asked if she would mind helping with the primary group. This delighted both Anna and Sarah, who now also had Miss Swenson for her teacher.

They were dismissed to their tables, with the larger children moving benches and tables back to their original location. Each class was separated by as large a space as possible so they would not interfere with each other. Mrs. Esther Pearson, the mother of one of Anna's pupils, third grader Victoria, was the primary teacher. Anna liked her immediately. She was effervescent and creative, was a good story teller, brought cutouts to paste, and the children and Anna all enjoyed the class. At the conclusion they marched to the front of the room to sing *Jesus Loves Me*. Before being dismissed Inger asked if anyone would volunteer to play the piano for the Sunday School for the rest of the year. Mrs. Simms, who played for the Sunday School as well as playing the organ for the church service, was hoping that someone would be able to replace her for the

9 o'clock hour. Her children had been grown for some time and while she would continue to play for church, it was somewhat of an inconvenience for her to come so early for Sunday School. Anna had occasionally played for the Sunday School in Fort Dodge, but was not about to volunteer for this job. For one reason she did not have a piano on which to practice, and she would never let herself submit to playing before a group without having rehearsed the songs. Surely there must be someone else who could do it. To her relief they were dismissed.

Davey asked if he could go home with George, as he had been invited, and since both Floyd and Walter were home Milly approved. To ask a six year old to sit through both Sunday School and church was asking for almost too much. Peter arrived with Lucy, who appeared presentable as far as her mother was concerned, and she joined Mabel, Sarah and Erica Larson in a corner of the basement, on blankets on the floor, where there was a supply of children's toys.

As they entered the sanctuary upstairs, they saw about thirty people including many men. Anna was pleased to observe that this was not mainly a women's organization. Hymns were sung, the scripture read, the sermon not too long, and they were out by eleven o'clock. A final announcement was made concerning the Labor Day picnic, which would take place in the afternoon of the following day, on the church picnic grounds. While Milly went to retrieve Lucy and Sarah, Anna visited with the various members, happy to meet some of the parents of her students.

As she was about to join the family for the walk home, she was met by Mrs. Simms, the organist. "Inger told me that you played the piano. Would you possibly consider playing it for the Sunday School? I would appreciate it so much as I would like to have the extra hour on Sunday."

Anna was nonplused on hearing that Inger had recommended her and could think of no excuses except the obvious. "But I don't have a piano, so I couldn't practice," she answered, "and I wouldn't like to play without going over the songs."

She was reluctant to give the woman an outright "No", as being a newcomer to the community she wanted to make a good impression, but also realized that she should not overextend herself. Worse yet, she didn't want to put herself in a situation where she would make obvious mistakes, as a wrong note on the piano is definitely very obvious. She could hear the children giggle and she would die of embarrassment.

"I know that Rev. Blakeley would let you come and use the Sunday School piano whenever you wanted."

"I am not sure I would be good enough to do it," replied Anna. "I haven't ever played regularly for a Sunday School."

"I am sure you would be fine from what Inger says."

Anna wondered how Inger could recommend her so highly. Probably Uncle Lars had sung her praises in writing to the district. That may have been why Inger mentioned getting back the pump organ without asking Anna if she could play it. Or were they so desperate that they would take anybody. Surely there were other people in the community who could play. Almost every farmhouse had a pump organ and many had a piano. In desperation she continued, "Also I am just starting school and there is so much to do. Could you let me have a little time to think it over?"

"Yes, of course. But do think it over. I would be so grateful to you if you could do it. I wouldn't mind playing for the next week or two if I knew that you might be able to take my place at some time." With that she warmly shook Anna's hand, and went to join her husband who had their horse and buggy ready to leave.

This was a surprising development. She had never mentioned to Inger that she played the piano, in fact she did not consider herself terribly good at it. It certainly must have been Uncle Lars who had informed her, no doubt to add a little more to her list of qualifications for teaching. Well, so it was.

On the walk home she thought of the piano her father had bought for her mother when they were first married. Her mother who played beautifully had always kept it in the parlor. When company came the sewing machines would be forgotten and they would stand around the piano singing. It was such fun. Anna had been taught to play by her mother although had never attained the proficiency she desired. Anyway, she would not worry about this for the moment, as it was most important that she make a good start at teaching. After that, perhaps she could think about taking on the responsibility of playing the piano. She knew that she might even enjoy it, that is if she had enough time to practice.

Chapter Eight

In the moments of first waking this morning, Anna felt a sense of calmness. The air was still, no breeze to billow the organdy curtains at the screened window. The coolness of the night had disappeared to be replaced by a gradual warming. As she lay with her head on the soft down pillow she could hear the sounds of the household downstairs. No need to stir herself so soon. This was Labor Day, the day of the picnic, promises of fun, a baseball game, meeting the rest of the community who had not seen fit to attend church on the previous day. It was also the last day of vacation before she would begin teaching. She daydreamed about that and continued to let her mind wander to other pleasant events which had occurred since her arrival. She found herself laughing about the Saturday night bath. And she loved the children, sweet, shy Sarah, and Davey so eager to please. Lucy was a dimpled darling. She sighed as she thought how fortunate she was to land in this wonderful home.

Suddenly dragging her out of her reverie was the sound of a thump, thump, thump, thump, which continued at a fairly steady rate. Puzzled as to the source of this noise she listened carefully. It seemed to be coming from the entry porch, and then she realized it was the washing machine. Of course, it was Monday, and Milly probably insisted on doing the laundry. Nothing to do but to hustle herself up and face the day and its waiting occupations.

Ten minutes later found her scurrying down the stairs to the kitchen. A fresh table had been set with a new red checked oilcloth and fresh napkins in the napkin rings. The Sunday cloth had found its way to the laundry. Milly was busily preparing breakfast and frying chicken for the picnic. She glanced through the door to the porch and found that it was Peter who was pushing the washer handle back and forth, which turned the agitator on the square shaped machine.

"Oh Milly! I had no idea you were planning to do the washing today. I should have been up ages ago to help. You must have been up for hours."

"Oh, no," answered the efficient rosy-cheeked Milly, who seemed to have several pairs of hands which moved continually. "We didn't get up until almost six. Peter pumped the water from the well last night and had it sitting on the stove in the copper boiler. We have to use the hard well water now because there isn't enough in the cistern."

"You must have had to get up in the middle of the night to heat the water."

"Oh, no, Peter lit the fire before he went out to do the milking. When he came in he poured the boiling water into the washer. Now he's pushing the handle to do the wash."

Anna realized that it was not quite so simple as it sounded. Doing the milking involved separating it, feeding the skim to the pigs, saving whole milk and cream, washing and scalding the separator and countless other chores she was not aware of. However this couple seemed to take everything as it came, and now Peter was doing the laundry.

"I certainly know how to do the wash, Milly," said Anna. "Let me go and do that. Peter probably has other chores." She quickly entered the steamy entry to find him dejectedly heaving the handle back and forth.

"I'll do that," she told him.

"You'll get mighty tired pushing this handle back and forth, better let me do it," he answered heaving a sigh. "Anyway, I guess this load is ready to be wrung into the rinse water." He took the lid off the washer, and grabbed a big wooden spoon to lift the clothes out of the hot water up to the wringer. Carefully he inserted the first article and turned the handle, squeezing the water back into the washer, and dropping the item into the tub of cold rinse water, which sat on the backless chair. "You can slosh the clothes in the rinse water if you will. Don't mind if the water gets scummy. The wash water has been softened with washing soda so the soap will dissolve but we don't soften the rinse water. When I get through here I'll get Milly to put in another load."

56

Milly soon appeared and took charge, added a new batch of clothes to the washer, and said that they should soak awhile before the agitator was turned. Anna swiveled the wringer so she could wring the clothes from the rinse water into the wicker clothes basket. Cranking the wringer for small items was not difficult, but turning in to wring out the sheets was hard work. In a few minutes Peter reappeared to continue the agitation process, and Anna was off with the basket full of clothes and the muslin bag of clothespins.

The six rope clotheslines were strung from the top "T" board of two wooden clothesline posts. The posts were about twenty feet apart, and situated next to the vegetable garden to the right of the back porch. As the lines were full of summer dust, Anna went over them carefully with the wiping rag before hanging up the laundry. She returned to the house in time to wring out the second load of clothes, but was interrupted by Milly who had breakfast on the table. The meal was hotcakes and fried eggs this morning, and was barely over before the chores continued. Davey and Sarah were off to collect eggs and were reminded that when they returned to the house they were to leave them in the egg pail and not put them with the old eggs as fresh eggs did not hard boil well and Milly needed to boil eggs for the potato salad.

By eleven o'clock the work was done, and Peter drained the water from the washer through a hose into the back flower garden. As usual Milly cleaned both tub and washer scrubbing the entry way floor in the process.

"I am sure you are exhausted Milly," commented Anna as she collapsed into a chair. She could feel the perspiration running down her face and reached for her hankie only to find it soaking wet from overuse during the morning, but wiped her face anyway.

"It is nothing," replied Milly, patting at her face with her apron. "I did the washing today because I have to pick the last of the peas tomorrow and can them. I'll miss Davey. He's a champion pea picker, but I am so happy to have him attending school with you, because I know that you will be a good teacher. Let's have a cup of coffee." She poured them each a cup and sighed as she took a chair. "You have worked too hard this morning Anna. I did not intend that you should do the laundry. It probably isn't right for schoolteachers to do family chores. I yust forget. I think you are part of the family and I give everyone a yob."

"Oh Milly," Anna laughed. "I want to be part of your family. I want to help you in any way I can." She noticed that Milly did seem quite exhausted, but not so much so that she did not have the strength to get up and go to the cookie jar and come back with a plateful of cookies. After passing them to Anna and taking one herself she brought them to the children who were outside. Sarah and Davey had been playing with Lucy so they would not be underfoot.

Peter returned with Milly, poured himself a mug of coffee and joined them at the table. "I wonder if Eddie Marson is coming to the picnic. We could use him on our baseball team. Last year we sure got beat by the Simms' gang, and Eddie is a first rate player."

The name sounded familiar so Anna asked if it were the same Simms family who produced Mrs. Simms who played the organ.

Two heads nodded in the affirmative. Peter explained that while the couple may have grown children, Mr. Simms was still young enough to organize a first rate ball team, at least one that was considered good enough to beat any team which would take them on at the local picnics.

"Are you the one who organizes the team from around here?" asked Anna.

"Oh, no, Elmer Marson does that," Peter replied. "Since we lost last year, I was hoping that he could convince Eddie to play. Eddie played on his high school team and was a darn good pitcher. The rest of us can't throw a ball for beans."

"Enough! Enough!" said Milly as she jumped up. "Time to get ready for the picnic. "I will pack the food in the boxes over there," and she pointed to two large cardboard cartons. "We will use the oilcloth and napkins from the table and they can go in around the plates, cups and silver."

The children had come into the kitchen by this time and were listening to the plans. Milly took one look at them and exclaimed that they would need a wash-down and perhaps some clean clothes, especially Lucy who had been allowed to crawl in the dirt.

"How are we going to all get into the buggy?" asked Peter. "With only one seat and all that food, we're not going to fit."

"I'll be happy to walk," volunteered Anna. "Perhaps the children would like to walk with me."

"Yes! I would," exclaimed Davey, and his answer was resoundingly echoed by Sarah. So it was settled.

At 1 o'clock Peter hitched up one of the horses and drove the buggy into the yard. He carefully loaded the boxes of food and utensils, and with Milly and Lucy beside him they started for the picnic ground. Anna, Davey and Sarah had been given a head start. Davey wanted to beat his parents, knowing that the path was shorter than the road, so he started off at a run. Anna and Sarah went carefully behind, each one walking in the grass on either side of the path, holding hands over the path itself.

Anna had never had a close relationship with a young child before, and she cherished the feeling of companionship with this youngster. To feel her sweaty palm, holding so tightly as she maneuvered through the bunches of grass, to answer her questions, to notice the adoring look in Sarah's eyes when she looked up, was an experience which brought out strong maternal instincts and made Anna feel very protective and happy.

As they neared the picnic ground they could see the men carrying the tables and benches from the church basement and setting them up in an area near the river in back of the parsonage, under the huge cottonwood trees. As quickly as they were in place, the women spread out the cloths, set the cutlery, plates and cups, to be followed by dishes and platters of food. Milly and Peter had arrived and were setting up a table next to Inger and Floyd, making one long table.

"I've asked Rev. and Mrs. Blakeley to sit with us," announced Inger. "I hope that is all right with you?" This was directed at Milly, but was not actually intended as a question, more for an affirmative assent. "I've got the coffee going in the church basement. One of the men can bring it out later.

Oh, hello Anna. Here you can help me with this pitcher

of milk, just put it over there. Milly probably brought one too, so we'll have plenty."

Anna immediately put herself to work. She recalled seeing Mrs. Blakeley at church but had not met her. She knew she would enjoy having an opportunity to get to know the Reverend better. It made their table seem special, but then Inger was an organizer.

As the horses and buggies rolled in they were driven up near the tables, unloaded and driven over to another shady area behind the church where the horses were tethered. Gradually the tables were filling up in what seemed like orderly confusion. Women were walking around visiting and examining the various dishes which had been prepared, adding their own comments. There was definitely an undercurrent of competition which seemed to be masked by smiles, however the general mood was one of lightheartedness.

The Rev. and Mrs. Blakeley appeared laden with their bounty, which included two large apple pies. In seems that Mrs. Blakeley was known for her excellent apple pies, and everyone was happy to see that her apples were ripe enough for pies this early in the season. Rev. Blakeley greeted everyone at the table and then made his way around the entire group shaking hands and chatting informally to make sure everyone was getting settled. He was jovial and sincerely interested in his parishioners. When he returned he called for attention by hitting his knife against his cup, which was repeated at tables throughout the area, resulting in the silence needed for saying grace. It was probably the only time in the afternoon when they would be so still. For a moment the only sound heard was the drone of a few bugs, and the occasional barking of a dog, and then he said grace. Following the chorus of "Amen" from the crowd, came the shuffling of people sitting down, the clink of silverware, wives giving instructions, and animated conversation.

Anna was seated between Sarah and Mrs. Blakeley, with Davey, his parents and Lucy, on Milly's lap, sitting across from her. At the adjoining table were Rev. Blakeley, Inger, Floyd and children. Mrs. Blakeley was physically small and seemed reserved, however Anna was to learn very shortly that she had a mind of her own and was not reluctant to express herself and stand up for what she believed was "right".

She had barely met the woman when she found herself busy passing platters and bowls of food, and serving herself and Sarah. As she took a big platter of chicken from Milly she glanced over at the Kloster cornfield to see a small boy standing at the edge, about fifty yards away, solemn and wide-eyed, observing the festivities. "Is that little boy Joshua Kloster?" she queried.

"Where?" asked Milly.

"Over by the edge of the cornfield," replied Anna.

All heads turned to look at the child. "Yes, of course," said Mrs. Blakeley. "Wouldn't you know but his family is the only one not attending the picnic, and there he stands, left out of the food and the fun."

"There's not much we can do about it Mother," replied the Reverend.

"Yes, there is!" she firmly announced as she rose and climbed over the bench which had been pushed close to the table. "I'm going to get him."

"His parents will never let him come," added Inger.

"I have known Grace since she was a little girl," replied Mrs. Blakeley.

"Grace don't make the decisions in that family," said Floyd. "And Kloster prob'ly has the kid so scared that he'll run as soon as you start walkin' toward him. And how're you gonna manage that fence?"

"We'll see," answered Mrs. Blakeley, and she started walking toward Joshua.

They stopped eating and watched her as she went across the field where they would later be playing baseball. When it was noticed what she was doing, heads at other tables turned to watch also. Conversation quieted and a few parents were heard to admonish, "Hush!" to a noisy child. Joshua didn't move. He stood there and waited for her to come to him. She stayed at the fence talking to him for a short time, and then he held up the top two wires while she pushed down on the lower two to make an opening , and she crawled through. They disappeared among the rows of corn, walking toward the house.

"Well! I'll be dad gummed. If that don't beat all," Floyd remarked as if he didn't believe what he had seen.

"I hope they will be nice to her," Inger commented.

61

"I think she knows what she's doing," commented Rev. Blakeley. "Now, we'll have to wait and see what happens."

It took a few moments before the group continued eating again, so surprised were they at this new development, but once again they settled down to their food. Two women volunteered to pour coffee and were kept busy refilling cups, which caused a great deal of lighthearted banter.

Anna kept an eye on the cornfield. In about fifteen minutes they were finished with dinner and ready for dessert and still no sign of Mrs. Blakeley or Joshua.

"Peter, why don't you go and see if everything's all right," Milly said nervously, her hands shaking in agitation.

"Would you like me to go check on them Reverend?" asked Peter.

"No, I don't think that's necessary. Thank you all the same Peter. When she finds that we are ready to cut into her apple pies, and she is not here, she will come a running."

No sooner was this said than the two of them came through the fence and walked across the field and over to the table.

"Here we are, so let's find a plate for Joshua so he can have some dinner too," Mrs. Blakely seated him between Anna and herself. "I knew it was time to come back as I see you were ready to cut into my pies. Well, go ahead. You have my permission if you save us each a piece." She took an extra plate for Joshua, which was quickly filled, and placed it in front of him.

"You folks probably didn't know that Joshua and I are friends. We often visit together at the fence, and sometimes he gets to come to my house for a piece of pie, isn't that right Joshua?" There was a nod in the affirmative. "Now Joshua, I would like you to meet your new teacher, Miss Swenson." The boy looked quickly at Anna and then bent his head toward the table again. "And you know Davey, don't you?" A small nod followed. "I think you know most of the rest of the people here, and if you don't, you can meet them later. So let's get on with our dinner, or they will have eaten all of our apple pie."

With dinner over, the women covered up the food, chasing off the pesky flies, and stashed away the dirty dishes. For the next half hour or so everyone visited, the women bringing coffee cups and sitting in groups at the tables, the children running around, and the men talking crops and farming over by the horses. Mrs. Blakeley asked Davey and Joshua to help her bring her dishes into the house. After they returned it was learned that she gave them an extra treat of candy. Milly suggested that Davey take Joshua over to where George and some of the boys were. She knew that if George were there he would see that they stayed out of trouble. He might be only eleven, but he was dependable. Joshua looked to Mrs. Blakeley for confirmation that this might be all right, and she smilingly assured him that it was.

"You go with Davey and meet some of the other boys, and when you want to go home I'll bring you back. I promised your mother I would look after you."

The main topic of conversation centered around the fact that Joshua had been allowed to come to the picnic. Mrs. Blakeley explained that both Roger Kloster and Bill Evans were in the barn when she appeared at the door with Joshua, and after much persuasive talking Grace finally gave her approval to letting the child come to the outing.

"Goodness knows what will happen when they find that the boy is gone, and that he has come here," replied one woman. "That is precisely the reason that I want to return him myself. If Grace can't stand up to those two men, I can. The poor child is deprived of all social contact. Thank goodness he will be attending school. I just hope he won't be a problem to you Anna. Oh, I don't think he will cause you any trouble, but it worries me that he is so quiet."

"It's not the quiet ones I am worried about at the moment," replied Anna. She was still thinking of tales told by teacher friends she had met at Cedar Falls.

The women noticed that the men were getting ready for the baseball game, so they all chose seats facing the field. The children were seated on the grass at the edge of the field. Lucy was asleep in Milly's arms and with Inger's help she transferred the baby to a blanket on the ground.

At sixteen Walter Parker was on the local team along with Jimmy Burns, who was fifteen, and Eddie Marson. Elmer had recruited ten locals, including Floyd and a few others who were not known for their batting or throwing skills, however the team looked as if it had some promise. Mr. Simms' team looked a bit better since he had more young men, but time would tell. Rev. Blakeley was asked to be the umpire, and he accepted the job knowing that the deciding would be all done before he could open his mouth. Floyd marked the bases by kicking a depression in the dirt with his heel, and then kicked up a small pile of grass and dirt for the pitcher's mound.

Teams chosen, a coin was tossed and the game began. The Grabney team was up first, and since it seemed respectful to let the older members have the first opportunities at bat, they made three strike-outs. The second half of the first inning Eddie Marson showed the other team that he could pitch. They had their best batters up and brought home only one run. During the game the women cheered no matter who made a hit. There were no favorites, however the children definitely rooted for the team where they had relatives or friends. It was not great sport, but it was great fun.

Joshua seemed to be enjoying the game as much as the other children until the first half of the sixth inning when Eddie hit a ball into his cornfield. Suddenly he froze, and then he took off in a wild run to where the ball had gone, and dashed through the fence to retrieve it. It was a fair ball a home run in fact, but Eddie did not run to first base. He stared after Joshua as if he feared some dreadful consequence. Soon the child re-appeared trembling and clutching the ball which he gave to Rev. Blakeley.

"I think I better go home now. Try not to let them hit it over the fence again. My pa can get awful mad."

Mrs. Blakeley had followed Joshua when he dashed after the ball, and now she joined him and her husband. "I will take him home. I promised Grace that I would, in case there is any trouble with Roger." She took the child by the hand, climbed through the fence and they disappeared.

The men decided to play through the second half of the inning and then call it a game. It was a hot afternoon and their enthusiasm had begun to dwindle. They probably paid more attention to watching for Mrs. Blakeley to come back than to what was going on in the game. As they called it a game, with the local Grabney men winning six to five, Mrs. Blakeley was

64

seen on the other side of the fence, and Roger Kloster was there to help her through it. She thanked him and he thanked her for giving Joshua a pleasant afternoon, which was witnessed by all.

"How was Grace?" asked her husband as they approached the picnic tables.

"I didn't get to see Grace. She was probably in the bedroom with little Elaine. I did talk with Roger about Joshua coming to school tomorrow and he said to tell the teacher that he would bring the boy himself. He also said, Anna, that he would be starting the fire in the stove in September and October, but assumed that you wouldn't be needing heat for this first month."

"That woman has always had a way with that family," said the Reverend shaking his head.

"Oh Thomas, how you do go on," she replied smiling at him. "Anyway, it is getting late and time to get the place cleaned up."

On the way home Davey walked with Anna, while Sarah rode with her parents. It had been a long day for her. As the two of them straddled the path to keep to the grass, Davey remarked that Joshua was so quiet, and it was strange that even though they lived across the road from each other, this was one of the first days that he had spent any time with him.

Chapter Nine

That Monday night Anna had difficulty getting to sleep. She lay tossing and turning with only a sheet over her in the stuffy upstairs room, still feeling the emotional excitement of the afternoon's events, and her brain refused to close down and rest. It was not that the day had been so extraordinary, simply that she had had several days of unceasing activity, and now she had to face up to tomorrow, her first day of teaching. The combination led to insomnia.

She mentally checked off all that she had done, to insure that there was nothing more she could do. She reviewed all the pupil's names and grades. She had met most of them either at Sunday School or at the picnic so formed a picture in her mind of how she would place them in their seats. And it went on, and on, until finally drowsiness overtook her and she fell into a fitful sleep.

The clatter of pans shook her awake. Had she overslept? She scrutinized her watch with bleary eyes. No, it was only 6:30. She felt limp, but at the thought of all that lay ahead a nervous energy consumed her. As she splashed the lukewarm water on her face and brushed her long, light brown hair her mind retraced each step of the plans she had so carefully prepared. She chose to wear a simple brown skirt and cream colored blouse, her most teacher-looking clothes. A last minute check in the mirror to make sure her hair was properly pinned with no loose ends, assured her that she did indeed look like a teacher.

She met Davey as she was going down the stairs. In his hands he carried his pencils and tablet, and the eager expression on his face left no doubt but that he was ready for this big day.

As usual Milly was busy preparing breakfast. Two lunch pails were on the counter, one had been a five pound honey pail and the other had held the same amount of peanut butter. Next to them were two enamelware cups.

"Oi! Yoi! Yoi! You look the perfect school teacher," exclaimed Milly with a wide smile of approval while carrying a platter of hotcakes to the table. "Sit down now, and don't hurry. You have plenty of time. It is only seven o'clock. Davey, wait for the rest of the family before you help yourself, and always pass the food to the adults first. Peter could you put Lucy in her high chair? Hurry Sarah and sit down so we can say grace. What time did you want to get to school Anna?"

"I thought it would be best if I got there about 8 o'clock."

"That sounds a perfect time. You will have an hour before classes start. Then you must leave here about 7:30 or a little after that. Ah, Peter. You are ready for the blessing." The simple prayer followed, with a wish that it be a perfect day for both Anna and Davey.

Immediately Milly continued with her information and instructions. "Anna and Davey, I have packed a sandwich and some cake in your lunches. Anna you take the honey pail. I had some small pieces of oilcloth left over from cutting the table-cloth so put one around the food so your napkin won't get soiled. Davey I gave you a napkin too, but Inger said boys don't like to have napkins in their lunch pail, so you don't have to use it. And, oh yes, I have an enamelware cup for each of you."

"I was planning to buy one at the store, but forgot," said Anna remonstrating with herself.

"Don't worry. These were left over from Peter's batching days. I don't like them. The cup gets so hot you can't drink the coffee until it gets cold, but they will be fine for water at school. I also have a huck towel for each of you. I embroidered them myself."

"Oh, Milly you shouldn't let us take your beautiful towels to school. I brought a towel, let me get it," volunteered Anna.

"No, no! You keep your towel, and when this one gets dirty, bring it home and you can use yours. These towels aren't so special, and I don't want anyone coming from my house without a pretty towel. You will see that some of the children will have very fancy ones. Davey, remember you must gather the eggs before you leave for school. I know you want to go early with Miss Swenson, so you will have to hurry."

Breakfast continued at a somewhat frenzied pace. Anna was not too hungry, but did not want to hurt Milly's feelings by not eating much, so she managed to get down enough to satisfy the cook.

At approximately 7:40 Anna and Davey were off for school. They glanced at the Kloster house as they left the yard and saw some activity there, but continued on without seeing Joshua. Ahead of them was Erica, who no doubt was on her way to Mabel's house. Davey's eagerness for school had somewhat subsided, and he became more solemn as they approached the building.

"Why don't you come in and put your lunch on the shelf, and your cup and towel on the hooks. Then you can wait for the others to arrive," advised Anna.

"But I don't know where to put them," he shyly admitted.

"Come in and you will see your name above your hooks. You know how to read your name I am sure."

"I think so," he muttered. "But I don't know if I can read your writing."

Anna laughed and led the way. Soon Davey had his things in the proper place and then spent some time perusing the room. He looked to make sure his desk was still there, and then went out on the porch to await the others. "Leave the doors open," Anna called after him.

She put her lunch pail by her desk, and her cup and towel in a drawer. She rechecked her notebook to make sure that her plan for the day was there, as well as the students' names. After winding and setting the clock, she realized that there was nothing more she could do and so it was a relief to hear Davey shouting to someone, and was pleased to see George appear in the doorway.

Greetings were exchanged and George, knowing what to do, put his lunch pail, towel and cup in the assigned place.

He then took the pail out to the pump, filled it with fresh water and lugged it into the building to replace it on the shelf. He let Davey put the dipper in, and they both watched as first it floated on top of the water and then as it filled, it gradually sank to the bottom.

The others arrived, searched for their names above the shelf, and put the things they had brought from home in the designated places. Victoria Pearson, the daughter of the woman Anna had assisted at Sunday School, brought a handful of neatly cut out pieces of flannel, each about three to four inches square.

"My mother cut these flannels for you. They were scraps left over from making winter nightgowns."

"How thoughtful of her," replied Anna, realizing that there were things which she had overlooked. "I know we don't have any flannels here, and I had hoped to start writing with ink very soon. Now we can start this very first day. Be sure to thank her for me." With a smile the child was on her way outside to play with the others.

At nine o'clock Anna was standing on the narrow porch, gripping the bell rope, and ringing the bell which was mounted on the building next to the door. The students entered and were asked to sit at a desk which fit them. The desks were bolted to the floor in three rows, with the smaller desks toward the front. As the seat was attached to the desk behind it, often a seat was a little high for a smaller desk. It took about five minutes for the group to get settled as there was a fair amount of changing seats and muted conversation regarding not only the size of the desk and seat, but who would be sitting next to or across from whom.

After the group had settled down Anna called the roll. "First grade: Joshua Kloster and David Jensen." Joshua had not yet appeared.

"Third grade: Annie Lindquist, Victoria Pearson and Carl Anderson." Annie and Victoria were sitting across from each other in the second row. Carl was in the third row nearest the windows near the boys. That was as to be expected Anna realized as she smiled to herself.

"Fourth grade: Philip Reed and Edwin Lindquist.

"Sixth grade: George Parker.

"Seventh grade: Lars Anderson and Edna Reed.

"Eighth grade: Mabel Parker and Erica Larson." Mabel sat in the back row behind Erica, with Edna the seventh grader, in front of them.

All looked well. Anna had just started to tell them a little about herself when there was a sound of footsteps coming up to the porch. Through the open door she could see Joshua Kloster and his father. They entered the room, and all heads turned. Mr. Kloster was tall and thin, very thin but very muscular. His hair was black and his high cheekbones gave him a gaunt appearance. There was a strong resemblance between the two, especially their deep-set brown eyes, however the father's face was stern, whereas the child's face looked innocent and frightened.

"Scuse me. Sorry to be late. Name's Roger Kloster. This here's my boy Joshua." He forcefully shoved the boy forward. "He was named after Joshua in the Bible. Are you a God fearin' woman?"

Anna was taken aback by the question. "I don't know what you mean."

"I mean, are you a God fearin' woman? That ought to be plain enough. Answer me woman!"

"I attend church, if that is what you mean. I was there last Sunday, and I am helping with the Sunday School." Not to be bullied Anna retorted with, "I don't believe I saw you in church."

"We worship at home all day Sunday, not just for an hour in the morning. We are a holy family and abide by the gospel. No work on Sunday. We read the Bible. We are true believers, not just Sunday Christians."

Anna realized that this was the beginning of a sermon, so broke in with a welcome for Joshua, walked over to him and explained where his seat was located. She asked Davey to take the boy to the lunch pail shelf so he could put his things there. The child glanced timidly at his father who nodded that he was to do as he was told.

"Now, if you go to church I guess that will do. But remember that Joshua is to have a Christian education. No bad language!"

"I assure you that there will be no bad language used in this classroom nor on the playground. Thank you very much for bringing Joshua. Perhaps in the future he will be able to walk to school with Davey and me," and with this she hoped he would be dismissed, but it was not to be.

"I haven't finished. He may walk with you and David Jensen in the morning only if he has finished his chores. Also you are to let me know if he is lazy and doesn't work, or if he disobeys. You do not need to whip him, I will use the strop at home. He knows what that means."

Horrified, Anna replied that there would be no whipping, not even a spanking in the school, and she turned and resumed her place at the front of the classroom behind her desk. "Good-bye Mr. Kloster. I must get on with the class work."

"It is my responsibility to start the fire for September and October. You won't need one for at least two weeks. I will light the fire after that. And Joshua, I don't want any bad reports about you. Understand!" With that he turned and left the room, continuing down the stairs and off to the road without looking back.

The class had been completely silent during this interruption, and now they looked around the room at each other and then at Anna. She realized that she as well as the students needed a complete change of pace, so she gave them her warmest smile.

"We all welcome Joshua," and she looked at him reassuringly. "Now I had started to tell you a little about myself and after I have finished, I would like you to tell me a little about yourselves and about Grabney. We will also discuss the rules you had last year. I am new here so you can help me learn, and then we will talk about the rules we will have for this year. You will notice that I have written a schedule on the blackboard which says that we will have a ten minute recess at 10:30. If we finish before that I will read to you from *Treasure Island* by Robert Louis Stevenson. When I arrived Mr. Parker could hardly lift my trunk and accused me of packing too many books." Giggles followed this remark. "He was right," she laughed. "I brought lots of books, some for you to read, and some for me to read to you."

After recess Anna asked the students to take out their pen holders and pen points, as they would have a writing lesson. "You know how to put the pen point in your mouth and suck off the oil, then wipe it off on the flannel I will pass to you. But only do this when the pen point is new," she advised, and they all laughed with her.

"I don't want one of Victoria's flannels," sneered Carl Anderson. "And I don't want to write with pen and ink. I have a pencil. That's better."

"Raise your hand if you wish to speak Carl," Anna commented brusquely, "and you don't need to learn to write with pen and ink. You may do this lesson with a pencil."

Next she poured a small amount of ink in the glass ink well in each desk. "Keep the metal hinged cover over the ink well when you are not writing in ink. I am sure many of you have had the experience of unintentionally getting ink on papers and making a mess. When you are finished wipe the ink off the pen point and put the pen on the pencil tray on your desk. Keep the flannel inside the desk, but off to one side so ink won't get on anything else. Each one of you will keep your own pen. I hope that you brought tablets with ink paper. Be sure to write lightly, because if you press too hard you will spatter the ink and may break the pen point. I know that this is the first time that the third graders have written in pen and ink so I would like to ask Mabel and Erica to help Annie and Victoria get started." The girls nodded with enthusiasm that they would be happy to assist, although it was obvious that Victoria and Annie had practiced at home as they tackled this new project with confidence.

"I am going to start the first graders with writing their name, and the rest of you follow the instructions on the board and write about yourself and your family, and perhaps what you did during the summer. This will be like a diary or journal and you will write another page or two every Monday. I will help the third graders when I have finished with Joshua and Davey."

The morning went quickly, with the students wiping off their pens about noon, and passing in their work.

73

"It is now noon and we have forty-five minutes for lunch. You may eat your lunch in here or outside," and she dismissed the class.

Anna ate at her desk while looking through the morning's compositions. The afternoon went quickly, with the students designing covers for their journals, and following the afternoon recess they were given arithmetic, reading, spelling and history or geography books, which they kept in their desks. She gave them a reading assignment. Thus Anna was able to spend time with the two first graders, helping them to learn to write the alphabet, copying letters which were thumb tacked above the blackboard, and for a change of pace they drew a picture of their family.

School was dismissed at three. Anna told Davey to go on ahead as she wanted to prepare for the next day, and she was pleased to see Joshua walk out of the building with him. It was pleasant to sit at her desk in her room. She felt a sense of proprietorship and belonging. The students had been well behaved, perhaps on good behavior for the first day. Now she must look over their books and have assignments ready for each subject for the next day.

As she made ready to leave, she collected the compositions and the pictures drawn by Davey and Joshua to bring home. She was amused at Davey's picture, cute stick figures of his family, tall Peter with Milly shorter carrying a plate of food, next came Davey carrying a school book, Sarah, and a very small Lucy. She next came to Joshua's picture, and at first couldn't make it out. There was a very tall father on the left side of the paper, then another medium sized figure in the middle, also a man, probably the grandfather. Then there were three very short people, all the same height, two were girls and one was a boy. They were off in the lower right corner, almost as if they didn't belong. Since there was only one other child besides Joshua, one must be his mother. "How strange," she thought and the picture brought back the bizarre episode following Joshua's arrival. "It's a very strange family indeed, but I guess there is always one in every community," and with that thought she put the papers to be corrected into her small satchel, grabbed her lunch pail, gave a last minute glancing check to the room, closed the doors and sauntered slowly home.

Chapter Ten

Anna turned to walk down the road to the Jensen farm and looked at the Kloster place, hoping that she would not have another confrontation with Roger Kloster. Her fears were allayed as there was no one in sight.

As she walked into the farmyard she met Peter who had completed the milking. "I'm later than I thought," she remarked to him.

"Teaching is a big job," he confided as he climbed the back steps and headed toward the basement door, which was behind the table in the kitchen, under the upstairs landing. "Preparing all those lessons is not easy. I am sure you will be burning the midnight oil many a time."

Anna nodded in agreement. She waved to the children who were playing in some tall grass and entered the house.

"Oh Anna," exclaimed Milly as she hovered over a hot stove removing jars of canned peas from the copper boiler. "Davey told me about Roger Kloster using the razor strop on little Yoshua."

"He did threaten to use it," Anna replied, "but he won't get any bad reports from me, so he can't use school as an excuse to punish the child. Let me bring these papers to my room and I will be back to help with dinner," and she turned and ascended the stairs.

When she reentered the kitchen, she found Milly pouring two glasses of cold tea, and they sat down for this quick refreshment. "Next summer we will have real iced tea," Milly proudly announced. "Peter is going to make me an ice house, and this winter when the river is frozen he will chop blocks of ice and bring it up to the ice house, and we will save them until next summer."

"Won't they melt?" asked Anna skeptically.

"Oh, no! You see he will dig a very large, deep pit, way over near the north fence. Then he will build a roof over it and cover the roof with the dirt he dug out. When he is finished it will look like a little hill, and grass will grow on the dirt. It will be strong enough to walk on."

"How will you get in it?" came Anna's second question.

"Oh, he will leave a doorway, with a proper door on it. We will have to go down several steps to get to the door. Oh, I am so excited that I can hardly wait. We had these in Sweden, so I know all about them. Lucky for us that we live next to the river, so the ice is close. Floyd is going to build one too and he will have a mile farther to haul the ice."

"How will you get the ice up here from the river?" came the next question.

"First you have to be sure it is frozen deep enough. When everyone goes out to skate on it then you know. Then the men go and chop it out. Oh, it's so much fun to watch. Getting it home, that's not too hard," she replied with a wave of her hands. "You yust tie a rope around the ice and the team hauls it home. With the ground all frozen, maybe snow, it slides real easy."

"Oh, I want to see that."

"You will, Anna. It will be fun. We line the ice house with straw and put lots of straw over and around each piece. That helps keep it from melting. You will see that in the summertime it will be there, just as cold as it was when it came out of the river. But I forgot to tell you the best part. I am going to get an ice box."

"How wonderful! Then you won't have to use the well for cooling things."

"And, oh let me show you. It is in the Sears catalog," and she jumped up to fetch the catalog from the parlor. "Here look! Doesn't it look nice, and it will fit on the back porch, in the entry way."

"I'm still not sure where you're planning to put it," queried Peter as he came up from the basement, having finished the separating. "You don't have too much room out there now and I don't want to build on to the entry."

"There is plenty of room. It will go where the coats are hanging."

"And where do the coats and the boots go?" he mused.

"There is still plenty of room. I measured it," she retorted. "The hooks will have to be closer together, that's all. And wait, I have more plans."

"Mind if I have some cold tea Milly, while I sit down and digest all these plans of yours." He poured himself a glass and joined them.

"I am planning to buy a six quart ice cream freezer, here let me show you. It's in the catalog too," and she flipped to the correct page.

"And we can have ice cream any time we want it," announced Davey as the children came into the room. "And we're going to get an ice box. Did you know that Miss Swenson?"

"Yes, I heard all about it. I even saw a picture of it in the catalog."

"And mama's saving the money for it from the money you pay her for staying here."

"Oh Davey! Shame on you! You weren't supposed to tell anyone that," scolded Milly.

"I thought she was part of our family now," he said with a puzzled expression. "You said to just keep it in the family."

"Oh, I do hope that I am one of your family," came Anna's reply. "And if my being here, and all the extra work I cause your mother can bring her something she wants, then I am all for it. And I do want a taste of that ice cream. Since I am part of the family," she said rising, "I will take charge of Lucy and get her changed while you continue with what you were doing Milly."

"I can't let you do that," Milly replied firmly as she rose to get Lucy.

"I have her first," said Anna as she picked up the baby.

"Let her do it, Milly," admonished Peter. "She's going to have kids of her own someday so she might as well start learning now."

"I've handled babies before," she told them as she carried Lucy into the bedroom, followed by the other two children who suspected that she would need their advice.

"And talking about having a family, stay clear of Inger or sure as shootin' she will go hunting a husband for you," Peter shouted as they entered the bedroom.

"She found one for me," Milly laughed, "and I didn't do so bad."

"If you say so," he countered with a wink as he left to carry the skim milk to the pigs.

The next morning Anna and Davey left home at eight o'clock. The weather still contained the shimmering heat of summer, however the mornings were cooler, and the walk refreshing.

At nine o'clock Anna went out to ring the bell hoping to see Joshua running up the road to make it on time. It was not possible to delay the bell while waiting for a tardy youngster, as many families checked their clocks by the school bell. If it didn't ring on time they would feel that the teacher had been negligent in carrying out her duties, and no doubt gossip would ensue. Ah, there he was, running for all he was worth, and he made it to the porch by the last ring.

"Good morning Joshua," she greeted. "I am glad that you made it on time."

"Me, too," he panted.

"We were disappointed when you didn't meet us so we could walk to school together."

"I didn't get up early enough to finish my chores," he hung his head.

"Who wakes you up?"

"My grandpa does. We sleep in the attic bedroom. He gets up first so he can milk the cows, but when he leaves sometimes I forget and go back to sleep."

"Is that what happened this morning?"

"Yes."

"Can't your mother get you up?"

"No, my dad says that being called once is enough. But I got here before the bell quit ringing, didn't I?" he asked hopefully.

"Yes, of course you did. However you should get up when you are called. We would enjoy having your company on the walk to school. By the way did you have any breakfast?"

"No, ma'am. There wasn't time, but I brought my lunch," and he held up his lunch pail and hurried into the classroom.

School went reasonably well during the rest of that first week. Joshua didn't appear for the walk to school, but managed to sidle in barely on time for the nine o'clock bell. As Anna had suspected, Joshua would be picked on by someone. Carl Anderson called him names during one lunch period, but was stopped cold by his older brother Lars who told him if he wanted to fight to pick on someone his own size. Except for the two first graders all the boys were older than Carl, so he gave up that idea and instead tried to antagonize Victoria Pearson and Annie Lindquist, the other third graders. However the girls showed that underneath their sweet demeanor, they were tough enough to handle any Carl Anderson.

Milly was right in that George was the brightest child in the school. Lars, who chummed around with George, was an average student, as were most of the others, although it was actually too early in the year to come to any definite conclusions. By the end of the week, however, she had sorted them out and was making a list of extra projects that she felt they were capable of attempting in small groups.

When she arrived home on Friday there was mail from her mother and Elsa. They had read her letter anxiously and were delighted that she had found accommodations with such a fine family and hoped that school was going all right. Immediately she sat down to write a reply, which she would mail the following morning.

On Saturday, after a breakfast of pancakes and home cured sausage, Anna mentioned that she would like to walk to town to mail a letter. Seeing the, "Please may I go too," look on Sarah's face, she asked Milly if the child might accompany her, and so they set off down the now familiar path.

As they reached the river they could see it was fairly shallow due to the long, dry summer, however at the part which became fairly deep they found Joshua, fishing pole in hand, patiently waiting for a catch. She was delighted to see him doing something he obviously enjoyed.

"Hello Joshua," Anna called as they approached him.

"Hello," came the reply as he quickly glanced up at her, and just as quickly returned his gaze to the river.

"Have you caught any fish?" asked Sarah.

"Nope!"

"Is this a good place to fish?" Anna questioned, trying to make conversation.

"Yup!"

"How do you know it's a good place to fish?" she questioned again, hoping for an answer that was more than one syllable.

"My dad says so," came the slightly longer reply.

"How does your dad know?" Sarah queried with a puzzled look.

"Well . . . you see how the water is running so fast over the rocks at the edge of the river, and upstream a bit beyond the bridge." They both nodded. "That's where it's shallow. You won't get any fish there. Too shallow. But see where it looks as if the river has slowed down and you can't see the bottom. That's where the fish is. I've catched them there before. That's where I have my line."

"Is that what your dad told you?" asked Sarah.

"Yup! He says to put your line where it looks like the water is still. Fish like the deep water, and still water runs deep."

"That's an interesting observation," thought Anna.

"Do you think you'll catch any fish?" came another question from Sarah.

"Sure! I've caught lots before."

"Good-bye Joshua," called Anna as they left. "And good luck with the fishing." He nodded in reply as his eyes continued to focus on the line.

They continued, chasing butterflies, listening to the buzz of insects, and smelling the occasional wild flower until they came to the bridge, which was built where the river narrowed. In the middle they stopped and Anna picked Sarah up so she could see over the railing and they both looked down at the water which was deep enough so they couldn't see the bottom. Then they looked downstream where Joshua was fishing, and could see that he had made a catch. While he appeared to be very cautious, Anna realized that the bank was fairly steep in that area. No wonder Milly was unwilling to let Davey fish there without his father.

She put Sarah down on the bridge and they laughed and skipped their way to the Post Office with a couple of jumps over the railroad tracks. Upon entering she saw the clerk's cage was empty, so she quickly stuffed her letter in the mail slot and they tiptoed out to avoid an encounter with the gossipy Mrs. Crawford, each giggling silently with a hand over her mouth.

"Since we are in town, let's go to the store," said Anna with lightheartedness, and they made their way across the dusty road.

"Are we going to buy something there?" asked Sarah.

"We might," Anna replied.

"But do you have any money?"

"I think I could manage to find a few pennies in my pocket," Anna answered as she jingled the coins there.

"Oh, good! Can we buy anything we want?"

"Not quite anything, and remember what we buy we have to carry home."

"What's Eddie doing over there?" asked Sarah as they noticed him busily engaged in conversation with another man on the south side of the store. Several others were gathered to watch. "And why are they digging that big hole?"

"I have no idea. Let's go into the store and find out. I'm sure Mr. Marson will know the answer."

"What can I do for you two lovely ladies?" came the greeting from the proprietor as they entered the premises.

"We came to look and see if there is something we would like to buy, but first what's going on out there?" asked Anna.

"A pretty important thing for this town. Yes, siree! Pretty important! Tell you this. I'll give you one guess little lady," and he stooped to talk to Sarah, "and if you guess right you can have a sucker.

"An ice house," she enthusiastically volunteered, remembering the many conversations they had had discussing it.

"That's a good guess, but our ice is brought to us on the train, so we don't need an ice house. But I'll give you one more guess, and here's a little hint. It has something to do with cars."

"I don't know anything about cars," she shyly answered and shook her head.

"Now dad!" came an admonishment from the back of the store followed by Vi Marson walking toward them. "Don't tease the poor child. Just because you think a gas pump is the greatest thing on earth doesn't mean that everyone does."

"What's a gas pump?" asked Sarah.

"You guessed it! A gas pump," laughed Elmer Marson. "So now little lady you get the all day sucker." It was obvious he was in a very jovial mood. He lifted the glass candy container off the counter and held it so Sarah could choose her favorite, which she did immediately. After putting the jar back, he volunteered to take her out to see the excavation, and she readily accepted the offer.

"Elmer's so happy you'd think that he reinvented Christmas," remarked Mrs. Marson as the two went out the door.

"I am sure the Reverend will be glad to have it here," Anna replied.

"Oh, yes! He and a lot of others. The Simmses are going to buy a car, and once the pump gets in there will be cars all over the place. Eddie wanted to put one in for a couple of years, but dad wouldn't hear of it, then suddenly he took a notion, and once he gets a notion nothing will stop him. Oh, by the way, I forgot. I'm sure you wanted something and didn't come to town just to see the gas pump, although a lot of others did," and she laughed.

"Milly said you took the *Ladies' Home Journal* and I was wondering if I could see one of your copies. I was thinking of getting a subscription."

"Of course, of course! I'll run upstairs and just be a minute."

"I don't want to bother you."

"No bother at all. Just take me a second. Be right back," and she dashed up the steps, returning quickly with the current issue. "Here! Look at this, latest fashions and all. Don't know if we would wear some of these outfits here in the country, but they are fun to look at. And the stories are good, real interesting. The one that's continued, I can hardly wait until next month." She flipped through the pages. "Look at this hair, so short. I wonder what dad would think if I cut my hair," and they both laughed as they perused the magazine.

Soon Elmer Marson and Sarah appeared in the doorway and Anna realized it was getting toward noon and time to be starting for home. Mrs. Marson insisted that Anna take the magazine with her, and after buying a small tin of candy for the family, the two left, with backward glances at the town's latest project while listening to Sarah's excited comments.

As they neared the fishing area Anna saw a woman cross the path and walk toward the river and she assumed it was Grace Kloster getting Joshua for lunch. She was anxious to meet her so hurried, before the woman would have completed her mission and disappear in the cornfield on her way back to the house. They met on the path and startled Grace. She was quite thin almost to the point of looking haggard.

"You must be Joshua's mother," Anna said warmly. There was an affirmative nod. "I am Anna Swenson, his teacher. I am so glad to be able to meet you."

"I am sorry I am such a mess," came the apologizing comment as Grace's hands went to smooth her hair. "I had no idea that I would be meeting anyone on the path, especially the teacher. I just came to get Joshua for lunch."

"I wouldn't expect anyone who works as hard as farm wives do to be dressed up on a Saturday morning," Anna replied as she smiled at the woman. "But I live with the Jensens, across the road from you. I would love to have you come over sometime," and searching for an excuse to issue an invitation she added, "and we could discuss Joshua's schoolwork."

"You mean he is not doing well?" Grace responded fearfully.

Quickly Anna realized her mistake and added, "No! To the contrary, he is doing very well. I am so pleased with him." At this point Joshua appeared with two freshly caught fish, giving Anna an opportunity to praise the boy so both mother and son could hear.

Thanking Anna for the compliment and looking somewhat frenzied, Grace hurriedly remarked that they must be getting home.

"Be sure to tell Mr. Kloster what a good student Joshua is," Anna called out after her, "and do try to come over sometime," and the two disappeared into the rows of corn.

Chapter Eleven

Anna had been so busy during the week that she had completely forgotten about being asked to play the piano during Sunday School, however one of the first people she met upon arriving at the church was Mrs. Simms. It appeared that this enterprising lady had contacted the minister and gotten approval for Anna to practice on the piano any time she wished.

"I would like another week to get settled at school before I take on any new tasks," replied Anna as politely as she could, "but I will try to make some time in my schedule for the week following. I would appreciate it if you could play through September. I am still not sure I am good enough. Are you certain there is no one else who could play?"

"I have asked everyone and they all have excuses. You know how people are. They have no idea how much time I have donated to the Sunday School all these years, and . . . well . . . they don't care. And I still play the organ for Church. They don't seem to think of that," came the self-pitying reply.

Not wanting to continue the conversation Anna repeated her request for another two Sundays reprieve, hoping that the woman would be agreeable. "Well, I suppose if you insist that you can't start until October, I will just have to, but I don't know what my husband will say." She was cut short by Mr. Blakeley calling the Sunday School to order, and Anna gratefully sat down with the ladies while Mrs. Simms took her customary place at the piano.

Anna assisted Mrs. Pearson with the Sunday School class of beginners as she had the previous Sunday, and sat with the Jensens during church. It wasn't until after the service, when she shook hands with Rev. Blakeley at the door that she was reminded of her promise to play the piano. "I am not sure I am skilled enough to play for the Sunday School," she protested. "I did play some for the Sunday School in Fort Dodge, but not on a regular basis."

"Don't you worry. You will do fine," he reassured her. "Mrs. Simms does want someone to replace her, so we would appreciate it very much if you would consider doing it."

"I am not sure I can play the *Doxology*. The only songs I know are *Jesus Loves Me* and *Jesus Wants Me for a Sunbeam*."

"Nothing wrong with those songs, and we don't have to begin with the *Doxology*. Don't you worry now. When you have time come over and practice on the piano in the Sunday School. Use the back door. We usually don't keep it locked, but it if is come to the parsonage and we'll give you the key." With that, and a second handshake, he bade her farewell until the next Sunday.

At two o'clock the family squeezed into the buggy and were off to Inger's for Sunday dinner. Walter met them as they pulled into the yard. "Don't bother to unhitch the horse," Peter told him as they climbed out of the buggy. "Just tie her up to the corral fence in the shade."

"Have you heard that they're puttin' in a gas pump at the store?" Walter asked with enthusiasm as he grabbed the reins. "Do you think that we'll all be gettin' cars then?"

"Those that can pay for them will," answered a bemused Peter.

"And those that can't, will borrow on their next crop just to prove that they're prosperous enough to ride around on four rubber tires," quipped Floyd as he came out on the back porch.

"Are we gonna get a car dad?" asked Davey, his eyes wide with excitement.

"Not for a while son," answered his father as he put his hand on the boy's shoulder.

"Who needs a car," Milly quickly chimed in, "when we have good horses and a buggy."

"I was thinkin' that I could hire out and earn some money," added Walter. "Then I could save up for a car."

"You'll stay home where you're needed," added his father. "If you left, I'd have to pay someone else wages and I'd be more broke than ever. Anyway, let's quit talkin' and come on in."

The marvelous odor of roast pork and apple pies came floating out of the kitchen as they climbed the back steps. The kitchen was immaculate. The table was covered with a linen cloth and matching napkins, each place neatly set. Bowls of hot food were being dished up by Inger and carried to the table by Mabel. The roast had been carved, and all was ready.

"Well, just you look who's here," said Floyd as he greeted Anna. "And I want you to know that Inger has been planning this spread for days. It's not every day that we have a real tablecloth and napkins, so you see you are bein' honored."

"Don't listen to him," advised Milly. "Inger always sets a beautiful table."

"Now ain't that just like you Milly," came Floyd's retort. "Here I was tryin' to make our little schoolteacher feel special, and you go and ruin it."

"Sit down before the food gets cold," came Inger's order, and so they took their places with Floyd and Inger at the head and foot of the table.

"Dive in!" came Floyd's loud voice.

"Not before we say grace," Inger scolded.

"All right!" Floyd answered. "Good food, good meat, good God, let's eat. Pass the spuds."

Looking at him with a critical but bemused expression, Inger responded with, "We will have the proper Swedish grace. Walter will you say the grace? Bow your heads please."

In a serious tone Walter prayed, "I Jesu namm till bords vi ga, Valsigna Gud den mat vi fa. Amen." This was followed by a brief silence accompanied by the quiet placement of napkins in laps.

"That is the grace that Inger and I were taught at home," volunteered Milly. "It means, In Yesus' name we go to the table, May God bless the food we eat."

"I like it very much," replied Anna. Perhaps I could learn it some day."

"I'll teach you," Davey enthusiastically volunteered. "I know it by heart."

"Thank you Davey," Anna responded. "I would be very happy to have you teach it to me."

"Let's eat," called Floyd. "I didn't butcher this pig to have it sit here and get cold." With that he helped himself to a good portion, and sent it around the table. Other dishes followed. There was an abundance of food that she had seldom seen before, enough to feed twice their number, and it was deliciously prepared. Floyd seemed to lead the conversation in his jovial fashion, joking first with one person and then another, occasionally interrupted by one of the women giving instructions to the children.

"I s'pose you never heard Milly's real name," he asked Anna. "Well it's not Matilda or nothing like that. As I told you before. It's somethin' unpronounceable."

"It's Gota," Milly announced.

"See, I told you it was unpronounceable," Floyd replied.

"I admit it is not easy to say, but how did she get the name of Milly?" asked Anna.

"I took one look at her and said, "It's goin' to be Milly. I can't pronounce that God-awful Swedish name.' and so Milly it is."

"Floyd wouldn't even try to say it," added Inger. "Now everyone calls her Milly, and so I do too."

"I like the name," said Milly smiling, and speaking in her Swedish accented English. "It sounds much more American than Gota."

"At least you had the sense to call Davey and Sarah by good honest names," Floyd commented, "and we got Lucy's name shortened a bit."

"Isn't Lucy her real name?" asked Anna.

"Oh, no!" answered Milly. "You see she was born on December 13th, and that is Lucia Day, so she was named Lucia. You know about Lucia's Day don't you?"

"Yes I know a little about it," added Anna. "I remember my mother telling us about it, but I never knew anyone who celebrated it."

"Not everyone does," added Inger, "not even in Sweden. "I think more people in western Sweden celebrate it. That's what I've heard anyway."

"And we came from western Sweden," added Milly proudly. "So we enjoy celebrating it because it makes us think of the old country. And it starts the Christmas time. Sweden is so dark at Christmas. I think that's why Lucia has seven lighted candles on her head."

"And on the 13th there was an old fashioned idea of fasting until Christmas," exclaimed Inger. "That's why they ate before sunrise. But there's never any fasting around here," and she looked around the table at her family.

"Some day I will get to be Lucia," added Sarah, "and wear a long white dress."

"Well, not for a while," added her mother. "But when you are old enough you may, and that will be very exciting, and then I won't do it. Every year I think I won't, and then I bake some buns and Peter and I have coffee and buns in bed."

"That's when I hear the cows bellowing to be milked," laughed Peter. "Anyway, Mabel has done it, haven't you Mabel?"

"Yes," she replied, "but Mother always helps me so I don't set fire to anything. And then she hurries back to bed so that I can serve it to them in bed the way it is supposed to be. I have to give the boys milk. Even Walter doesn't drink coffee. It's fun."

"Last year she baked the buns by herself the night before," Inger announced proudly, "and delicious cinnamon buns they were too."

"Perhaps I could help Sarah do it this year," suggested Anna. "We could make the buns ourselves, couldn't we Sarah?"

A shy nod came from the child in question and a comment, "I've never done it before. Maybe I won't know how. But I will be four years old by then, won't I mama, because my birthday comes before Lucy's."

"Yes, your birthday is also on an important day," replied Milly. "It is November 11th, Armistice Day, and you are right. This November you will be four years old."

"You'll have to get up early before I milk the cows," advised Peter.

"Maybe that's one morning the cows can wait a little," admonished Milly. "And it will be Lucy's first birthday. What a celebration! How wonderful to have someone in our family be St. Lucia. Oh, Anna it would be so good of you to do this for us," and she almost became tearful.

"It would be exciting for me too," answered Anna.

"When Lucy does it she'll have candles on her head instead of on her cake," Floyd joked.

"Won't she get a birthday cake then?" asked Sarah.

"Of course she'll get a birthday cake, and presents too," her mother confirmed. "Uncle Floyd was yoking."

The conversation continued happily with discussions on the harvest vacation, Thanksgiving and Christmas.

After the main part of the meal, Mabel and Milly cleared the table, and wouldn't hear of Anna helping. Soon Inger was passing huge pieces of apple pie, accompanied by cups of coffee and more milk for the children. Now the talk centered mostly on farming, the weather, and the time for harvesting. Lucy fell asleep so was put on Inger's bed for a nap. It was about four o'clock.

Suddenly they could hear the front parlor door open. They paused in astonishment, as who would have the effrontery to enter through the parlor without an invitation. Jimmy Burns burst through the doorway to the kitchen. "Fire at the Evans' place. Get all the buckets you can," and with that he was off running the way he entered.

The men nearly tipped over the table they got up so suddenly. "Grab the milk buckets," Floyd yelled to Walter. "I'll get the ones from the well."

"Let's go in my rig, it's all hitched up," shouted Peter, and with that the three were off.

"George you run and ring the school bell," directed Inger, and George shot out of the door.

"Can I go with him?" pleaded Davey.

"Yes, but stay with George. Don't you go anywhere near the fire," called Milly as Davey chased after George down the cornfield.

"I'll get on the phone, but I heard it ring a while ago and I know that you know who is on the line, but I'll try to break in," and Inger picked up the phone.

"Hello! Hello! Is that you Liza?" asked Inger.

"Yes, it is Inger Parker, and I will thank you not to interrupt when I am on the phone," came the reply which could be heard across the room.

"Get off the line Inger Parker. We are using it," shouted another angry voice, the one to whom Liza had been speaking.

"There's a fire at the Evans' place. We need all the men to help. Get off the line so we can give the emergency signal," commanded Inger.

"I don't see no fire," retorted Liza Crawford, "and I'm lookin' out a my window."

"Of course you can't see it from your place. Get off the line," shouted Inger. "We need help!"

"If there ain't no fire, and you're jus' . . ."

Inger cut Liza off telling her to get on the other line and get all the available men to the Evans' place.

At that moment the continuous clanging of the school bell filled the air, and Liza Crawford and her friend slammed down their receivers. Immediately Inger rang one long ring, which was the emergency signal, and phones were picked up by most of the people on the line. She gave them the message and cut short any curious questions.

"I'm worried about our place," said Milly.

"Mabel you stay here with Sarah and Lucy. Milly and Anna and I will run down to Milly's and see what the situation is," and the three women ran out the kitchen door, as was the usual custom, forgetting that the shorter route would be through the parlor.

When they arrived they could see that the fire was located in back of the barn and was burning a pile of dried hay with flames about fifteen feet high. It was possible that it could quickly cross to the barn and burn it down. The barn would be a tinder box as it was filled with dry hay. Men had formed a bucket brigade and were pumping water from the Evans' well. Milly took their horse, which had been tethered to the front post, and brought it and the buggy into the back yard.

Soon men were arriving from all over, and Inger and Milly found themselves stabling horses or putting them in the Jensen corral. Anna had not been around horses much, but volunteered to help with this activity, even though she was fairly frightened of the animals. The animals were also frightened and some were hard to control.

The smoke was so thick it filled the air, and Milly rushed into the house to shut all the doors and windows.

The fire started to burn hotter and higher, as they couldn't get water pumped fast enough from the one well to contain it. With the arrival of more men, Peter suggested they use his well also, and so they started a second brigade not only pumping water from the well, but lowering a bucket on a rope, filling it with water and emptying it in one of the brigade buckets.

Fortunately there was no wind to blow the embers onto neighboring property, and after more than an hour the fire was out. The acrid smell of smoke filled the air. Milly entered the house with Inger to make coffee for the men who wandered over to get their horses, but wanted to stay to talk about what had happened. Most of them wanted a cold drink, and well water was thirst quenching. A bucket was lowered and a dipper passed around, and they sat on the grass. Davey and George were among them, and from the looks of their clothes they had been in the thick of it. Some of the womenfolk had come by this time and were eager for information.

"How did it start?" asked one.

"You tell 'em Jimmy," said Peter. "You were the first one there."

"Well, I was thinkin' about goin' fishin', so I grabs my pole and starts walkin' down the road. I gets to the Evans' place and I sees smoke, and the old man has a blanket tryin' to beat out a blaze in back of the barn. I knew it was gettin' out of control with that pile of dry grass, so I ran to the Larson's first. I knew they'd tell Schmidt, and then hot-footed it to your place Floyd, 'cause I seen Peter's rig in your yard and I knew the Jensens was there too. That's when you all come runnin'."

"If it hadn't been for Jimmy, the whole place could have gone up," added Floyd.

"Well, I don't know about that," he said with a shrug.

"But what started the fire?" asked someone, "and where was Kloster?"

"I talked to the old man later," Jimmy said. "Seems he decided to go out in back of the barn to sharpen his scythe. Since it was Sunday, and Kloster don't cotton to no work on Sunday, he had to sneak out and do it. I s'pose he was tired of prayin'. Anyways, he decides to roll himself a cigarette, and started smokin'. He said he thought he heard someone comin' so looked back of him, and when he did that he cut himself. His cigarette must have dropped into the grass, but he was thinkin' so much about the cut that he didn't notice it. When he did see it he dashed into the barn to get a horse blanket to try to smother the fire, but it had got beyond him."

"Where was Kloster?" asked another.

"Just where you might guess," added Floyd with a disgusted tone. "We was all workin' and he was on the porch on his knees prayin'. I comes up to him and says, 'Get your God damned hide over to that bucket brigade.' Excuse the language ladies. And he says to me, 'This is God's punishment for workin' on Sunday. I told the old man God would punish us if we worked on Sunday. It's against God's law. I'm prayin' for forgiveness.' I tol' him that forgiveness would not put out the fire and I give him a kick that he will never forget, so he lumbered over to help with the brigade."

"The man's plain crazy. We've knowed that from the beginning," said Elmer Marson.

"Maybe we're the crazy ones to put out his fire, but if we hadn't it would've spread to the other farms," added Floyd.

"Where was Grace and the children?" asked someone.

"They stayed in the house," added George. "I could see Joshua lookin' out the kitchen window. He looked kinda scared."

"Prob'ly not half so scared as he will look when his dad gets ahold of old man Evans," commented Walter.

"Oh let's not talk about that," shuddered Milly." "Have more coffee," she insisted to the few who had chosen this drink. As Peter held out his cup she gasped, "Oi, yoi, yoi! Look at your Sunday clothes," and she glanced around at the other men. "Oi, yoi, yoi! Look at all of you. I can see that the women will be busy tomorrow. All of your Sunday clothes, black with soot and dirt. What a yob to scrub that out. I hope we can get them clean."

"Well, if you can't, then we'll just have to stay home from church," Floyd commented with a grin.

"No clothes are that dirty," said Inger.

Chapter Twelve

As Anna and Davey left the yard for school on Monday morning, they paused to look at the damage the fire had done the day before. The barn was saved, but the north side was badly scorched with the remaining paint blistered and peeling. The grindstone was lying on its side in a heap of ashes, although it would be salvaged to sharpen scythes again. A scattering of charred hay was all that remained of the small haystack which had been next to the pile of dry grass where the fire started. The entire area had been raked clean with the soaked hay in the middle and bare dirt surrounding it. Fortunately the livestock was in the south pasture, as all the grass near the barn had been eaten weeks before. The bare dirt helped prevent the spread of the flames.

Anna had not had a chance to examine the ruins on Sunday. As they were resting after the exertion of putting out the fire, one of Peter's cows started mooing, wanting to be milked. At this sound all the men realized that their chores had to be done, jumped to their feet, mounted their horses and were off. Even Mr. Simms, who had bought a new Ford a few days ago, rode in on his mare. Floyd had kidded him about not knowing how to drive yet, but the reality was more likely that in an emergency a person goes with the familiar without thinking.

Joshua was nowhere in sight, so they proceeded to school. The building was slightly chilly as no fire had been lit, however Anna decided that one was not necessary as in a short time the sun would warm things up. She was actually grateful that Roger Kloster was not there. If need be she could start a fire herself. There were corncobs for kindling, coal in the scuttle, and matches in the cupboard.

The talk in the school yard centered mainly on the fire of the day before. Anna joined the students, as eager as they were to acquire any new information, although she found that she and George were the center of attention in dispensing it. George had been part of the second bucket brigade, and was somewhat of a hero for running so quickly to give the alarm by ringing the school bell.

Nine o'clock and Joshua was nowhere in sight, however Anna rang the bell and school began without him. He came in about two hours later, hanging his head, and looking neither to right nor left, took his seat. His response to questions was lifeless. As he had neglected to bring his lunch, Anna shared hers with him, but he ate halfheartedly. At the end of the day he left the building as if in a trance. Davey tried to walk with him and make conversation, but it was useless.

On the way home she glanced at the Evans farm, trying to convince herself that she should go up to the house and inquire about Joshua, however her courage failed her and feeling somewhat guilty she turned into the Jensen drive.

That evening, after the children had been put to bed, Anna brought out the *Ladies' Home Journal* which Vi Marson had lent her. It was a pleasant change of subject after the grimness of the fire. She sat with Milly at the dining table, looking at the latest fashions. The length of women's' skirts and dresses was definitely shorter, and it appeared that long sleeves were not popular either. "It seems like every year they are showing more and more of womens' arms and legs," commented Milly, "and look at this dress. It hardly has any waist at all. This might be all right for people living in the big cities in the East, but these skirts are so short. I don't think the men here would let their wives wear clothes like this."

"At least it will take less material to make a dress, so they will cost less," added Anna, "and it will be faster to sew , especially if they are so straight up and down."

"And long sleeves are so hot in the summertime," agreed Milly. "I won't have to make new dresses, I will just cut off part of the sleeves and part of the bottom. Some of my dresses do have short sleeves, but for church I think that long sleeved dresses are the best. I'll wait and see if those straight dresses are being worn next year before I make one like that and I won't make the skirts so short."

"Yes, I will do the same," added Anna remembering that schoolteachers had to set a good example for the community and knowing that she would not feel comfortable in a dress with a skirt up to the knees. "Some of these clothes do look beautiful though. Do you think we could make some as nice?" "Look how thin the ladies in the picture are. Oi, yoi, yoi, I could never look like that even in a new dress. You could Anna, you are so thin, but me. I am yust fat."

"You are not fat," added Peter from his rocking chair where he was reading the newspaper. "You are just the way I like you. I don't want a bag of bones. I want something to hold on to," and he laughed with this remark as did the women.

"Look at the bobbed hair," remarked Milly. "Would we dare bob our hair Anna? It looks so much cooler and it would be easier to fix in the morning."

"I couldn't cut my hair," Anna confessed. "If I did, it would look terrible. I have thought about having short hair, but don't have the nerve to get it cut. Once it's cut it can't be glued back on again, and it takes years to grow out."

"If you ladies are serious you should let Floyd cut your hair. He cuts the boys' hair and Mabel's too," came a joking remark from Peter who found himself laughing at the very thought.

"No! No! I wouldn't think of letting him touch my hair. He would do something terrible to it and I would have to knit myself a cap to cover up his mistakes," laughed Milly.

"Let me see those pictures," said Peter as he came to the table and stood over the magazine. "Well, I'll be dad-gummed. Those women look almost like boys. Don't you ladies think of cutting your hair right away. I don't want you looking like that Milly, and those skirts are so short they aren't even decent."

"Some of the young girls around here have cut their hair, and they look nice," Milly answered. "Besides long hair is such a bother, because it always has to be pinned up. And yust think Anna, washing it would be so much easier, and it would take less rain water."

"If you say so," came Peter's reply as he stretched his long arms and sighed, which was his signal that it was time for bed.

As Anna returned from school the next afternoon she heard someone digging, and quickly walked over near the north fence, behind the barn, and found Peter had started on the ice house. "They say women's work is never done," he commented as he threw another shovelful of dirt on the pile which was accumulating nearby, "but I think a farmer's work will never be done." He leaned on the spade and took a breather. "Here I've been workin' on this nearly all day and I've hardly made a dent in the ground. It'll take me a week just to get it dug, and after that I'll have to build the roof, and shovel all this dirt back onto it."

"I think you're making great progress," remarked Anna as she looked at the hole which was about fourteen feet in diameter and about two feet deep.

"S'pose it'd be just my luck to get this thing finished and then have a warm winter where the river doesn't freeze enough to get any ice," and he shoved his foot on the spade, sending it the full length into the ground, and heaved the dirt out.

The sound of the dinner bell startled them. "Can't be time for dinner yet, I haven't done the milking," commented Peter, puzzled.

A shout was heard from Milly entreating them to come for a cup of coffee and rest a spell, and at this welcome idea, both of them hurried to the kitchen.

"I've yust baked a cake, so let's have it now with coffee. Peter you should take a rest, and I am sure that Anna could do with a little sit-down."

It was always pleasant sitting around the kitchen table, drinking freshly brewed coffee. The conversation went immediately to the events of yesterday. In her concern for Joshua and Grace, Milly told them that in the mid-morning, after Roger had gone out into the field, she took it upon herself to cross the road and inquire if there were anything she could do for the family. Grace answered the door, and proudly stated that things were fine. She seemed to want to make it known that she sided with her husband as she criticized her father for breaking the Sabbath and reiterated that if he had not strayed from the Holy law it never would have happened. She did add a thanks for all the help which they had received yesterday, with the additional comment that it was God's will which had sent the neighbors, in recognition of the rest of the family who had not strayed from Sunday prayer.

"I asked her again if there was anything we could do to help them, and she yust said that they were fine. She didn't even ask me in, so I left."

"Huh! At least she said thanks and that's more thanks than Kloster gave us," commented Peter. "He didn't say one word. It was as if he resented our being there."

"Did you see Mr. Evans?" asked Anna.

"No, but I think he was out in the barn because I heard someone out there," Milly replied.

"I'd hate to be in his shoes," laughed Peter.

"It sounds as if Grace sticks by her husband," Anna mused.

"Yes. In the few times which people know about, I understand that she has always stood by him, even in defiance of her father," Peter added. "People may want to believe that she was sweet on Ed Marson, but once Roger Kloster appeared, Ed had to take a back seat. The rumor is that the old man forced her to marry Roger, but I don't believe it."

"Well, Ed was yust a young kid barely out of high school, and I think that they were in love," added Milly.

"I would guess it was puppy love. They had known each other from childhood," said Peter.

"Knowing each other from childhood doesn't always mean that they are going to fall in love. I can't imagine Victoria Pearson or Annie Lindquist ever having anything to do with Carl Anderson," laughed Anna.

"Well, you never know," Peter contemplated. "I always thought Ed was more serious about it than Grace. He seemed to think that Grace was his girl, but he was so busy at the store that he didn't have much time to do any courting."

"And if he had tried it, Grace's father would've put a stop to it," added Milly. "He kept his eyes on her, wouldn't let her go anywhere."

"Is that why they had secret rendezvous?" asked Anna.

"Well, Ed would occasionally meet her in the field," Peter recalled, "but I always had the feeling that it was only a game with Grace. I once heard her arguing with the old man about running away, not with Ed mind you, but to her aunt's place. She definitely wanted to get away and being a storekeeper's wife was not what she had in mind."

"Everyone around here expected them to get married some day," added Milly.

"The Marsons may have encouraged that rumor because they knew it was what Ed wanted, but I don't think that they knew what was in Grace's mind," said Peter.

"But why on earth would she marry Roger Kloster?" queried Anna. "I don't see how anybody could be romantically interested in him."

"When Roger arrived he made a very nice appearance. I talked with him several times and he seemed like a good enough sort. He also did all the heavy chores. Grace didn't have to do any more farm work. We all thought that it was a blessing that he showed up when he did as Grace was skin and bones. Everyone had been worried that she wouldn't last long and follow her Mother to the grave. I'm sure she thought he was heaven sent. No wonder she took a fancy to him," Peter recalled. "She did the cooking and kept house and began to put on weight. And remember that Grace was always one who liked town life and city ways. She didn't get to live with her aunt after her mother died, as the old man would have nothing to do with that. Who knows what promises Kloster made to her, but he was the first person she had seen who could take control of her dad. I don't know how he did it, whether it was his Bible preachin', or what, but he sure took over the place."

"Perhaps she is, in her own way, happy with him," Anna commented.

"Happy with him or not, she is stuck with him, and it's not our problem, thank the good Lord," Peter said as he straightened up. "If you ask me, she went from puppy love to a dog's life. Anyways I've been wastin' enough time with you two. It's time to get the milkin' done," and he strode out the door with his usual long strides, grabbing the milk pails from the porch, and taking the back steps two at a time.

Chapter Thirteen

As they arrived at church on the following Sunday, September 17th, they could see several men gathered at the Marson store. Standing proudly beside his new Ford was Mr. Simms.

"Can I run over there and see his new car?" begged Davey.

"You'll have plenty of time to see it after church," answered Milly. "Your father won't want to go home without a look also. Well Anna, it looks as if Mr. Simms is just as happy to drive his wife to church an hour early this morning, otherwise he wouldn't be able to show off his automobile. I suppose he's spent the week learning to drive after Floyd teased him about not knowing how to run it."

"I hope he will be just as happy to drive early next week also," added Anna, "since I won't be playing the piano until the first of October."

"He probably won't get all this attention next Sunday," Milly remarked. "Come along now you two, it's time we were inside."

Peter wasn't the only one interested in seeing the Ford after church. "By the looks of it Mother," he joked, "I think the whole congregation has adjourned to the store."

Mr. Simms was proudly holding forth on the attributes of his new vehicle, not the least of which was paying for it on the new installment plan called "easy little payments". He had not needed to borrow on his crop, but paid $35.00 a month to the Ford Company. The farmers had heard of this arrangement, but not being completely familiar with it, and with interest rates fairly high, no one else had taken advantage of the proposition.

"So when's this thing goin' to be paid for?" asked Floyd. "Or will you ever get it paid for?"

"Of course I'll get it paid for," countered Simms rather defensively. "In the meantime I get to own it and ride in it while I'm still payin' on it. Just look at it. Ain't she a beaut?"

"And he don't have to go to town to buy gas now neither," added Elmer Marson, who was happy for the opportunity to show off his new pump. "Let me show you what's goin' to get you all to buyin' cars."

"Maybe you should be sellin' cars too," joked Floyd.

"And I'll bet you'd be the first one to buy," countered Elmer which brought laughter to the whole group as they moved to survey the newly installed mechanical device. It consisted of a round tank standing vertically, several feet high, topped with a somewhat shorter glass tank of equal circumference. On one side of the glass were gallon markings, and it was filled with the yellowish-orange gasoline. A metal lid covered the top.

"Fill 'er up Elmer," called Mr. Simms, "an' you can show 'em how she works."

Davey crowded to the front and was fascinated as Marson took the hose, which was attached to the bottom of the tank, and inserted it into the opening to the gas tank of the car, which was under the front seat. As the gasoline entered the car by gravity feed, he watched the gas in the glass top go lower and lower.

"Stop at five gallons Elmer," Mr. Simms advised, "otherwise it might overflow," and so it was stopped at the five gallon mark, which was visible on the glass tank.

"You can help me pump it up Davey," Elmer said as he winked at the boy. Davey grabbed the pump handle, which was on the side opposite the hose, and was the same style as on the washing machine at home, and with Elmer's help they slowly pumped the glass tank full again.

After Mr. Simms paid for the gas, he put the front seat back and carefully helped Mrs. Simms into the vehicle. He then took hold of the crank which was located in the front of the car, gave it a few hefty turns, which resulted in the vehicle jumping up and down with the most horrendous sound as the engine started running. He then jumped in, and with a few jerks, they were off, with Mrs. Simms waving somewhat imperiously to the crowd.

"By gum!" remarked Floyd. "I thought the dad-blamed thing was goin' to stampede."

"Ford's 'r like that," described Elmer. "I'm buyin' a Chevy myself. Should have it here by next week. Then you'll see a good car."

"I've seen Chevys buck as much as Fords," came a comment from the crowd.

"Well, we'll see about that," Elmer retorted.

As the good-natured crowd dispersed, the Jensen family headed for home. "You'll be seein' lots of cars around here now Milly," Peter said thoughtfully. "I just wish we could afford to buy one."

"But you can dad," Davey chimed in. "Mr. Simms said it costs only $35.00 a month. After we buy the ice box you can buy a car."

"Oh hush Davey," scolded Milly.

"Mr. Simms didn't tell you about how long he will be payin' for that car Davey. There's something called interest that adds a lot onto the price, and keeps a person payin' for a long time." After a few moments he added, "When Uncle Floyd gets a car I promise you that we'll get one too. How's that?"

When Anna arrived home on Tuesday she found Milly wearily hunched over the ironing board pressing Sarah's Sunday dress. She touched the middle finger of her left hand to her tongue to wet it and then touched the iron, which gave off no sizzle. "Dear me! This iron is cold again," and she quickly moved to the kitchen range where two cast-iron irons had been heating, unclamped the handle from the one she had been using and exchanged it for one which was hot, leaving the cool one to heat. She returned to the ironing board, placing the new iron on the metal plate sitting near the end of the board, rearranged the dress, tested the iron by touching it to the fabric on the board, and decided that it was not hot enough to scorch the dress, continued her task. "Club meeting is tomorrow and

I want Sarah to wear this dress," she commented. "And after I finish this I am through."

"I had forgotten about your club meeting. Isn't it going to be at the Lindquist's? I thought I heard Annie mention it at school."

"Yes, and next time it is probably my turn. I haven't had the meeting since Lucy was born, so I will invite them here in October."

"This is your ladies church group, isn't it?" Anna continued with her questions.

"It's not really a church group, but in a way it is because most of the ladies belong to the church, and we plan church affairs like those that raise money for the missions. And we also make improvements around Grabney, like cleaning up the picnic ground, and then when someone is sick or has a baby we arrange to help out."

"It sounds worthwhile to me," commented Anna, "but I hope it isn't all work. You ladies work hard enough."

"No, it isn't all work," added Milly smiling. "The real name is the Grabney Community Club, but we yust call it the Club. And we do have a good time, drink coffee and eat cake and cookies, and, well . . . I guess you would say we gossip too," and she gave a slightly embarrassed giggle which turned her face into a rosy pink.

"It sounds like fun. I hope you remember to tell me all that goes on."

"I'll tell you before Peter comes in," Milly continued. "He yust makes fun of the Club. Now with you here I have someone to tell the gossip to."

"I will be all ears," said Anna laughing. "By the way I see that Peter is starting to work on the roof of the ice house. How long do you think it will take him to finish it?"

"I don't think he is too happy about it," answered Milly. "It is taking so long to build. It is not so easy here as where I lived in Sweden. We had a hill in back of our house and my father and grandfather dug a cave in it. All they had to do was put on a door. They didn't have to put on a roof. The cave was so large that we could use part of it as a root cellar, where we would store vegetables like carrots and potatoes, and other vegetables that grow beneath the ground. By covering them with sand they would keep all winter. Did you know that Anna?"

"I had no idea," Anna replied as she thought how much Milly loved to talk about her native land, as much as Anna enjoyed listening. It was amazing all the things she had learned from this loving and practical woman. "By the way," she said as she came back to reality, "what do you do here with your root vegetables?"

"Peter has made bins in the basement. We use sand, the same as in the root cellar, but we leave them in the ground as long as possible, at least until the corn is harvested. Even if it freezes some they are usually fine, but it's easier to dig them up before the ground gets too hard."

"I don't think your work is ever done Milly."

"Oh yes, I have a cup of coffee now and then, and remember tomorrow I will go to the Club," and they both enjoyed the humor.

"Talking about tomorrow, I was going to stop by the parsonage to borrow a Sunday School hymnal, but I guess I had better go today, since Mrs. Blakeley might not be home tomorrow and I did want to talk to her about practicing on Saturday morning."

"Yes, you must get settled about the practice," advised Milly.

"After Mr. Anderson brings back the pump organ to the school I could practice on that, but I would rather practice on a piano. Anyway I hope he doesn't bring it back too soon as I have enough to do with getting started in school without learning to play songs for the students," and she got up from the table. "It's also getting dark earlier now and I think that it would be too late to practice after school. But I did want to help you with some of the work this afternoon."

"No, no!" ordered Milly waving her hands into the air. "I can manage fine, and you should get over to the parsonage."

As she walked up the stairs Anna could hear Lucy waking up from her nap, and she marveled again at how Milly managed so well.

The afternoon was brisk but not cold and Anna enjoyed the walk along the river. As she approached the parsonage she heard Rev. Blakeley's voice, and he answered her knock at the door. "Welcome, welcome!" he greeted her warmly as he shook her hand. "I was wondering when you would pay us a visit. Come in."

"This isn't an official visit, even though I did come to the front door," said Anna with a smile. "I wanted to talk to you or Mrs. Blakeley to see if it would be possible to practice on the Sunday School piano on Saturday mornings."

"Come on out here Tom," came a voice from the kitchen. "Don't keep her standing on the porch."

As they walked through the formal parlor, Anna could hear another male voice in the kitchen and was surprised to find Ed Marson there, sitting at the table. "You've met Ed Marson, haven't you Anna," asked Rev. Blakeley as he ushered her into the cozy room which smelled fragrantly of apple pie.

"Oh yes, I met him at the store," she answered.

"Glad to see you Miss Swenson," said Ed as he nodded to her and rose rather formally from his chair.

"Oh, please call me Anna," she quickly cut in. "And do sit down again. I didn't mean to interrupt anything."

"You're not interrupting anything," commented Mrs. Blakeley. "Eddie always knows when I've baked a pie. I think he can smell it from the store, so as soon as it came out of the oven, who should be at the door but Ed."

"And I must say that you make the best pies around here, but don't tell my ma I said so," the young man remarked with a smile as he sat down again.

"Anna please take a seat," and Anna pulled a chair up to the table as Mrs. Blakeley continued. "I remember the days when our Michael was home and you and he used to wait on the porch until the pies were cool, and then you would come in with long, hungry faces, and of course I had to feed you two starving boys. You probably went back to your mother and pulled the same trick."

"Maybe just once or twice," said Ed with a mischievous grin.

"Mike and Ed were friends since we moved here," added the Reverend. "They were inseparable. They finished grade school together, and went to high school together. After graduation Mike got a job in a hardware store in Des Moines and lived with my brother's family for a time."

"And I came back to work for my dad, and I'm still around to eat the pie, but Mike's missin' out on it," laughed Ed.

"I always wanted Mike to go on to college like his brother Stephen," added Mrs. Blakeley, "but he did so well at the store that I guess he has found his place in life."

"I didn't know you had two sons," Anna said with surprise.

"Oh yes indeed, but we don't see them much. Stephen is in Medical School, and after he graduates he intends to practice in some town in Iowa, but I doubt if it will be near Grabney."

"I sure wish I could've gone to Des Moines," Ed said dreamily. "I did try workin' in a couple of other places, but I knew that I'd always have to come back here, and I've been here eight years, off and on."

"And your folks need you at the store," added Mrs. Blakeley. "Why I don't know what they would have done without you."

Anna sat still and listened to the conversation, surprised at how at ease Ed seemed.

"I hope Mike can come home for the dance in Brewster next month," continued Ed. "By that time we'll have a car so we can go off in real style. Have you heard if he can make it?"

"You mean you're not going to try to borrow my car?" joked Rev. Blakeley.

"Well, I guess that's why dad and I had to get a car, so we wouldn't be running yours in the ditch any more." As they all laughed, Anna wondered what was the story behind this event.

"To get back to Michael, have you written to ask him?" queried Mrs. Blakeley. "It's just a month away, and I think he has a girl friend. She'd probably like to come too. I think her name is Emma."

"You know good and well he has a girlfriend and that her name is Emma and what you really mean is you'd like to meet her," remarked Rev. Blakeley, "and you think this would be a good excuse because it sounds serious this time."

"Now Tom!" she protested.

"What! Another girlfriend?" Ed commented in surprise. "Are you sure it's serious? I never knew Mike to be serious about anything."

"We think it's serious because he has written us about her," said Rev. Blakeley. "Mike was never one for writing."

"I'm not good at writing either. Anyway I just sorta thought that he would have heard about the dance and come if he could," added Ed.

"Well you better write him and make sure. I don't think the local Grabney news is listed in the *Des Moines Register*. And if you promise me you'll do that, since I want him to come even more than you do, I'll let you have a piece of pie," Mrs. Blakeley stipulated.

"Now Mother," complained her husband, "you mean you're going to give Ed some pie and leave us out, just because Ed promises to write a letter."

"Of course not!" she sighed in good-humored exasperation. "Stop your complaining," and she cut generous portions of pie for each and started passing them around. "While I am doing this pour everyone some coffee Tom."

As they ate their pie Anna realized that this was the first time that she had seen a warm side to Ed. He had always been rather businesslike or perhaps shy in the store. She had heard about the dance, but didn't know the particulars.

"You will have to go to the dance Anna," said Mrs. Blakeley. "You will have such a good time. Have you planned to go?"

"Are teachers here allowed to go to dances?" she shyly asked.

"Goodness yes," answered Mrs. Blakeley. "This isn't Kansas. Well, I guess even parts of Iowa might frown on it, but not here. That's one reason we like the place."

"Well Mother," Rev. Blakeley added, "I think it's the Scandinavian influence. You see Anna, I'm sort of a renegade myself. I'm a Presbyterian minister in a community where most people came from a Lutheran background. But that suits me fine. Somewhere someone got the idea of setting up a mission church so we wouldn't be outnumbered by the other faiths. So now, are you going to go to the dance?"

"I really don't know much about it. Isn't Brewster rather far away."

"It's less than ten miles, and everyone around here will go, children too," related Rev. Blakeley. "It's a real community affair. You see we may have a church here, but Brewster has a community hall. They have services in the hall on Sunday, and that's one of the places I go to preach. And I'll bet my bottom dollar that Mother here will insist on going if Mike is coming home with a girl." At this remark Ed gave a real guffaw.

"Now Dad!" she said with feigned exasperation, and then turned to Anna. "I am sure the Jensens will be going. They may not stay for the midnight supper, but they'll go for the early part of the dance. Milly always liked to dance, and she hasn't been to one since Lucy was born."

"Perhaps I can take care of the children while they go," added Anna. "I feel I owe them so much."

"No, they wouldn't let you do that," she continued. "You should see that Milly out on the dance floor. She's a wonder, never gets tired. I think she could dance all night. Well, I hate to eat and run," said Ed as he stood up, "but dad had a load of feed come in on the 3:15 freight and I've got to get it stacked. Thanks for the pie, and I will write Mike." With a good-bye wave and a smile he was out the kitchen door.

"See that you do," Mrs. Blakeley called after him.

"The pie is delicious," Anna remarked. "I have heard that you make the best apple pies around here, and I can believe it. I guess I came at a lucky time."

"You come any time you want," added Mrs. Blakeley. I won't always have a pie, but I can put on the coffee pot and you can count on cookies in the cookie jar."

"That's really nice of you. I would enjoy coming again. And oh, by the way Rev. Blakeley do you think it is possible that I could get a Sunday School hymnal and would it be all right if I practiced in the Sunday School rooms on Saturday mornings?"

"Of course I can get you a hymnal. I have one in the other room, and you may practice any Saturday morning you like."

"Thanks. I should be going," added Anna. "Milly will have supper ready soon. Thank you so much for the pie. I also enjoyed visiting with you."

As she walked down the front steps, hymnal under her arm, she waved good-bye and thought again of Ed Marson and his new car and Mike Blakeley and his girlfriend and the dance.

Chapter Fourteen

Thursday evening had been quite chilly, so that when Anna and Davey arrived at school on Friday morning, the building was like a tomb. The cold air which greeted them made them both shiver. It was obvious that they needed a fire. Anna asked Davey if he could lug in some coal from the shed, and while he struggled out the door with the coal skuttle, she started to pile corn cobs into the stove. Soon another voice was heard. It was George. "Thank goodness!" she thought. She could hear him talking to Davey as he filled the skuttle and he soon appeared smiling in the doorway with Davey at his heels.

"Mom looked out the window and didn't see smoke comin' from the chimney, so she sent me on early to start the fire," he explained. Quickly he took over and soon had the corn cobs blazing, adding coal at the proper time. "We'll have a rip-roarin' fire here soon enough, and that'll heat this place up." He looked at his clothes and was pleased that he managed to keep them clean. "Guess I'd better wash my hands real well 'cuz coal in sure hard to wash off."

Anna realized that washing in cold water probably didn't help either. "I don't know how to thank you enough for doing this George."

"That's all right," he replied. "I kinda like to build fires anyways. My dad says I'm real good at it."

"You certainly are," she added, "and everyone will appreciate it. I hope that Mr. Kloster will start making the fires next week, so you don't have to do it."

"I don't mind but we need more coal. My mom said she was going to phone Ed to make sure he delivered some today in case Mr. Kloster forgot. We've got plenty of corncobs and newspapers for awhile." As he put his hands into the icy water trying to get the soap to lather, he said thoughtfully, "I'm gonna put a bucket of water on the stove to heat. Then we won't have to wash in cold water."

"Thank you George," Anna replied. "You certainly think of everything. I don't know what I would do without you," and she thought that was certainly the truth.

In mid-morning she could hear a wagon pull into the yard, and looked out to see Ed pulling in with a full load of coal. The children dashed to the window to watch him heave the heavy sacks out of the wagon and empty each one into the shed. Anna joined them. As he left he gave them a big wave and a smile, which they returned, and with the excitement of the day gone, they all went back to their desks.

Anna was wondering how to approach Roger Kloster about lighting the fire beginning next week, but her fears were allayed as Joshua mentioned at lunch time that his dad had said he would come at eight o'clock starting Monday.

On Saturday morning Anna first walked to the store to return the magazine to Vi Marson, hoping to see Ed and thank him for the coal, but he wasn't around so she went to the church to practice. She entered through the kitchen door, which led to the Sunday School rooms, and felt the same tomb-like atmosphere which had greeted her at school the day before. It was also rather dark, and she stood for a moment wondering what she was doing there in the first place, but she quickly got hold of herself and pushed the piano over near the window. She moved the stool, gave the top a few turns to fit her height and sat down. Touching the keys she found they were like ice, and she knew she would have to start practicing with gloves on, which did not help her playing. Still her fingers became quite stiff and cold. She took off the gloves and rubbed them and blew on them, hoping that without gloves she would play better, but it did little good as the minute she touched the keys, the blood seemed to desert those appendages for warmer parts, so she put on her gloves again.

"Good morning Anna," came a voice which startled her, and she was surprised to see Rev. Blakeley coming into the room. "I see you're wearing gloves. That's a good idea. You might have to play with them on as the keys are usually cold."

"Oh dear!" thought Anna. "He has no idea how difficult it is to play while wearing gloves."

"On Sundays they get a bit warmer," he continued, "because the room is heated, but they still will be cold."

"I'll do my best," Anna informed him with a forced smile, "but this is certainly an added disadvantage that I hadn't counted on. I'm not all that good anyway, and to play with gloves on doesn't make things easier."

He could see that she was discouraged, so quickly added, "Whatever you do, we will be grateful. Don't let yourself worry about it. We don't care if you make mistakes. We'll just sing all the louder. I have to go now, so I'll let you practice in peace," and with that he was out the door.

Rev. Blakeley might not worry if she made mistakes, but Anna knew that she would feel terribly embarrassed, not to mention the giggles that she imagined from the children, and looks of disapproval from the mothers. Even Milly would feel sorry for her. Well no other choice so she bravely started on the *Doxology*. It wasn't all that difficult actually, being in the key of G with only one sharp. Playing the right hand chords with gloves was difficult, so she decided to simplify it and play only the melody line.

She was concentrating completely when Rev. Blakeley appeared again. "I'd say you were doing all right, but I have an idea. I just checked with my wife. You know we have a piano in our parlor, you may have seen it when we came through it the other day." Anna nodded in response. "Well, the parlor isn't heated much, but it is warmer than this room and since we have no one coming to see us this morning I thought you might like to practice there."

"That's very nice of you," Anna replied, "But I may make so many mistakes that it would bother you."

"Don't worry about that, we're used to mistakes in our business, and I daresay you play better than you think. So what do you say, close up that ice box and come with me."

Anna did as she was told. She was concerned that she would play too many wrong notes fearing that they would be listening to her, but as it happened she felt very relaxed at the parsonage. The first thing Mrs. Blakeley did was to give her a hot cup of coffee to warm her up. She held it firmly with both hands as she drank it and slowly the circulation returned. After that she sat at the piano and played a bit nervously, but she practiced well, and without gloves.

The next week went very smoothly. Each morning as she approached the school there was a curl of smoke coming from the chimney, and although she never met Roger Kloster going to or coming from the school, he did light the fire and the building was warm.

Peter completed the ice house with the finishing touch being an old door that he had resurrected from somewhere years before, and at last it was being put to use instead of taking up space in the barn.

He was also getting his hogs ready for market, although they wouldn't be shipped for several weeks. He had his eye on a prize one which he was planning to fatten and butcher for the family. Milly would take care of part of the meat, and he would get the smokehouse going for the hams and bacon. Floyd had a steer they were going to butcher between them, so both Milly and Inger would be busy canning corned beef. Perhaps next year Peter would raise a lamb or two. Milly had always wanted one for the wool and they made good meat.

In another month there would be the one week of school vacation which would mean that it was time for the corn to be harvested. After that the stalks and husks in the west field would need to be chopped and put into the silo for winter forage. He would let the stock graze in the east field nearest the house. His four cows were due to calve next spring, and with luck he would have at least one or two milkers until the first one calved. Of the four calves he had in the spring, three were steers he was going to ship and the heifer was a good one so he decided to keep it and breed her next summer. He shared a bull with Floyd, and that animal was good for a few more years. Plenty of work to keep him busy. It was a year round job, what with the haying in the summer.

Floyd and Walter would take his steers and hogs to the stockyard in Chicago. They had far more animals than he had, and Walter was eager to go and learn the system which led to selling at the highest possible price. He had a good teacher as Floyd was an expert in this business and always seemed to come back with one of the best prices, and he was happy to do Peter the favor of selling his stock also. Floyd didn't seem to mind riding in the caboose on the stock train and Walter couldn't wait for the trip to begin. Fortunately the stock could be loaded at Grabney so there wasn't far to drive the cattle, and with his lumber wagon he could haul the hogs.

Hogs seemed to be selling well and since they were the main source of income Peter thought that next year he would be in a position to increase his stock considerably. He had a couple of good breeding sows and the chance to pick up a third from a neighbor. He could always raise more from one of the litters. He had plenty of corn for feed and would build another corn crib this winter. It was a good system where the pigs and cows ate the corn off the cobs, and the surplus he could get shelled and sell. If he were planning to have more hogs he would have to build more pens this winter.

His corn crop looked good. It was already getting dry, so by the first part of November it should be ready to harvest. He could decide then how much he wanted to sell and when the corn shellers came around would have it ready for them. Since they usually came to his place he could keep the dry cobs for fuel. If they shelled it in town they would be more than happy to deliver them for a dollar a load. He also wondered what hired hands would be available for the harvest, but that was something he would face later.

These were his thoughts as he did the evening milking. He poured some milk for the cats, grabbed the two full pails and walked with his usual firm strides toward the house. Davey saw him coming and ran to meet him. "Can I turn the separator? Please dad!" came his earnest request.

"I think you might just this once," came the reply from Peter who looked very kindly upon his son.

"Me too!" shouted Sarah. "I want to turn it too."

"You're not strong enough. I tried it before and it's hard," came the answer from her brother.

"Not if someone else starts it first, then it's easy," retorted Sarah stubbornly. "It almost goes by itself. I did that once, didn't I daddy?"

"Now you two quit arguing. I'll give you both a chance, and let Davey start it first so he can show how strong he is.

Get the cream can from your mother Sarah and ask her if she needs any milk," so Sarah darted ahead up the steps and into the house.

Anna was sitting at the table mending some holes in the heels of her silk stockings, having borrowed a wooden stocking darner from Milly. "This is a job that is endless," she commented. "Always mending, mending, mending. I wish there were stockings that were stronger."

"It's too bad you can't wear cotton anklets like I do," said Milly. "I save my silk stockings for Sundays and meetings, but teachers can't do that."

"I didn't know that you could sew!" exclaimed Sarah as she dashed into the kitchen. "Could you make me some doll clothes? My doll has only two dresses."

"Sarah!" called her mother. "Shame on you! You don't ask people to do things for you. What will Miss Swenson think?"

"I would think that she has a doll that could use another dress and I would love to make one for her. In fact I'll write to my mother and she can send me some scraps of material. She sews lots of beautiful clothes and I am sure she has some nice material that would be just perfect for doll clothes."

As Sarah was beaming an appreciative smile, they heard a call from the basement, "Where's the cream can Sarah?" Quickly Sarah grabbed the can from the counter and hurried down the stairs.

"That's so nice of you to offer to sew clothes for her doll. I yust haven't had time to do it lately," said Milly.

"I think you have more than enough to do without having to sew doll clothes. I love to sew, and Mother would be more than happy to send me odd scraps. After all, remember I'm part of the family now."

Chapter Fifteen

It was Sunday, October 1st. Anna didn't feel like eating much breakfast. Somehow her stomach wasn't eager for food, however she managed to get down enough so Milly wouldn't notice her lack of appetite.

It was quite chilly, but they decided to walk to church and not take the buggy as the air was invigorating and the walk was always fun. At least the walk was usually fun. Anna tried to get her mind off the ordeal of playing the piano, and then she would look down at the hymnal and the Bible which she held clenched tight to her chest and her thoughts went back to gloves and cold piano keys.

As they were entering the church grounds, who should drive up but Mr. and Mrs. Simms. This caused some consternation with Anna, because she was under the strong impression that Mrs. Simms would not appear at Sunday School. "Had Mrs. Simms planned to play today?" she thought. "Perhaps there had been some rumor that she was not that capable and the lady had decided not to resign after all."

Rev. Blakeley was at his usual post at the door greeting everyone. Mrs. Simms and Anna arrived there simultaneously. "I see you have the hymnal," the lady commented in her usual humorless voice.

"Yes," came the somewhat hesitant reply.

"Well, I just thought I would come and see how you did, and if you have any trouble I'll be glad to take over," she added firmly nodding her head.

Before Anna lost her composure completely, Rev. Blakeley came to her rescue. "Anna's been doing fine. She even has practiced at the parsonage so we've been able to hear her.

Now she may have to play with gloves on this morning, and you know that is difficult, but she'll do fine. You rest easy Mrs. Simms. Come on in and enjoy the Sunday School." With that he shook hands with Mrs. Simms and then Anna, giving her a smile and a pat on the shoulder for encouragement.

Mrs. Simms marched down the steps and took a seat in the ladies' section. "The nerve of her," Milly whispered to Anna. "Don't you pay any attention to her. You'll do fine. We're so proud that you can play the piano," and with that Milly took a seat with the ladies.

Feigning an air of confidence, Anna walked quickly with firm strides to the piano, opened it up, took off her gloves and felt the keys. They were cold, but somehow her hands were quite warm, so she decided to play without gloves. She adjusted the stool and sat down to wait for the service to begin. Her heart was pounding and her stomach felt queasy.

Then Rev. Blakeley walked to the front of the room, greeted everyone, announced the *Doxology* and the group rose. He smiled at Anna and she played the last line as an introduction, so far so good, no mistakes. She started on the song itself, playing only one note of the melody when she felt unable to play both, and doing the same with the left hand, but everyone was singing loudly so hopefully no one noticed. At one point she thought she played an A instead of a G, but continued through the number. At last the "Amen" which in her nervousness she almost hit the wrong notes, and finally it was over. She gratefully could hear the group resuming their seats.

"This morning as you can see we are delighted to have Miss Anna Swenson as our pianist," announced Rev. Blakeley. "She has promised to play for the Sunday School so Mrs. Simms, who has given us such faithful and devoted service for so many years, can devote her full time to playing for the church service. Let us all give our thanks to Mrs. Simms for being such a loyal servant of the church." He started the applause which Mrs. Simms accepted primly with several nods of acknowledgment. "And now let us applaud Miss Swenson who has so kindly offered to replace her." Anna turned and smiled at the group, and felt relieved because they seemed genuinely glad to have her.

The next song, *Jesus Loves Me*, was fairly easy for her as she had played it so many times in Fort Dodge. She remembered the hours she had spent practicing it, to get it perfect, and she could still play it from memory. After the lesson and the class, they closed the service with *Jesus Wants Me for a Sunbeam*, which Anna also could play.

As she left to join Milly to attend church she gave a sigh of relief. At least she was reasonably successful this first Sunday. She would have to talk to Rev. Blakeley to see what songs he wanted next Sunday. Perhaps she could practice more than once during the week, and she was determined to learn the *Doxology* with no mistakes.

"I am so proud of you Anna," said Milly as she grabbed her arm. "You did perfect." Several others congratulated her on doing such a fine job and Anna wondered if they guessed at how nervous she was. Well, it was over for this week anyway.

On Monday evening as Anna was drying the last of the plates and putting them in the cupboard, she heard the clomp, clomp of a horse's hooves and the crunch of wagon wheels on gravel. "That will be Inger and Floyd," yelled Milly from the bedroom where she was getting Lucy ready for bed.

Peter went out on the porch and soon ushered the two into the kitchen, offering them seats at the table. "Any more coffee Milly?" he called. "We got a coupla folks here just hankerin' for some."

"Plenty in the pot," she called back. "I'll be out in a minute."

"I'll get cups and saucers on the table Milly," said Anna as she took them from the cupboard."

"Well, I thought we were hirin' a schoolmarm, and here I find that we have a hired girl," teased Floyd. "First I see her doin' dishes and now she's settin' the table. I don't s'pose she spends much time at school with all the work that she has to do aroun' the house."

"Milly doesn't let me do very much around the house," Anna quickly informed him, trying to be serious.

"That's enough of your yoking Floyd," chimed in Milly from the other room. "You know that Anna goes to school every morning."

"Well that's it. Just you two women stick together so you get your stories straight. If the truth were told Milly prob'ly spends all day just sittin' aroun'."

"Yer right Floyd," added Peter with a grin as Milly came into the kitchen. "Every time I come in there is Milly sittin' in the parlor, readin' some ladies' magazine. Doesn't do a lick of work. That's why she wanted Anna to live with us. Someone to do all the work."

Milly and Anna each pulled up a chair to the table and listened with mock patience, knowing that they would lose this battle of words.

"Well I'll be dad-blamed," Floyd droned on. "Wouldn't ya know it. What we really come for was to give the school-teacher her paycheck, but if all we got is a hired girl, well we'll have to take the check back. Isn't that right Mother?"

"That's enough Floyd," came the straightforward voice of Inger. "Here is your first paycheck Anna," and she handed her the important piece of paper on which was written the sum of one hundred dollars. "I'm sorry I didn't get it to you yesterday on the first of the month, but being Sunday I didn't think it was proper. And we are all agreed that you are doing a fine job and are happy to have you here."

"Thank you," replied Anna who was delighted at these welcome words.

"Now Mother," scolded Floyd. "You'll turn the girl's head and she'll get so uppity that we won't know what to do with her."

"That will never happen," Milly remonstrated with him. "Let's have some coffee, and I'll get the cookies."

"You pour the coffee and I'll get the cookies," said Inger who was as familiar with Milly's kitchen as she was with her own.

"I'll write you a check as soon as I go upstairs." Anna spoke softly to Milly who was next to her. "I have enough in my account to cover it until I get this one mailed in and deposited."

"Don't worry about that. Tomorrow will be fine," Milly whispered back with the usual waving of her hands in protest, rising at the same time to get the coffee pot.

"Do you have any plans for your money?" asked Inger forthrightly.

"Well, after I pay Milly, I will deposit it in the bank, and then send some to my mother and try to pay her back for what she spent on my normal school expenses. I am also saving so that I can go back to school next summer."

"That's a good plan," Inger agreed.

"Sounds like too much edjacation to me," Floyd interjected. "You've got a job teachin'. What more do you have to learn? My Walter ain't never even gone to high school, and I'll bet he'll be one of the best farmers aroun' here."

"That's enough Floyd," Inger intoned, and she meant it. "Anna has good sense to return to school."

"Sounds like a waste a' money to me," was his final comment on that subject. Looking directly at Peter he said, "By the way, I think that Walter'n me'll take the stock to Chicago in a coupla weeks. The price is pretty good now. How's that sound ta you?"

"Jake with me," replied Peter. "Good to get them out of the way before the corn harvest."

"How's your silo doin'?" Floyd continued.

"Just about empty. I'll have it cleaned out by November. Got just enough feed to last until we ship."

"That reminds me, talkin' about cleanin' out silos," continued Floyd. "Remember what happened to Charley Wheeler a coupla years ago?"

"That is such a funny story," said Milly laughing. "Tell it so Anna can hear it. Oh Anna, we laughed until we cried. We yust couldn't stop."

"I admit it was pretty hilarious," and Floyd paused to chuckle a couple of times. "Well you see Charley and Bill Wheeler, I don't s'pose you've met 'em, you know they live acrost from us, and neither of them boys is any too bright, but they're a good sort, but anyways Charley and Bill decided they was gonna raise pigs. They got their pigs all right and then built a silo and filled it up with corn stalks. I kep' on tellin' 'em to chop the stalks and the husks up pretty good so's they'd pack down in the silo. You've gotta keep the air out or the silage will spoil. Well, they prob'ly got tired of choppin' and figured, 'What's the use of doin' all that work,' so I guess they just shoved the stuff in. Well, one day in the spring, Charley comes runnin' over to our place hell bent for leather and says I gotta come quick cause all his pigs is layin' on the groun' dead. Well nothin' to do but chase back after him, and he was right, all his pigs was a layin' on the groun' lookin' for all the world as if they seen the last of it. But then I smelled somethin' pecul'ar, and I says to him, 'What you been feedin' these pigs?' An' he says, 'Silage, same as usual.' Well I goes over to one of 'em and pokes him and smells aroun' and I'll be dad-gummed if it wern't the strangest thing I ever did see. I said, 'Charley! Yer pigs ain't dead, they's dead drunk.' He looks at me sorta strange, like he didn't hear me right. 'I tol' you,' I said. 'You gotta pack the silage in tight so's the air can't get at it. Yer stuff not only fermented but it spoiled, and these pigs is on the biggest drunk that I ever did see."

By this time everyone was laughing so hard that tears were pouring from their eyes. "What happened to the pigs?" asked Anna. "Were they all right?"

"Oh sure," answered Floyd, "but they probab'y had one helluva hangover. When they fin'lly begin to come to they staggered aroun' and it was somethin' comical to see. By gum! I ain't never seen nothin' like it."

Their coffee finished, he added, "Peter here and I have got to get things settled about shippin'. Why don't you ladies go off in the parlor and leave us be, and you can talk your women folk talk."

Milly was the first to rise with a command to the two children who were hanging around the table listening to every word of their Uncle Floyd's story. "Davey and Sarah off to bed you go. I forgot it was so late. Now shoo! Come on Anna and Inger. Let's look at the catalogs." She lit another coal oil lamp, carried it to the parlor and set it on the table next to the sofa.

"I want to show you the ice box I'm going to get. It's here in the Sears catalog," and she opened it to show Inger. "Anna I'm going to keep the money I get from you in an old sugar bowl on the top shelf of the cupboard. Elmer Marson says he will cash my checks. When I get enough I'll send off a money order to Sears. Peter says not to put the money in the farm account, or it will yust get spent. This way I'll have my own money to spend. Oh Peter buys me all that I need, but my money will be for special things."

"Good idea," agreed the practical Inger. "This is the same one that I picked out for us. I can see that I'll have to talk Floyd into getting it."

"You manage Floyd yust fine," commented Milly. "You'll probably get yours before I get mine."

"Well I doubt that, but we'll see. How about you Anna? Is there anything in the catalog that you want? You know it takes more than a week to get the order. It comes from Chicago. I know that it won't be like shoppin' in town, but it's fun to get things in the mail, sort of like Christmas."

"I think it would be fun to order. There is something that I was thinking about. I don't have any pants to wear if I want to help in the garden or do any work outside. I couldn't do much in a dress, besides I might ruin it."

"Don't let Floyd hear you say that or he'll offer you a worn out pair of his overalls. What you need are farmerettes. They're attractive and practical, like women's overalls, with a bib on them, two pockets sewed on the front of the pants, and they are gathered into a cuff which buttons at the ankle."

"That sounds perfect," Anna said enthusiastically. "Would they be in the Sears catalog or in the one from Belles and Hess?"

"Let's try Sears. Belles and Hess have fancy clothes," Inger looked in the index and soon found the right page. "I think I'll buy a pair of anklets too," Anna added. "Then I won't have to wear my silk stockings if I want to help with the garden."

"You are not to help with the garden," Milly stated emphatically. "You have enough work to do with teaching."

"But it might be fun for me Milly," Anna replied. "I've never lived on a farm, and I know it's hard work, but I think I would enjoy doing it. I also could use another pair of shoes. Can we find the page for those?"

"Oh, don't buy shoes from the catalog," advised Inger. "Wait until the shoe salesman comes. We all buy our shoes from him. They are about the same price as Sears, and they always fit. Remember Milly when I ordered that pair of fancy black laced shoes from the catalog? They were so huge they would have fit Floyd. I have ordered other shoes which have been all right, but I have always been most satisfied with the shoes from the salesman. Haven't you Milly?"

"Oh yes. I think it is best to buy from the shoe salesman. I remember those big shoes. We couldn't imagine why the shoe box was so big until we opened it," and she laughed at the thought.

"Is he going to come this fall?" Anna inquired.

"Of course! He always shows up about this time of year," said Inger who had a general knowledge of most things.

"In that case I'll order them from him. I don't need the shoes immediately," Anna remarked.

From the kitchen Floyd's voice could be heard, "If you ladies have finished spendin' Anna's money we'd better be goin'. Come on Mother. Time's a wastin'. Five thirty comes early tomorrow mornin'." After they left, Milly carried the kitchen lantern into their bedroom and Anna walked upstairs carrying a lighted candle held in a blue porcelain holder.

Chapter Sixteen

The first week of October went quickly. Anna found time to practice the piano and thus on the second Sunday she made a noble attempt at playing the songs which Rev. Blakeley suggested. The few mistakes she did make were hardly noticed, and if she did say so herself, the singing seemed to be more lively than it was before she took over. At times it seemed as if the children were trying to outdo themselves.

On Monday as she arrived home she saw a package on the table addressed to her. "Peter was in town so he picked up the mail," said Milly. "I see it is from your mother. There is a letter on top underneath the string."

"I think it's probably the material I asked her to send for doll dresses for Sarah," Anna replied, as she quickly picked it up and started to pull off the string.

"Here, use the scissors," said Milly, handing them to her. "Your mother ties it so tight with so many knots that you'll never get it off without cutting it. I can see that her packages won't fall apart in the mail."

Anna laughed with amusement and excitement as she cut at the many pieces of string, freeing the letter which she set aside, and finally tearing off the paper. Beneath it was a box, also tied with string which Anna cut. By this time Sarah and Davey were in the room and peering with curiosity at the activity. Anna removed the top of the box revealing scraps of beautiful material. Milly, holding Lucy in her arms, was also in the group of onlookers. With each piece that she took out there were exclamations of wonder. Most of them were silk. One of them seemed to be wrapped around an object a little smaller than a teacup. With a tug she pulled off the material and there to her surprise and delight was a bell, a real teacher's school bell. She set it on the table and tapped the top and it gave off a clear ring.

"What's that for?" asked Sarah.

"That's for school," replied Anna. "All teachers have school bells, but I didn't have time to buy one before I left. It will go on the front of my desk and when I want the class to come to order and pay attention, I will just tap the bell. Mother knew I should have one, and so here it is."

"Will you put it on the front of your desk at school?" asked Davey.

"I certainly will, and tomorrow you will hear me ring it when I want everyone's attention. Would you like to try it?" she said looking at Davey.

An emphatic nod in the affirmative gave no doubt and soon he was tapping the top and listening to the clear ringing tone. Next Sarah had a turn and even Milly and then Lucy.

"I never thought I would get to ring a teacher's bell," announced Milly, "but here I am doing it. Maybe we should get one for home and then I can have everyone's attention when I want it," she laughed.

"Sounds like the schoolhouse has moved inside here," said Peter as he entered the kitchen. "I wondered what all the excitement was about, and I heard that last remark, and no we don't need another bell here. The dinner bell is bell enough."

"Look at all the beautiful material that Miss Swenson got so she can make dresses for my doll," shouted Sarah as she jumped up and down.

"Quiet down young lady," admonished her father.

"Give Miss Swenson time to read the letter from her mother," said Milly. "And while she is doing that, I think it is time for a little coffee."

The next morning at school Anna carefully set the bell on the front of her desk. It looked beautiful and in its newness gave a sense of authority. She felt very proud to tap it to call the class to order after they entered the room. She knew that other teachers at the school had used bells, and so the students were used to them. At the end of each period she could now tap the bell one single ring before telling them to change subjects or go to lunch. A bell on the teacher's desk was almost as much a part of the teacher's equipment as was a blackboard and chalk. She had managed quite well without it, but now that she had it she felt more professional.

School was also going well. The third grade was the most trouble with Annie Lindquist and Victoria Pearson far ahead of Carl Anderson, which he resented. It also didn't help that he was slightly older than the girls. He definitely wanted to be a farmer. School did not interest him. This was made more apparent when Anna had an informal conversation with him one day. He was telling her about a hired man they had.

"He has came all the way from North Dakota," Carl informed her.

"That's interesting Carl. That's a long way," she replied, "but I think it is more correct to say 'He has come' instead of `He has came.'"

"My dad says, 'He has came,' and if my dad says, `He has came,' then it's right," came the authoritative answer.

Realizing that she would teach him more if he could read and write about practical farming matters, she wrote to the state agricultural department for printed material they might have for her or information as to where she could obtain such. She could also use this with some of the other boys, even though it would mean rewriting much of it.

That evening as she was correcting papers in her room she kept thinking of how she could add to the curriculum to make school more interesting. She had been thinking about her Manual Training class in Cedar Falls and some of the things which they made. There were raffia baskets and hot pads, and the picture frame where she had so much trouble mitering the corners. She knew she could get some supplies from the county, but just what she should get was another question. She decided that the next afternoon she would tell the class that all who had finished their work by Friday noon, could spend the afternoon working on craft projects. They could have a discussion as to what they would like to make. Perhaps some of them would have good ideas. They could bring materials from home or she could order from the county. Anyway it was worth a try.

The idea was greeted with much enthusiasm. The five girls all said they wanted to knit or crochet, which Anna realized would be simple enough. Now for the seven boys. Activities for them might not be so simple. She asked for suggestions and Lars Anderson, the oldest boy, raised his hand and asked if he could bring some boards and make himself a chest for storing his things in his room at home which he shared with Carl. This seemed like a rather large project. (She had been thinking more of wood carving or whittling, perhaps making toys for younger brothers or sisters at home or even the picture frame). Anna did not want to dampen his enthusiasm, since at least it was an idea and the other boys smiled eagerly at the suggestion. She mentioned that there were no tools at school. He said he could bring tools from home, so she agreed to the idea, but asked him to check with his father to make sure that this was all right. She also didn't want this to be a financial burden on the family. George mentioned that Lars was very skilled at making things, and asked if they could watch him. This seemed reasonable, so with the added suggestion that they talk to their parents about a project they could work on at school, she dismissed the class for the day, reminding them that this Friday, October 13th, they would start their projects.

Thursday the 12th of October being Columbus Day, Anna wondered what she could do to make it special. At breakfast and on the way to school she talked to Davey about it and taught him the simple rhyme, "Columbus sailed the ocean blue, In fourteen hundred ninety-two." She realized that 1492 meant very little to him, and it probably was the same with most of the students, so when she arrived at school she drew a chalk line across the blackboard and wrote 1492 at the left end, and 1922 on the right, adding the other years in increments of fifty years. With comments from the students she filled in additional historical facts along the line, and after that they discussed Columbus' voyage. It had been a rather dull history lesson but one she felt obligated to teach. Perhaps next year she would do better.

On Friday morning she was surprised to see a wagon drive up to school about 8:30 with Lars, Carl and who she assumed was Mr. Anderson. He leaped easily from the wagon, throwing the reins of the horse to Lars to tie to the post. He was tall, blonde and muscular, with the weathered face of a farmer, and joked with Davey and George who were watching with obvious interest. "Good mornin' ma'am," he ventured, tipping his cap to her. "I brought the pump organ back for you. It's that what's wrapped up in the blankets. We've been real careful with it."

"Good morning Mr. Anderson," she smiled in reply as she hurried down the steps. "It was nice of you to bring it back, but there was no rush."

"Well, it belongs to the school, and my missus was right glad to have it for a while. She's busy now anyway with the harvest, and it's time we got it back. But before we unload it, Lars said that he could build a chest for his room. Is this what you wanted?" he said as he pointed to the lumber.

"Oh, yes," she hesitantly replied, not sure what she did want. "I am sure that will be fine."

Awkwardly he came forward to meet her, with his cap in his hands. "First I'd like to have a little chat with you and the boys, if that's awright."

"Oh, certainly," she answered apprehensively, not knowing what was coming next. She had so far had no problems with parents, and hoped that this would not be the first. Immediately she thought of Carl and how she often corrected him, especially the time he quoted his father's grammar.

He stood in front of her, with a boy on each side. The other students, sensing a private conversation, left reluctantly to gaze at them from another part of the yard.

"Well, you see," he began with hesitation and some embarrassment. "I want my boys to have a good ejucation. I . . . well . . . I never got to go to school much. We were dirt poor, and bein' the eldest I had to stay home. School warn't much anyways. Now I heerd that Carl has been givin' you trouble," he said as he looked at Carl who was standing hanging his head. "I want you to know that whatever you tell Carl to do, he must do. I want him to learn good. He's lazy but he's not good for nothin'. The same goes for Lars, but Lars thinks different about school."

"Lars is a very conscientious student," replied Anna. "I never have to worry about him."

"Lars is also good with his hands. You see, my dad was a good carpenter. He was a real Swede carpenter. He could build anythin', and I, well I guess if it's awright to say so, I tried to take after him."

"I have heard that you have made beautiful furniture and cupboards for your house," replied Anna.

"Well, they's not all that good," he self-consciously admitted. "You see on a farm they's too much other work to do to just to keep body and soul together, they's not enough time for buildin'. The wife 'n I've got four young'uns, lost a girl between Lars and Carl, that would've made five. But what I'm also sayin' is that if Carl gives you any trouble at all, tell Lars to tell me. Lars is not one to tattle on Carl, but if you tell him he will. Now I'm not goin' to beat the boys, I got enough of that from my dad to know it's just plain meanness, but I'll see that they mind you, especially Carl."

"I appreciate you coming to talk to me," Anna confessed. "It's not many parents that will take the time."

"Well, I had a good reason too," he admitted. "You see Lars wanted this wood at school, and I had the organ to bring back, so I thought I could kill two birds with one stone, bring the wood and the organ, and talk to the schoolmarm. Lars, you kin bring in the wood and the tools if it's awright with your teacher. Once they're out we'll bring in the organ."

"Put everything in the corner in the back by the window," directed Anna. "That's where you will be building your chest."

"Lars knows that he'll have to bring home the tools, 'cause I only have one set, and am lucky to have that. I promised Carl that if he helped Lars carry the tools and behaved hisself, I would help him build a chest for hisself. I think you've got a good idea here. Some boys just ain't cut out for school, an' if they could do a few extry things, like buildin' somethin', well prhaps they'd pay more 'tention to the book learnin'. Well I sees they got the stuff outta the wagon, so let's get the organ in and then I gotta be moseyin' along. Plenty 'a chores waitin' fer me at home."

Quickly the pump organ was unloaded and carefully carried into the schoolhouse. They put it against the wall, next to the windows behind Anna's desk. Before they knew it he had jumped into his wagon and was off, waving to them as he left the school yard.

Anna and the children returned the wave and everyone excitedly entered the classroom to see Lars' materials. They were far more interested in them than in the organ. "The wood ain't, er isn't, all that good, but it's all we got, and my dad said we could sand it and paint it to cover up the bad spots," Lars explained. "I know just how I want to make it 'cause my ma has one at home that my dad made for her. Mine won't be so big, and not so fancy, but I will make it the same way he made my ma's."

"How're you gonna get the hinges?" asked Eddie Lindquist.

"I'll make them out of leather," replied Lars. "We've got plenty of that at home."

"Oh, Miss Swenson! It's nine o'clock," announced Mabel with concern in her voice. "You haven't rung the school bell."

"Thank you Mabel," she replied as she dashed for the porch, and promptly several gongs were resounding throughout the neighborhood, and another day had begun.

Chapter Seventeen

After dinner on Saturday, Peter settled down to his evening pipe while Milly and Anna finished the dishes. At the sound of a buggy being drawn up in the yard, Davey ran outside and announced that Uncle Floyd and Aunt Inger had arrived.

"That's a surprise," commented Milly. "I didn't expect them. Usually they phone first. I wonder what it's all about?" She didn't have long to wonder as soon Floyd's heavy tread could be heard in the entry way. "Aw shucks!" he called out as he came through the kitchen door. "Here you got the dishes all done, and I was just a aimin' to help ya. Well, Mother, we better turn aroun' and go home. Seem's we ain't needed here." Anna and Milly looked at each other and shook their heads.

"Sit down Floyd, you too Inger," remarked Peter, looking up from his newspaper.

"Well, we might just as well set a spell, since we made the effort to come. Anyways, I been thinkin' . . ."

"And it plain wore you out, did it?" Peter quickly added.

"Shore did," came the answer as Floyd lowered himself into one of the kitchen chairs. "Yup, it shore did."

"What's on your mind?"

"Well, it's like this," he slowly began. "Prices'r pretty good for livestock now in Chicago. I think Walter'n me'll go this comin' week, if that's awright with you. I don't think they'll get any better and the stock is as ready as it'll ever be. That sound OK with you?"

"That's find with me. The sooner I get them out of here, the sooner I can get things cleaned up before harvest. What day do you think you'll go?"

The three women, realizing that this was an important conversation, moved to sit in chairs at the table, with the two older children hanging around them and Lucy still in her high chair.

"I called the freight office and we can ship on Tuesday. Is that too soon for you? That way we'll be finished before the weekend, and I can show Walter around Chicago before we come back."

"But you'll miss the dance in Brewster. It's this Saturday night," Milly exclaimed.

"Milly!" said Inger sardonically. "You know as well as I do that Floyd is no dancer, and he will not be crying over missing the dance. This is probably the best excuse he could think of to get out of going."

"Them's rather harsh words Mother," Floyd remarked, as he got out his pipe.

"And what about Walter," added Milly. "Doesn't he want to go to the dance?"

"With a trip to Chicago that he's been looking forward to for years, there is no way that Walter would stay for a dance, considering that he has never been crazy about going to dances anyway," Inger explained.

"Chip off the ol' block," added Peter laughing to himself.

"Does that mean that you can't go?" asked Milly. "And what about Mabel? She loves the dances."

"George and Mabel and I will go. I'll probably dance just as many dances as I usually do even without Floyd," Inger said nodding her head knowingly. "And anyway I promised the Brewster Guild that I would bring potato salad for the supper."

"Now that's just her excuse for goin'," Floyd chimed in. "I no sooner told her about goin' with the stock, than I hear her on the phone promisin' to bring the potato salad. Jus' like a woman. A man can't get out of town before she's off to some local do."

"With you and Walter gone we'll have enough room in our buggy to take Anna with us, and we could perhaps take Davey too since we have a two seater," Inger retorted pragmatically.

"That's what I had in mind all the time, jus' my gen'rous nature," Floyd added with feigned graciousness. "As a gentleman I will go to any length, even to Chicago, to make sure the school teacher gets a ride to the dance."

Milly had told Anna the week before that Inger had planned to take her to the dance, even if their entire family went, however Anna was relieved to hear this confirmed and replied, "Thank you Inger, I'd love to go with you."

"Well, on second thought, if this ain't a fine state of affairs. It's enough to make me change my mind. Here I am goin' to Chicago, when I could dance with a purty schoolmarm. It's enough to keep me from goin'," Floyd retorted.

"After dancing with you she'd be lucky to have any feet left," laughed Inger. "She'd be on crutches the rest of the year."

"Well, I can see that I'm goin' to lose this one, so I'll give up the fun and be the workin' one. I'll go to Chicago and slave my fool head off just to provide for my family even though no one will 'preciate this sacrifice."

In the midst of this Davey shouted, "Can I go with them Mama?"

"Hush," came his Mother's admonition. "We'll decide later."

Amid much laughing and teasing, Milly chased the two older children off to bed, and Inger put Lucy down while Milly put on the coffee pot. Then she, Inger and Anna sat at the table discussing local events, including the new Chevy that was recently delivered to the Marson family, while Floyd and Peter made plans to ship the stock.

The next morning on the way to church the grass was crisp with frost and crunched underneath their shoes, however by the time they walked home the sun had succeeded in warming things up, enough so that while the ground was still firm, the vegetation was dewy wet. Peter walked first, carrying Lucy, with Davey by his side, followed by Anna, Milly and Sarah.

"How'd you like the Marson's new Chevy?" he called back to them.

"Looks expensive to me," answered Milly. "I wonder who is going to drive it most, Ed or Elmer?"

"Well, from what I've seen around here, it's the young folks that will be doing the driving. I reckon that's why so many folks have held back on buying a car. Most men are satisfied with their teams, and if the truth were told, probably are too scared to learn to drive a car. I was surprised that Simms bought one."

"He yust wants to show off," replied Milly. "You know how they are."

"Well, guess you may be right," and he laughed.

"Is Uncle Floyd going to buy a car?" asked Davey. "He wouldn't be scared to learn to drive. And anyway Walter could drive. He told me he's going to learn."

"Well, I don't know about the scared part," mused Peter, "but your Uncle Floyd doesn't take to new ideas, especially those that cost money. Isn't that right Mother?"

"That is yust so right about Floyd," and the three adults joined in laughter.

"Anyway, I heard that Ed is squiring a girl over Brewster way," Peter continued. "I imagine that he intends to use their car a lot."

"I didn't know that he had a girlfriend," Milly cried with astonishment.

"Oh he gets around more than you'd think. He doesn't spend all his time in the store. I think he's had several girlfriends, but nothing that's lasted," her husband added.

"How come I didn't know about it?" she asked, hurrying to catch up with Peter's long strides.

"Well, he keeps pretty much to himself," said Peter, walking sideways so they could hear him. "Living so close to Liza Crawford I think he has to. I'm surprised that she hasn't heard about his social life. Elmer told me that she often comes to visit with Vi and tries to pump information, but Vi's on to her, so keeps her mouth shut."

"When I was at the Blakeley's about a month ago, I heard that their son Mike might come to the dance and bring his girlfriend," added Anna. "Ed was there and said that he would write to Mike and ask him to come, and that they could use the new car they would be getting. Mrs. Blakeley was very anxious to meet this girl, and Rev. Blakeley was teasing her about it."

"Inger told me this morning that Elmer and Vi intend to drive to the dance, and if Ed goes, he will have to ride in the back seat," Milly laughed. "That would mean that Rev. and Mrs. Blakeley would probably go to the dance, with Mike and his girl in their back seat."

With a chuckle Peter answered, "Mike better be on his good behavior. His mother doesn't miss much."

"I didn't know that ministers went to dances," Anna said in surprise.

"I suppose most ministers don't," added Milly. "The Blakeleys don't go too often, but the ladies like to have them there. It keeps things more orderly, not that the crowd gets rowdy, but when they are there, there's never any trouble."

"And the Reverend is a nice guy. Everyone likes him. He's part of the community just like the rest of us," Peter added.

"How many people come to the dances?" asked Anna.

"Oh, about a hundred, maybe a hundred fifty counting the children, is that about right Milly?" asked Peter.

"I think that's about right," she answered. "There's not that many for supper though, because those with families sometimes go home early."

"Can I stay for the supper?" asked Davey as he ran to keep up with his father.

"You've stayed for the supper many times," he answered, "but you're always asleep so you don't know it's going on."

"This time I'm going to stay awake. Will you help me stay awake?" He looked at his father who was shaking his head and laughing. "Miss Swenson, will you help me stay awake."

"I'll do my best Davey. And since I won't know many people there, maybe you will dance with me. That should help to keep you awake."

"But I don't know how to dance," he sighed.

It was a busy week with the club meeting at Milly's on Wednesday. Thursday and Friday were filled with preparations for the dance, and then it was Saturday.

After the supper chores were finished, the family dressed in their best, and Anna and Davey walked up to the Parker's for their ride to the dance. On the trip to Brewster, Inger and Anna sat in front, with the three children in back. Ten miles was a fair distance to go, but the evening was not too cold, and they were well bundled in coats with a blanket over their knees. The children were quite excited, and Anna gleaned a great deal about the dance from the bits of conversation she overheard.

Inger mentioned that Floyd and Walter had gotten off fine on Tuesday with the stock, Walter being so excited that he could hardly keep his mind on what he was doing, yet he was trying his best to appear grown up and work as hard as any man.. "Floyd's not had much education, but there's no one around here who can beat him at getting a good deal on his livestock and his grain. He's a true farmer, and knows his stuff," she proudly commented. "I always wanted Walter to go to high school and get a good education, but now I realize that he isn't suited for schooling, and can get a better education from his father. Walter will be just as good a farmer as his father. Farming's in their blood."

"Walter seems a remarkable young man to me," Anna added. "You have a wonderful family. Mabel has a good head on her shoulders. She is a marvelous help both at school and at taking the nursery during church."

"Well, she's smart enough, and can go through high school, and perhaps go to normal school. Floyd may want to keep her at home to help around the house, but that wouldn't be fair. She needs to have the chance to go on to college if she qualifies. But the one in the family that I really want to go to college in George. He is definitely the brightest of our children," she admitted.

"I believe you are right," Anna replied. "It would be a pity if George did not have the opportunity to attend college. He is not only bright, but he has a great deal of common sense."

"Floyd may want him to be a farmer," Inger continued, "but this may be partly because Floyd never had the chance to continue his education beyond grade school. He feels that if he could get ahead without having any more education, then his children can do the same. Also he is overly frugal, and says it is a waste of money to spent it on schooling. You heard what he said to you when I gave you your first paycheck. Well that sums up the way he feels. He doesn't realize that times have changed since he was a kid."

"Miss Swenson," Mabel called from the back seat. "Look ahead! See the lights. That's Brewster."

Anna noticed that there were more wagons going toward the town, and now and then a car. It was not easy to pass on the narrow dirt road, and when one car went by Inger had all she could do to keep the horses reined in. At last they were in front of the hall. Inger took the side road which led to the back of the building where they tied up the horses.

"I'm going to bring the salad the back way into the kitchen," announced Inger. "Mabel, you take Miss Swenson around to the front, and George you and Davey go with them. Women don't have to pay to attend, but the men pay $1.00. Children also get in free. George can hardly wait until he's charged admission. Get a good seat along the side and save one for me. See if Milly and Peter are there. If not, save seats for them too. We're a little early, so you should be able to get seats together."

They walked to the front of the building. A lean, tall farmer was at the door collecting a dollar from each man, and he joked with George and Davey that they'd better start saving their money because soon they'd be paying. The room was large, with a stage at one end. Wooden folding chairs were lined up along all four sides, and people were entering, and putting their coats on the chairs. One woman had brought her baby in a buggy. This was definitely a community family activity. Milly and Peter had not arrived, so they held seats for them.

A four piece band was on the stage, getting ready with a piano, two fiddles and a saxophone. They were tuning up and jovially talking to members of the audience. The hall was gradually filling, and soon Inger appeared. She gave her approval of the seats they had chosen, which were at the end next to the stage. Milly and Peter soon appeared, with Lucy nearly asleep on Peter's shoulder. Milly was carrying the clothes basket, piled high with blankets. She hoped Lucy would be so tired that she would lie down in it and sleep through most of the evening.

Anna had never attended anything like this. There were a few dances in Fort Dodge, but for adults, and she and Elsa had been to only a couple. They used to practice dancing at home, singing the tunes. Occasionally their Mother would play the piano for them. At least she felt that she knew how to dance, and was hoping that she would be asked.

Soon the music began. Couples swarmed onto the floor and she was fascinated to watch them. There was every degree of dancing ability, but no matter how good or how unskilled a person was, everyone seemed to be having a good time. Inger volunteered to hold Lucy, who by this time was wide awake, so Peter and Milly could dance. Sarah sat next to Mabel, with Davey next to George. Soon the two boys were off visiting with friends. Peter asked Inger for the next dance, so Mabel took Lucy. Milly was not seated for long, as someone Anna did not know, asked her to dance. Ed was right. She was a good dancer, and very popular. There was so much activity, that Anna was fascinated.

Soon Anna realized that someone was standing in front of her. It was Rev. Blakeley, asking her to dance. "I think that the minister should be the first one to dance with the school teacher," he reasoned out loud, "so Miss Swenson, will you do me the honor of giving me this dance." He was his usual warm, friendly self.

"Yes, I would be happy to," she replied, and they soon were gliding across the floor to a slow waltz. As they danced she saw several others that she recognized, including Ed Marson and his girl from Brewster. Rev. Blakeley pointed out his son Mike and girlfriend Emma, adding that so far Mrs. Blakeley approved of her. "Well, at least I'm sure she approves because she suggested that Mike drive the car tonight, with his girl in the front seat with him, and we could sit in back. But on the other hand, it might be that she just wanted to keep an eye on them," he laughed.

At the end of the dance, Anna thanked Rev. Blakeley as he brought her back to her seat. A short time later Peter asked her to dance. He was a good dancer also. She was enjoying herself more than she thought she would.

As the evening progressed she was asked for two more dances. She had not met the men before. Both were farm hands from the area and it was obvious that they loved to dance. Milly knew them, but then Milly seemed to know everyone.

She saw Peter dancing with Sarah, holding her in his arms, and she was smiling with delight. Other fathers did the same. Mabel and Erica danced several dances, as did other girl partners. Peter tried to tease George into dancing with one of the girls, but he firmly shook his head no to this suggestion.

Lemonade was sold, so at the break Anna bought Sarah and Mabel a glass, and the three sat down and enjoyed drinking it, since it was cold and the room was fairly warm with all the bodies milling around. By this time Lucy was asleep, and Sarah was close behind her. Milly had brought a blanket for her, so when she finally couldn't keep her eyes open any longer, she was laid to sleep across two chairs.

The music started again. At the second number, Ed Marson came over and asked Anna for a dance. Anna thought he was heading for Milly, and was quite surprised to find him standing in front of her, and felt somewhat self-conscious as she happily rose to accept. He was a smooth dancer, and while he didn't say much, she enjoyed dancing with him and was flattered that he had asked her.

She danced with Peter again, plus two other young men, one of whom had a very jerky style which was hard to follow, and another person who turned out to be the shoe salesman, Jack Jarvis. Anna had noticed that he danced nearly every dance. He was very friendly, and introduced himself to her mentioning that both Inger and Milly had told him who she was. He also added that he would be coming by this week in case she needed any shoes.

She tried to coax Davey to dance, but he shyly declined. Soon the song, "Good Night Ladies" was being played. This was the last dance. Inger and some of the other women had already left to get the supper ready. Babies and sleeping children were left on the chairs, or in baskets or baby buggies. Everyone else filed downstairs to sit at long tables and partake of the fried chicken, potato salad, cake and hot coffee or lemonade, served by the ladies for an additional fifty cents. It was midnight.

Davey was barely able to keep awake, and half way through the supper he fell asleep leaning against Peter. Milly was as vivacious as she had been four hours earlier, and she had danced almost every dance. Mabel and George were managing to keep their eyes open and eat their supper, but it was a struggle. Inger went upstairs once to check on Sarah and Lucy. Anna felt tired but not sleepy. The food also revived her, especially the hot coffee. The crowd was a little less lively than it had been a few hours before, but remained quite animated. Conversation was plentiful, and everyone was still having a good time. There was lots of joking. It was like a big picnic.

Soon people finished and began to leave the tables. Peter awakened Davey and left him with George. Then he and Milly went upstairs to get Sarah and Lucy and head for home. Davey fell asleep on the bench again, so George left him and he and Anna and Mabel helped clear the tables. There was plenty of help, so it did not take long. Soon Inger appeared from the kitchen. "We don't have to stay to wash the dishes. They told me to take you folks and go home. They live closer than we do, so I'll get my potato salad bowl and meet you out front. George can you manage Davey?" George nodded. "Then Mabel and Miss Swenson you get the coats, and check around to make sure none of us left anything."

As they arrived at the top of the stairs they saw the men setting up chairs for the church service. "It's hard to believe that in 18 hours or so, Rev. Blakeley will be preaching here," commented Anna. "And I'm sure that it will look more like a church than a dance hall. Already I can see the difference." Together they made their way, carrying coats and belongings, to the buggy and Inger.

On the way home Mabel and George joined Davey in sleep, all three snuggled under the blanket in the back seat. The stars were out. It was a clear, cold night. Frost was in the air. Inger grabbed the reins and off they went. It had been a wonderful evening.

Chapter Eighteen

It was well after 4 AM when Anna crawled into bed, and it seemed like five minutes later when she heard Milly in the kitchen getting breakfast. Looking at her watch she realized that Peter must have been up for at least two hours as it was eight o'clock. She roused herself as quickly as she could, and splashed the cold water from the pitcher on her sleep filled eyes to help wake up. In a few minutes she was dressed, combed and in the kitchen apologizing to Milly for sleeping so late. Close on her heels were Davey and Sarah.

"Let me go to Sunday School Milly and you stay home," suggested Anna. "You must be exhausted, and then getting up so early."

"Oh, no. It is my responsibility to go," answered Milly. "But Peter is staying home and Lucy too. Peter was up so early and got to bed after I did. Sarah and Davey, you can stay home with your father if you wish."

"Oh no! I have to go to Sunday School," wailed Davey. "I want perfect attendance."

"Me too," echoed Sarah. "I want perfect attendance." So the four of them dragged off to Sunday School and Church, to what was a rather sparse attendance for both groups.

On Monday afternoon Jack Jarvis the shoe salesman appeared about four o'clock. He was in perfect time for a cup of coffee and cookies. As they were consuming this repast, he filled them in on the local news, which was his custom, although most of it had been transmitted at the Saturday dance. As he put down his cup after finishing the last drop, he got down to business and measured Sarah and Davey, as they had clearly outgrown the shoes from the year before, although they still could wear the dress shoes they had purchased before Easter. Lucy would wear Sarah's baby shoes. Peter and Milly decided that they could wait until he came around again. This was now the time for Anna to order some heavy shoes if she wanted to do any outside work. It was a new experience for her as she had always bought shoes in the store in Fort Dodge.

Jack had two suitcases full of sample merchandise, drawings to illustrate the types of shoes which he sold, and materials for measuring feet. He turned to Anna. "Just what kind of shoes were you thinkin' of Miss?"

"Some sturdy shoes I can wear if I want to work in the garden," answered Anna. "I have boots for snow, and dress oxfords for school, but nothing in between."

"Take a look at these pictures then, and let me know what you like," he said as he handed her several sheets of paper. "I think that this pair would suit you fine, the one on the second page," he continued.

"Those would be the best," Milly volunteered as she looked over Anna's shoulder. "But I don't see why you want shoes to work in the garden. Oh you are hopeless," she laughed and waved her hands in defeat.

"Maybe I will even help to harvest the corn," Anna added in a mocking tone with a firm nod of her head.

"I hope you learn quick," Peter remarked. "Then maybe I can leave Mother in the kitchen and she won't have to."

"Now Peter!" Milly scolded. "Don't listen to him Anna. I can't go into the fields any more, not with three children to watch. I used to do it though."

"I was up at Anderson's before I come here," said Jack. "They were sayin' the same thing. Lars and Carl can help with the harvest, but Mrs. Anderson has to take care of Elsa and Birgit. They really can't afford to hire any help, and the boys work hard, but one more hand would sure help out."

"Why can't I take some of the younger children at school?" asked Anna. "I know that all of the older children will be out working, but I would be happy to help out by keeping the school open during the week for the young ones."

"Would I be a young one?" Sarah chimed in.

"Oh Sarah!" her Mother admonished. "We can't ask Miss Swenson to have little children in school during the harvest week."

"Of course you would be a young one, and you could come to school Sarah," Anna replied. "But I think first we would have to talk this over with your Aunt Inger, to see if it's all right."

"I think it's a good idea," Jack added. "I know most teachers stick around during the harvest. If there are plenty of hired hands around they keep the younger students in school with only the older ones working."

"Hired hands cost money," announced the frugal Milly.

"And I don't think there are too many around this year," Jack continued.

"I think she'd be a darn site better off with the little kids at school, than trying to harvest," laughed Peter, "and it would sure be a big help. And from what I've seen of you Anna, you'd rather be busy than just sit around for a week."

"I know I'd never really be able to harvest," Anna said, "but I'd like the experience of trying, just to see what it's like. I've heard of walking behind the wagon and pulling off the ears and husking them."

"By the time you've done it an hour or two, you are really tired," Milly added. "It's not an easy yob, I mean job."

By this time Jack had completed Anna's order, and loaded and closed his suitcases. "Let's see . . . I should have your shoes here in two weeks time, that would be about the first week of November if I'm not mistaken. Maybe not in time for harvest, but almost. That starts the sixth, doesn't it?"

"That's right, if not before." Peter replied, "just as soon as the corn dries out."

"Don't bother to let me out. I know the way," and Jack left to continue his busy route, possibly getting supper at the next farm.

"If you really want to know what it's like to harvest corn, I'll explain it to you," said Peter as he resumed his place at the table, and Milly poured him another cup of coffee. "Well, you see we hitch up the team to the lumber wagon, the same wagon I use for hauling the pigs and for everything else around here. Anyway I put up a big board in the front of it, behind the seat. We call that the bangboard. The rows of corn are wide enough for the team and the wagon to go through, and the horses know just about how fast to go, if they don't move you just yell 'Giddap' or to slow them down you yell 'Whoa'."

"Can I ride in the wagon this year daddy?" asked Davey.

"We'll see about that. Anyway, if two people follow the wagon, one to each row of corn, that works out best. You grab an ear. Then with the husking pin, which is attached to your hand with a leather strap, and you also have to wear gloves, you slit the husk, and if you do it right, and this isn't easy if you haven't done it before, the ear comes free and you snap it off at the bottom."

"Then you hit the bangboard," shouted Davey as he demonstrated with a wild pitch which clipped Sarah on the ear, eliciting a howl from her.

"Davey, stop that," remonstrated Milly as she took the tearful Sarah on her lap. At this point Lucy felt neglected, so Peter grabbed her and sat her on his knee.

"Anyway, you get the idea from Davey. You throw the cob at the bangboard," Peter continued, "and it ends up in the front of the wagon. The corn is very dry, not like when you eat corn on the cob which is picked fresh during the summer. Eating corn is a different kind of corn anyway. You wouldn't want to eat corn that we use for feed, too tough. So after that you keep going until you fill up the wagon, and then you load up the corn cribs. The pigs and cows gnaw it off the cob, and we would use the cobs for kindling or for fuel, but by that time they're too dirty so we plow them back into the ground. The kindling cobs are what the corn shellers leave."

"Tell her about the corn shellers dad," chimed in Davey.

"You're sure feeling your oats today," his father said smiling and tousling Davey's hair. "For the corn I sell, and it should be a fairly good crop this year, but I don't count on a thing until it's all in, well, anyway for the corn I sell, we hire the corn shellers. They have equipment which rips the kernels off the cob, and are they fast. They come around and shell it when it is to be shipped to market, then haul it down to the railway. If we lived near a big town that had a grain elevator we would haul the corn to town ourselves, and the shellers would shell it there. That's where they sell the cobs for fuel for a dollar a load. But we don't live near an elevator and they like to come here. I think it's because Milly puts on such a good feed."

"Oy, yoi, yoi," Milly exclaimed as she got up and put Sarah down. "If I don't get busy we'll not have any kind of feed at all, not for tonight anyway."

"It sounds like hard work. I knew it wouldn't be easy, especially hour after hour. I think I'd rather teach school," Anna commented. "But I'd like to see it done," and she rose to help Milly with the supper.

"You'll have plenty of time for that. Every day when you come home from school, we'll still be at it," Peter said as he got up to go milk the cows. He took the two older children with him.

As they finished eating, the telephone rang. Milly got up to answer it, and it was Inger.

"From their conversation, it's just as I suspected," Peter commented. "Jack's been to their place and told Inger about you wanting to take the younger children at school while we are harvesting. I was wondering how long it would take before she called. You don't need a phone with Jack around. Of course he doesn't come that often, but when he does you can bet that what you've told him will soon spread around the country like wind blowing chaff from a haystack."

After Milly hung up, she reported to her audience. "Inger says that maybe it is a good idea, but we've never done it before. She'll have to see how the other folks feel about it. And then you'll have to decide how many children you can take, and how old they should be. We'll have to wait until everyone is told."

"I think everyone will know by bedtime," mused Peter. "And by the time that school opens tomorrow morning, Anna will have notes from all the mothers who want their children to be taken care of during harvest. You may have bitten off more than you can chew Anna."

"Oh dear," Anna said, giving the matter a second thought. "I thought it was such a good idea. I was sort of thinking out loud, and I hadn't counted on Jack being such a good messenger. I guess we'll just have to wait and see what happens."

Chapter Nineteen

There was great excitement at school the next morning as most of the children had heard that Miss Swenson was planning to take the younger children at school during the harvest week. However it was also reported that many of the mothers felt this was an imposition, even though they would like to take advantage of the offer. Anna tallied up the number of children she might have, and found that it would be no more than eight, including one from a family who had no children of school age. She told the class that the children should be three years old, the same age as entering Sunday School, and all agreed that this was fair. Lars Anderson mentioned that his sister Birgit was almost three, and as she acted three it was decided that she should be able to come. Joshua raised his hand and said that his sister Elaine would be three in January, and wondered if she could come too. Anna hadn't counted on this, but on second thought realized that this might be a way she could get closer to the Kloster family. That would make ten children. Thus it was that she started that day of Tuesday, October 24th, not knowing what she was getting into. Perhaps she had inadvertently opened a Pandora's box.

After school she was delighted to learn that Liza Crawford had called and said a package had arrived for her at the Post Office. No doubt it was her order for the farmerettes and anklets from Sears.

They sat down to the usual afternoon coffee and a catch up of the day's activities. "I think I may have ten children in school during harvest," mentioned Anna. "I had counted eight, but Lars has a sister almost three, and so does Joshua. I thought I could take them too."

"Oh, Anna, that is too many," said Milly shaking her head. "There's those of us who would appreciate it, but you can't take on such a big yob, job," she corrected herself.

"Who will take care of Lucy?" asked Davey.

"I'm lookin' at that person right now," added Peter nodding his head.

"Oh, not again!" wailed Davey. "I thought I could go out and help harvest."

"When you grow a little bigger you can," his mother commented. "Most of the younger children from school will be taking care of the babies in the family."

"But Joshua said he will help with the harvest, so why can't I?" came the whiney voice.

"Never you mind," counseled Peter. "They don't have a baby in their family, and we do. By the time you are old enough to harvest you will find that you'll be plenty tired of the whole thing. Now that's enough of this discussion."

"I'll stop over at the Klosters on my way to the Post Office, and mention about taking care of Elaine during the harvest," Anna informed them. "I've never had a chance to really talk to them, and this would be a good excuse."

"And I think that Roger would not be in the house, so you'll have a chance to talk to Grace alone," Milly volunteered.

"I'd better get going then," said Anna as she pushed herself from the table. "I don't know how long this will take and I want to get to the Post Office before it closes."

"I doubt if she'll invite you in for coffee and cake," added Peter as Anna went into the entry way to put on her coat. "I'll be interested in what she says, especially since we haven't heard a single word from them since the fire."

With a light heart Anna walked down the back steps and out the road which led to the Klosters. As she approached their driveway she could see Joshua and his grandfather heading quickly for the barn with the milk pails. "A little early for milking," she thought as she glanced at her watch to make sure of the time. She looked around the farm to see if Roger were anywhere in sight, and could not see him so headed for the kitchen door, hoping to find Grace and Elaine by themselves.

She was about ten feet from the house when she heard someone yelling. Was it Grace? No it was Roger. No, it was both of them, having an argument. By this time she was close enough so she could hear their words. She stood there almost frozen in shock as she heard Roger yell, "I was the one who saved this place. You an' your ol' man wouldn't have lasted another six months here."

"Please Roger," came Grace's plaintive cry.

"Shut up!" and with that came the sound of something falling. "Get up and get on your knees to me. The Bible says that a husband is the master of the house. It's time you learned that."

"Don't hit me again," Grace begged as she cried.

"You are a sinner. Sinners need to be punished. I've a good mind to leave you all here to rot, and that's exactly what you'd do without me."

Anna turned, half terrified, and quickly walked back to the road, his last words ringing in her ears. She didn't want to hear any more of this, and knew that there was nothing that she could do to help Grace. She would have gone back to the Jensens but knew there was nothing that they could do either. Her every fiber seemed to tremble, and she hoped that the walk to the Post Office would calm her down. What had started out as a happy jaunt, had turned into a nightmare. "What kind of life did Joshua have? Is that why they were hurrying to the barn? And what about Elaine. Where was she during all this?" she kept asking herself.

She reached the river and turned right toward Grabney. About one hundred yards in front of her was Ed Marson, carrying what looked like a posthole digger. Peter didn't order a posthole digger, she was sure. Where was he going? Of all days to meet him. What would she say to him? Her mind raced to solve this problem. She had so wanted to be friendly and pleasant when she saw him again, remembering the afternoon eating the pie at the Blakeleys and dancing with him at the dance.

He was closer now and waved his free left arm in greeting. She waved back, hoping that it looked friendly and casual. As he approached he smiled, "Goin' to practice at the church this time of day?"

"Oh, just going to the Post Office," she replied, surprised and a little flustered that he should remember that.

"Well, I'm on my way to Klosters'. He ordered this posthole digger, and said he wanted it soon as it come. I don't see how he thinks he can get this fence fixed up by the time he turns the cattle in," said Ed as he turned to look at the rotten posts and sagging wire, shaking his head. "Had all year to do it. A coupla cows got out last year. Well I better be on my way, see'n as he wants it sooner rather than later," and with that he smiled and turned and strode firmly along the path.

Anna started to say, "Good-bye," but her throat stuck on the first syllable as she realized that Ed was heading for the Kloster house. There was no way she could have warned him of what he might find, and then she thought it possible that by this time the confrontation between Grace and Roger had ended. At least she hoped so. She quickened her step to force herself to think of other things than that horrible scene. Although she hadn't witnessed it, she had heard enough to imagine what was happening.

As she approached the Post Office she heard a familiar voice which could be no one else's but that of Floyd. "Well, I tell you now Liz, if Chicago ain't the durn biggest city I ever seen. I shore wouldn' want to live there, but me'n Walter had a real good time. It's jus' mighty excitin' bein' there, right Walter?"

"Sure is Pa," came the answer.

"How come yer train was late?" asked Matt.

"Well I tell you now, it was this a way. The conductor and I jus' got a talkin' and he plum fergot to tell the engineer to start."

"What about that herd of cows that wouldn't move off the tracks Pa?" added Walter.

"Well, that jus' may have had somethin' to do with it also. Anyway, let's get the mail. I think I heerd George drive up with ol' Nellie." Floyd turned around to see if it really were his wagon when his eyes lit on Anna. "Well, look who's come to welcome us home from Chicago, if it ain't the schoolmarm. Howdy Miss Swenson, mighty nice of you to come meet us. See Walter, this jus' shows how we rate aroun' here, with the teacher comin' to meet us."

"I'm glad you're back," Anna smiled in reply. "Sorry the rest of the welcoming committee couldn't make it, but they're home doing chores." For once she was grateful for Floyd and his brand of humor which took her mind off the events of the previous half hour.

"I've got that package for you Anna, and there's some mail for the Jensens too," Liz interrupted.

"Thank you," said Anna as she took the parcel and the few items of mail.

"Well, I can see that you're never goin' to make it home with that heavy load," said Floyd, feigning seriousness, "so we might as well give you a lift. I've got to get to Peter's anyway, 'n pay him the money that's comin' to him. Let's see now, gol darn, where did I put that money. I must have it somewhere," and he pretended to search his pockets.

"Hey Pa, George is waitin'," called Walter. "Let's go!" so the three of them trooped out of the Post Office.

Anna could see that George had been to the store, because the back of the wagon was full of supplies. She climbed up between the boys, with Floyd driving. As they crossed the bridge she suddenly thought of Ed and looked up the path to see if he were coming. He was nowhere in sight, and not giving him another thought she was immediately engrossed in the tales of Chicago.

Chapter Twenty

It was a chilly Wednesday morning as Anna and Davey walked to school, but they didn't notice the cold as they talked about Uncle Floyd's visit the evening before. He had sent the boys on home and stayed to talk with Peter and settle up on the money he owed him. Peter was delighted with the price Floyd had gotten and Davey was very excited to think that now they had so much money, not realizing that it would be plowed back into the farm.

Suddenly Davey looked up at the school and exclaimed, "Hey! How come there's no smoke coming from the chimney."

Anna was puzzled as Roger had always meticulously fulfilled his obligation to start the fire. They hurried on to the school, and when they opened the door found that it was freezing cold inside. It seemed worse than outside. Nothing to do but to get busy and light the fire themselves. Davey was delighted that he could participate in this event, and immediately started putting cobs in the stove. "Can I light it Miss Swenson?" he begged. "I hope George doesn't come."

" I wish he would," thought Anna. "Let's be sure we have enough coal first," she reminded him. "Otherwise we'll burn up the cobs and they'll go out, and we still won't have a fire." So they took the coal scuttle to the shed, and Davey volunteered to fill it. "Be careful Davey, don't get the coal dust on your clothes," but she was too late. In his eagerness he had a fair amount on his sleeves, not to mention his hands.

Together they carried the coal into the schoolhouse. Anna could have managed alone, but Davey insisted on helping making the trip up the steps rather awkward. "Just put a few pieces of coal on the cobs for now," Anna directed. "Once the fire begins to catch we'll add more, and here I'll let you light it, but be careful." On the second try some of the cobs caught, and slowly the fire started to fill the cavity of the stove. Anna used the coal shovel to add more coal, as was her custom during the day when the fire got low, so she was spared the oily grime.

Davey tried to wash his hands in cold water, but was not very successful, so Anna put a basin of water on top of the stove to heat, and insisted that he shake his hands dry and not dry them on his towel as he nearly did. When the water was warm, he could have a proper wash up.

It seemed to take forever for the room to get warm, although by standing near the stove they were quite comfortable, they still left their coats on. As the children arrived, they too stood by the stove, while Davey proudly explained how he had built the fire. George didn't come until nearly nine o'clock. His family had been so interested in listening to his father's and Walter's stories of Chicago that no one noticed the lack of smoke from the school chimney. By nine o'clock all had arrived except Joshua, and as Anna walked out on the porch to ring the bell she searched the road for him, but couldn't see him anywhere. Anna wondered if the quarrel the day before had anything to do with his not being on time, but dismissed the thought from her mind. No doubt the child was used to such things, and this might be the reason he was often late, and at times did not look well. He would most likely show up later. More perplexing was the fact that Roger had not lit the fire, but no doubt there was a logical reason for this also. In any event she had a day's teaching to do, and could not let her mind be occupied by other things.

As the children left the school that afternoon Anna called to Davey, "Be sure to explain to your Mother why you have coal dust on your coat. Tell her I'm sorry that it happened, but that I'll be home in another hour and I can clean the coat for her." She wasn't sure Davey heard, he was so anxious to get home and tell how he lit the fire.

As Anna climbed the back steps to the kitchen she could hear Inger's voice. "I think we should just ignore him. I'm certainly not going to beg him to light the school fire."

"I see you've heard that we have a new fire lighter for the school," joked Anna as she came into the room.

"I've just told Milly that I'm certainly not going over there to beg him to do his duty. Let him be stubborn and independent if he wants to, if that's what he wants anyway."

"Joshua wasn't in school today either," added Anna. "Perhaps the family overslept, or maybe Roger is ill." She considered telling them about the quarrel the day before, but decided against it. Somehow she didn't feel right divulging what was rather private information. "Anyway, if it happens again, I can light the fire. To be prepared I'll have the boys carry coal in for me in the afternoon."

"I'll light it," called Davey enthusiastically.

"I think Mr. Kloster will probably be back tomorrow Davey," added Anna. "He has lit it every morning, and something must have happened today to keep him home. And by the way Milly, I'm sorry that Davey got coal dust on his good coat."

"That was nothing," she answered shaking her head with a smile. "It's all cleaned off by now."

"You should not have to start the fire, so just to make sure it gets built, I'll look over in the morning, and if there's no smoke coming from the chimney I'll send Walter to do it," Inger added with the satisfaction of having solved a problem. Peter's firm steps could be heard in the entryway, and as he opened the kitchen door he called out, "I hope you've saved some coffee for me."

"No, not a drop," Milly laughed. "We never have a drop for you," and Peter pulled up a chair to the table as his mug was filled.

"I got to light the fire in the stove this morning at school," Davey exclaimed excitedly to his father.

"What'd you do, tell Mr. Kloster that you'd take over for him?"

"No, he didn't come, so Miss Swenson and I had to start the fire."

"Sounds peculiar to me," thought Peter out loud. "I know the man's a little strange, but I thought he was someone who would take his duties to heart. Well, maybe he has other

problems. It's been quiet over there today. I haven't seen anyone around. Did Joshua come to school?"

"No Pa, he never showed up."

"How were they doing when you went over yesterday
Anna?" asked Peter. "Was anyone sick?"

"I saw Joshua and his grandfather going to the barn,"
Anna answered quickly, trying to think of what else to say.
"And when I got to the kitchen I could hear that Grace and
Roger were talking, so I didn't bother them. I wanted to talk
to Grace alone anyway."

"That was a good idea not to go in when Roger was
there," added Milly.

"Well I dare say, things'll be back to normal tomorrow," and with this Peter dismissed the topic. "By the way, did
you know Inger that Anna here got her overalls from Sears
yesterday? I'm goin' to have her work a two hour shift in the
fields before she goes to school." There was a fair amount of
merriment at this suggestion.

"Speaking of school," Inger interjected, "Anna are you
serious about taking the youngsters during the harvest? That
might be too much for you."

"I may have overstepped my bounds by asking for them,
but I am sure I can manage," she replied.

"The little girls would probably like to bring their dolls,
but I think you'll have a couple of boys if not more. What will
you do with them?" Inger asked.

"The most I will have is ten, about six girls and four
boys. I thought I would read to them. We could sing, and act
out some of the stories. Of course the boys may want to stay
home and help their fathers."

"Well, if you do have the boys, I'll get some toys out of
the attic that our boys had when they were little," Inger added
as she rose to go. "It will be a great help to the families around
here, but just don't keep on taking on chores that aren't necessary." With that she bade them farewell, and set off for the
walk home.

It wasn't until Friday that Joshua came to school, looking very haggard. Anna realized that he was not well and tried

to make the day easy for him. "Joshua, why don't you go home after lunch?" she suggested.

"No, I can't go home. My Ma says I'm to stay in school all day."

"How is your father?" she asked. "I hope he's not sick." She didn't want to mention about his not lighting the fire, but hoped she could get some information that would shed some light on the situation.

The child didn't reply, but sat at his desk looking lost.

"Are you sure you're all right?" Anna asked.

He nodded his head, with that same lost expression.

"Is he gonna come back and light the fire?" asked Davey with childish curiosity, from the desk across the aisle.

Joshua looked up at Anna with a stunned expression, and spoke very slowly. "No! He ain't comin' at all. He's gone. He done left us."

Chapter Twenty-one

Anna bent over and put her hands on Joshua's shoulders in the hope of comforting him and as she did so the child looked at her with bewilderment in his eyes. The memory of the quarrel between his parents suddenly assailed her and she could hear Roger's words as plainly as if he were standing defiantly in the room, "I've a good mind to leave you all here to rot, and that's exactly what you'd do without me." She realized that she might be the only outsider who knew of the quarrel, unless Ed Marson heard them fighting when he delivered the posthole digger. No one had checked on the family since that Tuesday night. Perhaps Grace was seriously injured. Quickly she regained her composure. "I'm sure your daddy will come back. Things will be all right," but the boy only shook his head. She hesitated to ask the next question but knew she had to, "Um, . . . how is your mother?"

With lifeless expression he replied, "Not so good. She looks somethin' terrible. She's in bed."

Anna looked up and saw eleven pairs of eyes riveted on her and Joshua. "Well class," she fumbled for words. "Joshua is not feeling very well, and perhaps he did not have his breakfast this morning. Did you have any breakfast Joshua?"

Shaking his head, Davey volunteered, "He didn't bring his lunch either."

"Well, in that case, I am sure he is hungry, and when you're hungry things look a lot worse. I have a sandwich in my lunch I will be happy to give to him, and I think some cookies too. Joshua would you like to have my lunch?"

At last a faint smile twitched on his lips, and he slowly nodded his head. "Well then, that's settled. The rest of you get back to work, and Joshua can have a late breakfast," said Anna as she went to her desk, opened the drawer and brought out her lunch pail, which she gave to him.

"Now you're not going to have any lunch," commented Davey so all could hear.

"I know just how to solve that problem," she said as confidently as she could. "Let's see, George your farm is the closest, and you are a fast runner. Do you have most of your work finished?"

"Yes," came the strong affirmative reply.

"Well then, I think George can dash home and bring lunch for both me and Joshua. Come out on the porch with me George and I'll give you instructions." She walked toward the porch with George following. "I know your mother will be happy to help us out. The rest of you get back to work now. I'll only be a minute," and as she and George left the room, Anna quietly closed the door behind them.

She faced the boy and said to him in a confidential tone, "George I want you to get more than two lunches when you go home, but you are not to tell anyone else in school what I am asking you to do. Do you understand?"

"Yes," he replied seriously.

"You heard what Joshua said in the classroom, didn't you?"

"Yes, everyone heard it."

"Yes, I know that. Well, and I may be wrong about this, but I think that Joshua's mother may not be well at all."

"You mean because he said his mother was in bed and looked terrible?" the boy continued.

"Yes," she hesitated. "Tell your mother what happened here at school, and ask her if she could go to the Klosters right away to check on things. Tell her that I think it's important. Do you understand?"

"Oh, I understand. And you want me to bring back two sandwiches too."

"Yes, that would be fine, if it's not too much trouble."

"Oh, I can make the sandwiches," he assured her.

"Well then, hurry now, and remember not a word to anyone but your mother." With that the boy was off running through the rows of corn to his house.

All heads swiveled toward the door when Anna returned to the room, but she smiled her get back to work smile, and so they resumed their tasks. It was no time at all before George walked in with a lunch pail with enough lunch for two, which he gave to Anna with a smile indicating that the task had been satisfactorily completed.

Anna was very preoccupied the rest of the day, wondering if Inger had been able to go to see Grace, and what she had learned. After recess it was time for Friday spelling tests. She divided the school into two groups for this, first giving the first, third and fourth grade words simultaneously, and then following with those for the sixth, seventh and eighth grades. She managed fine until she came half way through the older grades, and mixed up the words so that she was not only giving the wrong word to the wrong class, but skipped some words and had to go over the lists separately with each class to make sure they covered all the words. At last she was finished and they were kept busy writing the definitions and sentences, and completing their other assignments for the day.

After lunch was time for crafts, for which she was grateful. The boys were doing a good job on their projects, and the girls sat and worked and visited as though they were at a club meeting. Anna could imagine them ten or fifteen years in the future, wondering how many of them would be in Grabney to attend the monthly club.

At last is was 2:40, and time to clean up. She had given Lars and George, the two older boys the responsibility of tending to the heavier housekeeping chores and seeing that the room was left clean on Friday afternoon. They assigned jobs to everyone, including sweeping the room with sweeping compound. Each person was responsible for his or her own desk, which often had to be scrubbed. Mabel and Erica checked the towels and sent home with its owner any which needed laundering. Anna put the spelling tests into her bag to carry home. This was one day when she was not going to remain to finish correcting papers.

Just before three o'clock all were seated at their desks and the room was in order. She wished them all a happy weekend and school was dismissed. "Davey and Joshua, if you will wait a minute I am going home now too," she called. "We can walk home together."

She closed the door firmly and followed them down the steps. Joshua had been quite uncommunicative all day. In the past month he had become fairly outgoing, and now that this happened she feared that he would retire into the protective shell which was so evident during September. Fortunately George and Lars had seen to it that the boys had not peppered him with questions. She had hoped that walking home with him would provide an opportunity to learn more about the situation at his house, and if there were anything which she could do.

"Well boys, what do you plan to do this weekend?" she asked with feigned cheerfulness as they ambled down the road.

"I dunno," answered Davey. "What do you think we'll do Miss Swenson? Do you think Uncle Floyd will come over?"

"He just might," she answered. "And then we'll all laugh at his funny stories."

Remembering some of the stories occupied them until they turned the corner to the road which led to their places. Joshua walked silently beside them, his eyes on the ground. "Now, what about you Joshua? Do you have any plans?" she inquired. To this he shook his head and looked more morose than before. Anna looked down the road and could see the path which led to the river, and suddenly thought of his fishing. He loved fishing. Perhaps this would bring him out of his lethargy. "What about going fishing Joshua? You love to fish and as I recall you always catch some."

"No," he said quietly but firmly. "No! I ain't never goin' fishin' again!" Without another word he ran off toward his house leaving Anna and Davey to stare in astonishment.

"I guess I said the wrong thing," Anna commented dejectedly. "I was only trying to cheer him up."

"He always went fishin' with his pa," Davey said. "I think he misses him a whole heap."

"Yes, you're right Davey."

"Why'd his pa go away anyway?"

"We don't know the answer to that," Anna answered shaking her head sadly.

"When's he comin' back?"

"We don't know that either, but he probably won't stay away too long. Maybe he's there now. Let's hurry home to see if we can find out some good news," and together they ran to the Jensen home. In the entryway, as they took off their coats, they could hear conversation in the kitchen with Inger's voice dominating the discussion.

"You've never seen such a mess. I know that Grace was never a housekeeper, and she's been in bed for days, but that place hadn't had a good scrubbing for ages. And that ol' man Evans, he's useless, milks the cows and leaves the milk to sour. When I came he was sittin' in a chair, jus' lookin' out into space. Oh hello Anna."

"Oh Anna," Milly said excitedly. "Sit down and listen to what Inger has to tell us. She yust came back from the Klosters. Here have some coffee." Without waiting to bring her schoolwork upstairs, Anna sat down immediately, eager to listen to Inger, joining Peter, Milly and Sarah.

"I'll start from the beginning. Thank goodness you sent George running home. I knew it was important from the way he told it, so I left him to make the sandwiches and hurried to see Grace. I hope he did all right with the lunches."

"Oh, they were fine," Anna added quickly, eager to get back to the main subject.

"Well I knocked on the door and no answer, so I just barges in, and see that old man settin' there sort of stupefied. But when he sees me he gets up and starts hollerin' to me to get out, that they can take care of themselves and they don't want no busybody interferin'. Well, ol' man Evans isn't goin' to push me around, so I holler back at him, 'Where's Grace and Elaine?', and he keeps on rantin' and ravin', so since I hear Elaine cryin' I guess they're in the bedroom, and I open the door and go in.

"I nearly fainted at the sight I saw, and believe me it takes a lot to make me feel squeamish. There was Grace lyin' in bed, her face half purple and greenish yellow from bruises. There was blood on the bedding. Elaine was in her crib, filthy dirty. It was a sight I couldn't believe.

"I looked at Grace and she started to cry and said, 'Oh Inger. I'm so glad you came. I don't know what to do.'

"I tell her the first thing is to see how badly she is hurt. By that time the old man is at the bedroom door tellin' me to get out. Well I give him a piece of my mind and told him if he didn't clear out I would get both Floyd and Walter to come down and they would take care of him proper."

"What does take care of him proper mean?" asked Davey.

"Hush Davey!" Milly admonished. "Children should be seen and not heard, so keep still."

"Then as he was leavin' I told him to get Sylvia Larson. She saw me running down the road and probably wondered what was goin' on, so I knew she would be about. He made a fuss about this, but I said that if he didn't go get her, I would call her on the phone and then everyone would hear about what happened. Sylvia's a good worker and no children at home, so I knew she would come. With the mess that place was in I needed help, and I wasn't about to ask you Milly with two little ones." Milly nodded an approval.

"Before she come, and with the old man out of the place, I got to talk to Grace. I told her how you had talked to Joshua, Anna, and how George ran home and all that. Well, Grace tells me that her dad wouldn't let Joshua go to school, that he kept him home to do the chores, but it seemed to her that all he did was yell at the boy."

"I thought Joshua and his grandfather got along fine," Anna interrupted.

"Grace says they did as long as Roger was there," Inger continued. "But with Roger gone, the old man became just as tough as he was before Roger arrived. I guess the poor kid tried hard to please, but he was too worried about his father leaving and his mother being so sick to do much of anything. She was the one who sent Joshua to school this morning, told him to slip out when Evans was in the barn. Well, he raised a mighty ruckus when he comes in and finds the kid gone.

"I was still talking to Grace when Sylvia comes in with Jonah. Anna I don't think you've met Jonah. He's four years older than Walter, I guess a little more than that, and has been away working. You might have seen their other son William around. He graduated from high school last June."

"Get on with it Inger," begged Peter.

"Oh yes, where was I? Well in come Sylvia and Jonah. Sylvia said she was so scared when Evans came that she didn't want to come down alone but she knew the situation was desperate if I would send him for her. The old man didn't even come back into the house, probably stayed in the barn for all I know. Anyway Sylvia comes into the bedroom, takes one look at poor Elaine, goes over to the crib, picks her up and tells Grace that she is taking Elaine home with her. I am sure Grace was relieved, but I lost my worker or so I thought.

"The next thing I knew Jonah was knocking at the bedroom door, even though it was open, asking if there was anything he could do to help. He took one look at Grace and turned around. I thought he was going to leave, but no siree, I could hear him busy putting dishes in the sink, stoking the fire and putting a pan of water on to heat. And if that wasn't good enough, Sylvia sends down William to give him a hand. 'Heat lots of water boys,' I call out, 'we have a real scrubbin' job here. And the first thing I want to do is to give Grace a bath and put clean bedding on her bed.'

"While the water was heating, I swept out the bedroom and picked up all the dirty clothes. I also cleaned up the crib. The smell there was terrible. Grace seemed to relax a little and I thought she slept. I was real worried about her though and thought maybe she should see Dr. Bailey. Could you give me another cup of coffee Milly?"

Milly quickly poured Inger a second cup and pushed the plate of cookies toward her. "Have some cookies Inger. You have been working so hard."

"Gol durn it! Where did Roger go and why did he leave? Did you ever find that out?" asked Peter.

"I found out what Grace told me anyway. She talked to me while I was cleaning her up, and by the way I don't think that she needs the doctor. She looks terrible with so many bruises, but she doesn't seem to have any broken bones. Well to get back to the story, it seems that Roger would hit her occasionally when she didn't move fast enough or did something to displease him. When they got married he understood that before too long he would be given the deed to the place. Well, the old man kept putting this off. The more Roger hounded him about it the more stubborn he became. So Roger tells Grace she has to get her father to sign over all the property to him. Of course Evans won't listen to her and tells her that Roger is getting her to do his dirty work. I never thought Roger was a real farmer anyway, and I knew that Grace didn't want to spend her life as a farmer's wife. Grace admitted that as soon as Roger got the deed he was planning to sell the place, and he and Grace and the children would move to some city. Oh he had great plans."

"But where would Grace's father have gone?" asked Milly.

"I didn't go into that one, but I don't think that Roger cared and the old man knew this. Old Evans isn't really stupid. You know Milly, we've often thought that he sacrificed Grace to get a free hired hand."

"The whole country thought that," added Peter. "We never could figure out why she married him."

"That's for sure," Inger continued. "Anyway Grace said that on Tuesday afternoon, before milking time, Roger came into the house furious. Her father had just told him that he would be damned if he would sign over the place so it could be sold and they could skip out and leave him. She said they got into a terrible argument."

"Anna, wasn't that the day that you were going over to talk to Grace about having Elaine come to school during harvest?" asked Milly.

"Yes it was," Anna answered.

"Did you hear them fighting?" came her second question.

"Yes, that's why I didn't go up to the house. I didn't talk about it because there was nothing that we could do. It was awful. I heard what I thought was Roger hitting Grace. She was crying and begged him not to hit her again."

"That's terrible, and right across the road from us," said Milly as she shuddered. "Do you remember what he said? Did he say anything about leaving?"

"Yes. He said something about punishing sinners and her not obeying him like the Bible says, and that he had a good mind to leave them to rot, because without him that is what they would do."

"That's about what Grace told me," Inger added. "She didn't know that you had come, but she did say that Ed Marson came to the door with a posthole digger that Roger had ordered."

"That's right," said Anna. "I met Ed on his way to the Klosters. He was carrying a posthole digger and said that Roger would have a busy time of it to get his fence fixed before he turned the cattle in after harvest."

"I guess he had to bang pretty loud on the door before anyone heard him, and then when he saw what was happening he and Roger got into a real argument. Grace told me that Ed said he had half a mind to bash his face the way he had bashed Grace's. Grace said after that Ed left pretty quickly, and Roger calmed down and started to cry and beg her for forgiveness and that he would never do it again. She said he always was sorry after he had hit her, and she felt he always meant it and didn't understand why he would do it again. This time he picked her up and laid her on the bed, and told her to lie down for awhile. He started pacing the kitchen floor and couldn't seem to settle down, then after about half an hour he said he was going to start digging the postholes. She could see that he had become angry again. The last thing he said to her before going outside was that she had to get the property signed over, and that he meant what he said."

"Where were Joshua and Evans while this was going on?" asked Peter.

"I saw them go to the barn as I was walking across the road," answered Anna.

"Well no doubt they heard the beginning of it and wanted to get out of the way," Peter continued. "It probably wasn't the first time they ducked out on a quarrel. But when did Roger leave? Did he get up and go in the middle of the night?"

"Grace said that she tried to finish the dinner. She had some stew on the stove, but felt too sick. After awhile Joshua came in, so she asked him to set the table, then he went back outside. After that she guesses that Joshua had come in again because she remembers asking him to ring the dinner bell. Her father came in but Roger didn't. She thought he was being stubborn. Grace was too sick to eat, so went to bed, and the others ate in silence, even Elaine. They kept thinking that Roger would come back, but they haven't seen him since."

"Did you meet Roger when you walked home from the Post Office Anna?" asked Peter.

"No," she answered, "because that was the day that Floyd and Walter came home from Chicago, and they gave me a ride. I looked down the path to see if Ed were coming back, but I didn't see him either."

"Well, who knows where he had relations," Peter continued. "We never did know much about him. It isn't too far from here to Minnesota, or South Dakota or Nebraska. Now somehow I don't think he would take the train, he would probably just keep walkin', and then he'll turn around and walk right back again. When he arrived I thought he looked like a drifter. Well this time he drifted into a pretty nice set-up, so I don't think he'll leave it for good."

"That's about what I told Grace," Inger said. "Now let me get to the phone and call Floyd and get a ride home."

"No you don't," said Peter getting up. I'll hitch up and be ready for you in a jiffy," and he was out the door.

"I'm exhausted," Inger exclaimed, "and I don't know what I would have done without those two Larson boys. They pitched right in and cleaned up the place spic'n span. Sylvia's going to keep Elaine for the weekend at least, and said that Erica would be excited about having a toddler in the house, so she figures she wouldn't have much work to do. Now I'll have a hard time explaining to Mabel why I didn't bring Elaine home with me."

"Is there anything we can do?" asked Milly.

"I think it would be a good idea to check on the family later on this evening. If you go over there, take Peter with you. No telling what that idiot Evans might do. It also might help Joshua to know that there is someone close that he can call on if he needs to. I didn't see the boy this afternoon, but then I left right before he came home from school.

"Well, I hear Peter outside so I'll be on my way. Thanks for the coffee Milly. I'll check with you in the morning. I think Mabel and I will go over and do their washing."

"Let me help with that," suggested Anna. "It would also give me a chance to get to know the family before Roger returns. Let Mabel go to the Larsons and she and Erica can take care of Elaine."

"All right," said Inger. "Mabel will be the first one to agree with that. I'll phone you when I'm ready to leave. Goodness knows the whole of Grabney has heard the story by this time since Joshua came to school and said his father had gone. See you tomorrow then," and she was gone.

At that moment the phone rang. "What do you bet that it's Liza Crawford," said Milly, and as she picked up the phone she nodded her head. The word had indeed gotten around.

Chapter Twenty-two

At nine o'clock the next morning the phone rang and it was Inger ready to go to the Klosters. Anna jumped up from the breakfast table eager to have an opportunity to get better acquainted with that family even though it meant a day of hard work.

"What will you do if Roger has come back?" asked Milly. "Inger said that if he did she would yust I mean just as soon stay and give him a piece of her mind for what he did to Grace."

Anna paused "I really don't want to tangle with him," she admitted. "If I saw him I would probably come back home. Inger can handle him, but he frightens me. If she needed me I would stay for moral support I suppose, but somehow I think that Inger can manage on her own."

"That's for sure," added Peter. "I looked over there this morning to see if there was any sign of him but I didn't see any. I don't always see him, but he's sometimes out by the barn, and then once in a while he gets the cows in to be milked."

"Well I'll go now," Anna said. "I was really looking forward to getting to know Grace better and Joshua too and hadn't thought too much about Roger. I don't want anything to do with Bill Evans either."

"I'm going to bake some cookies this morning so I'll bring them over after awhile," said Milly. "I'm sure they can use some and this will give me a chance to talk to Grace too."

"I'll bet every woman in Grabney is thinkin' the same thing, that they'll bake cookies to bring so they can see Grace and get all the gossip," Peter mentioned drolly.

"Oh, Peter," Milly countered, "that is not my idea at all."

"Now Milly, I didn't say it was your idea, but what do you bet that by this evening that house has enough cookies to start a bakery, and perhaps a few pies and cakes too. I can see ol' Bill Evans on the porch with his shotgun in one hand, and takin' the pies and cakes with the other, and the women runnin' up the road scared he's going' to shoot 'em."

"But dad, you can't shoot people," chimed in Davey. "It's not right."

"What's more it's against the law," his father added as he pushed back his chair and got up from the table. "But it should also be against the law to beat up Grace as Roger did."

"Oh, Peter, not in front of the children," warned Milly as she shook her head.

" OK!," he replied shrugging his shoulders. "Come on Davey, it's time you got the eggs collected."

"I'm coming too," Sarah said as she jumped down from her chair.

"Get your coats on then. Time's a wastin'."

The three hurried down the back steps with Anna following, leaving them when she turned down the road which led to the Klosters. She met Inger coming from her place, and they went up to the house together. They heard voices and paused, thinking one might be Roger's, but it was that of Bill Evans.

"What are these busybodies comin' here again for. Get up and get to work. I never did like neighbors interferin'."

"You can't boss me around any more like you used to. Wait 'till Roger comes back, then you'll see who's boss," came Grace's plaintive response.

"He's never goin' to shove *me* aroun' again, you'll see."

"At least we know Roger's not here," whispered Inger. With her firm knock at the door the conversation ceased.

"Come in," was uttered by Grace, weakly.

Anna noticed that the house was fairly small. The main room was the kitchen, with only a small open porch for an entryway. Two doors led off the kitchen, one was the parlor and the other Grace's bedroom. The congoleum was worn out in front of the sink and the stove.

"Well, how's the patient this morning. I see you're sitting up in the rocking chair. That's good news. By the way,

Elaine's fine. I stopped off at the Larsons on my way here and she and Erica are having a grand time. How do you feel Grace?"

"She feels fine and don't need no one to come and do her work," came the surly comment from Evans. "She's just lazy like her mother, another lazy one."

"I'm not goin' to stand here and listen to talk like that from you Bill Evans, so if you don't have anything better to do you can get out and do some chores around the farm. Get that fence mended for one thing," Inger commanded. "I suppose you don't know where the posthole digger is, and you'll use that for an excuse."

"I know where things is around my farm. It's lyin' on the ground where the fence is broke, and I'll thank you to mind your own business." With that he went out the kitchen door and slammed it behind him.

"Well, if I do say so, we can get along better without him," Inger said. "Now, Anna let's get that washing machine out of the corner and get some water on to heat."

"He didn't mean what he said, I'm sure," apologized Grace.

"He meant every word of it Grace," Inger said matter-of-factly. "I've known him a long time. He's a bully and a coward. He was mean to your mother and mean to you, and neither one of you should have had to put up with it. Help me with the water Anna, we can heat it up in these two pails. Is this what you usually use Grace?"

"Yes, I don't have a boiler. You're right about dad. One thing I liked about Roger is that he always protected me from dad. I know Roger hit me, but maybe it was my fault. I know he really loves me and things will be different when he comes back."

"I sure hope so," added Inger. "Anyway, you better get back to bed. You look like you still need to rest. Where's Joshua?"

"I guess he's still in bed. I'll go up and get him."

"No, you stay here. Anna you go up and get the boy, and take the bedding off his bed. I'm sure it needs changing too. Get him to help you collect all the dirty clothes around the house and we'll sort them in piles from white clothes to work clothes."

"Oh, Miss Swenson, you shouldn't have to come here to work. I'm so ashamed to think of you seeing our place in such a mess."

"Call me Anna," she replied in a friendly manner. "And I'm sure Joshua will be surprised to see me coming into his room to get him up." As she went quickly up the steps she understood why all the neighbors called Inger in to help when there was a family crisis. She was definitely a no nonsense person.

The upstairs was a partly finished attic bedroom and there was no door, so she went over to the bed and shook Joshua a little saying, "Time to get up Joshua."

"Oh ma, do I have to?' came the sleepy reply, and then he opened his eyes and saw Anna and was shocked. "Oh, Miss Swenson! What are you doin' here? Is my ma all right? Did my dad get home? How come you're here anyway?"

"Just one question at a time Joshua," and Anna smiled at him. "Yes your mother's fine. She's been up and had some coffee and is going back to bed to rest. Your dad hasn't come home yet, but he probably will soon. Now I want you to get dressed because Mrs. Parker and I are here to do the wash, so we need to take your bedding." Quickly the child jumped up and helped her strip down the bed. "Pick up all the dirty clothes that I see lying on the floor. I'm going downstairs now and make your mother some breakfast, and while I'm doing that, you get dressed and haul all these things down so we can wash them. Can you do that?" She grabbed the dirty sheets and pillow cases which probably hadn't seen the inside of a washer for a couple of months at least and turned toward the stairs, feeling fortunate that she was staying with Milly and not with a family such as this.

"Yes, Miss Swenson. And I'll hurry fast as I can."

When Anna came downstairs Inger was already making oatmeal for both Grace and Joshua, and had toasted the last piece of bread that she could find. "Get this piece of buttered toast inside you Grace," she said as she brought the toast on a plate to the patient's bedside. "I'm making oatmeal now. I can see that you're out of bread. I guess you usually buy it, but you won't mind if I make a couple of loaves will you? It's easier than going to town. I checked and you seem to have enough of everything else."

As soon as the water was heated, they poured it into the washer, along with soap shavings and a pile of dirty clothes. Joshua ate his oatmeal and was sent to collect the eggs. Between them Inger and Anna found themselves busy washing, rinsing, and hanging up the laundry. They saw Joshua dragging, one at a time, fence posts for his grandfather.

About noon a knock was heard at the door. It was Milly bringing over a plate of cookies. "You're a sight for sore eyes Milly," said Inger. "We could use a little rest. Let's see if Grace can get up and we'll all have coffee and cookies around the table. I made the coffee about an hour ago."

Milly glanced at Grace as she came through the bedroom door and had to control herself so Grace wouldn't see the shock she felt. Soon the four women were visiting and enjoying themselves.

"Goodness me!" exclaimed Milly. "It is time for me to go home. I can't sit here all day," and she rose to leave. "You take care of yourself Grace, and if there is anything you need at any time of day or night, send Joshua over."

"We'll be all right, but thanks Milly," answered Grace.

"Speaking of Joshua, if you see him Milly, tell him to come in and have something to eat. That way he can get a rest," suggested Inger.

"Yes, I'll do that," Milly answered as she let herself out the door.

Before too many minutes had passed, another knock at the door brought Inger to her feet. "That's not goin' to be Joshua. He wouldn't knock. I s'pose someone smelt the coffee." She opened the door to Lars Anderson who was carrying a loaf of freshly baked bread.

"My Ma baked this morning and she thought that Grace might be able to use this," and he handed her the loaf.

"That's mighty nice of her. I was bakin' some, but we're clean out now, so this will come in real handy," Inger said as she took the bread. "I thought you and George were goin' fishing?"

"Yep," came the answer. "I'm on my way to get him now. I told him I'd be up when my chores were finished."

"Good boy! You tell your mother how much we appreciate this," she called after him. Going over to the counter she sliced off several slices and put them with some butter on the table. "Might as well not let this go to waste. Besides we could do with a little nourishment, so help yourselves. There'll be three loaves more by this afternoon."

Grace was overcome with the generosity of these women. It seemed to put a new pink color into her face, which was a good change from the former pale look, touched up by the terrible bruise colors.

By three o'clock they had finished the laundry. Fortunately the day was sunny and dry, so Inger could bring some of Elaine's things to the Larsons. She left with these and with the promise from Anna that she and Milly would take down the dry clothes before it got dark. The rest could stay out all night.

Grace got dressed and had plans for dinner. She thought she should get Elaine back from the Larsons, but Anna assured her that Erica would be disappointed if she did, and that a young child would be a hindrance more than a help. "What if Roger comes back and finds that Elaine is gone?" she questioned. "I'm sure he will be back for Sunday prayers."

"If he comes back, then he can go get her," said Anna. "Explain to him that she is there so you can get a rest. I'm sure he will understand that."

"I don't know," came her answer, "but I know it is better for me not to have to worry over her. Joshua and Dad can take care of themselves."

Feeling that the household was in good order, Anna left, reminding Grace that she and Milly would return in an hour or so to bring in the laundry. As she walked across the road she saw Bill Evans look up her way, and soon he was walking toward the house. He hadn't been back since he left in the morning and no doubt was hungry. Anna hoped that he would not be angry with Grace, but this was something that Grace would have to learn to cope with. Hopefully she could take a page out of Inger's book.

Chapter Twenty-three

The ladies may not have shown up at Grace's with cookies and cakes on Saturday, but they made up for this by the interest they showed on Sunday. Most of them said that they would have brought over something, but they were afraid Roger would be there. During both the Sunday School and church services an undertone of whispering could be discerned, followed by a "Shhh". It was amazing that Rev. Blakeley could get anyone's attention. He had heard rumors about the situation, but not one to take stock in rumors decided to find out a few facts for himself.

After the service he took Inger aside, as he knew she was a reliable informant and did not tend to be gossipy. Inger beckoned Anna to come over and between them they filled the minister in on the information they had. The Klosters may not have been members of his congregation, but he was a truly kind man, was concerned about everyone he knew and humanitarian enough to want to help them when they needed it. He decided at this time a call might not be welcomed, but asked Inger to keep him apprised and let him know if there were anything he could do.

On Monday morning Anna and Davey left a little early for school so they could stop by the Klosters and see if Joshua would walk to school with them. To their happy surprise, he was up and ready to go, and Bill Evans was in the barn so they didn't have to deal with him. Joshua looked nice in clean school knickers and shirt, thanks to the Saturday laundering. It was the first time since the beginning of school that she had seen him so well dressed. He also seemed to show a new sense of pride, so she felt it was appropriate to comment on his appearance. "How nice you look Joshua. I am so happy that you can walk to school with us this morning."

"Yes'm," came the shy but proud reply.

"Maybe you can walk with us every day," added Davey.

"Mebbe, but I don' know. Mom says I should go to school, but Grampa says I'll have to stay home sometimes and help with the work. Grampa says he's goin' to start harvestin' this week."

"My dad said he might start this week too," Davey chimed in, not one to let another family get ahead of his.

"I can see that the fields are ready," commented Anna as she looked around the area. The countryside had changed so much since her arrival at the end of August. By now the cornfields were a light brownish color, instead of a beautiful green, as the stalks had dried. In another two weeks much of it would be cut and made into silage, leaving the ground covered with a bare stubble. The cattle and hogs would then be turned into the fields to forage.

"Your dad will prob'ly be back this week," said Davey, "then you won't have to stay home."

Joshua's face suddenly turned solemn. "Grampa said he's not comin' back. He said he heard Dad tell Mom that he was goin' away for good. Do you think that's true Miss Swenson? Do you think my dad won't come back?" His lower lip quivered and he bit it to keep from crying.

"Oh, I'm sure he will come back," Anna replied, not sure at all considering the conversation she had overheard between Roger and Grace. Her second thought was that perhaps it would be better if he didn't return.

"Dad's just don't leave their families," Davey espoused confidently as he kicked a clod of earth. "Maybe he went to Chicago to check on the price for hogs."

"Yeah, mebbe, 'cause Grampa said they need to be sold. I heard Grampa tell Mom that he was goin' to take charge of things now. He told Mom that he could do just as good a job as Dad, but I don't think so. I hope my dad comes back soon."

This was the longest conversation that they had ever had with Joshua, prompting Anna to add, "I think things will work out just fine Joshua, and if you have to stay home a day or so this week we will understand that you are helping your grandpa with the work," and they turned into the school yard to begin another day.

"Yack Yarvis was here with your shoes," Milly excitedly exclaimed when Anna came into the kitchen after school. "Here, try them on."

"Better yet," answered Anna, "I will go upstairs and change into my new farmerettes too," which she did. Soon she reappeared, looking quite perky. "Now, how's that. How do I look?"

By this time Peter had come into the house and was drinking his afternoon coffee, so gave her the once over. "I can see that I'm not going to be needed around here any more. Just take my old work jacket, hitch up the team, and see if you can bring in a load of corn before dark." Milly's and Anna's laughter filled the room. "Don't you ladies laugh. I may just decide to let Milly go out into the field with you. It's pretty comfortable stayin' in here drinking coffee. Maybe I'll take on the housekeeping, let the ladies take over the farm work."

"Joshua said his grandpa was going to start to harvest this week. Can we do it too Dad?"

"Well, we just might. I was talking to your Uncle Floyd. He says he likes to begin about the first of November. That's Wednesday, and the corn sure is ready. I'd like to get a head start."

"Can I stay home from school like Joshua?" came Davey's anxious question.

"Well now, with you and Miss Swenson working the harvest with your mother, I'd say you could both stay home, but then I'd get in trouble with your Aunt Inger and we wouldn't want that would we?"

"Oh, dad!" said Davey with a disappointed sigh.

"Speaking of Joshua, this morning I saw Bill Evans talking to the stockman from Des Moines, and sure enough by this afternoon they came and hauled away his hogs. Guess he's not waiting for Roger to come back to sell them. Anyway, the price is probably as good now as it will ever be and he needs to get them sold before he harvests."

"This way he can keep the money himself," added Milly.

"I imagine that was part of his reasoning. They never did get along too good. I just hope I'm not around when Roger shows up. There'll be one huge blow-up."

"With Grace in the middle," said Milly.

"Grace will have to learn to take care of herself I guess."

Davey, who was listening with great interest to this conversation, suddenly thought of something. "Joshua said his grandpa told him that his dad wasn't coming home. That he was going to stay away for good." His parent's eyes focused intently on him.

"That's right," interjected Anna. "Joshua told us this morning on the way to school that his grandfather had heard his father tell Grace that he was going away for good."

"I have a feeling that words of that nature may have been said more than once," commented Peter, "but as to whether he really meant them or not who's to tell. He fell into a rather good thing here and he'll possibly stay away just long enough to scare them, and then show up. My guess is that he may come home tomorrow. It's Halloween, and you know what happened last Halloween at their place."

"Oh yeah!" said Davey wide eyed. "You know what some of the big boys did Miss Swenson? They came and tipped over the Kloster's outhouse, and carried it out into the field."

"Roger was so mad," added Milly. "The next morning when he found out what had happened he ran in a fury up to Floyd's and said he knew it must have been Walter and his friends. Oh he was in a rage, Inger said."

"What happened then," Anna asked curiously. "Was it Walter?"

"Walter denied it, but then we'll never know really," Peter said. "Floyd got Roger calmed down and he came back with him to put the thing back up. I think most everyone around here was secretly glad it happened, and some were not so secret about it."

"We were all laughing," giggled Milly. "No one around here likes Roger very much. But I think that Floyd shouldn't have had to help put it back up."

"Floyd enjoyed every minute of it, seeing Roger's misery first hand as they struggled to haul it back and set it up again," laughed Peter. "If he were younger he probably would have tipped it over himself. Why I remember when I was young we did things like that. It was great sport."

"Dad did you ever tip over an outhouse?" exclaimed Davey.

"That was before I knew him Davey," said his mother. "And I don't want you to think of doing anything like that."

"Tomorrow being Halloween, will we have to watch out for pranks like that?" asked Anna.

"Probably not," said Peter. "But just to make sure, I do keep a look out. Anyway it's time for the evening chores. Come on kids," and soon he, Davey and Sarah were on their way to the barn. Anna took charge of Lucy and Milly started the supper.

Halloween passed without any serious events, and without Roger coming back. To make sure that nothing happened to their place, Bill Evans sat on the back porch all evening with his shotgun. Peter made the wry comment that he probably would use it on Roger if he returned.

Peter and Floyd both started harvesting on Wednesday, and Thursday Bill Evans had his wagon hitched up to do the same. Joshua was not in school either Thursday or Friday. Milly reported that Thursday morning she could see him struggling to pick the corn along with his grandfather. He was too young for that kind of work, the gloves being far too large for him, and he was not tall enough to reach the corn easily. In a short time Grace had replaced him sending Joshua into the house to watch Elaine.

"It's the same old story," Peter remarked Friday afternoon after school when they were sitting down to coffee. "This is just as it was before Roger showed up, Grace out in the field, killing herself off, with the old man continually shouting at her to hurry up."

"It's not fair. He could hire someone to help," Milly said. "He sold his hogs so he has money. And their place is paid for, so there's no mortgage. Grace is so small and thin. She's skin and bones."

"Well," Peter said thoughtfully. "He never did worry about overworking the womenfolk, and he's probably thinkin' of those who've lost their farms. Anna, I imagine you didn't know this but lots of folks have borrowed too heavily in buyin' new machinery. In the fall it always seems like farmers are rich 'cause they get paid for their hogs and corn, but then the mortgage comes due about November, so they pay that. And then the equipment salesmen show up. Well, by the time spring comes around they find they've got to go to the bank to borrow for feed corn, and before too long some of them are broke. I know it's hard on Milly to work in the field, but goin' broke is somethin' I don't want to do."

"I hadn't thought about farmers getting paid just once a year," Anna commented thoughtfully. "I can see how it would be easy to forget about having to save for the rest of the year. Anyway, I think you are right about trying to do the work without having to hire anyone." To this Milly nodded her agreement. "So for tomorrow I'll be your extra hand," and she laughed. "I may not be very good at it, but I would like to try"

Milly quickly lamented, "Oh Anna, you can't do that. You'll get your new clothes all dirty and what will the neighbors think?"

"Well, there aren't too many neighbors, and I don't think any of them will care," laughed Anna. "Anyway, I want to try it just to say that I have done it."

"It can get pretty exhausting for someone not used to it," said Peter, "but come along if you want to. We'll start right after breakfast tomorrow on the south side of the field with the rows next to the river."

After breakfast Anna put on an old jacket of Milly's and she and Davey went to meet Peter who had the team hitched up ready to go. He gave her a pair of gloves used for husking.

"There're a coupla kinds of husking pins. I'll use the one that straps on, but I'm gonna give you this one, as it's the one that Milly likes 'cause it's easier to use." It had a handle like a small knife, attached to a sharp pointed blade and a round ball-like metal piece at the end to separate the ear from the husk. "Now what you do is grab the ear with your left hand, take the pin and start from the top to separate the husk from the ear, then snap off the ear, and that leaves the husk attached to the stalk. The ears are so dry they'll snap off easy." After a demonstration from Peter which made it look easy enough, she started out. At first she could husk the corn fairly rapidly. However it was a tiring job, and her hands and arms soon ached.

Peter was taking one side of the row and she the other. He noticed that she was slowing down, so at times would work both sides.

Davey trotted along quite happily. Sometimes to amuse him Anna would give him an ear to throw at the bangboard, but often he missed and would then be kept busy trying to retrieve it. At other times he sat on the wagon seat, and pretended to drive the horses, which paid no attention to him as they seemed to know just how fast to move. Occasionally Peter would have to utter a "Giddap" or "Whoa". The rows were about a mile long, extending along the entire south border of the property. No matter which way Anna looked, the corn had been planted so evenly that the rows could have been going north and south or east and west. Peter had said that corn liked air. The pace was slow but steady. Finally the wagon was filled.

"I'm going to dump this load in one of the cribs, so I'll give you a lift up to the house and you can grab yourself a cup of coffee," suggested Peter. "I can't believe you have stuck it out this long. Don't you think you've had enough?"

"I must say I am tired," admitted Anna. "I knew it would be a tough job, but if you can put up with me I'm willing to continue."

"OK with me," said Peter. "Here you two, let me boost you up on the wagon." Slowly they made their way toward the house and barn. Anna left Peter and Davey and wearily climbed the back steps, leaving Milly's old jacket and the gloves and husking pin in the entryway. She didn't know that she could get so tired in such a short time.

As she opened the door to the kitchen, Milly exclaimed, "Anna, yust look at you!"

"I'm fine Milly," Anna said as she collapsed into a chair. Sarah quickly came and sat in the chair next to her, leaving Lucy crawling across the kitchen floor. "This farm work is no picnic. I really pity Grace out working all day long, and then having to come in and do her own chores."

"Well, we've all had our turn at it. It's not so bad once you're used to it. I'll be doing it myself next week, but I must say that Peter does let me come in and fix the coffee. Then I get a rest. He says he wants me to fix coffee for him, but he knows I get tired. He'll be in for a cup as soon as he's dumped the cobs in the crib. Here, I'll pour you some. You drink this and have some coffee cake. And don't you think of going back out there."

"Thanks Milly. Guess I could have done that for myself. I'm not really all that tired, and I am going back out there, that is if Peter will have me. I may be more of a hindrance than a help."

"I know you're a help, and anyway it's nice to have company out there," said Milly as she cut some more cake. "I remember the fall after Davey was born I bundled him up and put him in the clothes basket and moved him along as we worked the rows. He was six months old and not too happy about being kept bundled up so tightly. But we got the work done, and that was important. Peter said he might hire one of the Larson boys to help this year, but knowing Peter he will do all he can himself before he pays anyone to help. Any money we have he wants to put back into the place."

"I've seen William but I haven't met Jonah. What does he do?"

"He has a yob in the county seat, but I'm not sure what he does," answered Milly. "But he's smart and has been taking correspondence courses from Ames Agricultural School."

At the sound of footsteps in the entry way, they turned to see Peter and Davey coming in the door. "I see my help is sitting down on the job," said Peter with a touch of humor. "Well, guess I'll have a little sit down myself."

186

Chapter Twenty-four

"You take the buggy this morning Milly," Anna heard Peter say as she came down the stairs for Sunday breakfast. "I can get by with Belle. Don't really need two horses for harvesting anyway. Sure you can manage Ginger OK, or would you rather have Belle?"

"I'll take Yinyer. I think Belle is better for walking the corn rows," she answered. "Oh good morning Anna. We're talking about taking the buggy to church. Peter is staying home to harvest so you and I will have the children."

"Why can't I stay home?" whined Davey, as he poured a more than adequate amount of syrup on his pancakes.

"Because you want to get a gold star for perfect attendance," answered his mother.

"Oh, that's right. I forgot. But I'll help you when I get home Dad," he replied.

"It will be a women's club in church this morning Anna," Milly stated. "All the men and older boys will be staying home to harvest."

"That means that Elmer Marson will be the loneliest person in town," Peter said smiling. "He has his own club meeting on Sunday morning. I'm sure you've noticed Anna how many men lose track of the time and miss the service."

"I didn't think that they were in the store buying the week's supplies," added Anna.

"And they criticize the women for gossiping," Milly stated emphatically. "Vi has told me some of the things that she's heard as she's leaving to come to church. Oh, you wouldn't believe it!"

"Yes, I think I could believe it," replied Anna as she pulled up her chair and sat down to the usual sumptuous breakfast. She took Sarah's plate to cut her pancake.

"Say the poem," asked Sarah.

"All right. One, two, three, four. Turn it around and cut some more. Five, six, seven, eight. Now you can eat what's on your plate."

"I like that one," the little girl smiled at Anna.

"I can cut my own. I don't need any help," Davey bragged.

"Quiet down now and eat your breakfast or you'll be late for church," his father warned.

After breakfast Peter hitched up Ginger to the buggy and soon they were off. The canopy top was up and their knees were covered with a blanket. Each breath was visible in the crisp morning air. Sunday School was much the same, except that the older boys were gone, but church was as Milly had predicted. The men were noticeable for their absence.

Dinner was a hurried affair with Peter coming in for only a short time, and then going back out to the field. Anna didn't need much convincing to stay inside, so she played with the children until it was time for Lucy and Sarah to take a nap. After that she read to Davey who decided it was more fun to be read to than to go with his father.

About four o'clock they heard Peter's weary steps come up to the back door, and then suddenly stop. They heard him shout, "What's the matter Anders? What's wrong?"

Anna and Milly both rushed to the door, followed by Davey, and found Anders Anderson, Lars's father, struggling to regain his breath as he approach the house.

"It's George and Lars," he struggled breathlessly to say. "They been fishin', down by our place."

"What happened to them?" Peter demanded as he ran to the exhausted man.

"No! No! Nothing happened to them. But they found somethin' in the water, somethin' terrible. I had to tell you, to get help," he continued, still hardly able to speak he was so short of breath.

"You must of run over a mile to get here. Why didn't ya use the phone?" Peter queried.

"Damn it! I was so scared. I forgot about the phone."

"Tell me what happened? You said the boys were all right," Peter continued questioning.

"Yes, yes. They're not hurt. They wanted to go fishin' this afternoon after they helped with the corn, so we said it was all right," and he plunked himself down on the steps to rest.

"So . . ." Peter was becoming anxious.

"Well, they been fishin' for about half an hour, not catchin' anythin' when Lars throws in his line and feels it pull on somethin'. I guess he keeps on tuggin' thinkin' he has a fish and then I hears him yell, 'Dad! Dad!' and then he screams, and George screams, and I leaps over the fence like I was a jack rabbit and runs to them." Anders puts his head in his hands and shudders. "The hook was caught in a man's coat, and the man's still in it."

"Just a minute Anders," said Peter as he was trying to put some calm and logic into the situation. "Are you sure it wasn't someone's scarecrow thrown in the river. We've just had Halloween you know. It sounds like some kids' prank to me, meant to scare the livin' daylights outta someone."

"No, it warn't no prank. When I gets to the river I look at the coat, well a part of the front of it which was the only thing showin' above the water and think the same misself. It was sorta hard to see, and it was out about ten feet or so. So I gets me a branch from one of the trees and slowly pulls it toward us." He was getting his breath back and speaking less frantically. "You know it's deep there so I couldn't wade out. Anyway we slowly pulls it into us and it was heavy and all bloated like a cow gone off. And then we saw his head, or part of it, and then I knew."

"My God! Are the boys still there?" Peter demanded.

"I tol' them to stay there, jus' keep the line hooked on. I said I'd get you, and then I runs fast as I can and here I am. I didn't stop to think if they'd be skeered to stay."

"The wagon's hitched," said Peter as he jumped up. "Let's go!" and the two men leaped into the wagon and were off.

Anna and Milly were left on the back steps staring after them, unable to say a word. Even Davey was quiet. The women shivered, whether from the cold or the gruesomeness of what they had heard, they were not sure, but the three of them went into the house and closed the doors.

"What do you think happened?" asked Milly. "I have never seen Anders so shaken. He is always so calm. Maybe I should phone Inger and let her know. Anders said George was all right."

"I don't think you should phone anyone Milly," advised Anna. "You know the party line. This sounds as if it is something serious, and we'd better let Peter see what has happened before we do anything. If he needs Floyd's help, he will send George to get him."

"I don't understand. What happened Mom?" asked Davey. "Why did Dad leave with Mr. Anderson so fast?"

"We don't know any more than you do," answered Milly. "Yes, I think it is best if we sit and wait for them to come back." Then putting on her jolly self she continued, "Maybe it's not so bad as it sounds." And the three of them waited for further word.

It was nearly an hour later when the girls awoke. Milly and Anna were still sitting at the table staring at their uneaten pie. Davey had gone to his room long before to play with his toys realizing that he was not going to get any answers to his questions, and slowly losing interest in the event which seemed to have such a paralyzing effect on the others. The two women rose, grateful to have something to do.

"If Peter doesn't come back soon I'm going to have to milk the cows," exclaimed Milly with reality hitting her as she changed Lucy. "It's getting dark. What's keeping him?"

"The cows can wait for another hour Milly," advised Anna. "It's hardly 5 o'clock. I'm sure they've gone this long before."

Hearing the activity downstairs, Davey had returned with a favorite book, so Anna seated herself at the table with a child on each side and began to read. Milly had put Lucy in her high chair with a piece of bread and butter, and divided her time between pacing the floor and looking out the kitchen window. "Here comes someone," she said excitedly as she ran to the back door. "Maybe it's Peter."

A wagon stopped in the yard and soon Inger and George were coming into the house. "Where's Peter?" Milly questioned anxiously.

"He'll be coming," answered Inger in a preoccupied fashion, "but it may take awhile. We've got other things to do first." She took off her coat slowly, put it carefully over the back of a chair, and slumped down in the one next to it. Inger was used to moving quickly, and it was obvious she was pondering something serious.

George staggered in as if he were in a trance. He didn't even bother to say, "Hello".

"Have some coffee," offered Milly, as if this was the solution to all problems.

"No thanks," came the reply. "I've got other things on my mind. I'll have some later," and she waved Milly off. Turning her head suddenly she said, "George, you take the kids out and do the milking. It'll do Milly a favor, do you good, and get the little ones out of here. Best thing for you is to keep busy, and with cows and kids you'll have plenty to do."

"Sure Mom," he answered. "I know where the buckets are."

"I'll help get the cows in," volunteered Davey, as he opened the kitchen door to get his coat from the entryway.

"I can help too," added Sarah. Milly hurried to put Sarah into her coat and hat, and soon they were out the door and on their way, closing the entryway door with a bang before they went down the steps.

"Tell us what happened Inger," Milly asked earnestly.

"Well, I don't know where to begin. What time does Rev. Blakeley get home from Brewster?"

"You know more about that than I do Inger," answered Milly.

"Right. I guess he usually gets home from Brewster about four o'clock, and then has time for some supper, and leaves for Langton about six, to do their evening service at seven, if I'm not mistaken. So he should be home now. I've got to call him, but just not sure how I'm goin' to do it. I'm too tired to drive around to see him, and besides it would waste too much time." She went to the phone and rang the Blakeley number. Soon she was heard to say, "Rev. Blakeley, this is Inger. ————You remember talking to me and Anna about having a meeting at Milly's house about the Sunday School? Well, we're here waiting for you, and we need you right away so we can get some of these things settled.————OK, hurry over then because we don't have much time before you leave for Langton.————OK. Good-bye." She hung up the phone. "Well, at least he caught on to the fact that we need him, and I don't think we set too many ears on fire."

"What meeting?" asked Milly. "Inger, I don't know what you're talking about."

"I think he'll be here soon, and I don't want to have to go through the whole story twice, so I'll take that cup of coffee now and let's wait for him."

Anna guessed that the meeting idea was a ruse Inger was using to keep the party line quiet. Inger could be very resourceful. She had a feeling that her original fears were confirmed, that the body in the river might be Roger's. She shuddered at the thought. Rev. Blakeley was pretty shrewd if he guessed that the call would be related to the Klosters, but then any call from Inger would be taken seriously, no matter what the pretext.

Inger was definitely preoccupied as she waited for the sound of the Blakeley car. Milly was torn by feeling she should be out helping George with the milking, and wanting to stay inside in case she would miss out on something. Their concentration was interrupted by Lucy yelling to get out of her high chair. As Milly picked her up, the car could be heard coming into the farmyard.

Milly rushed to the door with Lucy in her arms, welcoming Rev. Blakeley. This time he came to the back door. It was not an official visit. Putting Lucy down she welcomed him and took his coat. "Please do sit down, and have a cup of coffee."

"Thanks Milly," he replied. "Hello Inger, Anna," accompanied by a nod to each woman. "I can only guess that something serious has happened. No Milly, just finished supper. Maybe later."

"I guess Anna and Milly can tell you what happened first, but the crux of the matter is that George and Lars found the body of a man in the river and it is possible that it is Roger Kloster."

"Whew! Let me catch my breath on that one. Oh that poor family. When you phoned with that lame excuse of a meeting I knew it much be something serious, but this is more than I expected," and he sat thoughtfully for a few moments. "Where's the body now?"

"Peter and Floyd and Walter will bring it here. Anders has had enough of this for one day so he and Lars decided to stay home. Anyway they wouldn't be needed. The body will have to be officially identified too," Inger continued.

"And if it is Roger, you will want me to tell Grace," he added.

"Yes, that's right. You're the only one around here to do it. But we are sure it's Roger. It will be terribly upsetting to both her and Joshua. They thought for sure that he would be coming back. Anna says that's all Joshua talks about."

"And the sheriff will have to be notified," added Rev. Blakeley. "If he were a drinking man I would say that he might have fallen into the river. Anyway it's not up to us to determine the cause of the death. Tell me a little more about it, and then I'll call Jim Wilson."

"Anna you tell him what happened when Anders came over this afternoon," said Milly. "You do a better yob than I do. I get so excited. Oh I am so nervous. I will have to sit down again. Come Lucy, you can sit on my lap," and she picked up the child.

Anna recalled as carefully as she could the events which led to Peter and Anders jumping into the wagon and tearing out of the farmyard. "I don't know what happened next, because after they left, Milly and I just sat here. We couldn't even eat our pie," and she looked at the two pieces which were sitting untouched on their plates.

"I guess I come in next," added Inger. "The first I knew about it was when George came running home. He said Peter had asked him to get Floyd and Walter. It didn't take too long to hitch up Nellie to the wagon and I jumped in with them. When we got there they were trying to ease the body out of the river. Lars was coming with some old sacking and we had an old blanket in the back of the wagon, so they thought they could use those to wrap the body in. The body was so messed up that Anders suggested they get a board to lay it on, so he went back to his place to get one. I took one look and that was enough for me, so I tell George that he and I are getting out of there and coming over here. Poor George threw up, and I nearly joined him. It was awful." She shuddered and Milly wondered if she needed to go outside. Inger saw her concerned look and said, "No. I'm all right Milly. Still haven't gotten over the shock. Anyway I told the men that I would get you, Rev. Blakeley and that I hoped you would be here by the time they arrived."

"They're coming here!" exclaimed Milly. "But where will they put the body?"

"Calm down Milly," Inger said. "You have nothing to worry about. It will be here only a short time."

"But where? Not in the house or anywhere near it," she stated emphatically with frantic waving of her hands.

"Peter wouldn't let it be anywhere that would bother you," Anna consoled.

"I don't want to hear any more about it," Milly protested. "I never liked the man, and I'm sorry if he is the one who is dead, but he's not going to be dead on my place."

The sound of a wagon interrupted the conversation. "Luckily the children are in the barn," commented Inger. "Come on Reverend. Let's go outside and see what's happening." The two of them put on their coats, and left the kitchen.

"I'll stay with you Milly," said Anna. "I'm not that interested in going outside either. Here let's get some supper going. When they come in they will be ready for a meal, and we will have Inger's family too."

"I don't see how anyone can eat a bite with this going on," said Milly. "But let's see what we can do with the leftovers from dinner. I could make some biscuits."

Within ten minutes Rev. Blakeley was in the house again. "It's Roger all right as far as I can tell. I've got to phone the sheriff, and then tell Grace before the party line catches on." He lifted the receiver of the phone and asked Liza Crawford to connect him to the county seat. He would have to talk through Liza, which was the only way he could make the call. It would mean the whole country would soon know, but there was not time to drive to the Post Office and make the call himself. Even when a call was made from the Post Office phone, Liza was a willing listener. It was a while before he got Jim Wilson on the phone. "Liza, tell Jim this is Rev. Blakeley from Grabney.———Tell him we're not doing so fine and that's why I'm calling him.———Tell him there is a problem here, which I think he should look into right away.———I can't tell him about it now. Does he think he could drive over to my house this evening?———I'll tell him all about it when he gets here.———What time can he come?———About eight?———That'll be fine. Ask him if he knows where I live?———Fine.———Fine. Thanks Liza. Tell him I'll see him about eight o'clock then.———Good-bye." He hung up the phone. "Well I hope that doesn't set too many ears on fire, but the word will get out soon enough anyway."

"What about your service in Langton Reverend?" asked Milly.

"Guess I can't make it. I'll phone the wife and she can call them. One person will be pleased and that is Joe Peterson. He's always been itching to give a sermon, and this is his big chance. With the harvest going on there aren't too many people going to attend anyway." He picked up the phone, and informed his wife to let Joe Peterson know that he would be unable to come that night. "Now for the hard part. I'm going to have to go over to the Klosters."

"Do you want someone to come with you?" asked Anna.

"No. Thanks anyway Anna. This is a job that I will have to do myself. If I'm not back in half an hour though tell Inger to come over and knock on the door. There may be something that she can do." With those parting words he opened the door to start on his sorrowful mission.

"Let me walk out to the road with you anyway," Anna suggested. "I'll be back in a few minutes Milly, and I'll check on the children and the milking for you."

"Thank you Anna. I don't want to go outside and take a chance on getting anywhere near a dead body."

It was dark as they walked along the roadway. Anna's main concern was about Joshua. She felt that he would take his father's death very hard and in the brief walk mentioned this to Rev. Blakeley. She left him and turned back toward the barn, and noticed that the wagon had been pulled in front of the ice house. Walking over she met Inger on her way to the house.

"What are they doing?" asked Anna.

"They needed a place to put the body so animals wouldn't get at it, and the one safe place Peter said was their ice house. It's solid dirt and has a stout door. Just don't tell Milly. If she knew she would never use it. If she really insists on knowing we'll tell her the body is over at the Klosters. Somehow I don't think she will ask, but if she questions you, tell her you don't know where it is."

"Won't Rev. Blakeley tell?" asked Anna.

"No. He thought it was a good idea."

"He left to go tell Grace."

"Yes, I saw him go. That's a part of his job that I wouldn't want for anything," Inger added.

"He asked me to tell you that if he didn't return in half an hour to come over and knock on their door That there might be something you could do," Anna replied.

"I don't know what it would be," came her answer, "but if he wants me to come over I will. Right now I'm going in the house to see Milly."

"I told Milly I'd go to the barn and check on the children and the milking."

"Walter left to do our milking as soon as they lifted the body off the wagon. But he'll be back and no doubt bring Mabel with him so we'll have some hungry mouths to feed and they'll all feel better if they can sit around the table and have supper. It'll make things more normal like. Oh, I see Peter and Floyd headed for the barn now. They must be finished. No need for you to check on the children. Let's go in and help Milly."

Chapter Twenty-five

Milly and Inger were busy preparing supper while Anna set the table. Suddenly Inger looked at the clock. "It's been half an hour easy," she commented. "Guess I'll put on my coat and head over to Grace's. Don't know when I'll be back so don't wait supper for me," and she was out the door.

"Inger's the one they always call on to help," Milly said emphatically. "I don't know what Grabney would do without her." No sooner had she said this than they heard a thump, thump on the back steps and then silence. "What was that?" With everything that had happened, Milly was obviously frightened.

"I don't know. I'll go see," volunteered Anna. She went through the entryway and opened the outside door. With the dim light coming from the kitchen she could barely make out a form at the bottom of the steps. It was Inger. She had fallen. "Oh, Inger," said Anna as she hurried down the steps. "Are you all right?"

"I should have known to bring a lantern with me. I missed the top step." She struggled to get herself up, and groaned when she stepped on her right foot. "Oh, it's my ankle. I think I must have sprained my ankle."

"Here let me help you," said Anna. "Let's get you into the house. Do you think you can step on it?"

"I can step on it all right," she groaned, "but sure hurts to beat the band. It's times like this I wish I could swear. What a stupid thing to do. Don't know how it could have happened." Together they worked to get Inger up the steps and into the kitchen. It was a painful ordeal for her, but at last they were in the entryway, just as Walter and Mabel came around the corner of the house and up the steps.

197

"Ma! What happened to you?" asked Walter. "Here, let me help you." He quickly took over from Anna. "Lean on me. Did you hurt your foot?" He then grabbed her under the arms and propelled her into the kitchen, shoving her into the chair closest to the door.

Mabel took her mother's coat. Milly had been busy with the supper and when she turned around was shocked to see Inger obviously in pain. "Inger, what happened?" was all she could say.

"I missed the top step and fell plumb down to the bottom. Guess I sprained my ankle. Isn't this a mess. Me with a sprained ankle and all I have to do."

"I have an old sheet we'll tear up so we can wrap it," said Milly as she came over to examine the injury. "Oh, look, it's swelling already." She was full of sympathy, and quickly dashed off to get the sheet.

"Since I can't go over to Grace's, someone better go. Rev. Blakeley might be in one heck of a mess with that old man, and Grace isn't much better. Anna would you go? Milly's got plenty to do here and I don't think she's eager to leave."

"I'll be happy to go. I'll take one of Milly's candles. At least that will give me a little light."

"I'll walk you out to the road," Walter offered. "We don't want two people tied up with sprains."

"Just be sure you don't fall and land on Anna," came his mother's advice. "And maybe you can stop off at the barn and see how they're coming along with the milking. Mabel, you help your Aunt Milly with the supper."

"Inger might be down, but she was not out," thought Anna. She quickly put on her coat, got the candle and lit it, and with Walter beside her she was out the door. She was careful going down the steps, and continued slowly. As they passed the barn they could hear Floyd teasing George and the children, and all of them guffawing with laughter. They both laughed at the thought of what was going on. "Go ahead into the barn Walter. I can make it fine to the road." Floyd was a good person to have around at a time like this, especially for George who had had a terrible shock.

"If you're sure," he said, and with little hesitation was headed for the barn.

Grace's house seemed fairly quiet. She approached the back door with caution and was startled when Bill Evans called out to her, "What you doin' here." He was coming from the barn with the milk pails. "Haven't we had enough trouble without you pokin' your nose in. Busybodies! That's what you all are, and that Reverend ain't no better'n the rest of you."

Anna knew that talking to him would do no good, so she ignored him and knocked on the door. Rev. Blakeley opened it, surprised to see her instead of Inger. "I hope you don't mind if I came over." She wondered if Grace knew that Rev. Blakeley had asked someone to come, so quickly added for Grace's benefit, "You see Inger was coming over to see how you were, but she fell down the back steps and sprained her ankle so badly she can't walk." She noticed Grace sitting in the rocking chair, almost lifeless. Her face was tear-stained. Elaine was sitting on the bedroom floor playing with a doll. Joshua was not around, perhaps he was upstairs.

"I'm glad you came Anna," said Rev. Blakeley. "I'm going to have to be going soon and I think that Grace could use some company." Turning to her he asked, "How are you doing Grace? I know it is a terrible shock, and I am so sorry to have to tell you news like this."

"I'll be all right. I just don't understand how it could have happened. Roger was always so careful. He wasn't a very good swimmer though. He always sank. Maybe he fell somehow and got knocked out. Oh, I just don't know," and she burst into tears again.

"Oh Grace," said Anna sadly. "I am so sorry. I wish there were something I could do. Could I make you a cup of coffee? Would you like that?"

"I don't think so," was the reply. "I don't think I want anything."

"Where's Joshua," asked Anna as she looked around.

"In his room," came the answer.

The door opened and Bill Evans walked in, surly as ever. "I gave all the milk to the hogs. We have plenty in here. You can wash out the pails," and he threw them on the floor next to the sink. "Looks like from now on you'll have to work a little harder. I'm goin' upstairs. Don't like the company." Soon he could be heard yelling at Joshua to get out of bed.

"Oh no, not that again," moaned Grace. "Ever since Roger left he's been so mean to him. I can't stand it."

Joshua could be heard sobbing uncontrollably. "I'm going upstairs to get him," said Rev. Blakeley, and he took the steps two at a time, making a quick return trip carrying Joshua in his arms. "Grace, if you will take my advice, let me bring him over to Milly's. Davey will be glad to have the company, and I think the atmosphere will be much better there than here."

"I don't want to go anywhere," screamed an angry Joshua. "I want to wait here for my dad. He is too coming home. He is too!"

"He ain't comin' home, you stupid brat," called Bill Evans from the top of the stairs, "and the sooner you get that into your head the better."

"Joshua," said Anna softly as she came over to him. "You can wait for your dad at the Jensens just as well as wait here. Why don't you let the Reverend take you over there?" The child shook his head and started to cry. "Will you let me take you over there? I live there too you know."

"Joshua," said his mother. "Go with Miss Swenson. Please. You know how it is around here."

"You're all babyin' him," shouted Bill Evans. "Gotta grow up and face facts. If no one else will, I'll beat it into him until he understands. You got that Joshua. I'll thrash the life outta you."

Grace got up and got Joshua's coat, which had been lying on a chair, and slowly helped him into it. "You're just going to visit there, maybe just have dinner there," and she put the child's hand into Anna's and they went out.

"I'll come back Grace and see how you are," Anna called as they went out the door. "Just a minute Joshua, let me light this candle. It's rather dark and I don't want to fall and sprain my ankle like Mrs. Parker did."

"How'd she do that?" came the soft spoken question.

"She was coming over here and fell down the Jensen's steps. Here hold my hand so you can help me. I don't want to fall in the roadway either." They made a silent progression to Milly's back yard, and heard laughter coming from the kitchen as they went up the steps.

"Is this where she fell?" he asked.

"That's right. Right here." Anna opened the kitchen door and when they saw who was coming in, silence fell on the room, but it didn't last long.

"Well, we got a new little boy here," said Floyd in his most jovial tone. "Jus' come in and make yourself at home. Glad to have you. Had your supper yet?"

"No," was his barely audible answer. He stared around the room at all the faces, and looked relieved when he spotted Davey.

"I'll put a chair for you right next to my Davey," said Milly, and she got him a chair and Anna took him over to it. "Let me take your coat."

"No, I want to keep my coat on," he replied.

"That's a good idea," remarked Floyd. "This house gets plenty cold sometimes. Milly's pretty stingy with the coal."

"I told Rev. Blakeley that I would come right back," said Anna to Milly.

"But you haven't had any supper. We were yust starting. Here let me send some biscuits back with you, and some of that pie that I made," and she put these things on a plate.

"That's my piece of pie that you're takin'," said Floyd. "I knew I shoulda stayed home fer supper. You gotta watch these ladies around here Joshua. They'll take your dessert every time." A slight but puzzled grin crossed the child's face.

Anna walked quickly across the road. Rev. Blakeley was waiting for her before he left. He opened the door, saying that he would be back in a couple of hours to see how they were, but that Anna didn't have to stay that long. She closed the door and went into the house.

"Milly sent some biscuits and pie Grace. Has Elaine had any supper?"

"She had some bread and butter this afternoon. There's some soup on the stove."

"Here, let me fix a bowl for both of you. Why don't you come to the table and have some soup and biscuits. Milly also sent over a couple of pieces of pie." By this time Elaine had come into the kitchen. "Here Elaine, let's sit up in your high chair and have some supper." She picked the child up, put her in the chair and tied a bib on her. The soup looked good and Elaine ate hers with gusto, as well as drinking some milk and eating a biscuit. The child was thin, and Anna wondered when was her last good meal.

Grace came slowly to the table and tried to eat some soup, but couldn't get much down.

"Do you think you'll be all right here if I leave," asked Anna. She hadn't heard a word from the upstairs and was wondering if Bill Evans was still there. "Would you like the Larsons to take Elaine?"

"No. Elaine and I will be fine," and her voice lowered to almost a whisper. "I'm used to what goes on around here, and so is she. He doesn't pick on her, so she'll be all right. But I'm glad Joshua is with Milly. I hope he won't be too much trouble for her. Do you think it would be all right if he spent the night there? I don't like to ask favors, but just this once."

Anna nodded her head, "I think that will be fine. Did you want Elaine to come with us to the little children's school tomorrow morning? We start about nine."

"No, I think I want her home with me."

"I understand," replied Anna. "I'll be off then. Rev. Blakeley said he would be back later."

"Thank you for all you've done, and oh, take the plate back to Milly. I'll put the biscuits and pie on one of mine," and she rose to do so, handing the plate to Anna. "And thank her for me."

"I will Grace," said Anna as she went to the door. "Do take care of yourself. Eat something if you can. You'll need your strength. And if we can do anything for you, don't hesitate to phone us." With that she left to return to the Jensens.

About 8:30 Rev. Blakeley arrived with Jim Wilson the sheriff. Anna was eating supper. Joshua and Davey had gone upstairs to Davey's room to play with his toys. Lucy was in bed and Mabel was reading a bedtime story to Sarah in her room. Poor Inger was having a time with her foot. She was sitting in the rocking chair and had it elevated on a footstool. Milly had done a good job bandaging it, but it looked as though she would have a difficult time walking for several days. When they heard Rev. Blakeley's car come into the yard, Peter, Floyd and Walter went out to meet them. George was already sitting off in a corner reading a book. He had had enough excitement for one day.

Only Milly, Inger and Anna were sitting around the table and Anna thought that this would be a good time to discuss what to do with Joshua. "Milly," she said in a confidential tone. "Rev. Blakeley thought that it would be a good idea if Joshua stayed here all night. His grandfather was terribly mean to him when I was over there. I'm afraid of what will happen to him if he goes back."

"I'm sure he threatened to beat the life out of the kid if he didn't do exactly as he was told," added Inger.

"And he doesn't seem to understand why Joshua is so upset," replied Anna, "and he did threaten to beat him."

"That was no idle threat either I can tell you," Inger continued. "I've seen Grace with horrible black and blue marks from where Evans hit her. That boy is in real danger. The old man is crazy."

"I'm glad to have the poor little fellow stay here," said Milly. "Oh, poor thing! To have to live with that crazy man and then to find out that his father drowned," and she was filled with sympathy.

"I suppose that he can sleep with Davey," suggested Anna.

"Oh I don't like to think of Yoshua getting into bed with Davey when he is so dirty. Oh no! It yust wouldn't do. To put a pair of Davey's clean pajamas over him. Oh I can't even think of it," and she waved her hands in exasperation.

"Calm down Milly," said her practical sister. "There's no where else to put him. Get some water heated on the stove and let him have a bath. Looks to me like his hair could do with a washing too."

"Then after he's in bed I'll wash out his clothes. They'll be dry by morning if I hang them over the stove," remarked Milly with her usual efficiency.

"Has he taken off his coat?" asked Anna."

Both women shook their heads. "Not so far as I know," said Inger, "unless he's taken it off upstairs."

"He might put up a real fuss about spending the night," added Anna. "And then to think he has to have a bath. He might not like that at all."

"I think the one to solve this problem is Floyd," advised Inger. "Get the water heated Milly, and when Floyd comes in we'll ask him to give the kid a scrub-down. He can accomplish all this without Joshua even knowing what's going on."

"Oh, that's a good idea Inger," said Milly, relieved of the responsibility. "I'll get the water on now."

In about thirty minutes the men could be heard saying good-bye followed by the sound of Rev. Blakeley's car leaving. Shortly after Peter, Floyd and Walter came into the house. They were solemn.

"Well, don't just stand there," demanded Inger. "Tell us what's been going on."

"Well, Mother, it just ain't so easy to talk about," said Floyd slowly, who for once was at a loss for words. The three sat down at the table. "Peter, why don't you tell them. I'm plumb wore out."

"Well," he began, "and nothing's certain you understand. We'll not know until tomorrow for sure, but Jim thinks that Roger was hit on the head, knocked unconscious, and shoved into the river. There's a mark on his skull which shows that. His skull was really bashed in."

"But that's murder," said George in a shaking voice as he looked up from his book.

"Yup. Could be," nodded Peter. "But let's not talk any more about it tonight. Jim will be back tomorrow morning to get some pictures and bring Dr. Bailey with him. Then we've got to get him buried."

"Is Rev. Blakeley going to tell any of this to Grace tonight?" asked Inger.

"I doubt it," said Peter. "He said he was going to stop by to see how she was doing, but Jim was anxious to get home. He left his car at the Blakeley's place, so as far as I know the Reverend was just going to stick his head in the door and leave as soon as he could. We gave our word that none of this would spread any farther than this room."

"Well, I guess we should be moseyin' on home Mother," Floyd said as he stood up.

"Not so fast," replied Inger. "Anna could you tell Mabel to get Sarah to bed, then she can come down and help with the dishes. And Floyd we have a chore for you. Joshua is to spend the night here, and he is filthy, so before he crawls into bed with Davey you get to scrub him down. He doesn't even know he's to stay here, so you might have a problem on your hands. And he needs his hair washed too."

"Yes siree that may be a problem but I think I can handle that Mother," he replied somewhat relieved to have something else to occupy his mind. "Is the water hot?"

"The water's hot, and you can bathe him in the entryway," Inger directed. "Lucy's asleep in the bedroom, so you can't go in there."

"All rightee," he said in as jovial tone as he could muster. "Walter you get the water in the tub and I'll see if I can't coax this young pup to get cleaned up." He slowly climbed the stairs.

Inger was not through giving directions. "Walter, after you're through with that, you can help with the dishes." She saw Mabel coming down the stairs. "Mabel call Erica Larson now. You both want to be teachers, so you should be at school tomorrow to help Miss Swenson. You can also bring some toys."

"I thought they both had to help with the harvest," Anna questioned.

"No, the Larson family has four good hands without Erica, and she's too young to do much good. And Floyd has hired Jimmy Burns, that way we can have two teams. George isn't very big, but he's a hard worker."

"He's sure a lot better'n Mabel," added Walter with some authority in his voice.

"Never you mind, Walter," said his mother. "Get that bath water poured."

Soon Floyd could be seen carrying a sobbing Joshua downstairs. "Never you mind son," he said soothingly patting him on the back as one would a baby. "Things'll be all right. We'll get you scrubbed up and into some of Davey's clean pajamas, and you 'n Davey'll have a good night's sleep. An' we won't think about tomorrow. That'll just have to take care of itself."

Chapter Twenty-six

The air was crisp and cold as Anna and Sarah started off hand in hand for school. They were dressed warmly with heavy coats, hats, mufflers, mittens and long stockings. Sarah clutched her doll tightly to her chest. Their noses stung with the frosty cold, and their breath looked like steam from a kettle. Anna carried their lunch. Peter was already out harvesting, and Milly was organizing Davey to look after Lucy, so she could join him. After breakfast Joshua went home, and as they passed the Kloster place all seemed quiet.

Erica was waiting for them as they went by her house, and Mabel met them at the corner. "How's your mother this morning Mabel," asked Anna. "I am worried that she will need you at home today?"

"No, Mom said she's fine. Dad got the breakfast, and she said she could hobble around enough to get dinner. I'll be home to help with supper. She said she was looking forward to a day of peace and quiet."

Anna wondered if Inger ever had a day of peace and quiet. They made quite a procession as they walked toward the schoolhouse. Both Erica and Mabel were carrying bags of toys.

Thanks to Walter the room was warm when they entered. Shortly after they arrived Lars brought his sisters Elsa and Birgit, who stood hand in hand, smiling apprehensively at Anna. Their pale blonde hair was braided into two braids and tied with a piece of ribbon. Mabel and Erica showed the little girls where to put their wraps, and more or less took charge of each newcomer. The total was five girls and four boys, one girl short of the planned total as Elaine was staying home with Grace.

The youngsters were very excited when Anna rang the school bell at nine o'clock. She had debated whether to ring it or not, but then decided that since these children felt they were in real school, she would continue with this part of the routine. She also took attendance and while doing so tried to elicit comments from each child. Reading stories, doing simple jigsaw puzzles she had made from magazine pictures and singing songs took up most of the morning. They seemed to love standing next to the organ, smiling at Anna while she played and they sang. In the afternoon they drew pictures and played with the toys which had been brought, and before school was out, another story. Thanks to Mabel and Erica, who knew the children from the church nursery, the day went quite well. At three o'clock they bundled up ready for the trip home. As they left the building some of the mothers were seen walking toward them to meet their youngsters.

Anna had been anxious all day to know what the developments were in Roger Kloster's death. She also was concerned about Inger. Fortunately Milly saw her and Sarah come into the yard and came in from the field. Davey was more than a little happy to be able to leave Lucy and go out with his dad.

"Oh, what a day this has been," said Milly as she plopped down in a chair.

"I see the coffee's hot. I'll pour each of us a cup," Anna volunteered. "Have you heard from Inger?"

"Thank you Anna. Yes, I called her at dinner time and she said she was managing to hobble around. You know Inger. Nothing will keep her down. Maybe you could get some cookies out of the cookie jar too."

"I'll do that, but while I'm getting the coffee and cookies, can you tell me what happened today? I've been so anxious to hear."

"Oh there isn't much to tell. First Yim Wilson came. I was in the house with Lucy, and Yim asked for Peter so I sent Davey out into the field to get him. By the time Peter got in Dr. Bailey had arrived. Before I knew it they were gone. I am sure Peter will tell you more when he comes in. All he told me was that Yim suggested we have the burial right away, and that there might be a few problems."

"Well," thought Anna, as she helped herself to a cookie, "I've waited this long, I guess I can wait a little while longer." To Milly she said, "After you've had your coffee, I'll take care of Lucy and start dinner, while you get cleaned up."

"Thank you Anna. Hot coffee is so good. And yust to sit down and rest, and have a cookie," said she as she helped herself to a second one. "It won't take me too long to get cleaned up, but I am so tired."

"Lie down awhile and take a rest. Lucy and I can manage fine."

"Oh, I couldn't do that. No. No. If you can keep Lucy out of my way I can hurry, and then I will feel more like myself again."

The sound of a car in the yard surprised them, but both assumed it was Rev. Blakeley coming back to check on Grace. Instead it was the county sheriff Jim Wilson who knocked on the back door. He was reasonably tall, with a husky build, but not fat. In fact he looked like any one of the farmers. His farm was near the county seat.

"Hello Milly," he said as she opened the door. "I'd like to have a word with Miss Swenson, if I may. Are you Miss Swenson?" he said looking at Anna.

"Yes I am," she replied.

"Pleased to meet you," he responded, and then smiled slightly as if to make the situation less tense. "Do you think I could talk with you for a few minutes?"

"Of course," answered Anna, not having the slightest idea what this was all about. "If it's all right we can sit down at the table."

Milly picked up Lucy and started to leave. "Oh, you don't have to leave Milly. This won't take long. Think I could have a cup of your coffee?" Sheriff Wilson asked.

"Oh, my yes." She slung Lucy over her left hip, quickly poured him a cup with her right hand and passed the plate of cookies. Looking over at the center of the table she checked to see if there were enough cream and sugar. Satisfied, she said, "I'm going to take Lucy into the bedroom and get us both cleaned up, so you go right ahead and talk to Anna. Davey and Peter won't be in until it gets dark, and then he'll have the cows to milk. Sarah you come too," and she motioned to the child as all three left the room.

"You're probably wondering what this is all about," he began. "Well, Peter told me that you went over to the Klosters the day that Roger disappeared, that was Tuesday, October 24th, but he also said you didn't go into the house. Can you tell me about it? Just take your time, and try to remember everything that happened. It may be important, and it may not be important, but I will decide that."

Anna quickly realized that he was no ordinary farmer. He was trying to find the answer to Roger's disappearance, and he intended to do a thorough job.

"Well," she began slowly. "I was going over to the Klosters on my way to the Post Office."

"Why were you going there?"

"I was going to ask them if Elaine could come to the school program I planned to have for children under school age for the week of harvest. That's this week."

"Yes, I know," and he shook his head. "I've had to hire a couple of men to do my harvest for me, but please go on."

"It must have been after four o'clock, because I know I wanted to get to the Post Office before it closed at five, so I was trying to hurry. As I got near their house I could hear yelling. Grace was crying. Roger was telling her that he was the one who saved the place and that she and her dad wouldn't have lasted another six months without him. I know he hit her because I heard a thump and she begged him not to hit her again. He quoted something from the Bible saying that wives were to obey their husbands, and she was a sinner. It was so awful." She shuddered at the thought.

"I know that this isn't too pleasant for you, but think now, did he say anything else?"

"Oh, yes," and she paused. "He said that he had a good mind to leave them to rot, and that that was exactly what they would do without him. I can never forget that part. His voice was so cruel."

"Is that all?"

"Yes, I think so," said Anna trying to recall that horrendous experience. "I left then, because I didn't want to hear any more and I knew that I couldn't do anything to stop him."

"Was anyone with you to hear this?"

"No, I was alone."

"Do you know if anyone else heard the argument."

"No, I don't know for sure, but I did meet Ed Marson after I left there. He was on the path to Grabney. He was bringing a posthole digger to Roger."

"Did he say anything to you?"

"Only that he was bringing the posthole digger to Roger because Roger wanted it as soon as it came in. I guess it had come in that afternoon."

"But you don't know for sure when it came in," Jim continued with his comments.

"Oh, no. I don't know for sure. I do remember Ed saying that he doubted if Roger would be able to fix the fence in time for the cattle to be turned in after harvest, and then he walked on. I felt so uncomfortable because I knew that Ed might hear them arguing when he got there."

"Why would that make you feel uncomfortable?"

"Well, everyone around here has talked about how Ed was sweet on Grace before she married Roger, and how they were so surprised when she suddenly ups and marries Roger, that I thought it might make Ed mad to hear Grace treated so badly, maybe not mad but just make him feel bad."

"You got to the Post Office all right then."

"Yes, and I picked up my package," she answered.

"Did you meet Ed when you were coming back home?"

"No, I didn't, because Floyd and Walter were just in from Chicago. George had met them and they gave me a ride home."

"I see. Did you happen to notice if Ed was walking along the path back to Grabney?"

"Well, I did look to see if I could see him coming," and she was somewhat embarrassed in admitting this, "but I didn't see him at all."

"Did you ever talk to him about this?"

"No, I didn't."

Jim Wilson rose from his chair. "Thank you Miss Swenson. I may talk to you again. And thanks for the coffee and cookies Milly," he called so she could hear him.

211

"You're welcome Yim," said Milly as she and the children came out of the bedroom. It was obvious that she had waited for him to finish.

"I'm going out to talk to Peter. I think I heard him come in so he's probably in the barn, then I'll be on my way," and he left the kitchen.

When Peter came in he had nothing much to add to what they had learned from the day before. He sat down and as usual poured himself a cup of coffee before he began talking. "Doc. Bailey said that Roger's skull had been cracked by being hit with a heavy, blunt object. We told him that we thought Roger had been digging holes with a posthole digger, since Ed had brought it to him that afternoon and he was anxious to get the fence mended. Doc said it could be the likely weapon, but Jim is not one to go on hearsay, so he will investigate thoroughly you can bet yer bottom dollar. Jim got his pictures, and suggested that the body be buried as soon as possible. It's decomposing rapidly."

"Oh Peter," Milly shuddered. "Do you have to go into all that?"

He looked at her and nodded understandingly before continuing. "I asked the Doc why Roger's body took so long to be discovered. I thought it was strange that it hadn't floated to the surface and drifted downstream." Another shudder from Milly.

"I heard Grace say that Roger couldn't swim very well, that he always sank," Anna added.

"Dr. Bailey said almost the same thing. He said that Roger was so thin that he didn't have hardly an ounce of fat on him, and sometimes people who are so thin, well they just sink. It's the fat mostly that makes them float. Then the water is so deep there. The water looks still, and still water runs deep."

"Joshua told me how his father had told him that was a good fishing area because it would have lots of fish since it was so deep," Anna said. "Joshua used those very words that still water runs deep. But why would his body suddenly appear almost two miles downstream by the Anderson's?"

"Bodies start to bloat, and with the current being what it is, it would carry the body downstream, even though it is fairly deep. What happened is that it caught on a snag under the water, and when Lars put in his line the hook caught on the coat. And you know what happened after that."

"Let's not talk any more about it," said Milly waving her hands in the air. "No! No more!"

"Just let me finish Milly. There's not much more to tell. Jim asked Anders to make a coffin, and he's goin' to try to do it this evening. With harvest he can't do it in the daytime. He always keeps lumber at home. He said it would be nothing fancy, but Jim said just to get it done so we can get the body in the ground. I guess Rev. Blakeley is to go over to talk to Grace tonight to see when the funeral will be. The Reverend will also get someone to dig the grave, providing Grace wants him buried here. These are all things which have to be settled soon."

"Has anyone seen Joshua today?" asked Anna, suddenly concerned about the boy.

"No, we haven't," answered Milly. "Have you seen him Davey?"

"Not since this morning," came the answer. "Remember he left right after breakfast."

"I think I'll go and see how things are over there," said Anna, and she rose to get her coat from the entryway. "It was so terrible yesterday. I don't trust Bill Evans. Is it all right if I bring him back with me if he wants to come?" she asked.

"Of course," answered Milly. "Tell him we'll be glad to have him. You would like to have him come again Davey, Wouldn't you?"

"Sure! And tell him we can play with my farm animals again," called Davey as she left the room.

She walked carefully since it was dark. As she approached the yard she noticed a car and thought it might be Rev. Blakeley's. She heard Grace talking and knocked on the door. It was opened by Jim Wilson. "Oh, I'm sorry," she apologized. "I didn't know you were here. I thought it might be Rev. Blakeley's car."

"Just don't know a Ford from a Chevy, I guess. Come in. I'm about finished, and maybe you can do me a favor."

"I will if I can," she responded, and looking at Grace she asked, "How are you Grace? And how is Joshua?'

"Joshua's hiding in the parlor," she said with a pained expression. "He's so afraid of my dad. He refuses to go upstairs. Dad's out doin' the milkin'. He's mad 'cause Dr. Bailey said I wasn't well enough to do any work this week. He wanted me to harvest with him. Now he says he goin' to have to harvest at night. He can't see to harvest in the dark. He doesn't have to do it all this week. Oh, I don't know what to do." Despair was in her voice.

By this time Joshua had opened the parlor door, and Anna spotted him. "I came to ask if Joshua could come over to Milly's again for dinner and to stay all night," said Anna. "Would you like to do that Joshua?"

To the surprise of everyone, the child nodded his head, hurried to the back door, opened it and ran out.

"I guess he knows what he wants," said Jim. "He sure went lickety-split out of here."

"He knows my dad will be comin' in soon from milkin' and he's really scared of him."

"Why is that?" came the question from the sheriff.

Grace hung her head. "He said he would beat the livin' daylights out of him. He yells at him all the time, never gives the boy a minute's peace. Anna can tell you. She heard him yesterday. That's why he spent the night at the Jensen's."

"Maybe he can stay there for a few days, until the worst of this is over," came the sheriff's evaluative reply. "Here, why don't we sit down Miss Swenson. Pull up a chair. I do have a little more to discuss, and Rev. Blakeley should be here soon."

"Oh, call me Anna," she stammered. "Everyone does, except the children of course."

"Fine with me, and I'm Jim to everyone. So that's settled. I've told Grace all I know about how Roger was killed. It looks like someone hit him with the posthole digger." Grace shuddered, and took Elaine, who was standing close to her, onto her lap.

Seeing her agony, he continued, "I'm sorry to have to bring this up, but it looks like someone killed him. Now I'm not saying that it couldn't have been an accident. You've told me that a lot of folks didn't like him, and I pretty much have heard all the gossip around here, but we have to find someone who at least was ready to pick a fight with him." A car could be heard pulling into the yard. "That'll be Rev. Blakeley I imagine," and he rose to go to the door.

Grace gave a groan and her head sank. "This is too much," she muttered shaking her head.

"Come in Reverend," welcomed Jim. "We've been waiting for you. You know Anna Swenson of course."

"Hello Anna," came the greeting to which Anna responded.

"Reverend I have a couple of things to get cleared up before I leave, and then I'll go and let you make the funeral arrangements with Grace. Anna just happened by, but I would like her to stay."

"You go ahead Jim," said Rev. Blakeley. "Then you can get on your way. I have plenty of time."

"We were discussing that Roger had been hit on the head by what we assume was the posthole digger. Doc. Bailey examined the body and agreed that it was the likely object, which probably knocked him unconscious. Since the river's a good fifteen feet away from the place where the fence is, the body was probably dragged to the river and heaved in. Of course they could have been fighting and gotten closer to the river, and the blow could have shoved him into the water. These are things we don't know."

"Dr. Bailey has completed the coroner's examination then," said Rev. Blakeley.

"Yes, and as soon as we see if the photos we took come out all right, you will be able to bury him. We should know by this evening, or tomorrow morning at the latest. Now to get back to who hit Roger. I know it wasn't a robbery because his billfold was on him," and the sheriff reached into his coat pocket and pulled out Roger's thick black leather billfold.

Grace gave a gasp, "Yes, Roger had one like that."

"And apparently he kept most of his money on himself, because inside I found $473.00 in bills, and twenty-six cents in change."

"That's a lot of money to be carrying around," commented Rev. Blakeley. "I'm surprised it didn't get ruined in the water."

"I'm surprised too, but the billfold was pretty thick, and the bills crammed in there so tight that they barely got wet," Jim continued. "Anyway, this money belongs to you Grace, and while I could hold it as evidence, I think it is best to let you have it. I brought along a paper for you to sign saying you have received the money, and I need two witnesses, so I am asking Rev. Blakeley and Miss Swenson to do that. I think you should first count the money, to make sure it is the amount written on the paper."

"I couldn't," she sobbed. "I just couldn't"

"Would you let Rev. Blakeley and Anna count it then?"

"Yes," she said wiping her eyes and nodding.

"Here Reverend," Jim said as he handed the billfold to him. "You open it up and count it, and Anna can vouch for what you come up with."

Slowly he opened the wet billfold and took out the bills. They were a bit damp and needed to be dried out, but together they counted them, and with the change came up with the same amount as the sheriff. "You're right Jim, $473.26."

"Doc. Bailey found the wallet when he was examining Roger, and we counted the money and came up with the same amount. Just wanted you to know that nothing had been removed. That seems to be a rather large amount to be carrying with him. Since Roger had threatened to leave, and I don't mean to be unkind, but do you think that he took the money so he could skip out on you Grace?"

"No," she replied shaking her head. "He always kept all of his money on him. He didn't trust banks. And anyway that wasn't the first time he had said he would leave."

The door suddenly opened and Bill Evans stomped in. "What's goin' on here anyway? Why don't you folks clear out and leave us alone?" Seeing the money on the table he added, "An' what's all that money doin' there?"

"Evenin' Bill," said Jim. "This was money that Roger had on him, and I've just given it to Grace."

"Money he stole from me," he shouted. "That's money he stole from my farm. That's my money."

"No," said Jim in his sheriff's voice. "That money was found on Roger, and as his widow it belongs to Grace. You are not to touch it. She can keep it here, or put it in a bank, but you are not to lay your hands on it. Understand?"

216

"Don't you go tellin' me what to do you young whippersnapper, you uppity farmer pretendin' to be sheriff. You think you can come here from the county seat and run our affairs. Well there's plenty I can tell you. There sure is."

"Why don't you have a seat and tell me then," answered Jim. "I would be happy if you could help us out."

"Askin' me to sit in my own house. This is my house I tell you and my farm. And over there sits my daughter who tried and tried to get me to sign the deed to the place over to her husband. And for what? So they could sell it and skip out on me."

"No!" shouted Grace. "That's not true."

"Hah! You tell me it's not true, but you don't know. I would come downstairs at night an' hear you and Roger talkin' in the bedroom when you thought I was asleep, plannin' to get your hands on my place," he screamed.

"That was Roger's idea, not mine," and she was sobbing again. "You know he beat me if I didn't do as he said."

"You lazy no-good, I would have beat you too. You're lucky he came along and married you, after you'd been hangin' aroun' with that worthless Ed Marson. Another uppity one. Wanted to go to high school and graduated. Didn't do him any good did it? He can't even farm. Doesn't know how."

"Let's leave Ed out of this," said Jim. "What we're trying . . ." and he was interrupted by Bill Evans.

"Whadda you mean, leave Ed outta this?" he continued ranting. "Ed was the one who brought the posthole digger over here. I saw him listenin' to you and Roger fightin', an' then he knocked on the door an' shoved it in Roger's face and left. Oh yes, I saw you too missy school teacher," and he sneered at Anna. "You came over too, but you heerd the fightin' and then left to go down the path to the river. You thought no one saw you, but I did. I sees everythin' aroun' here. But did Ed leave? No, he stayed. He walked over to the field and waited, jus' like he waited for Grace right before she married Roger. Only that time she went to meet him, Roger found them and I had to drag her away, screamin' she was. After that I'm surprised she got someone decent like Roger to marry her."

"Stop! Stop!" Grace shouted angrily.

"You can't stop me now. You and Roger thought you had me stopped, but now it's my turn. Well, let me tell you what happened that night. Ed waits in the field until Roger comes out. Roger has the post hole digger and goes down to dig next to the river. And Ed follows him, and they get into an argument. I saw it and I heard them. So! You think that I am a know nothin', but think again."

"Are you saying that Ed Marson was arguing with Roger down by the river?" questioned Jim.

"You bet I am."

"Did you see him hit Roger with the post hole digger?"

"No, I didn't see nothin' like that. I was up near the house. I got my own chores to do. But I heerd them. It's a wonder the whole countryside didn't hear them."

"Why didn't you tell us this before?" asked Jim.

"No point to it were there," the old man continued. "I thought it was jus' a argument. I heerd Roger say that he was thinkin of leavin' us, an' I thought that was what he did."

"What you are saying is that after the argument with Ed, you thought that Roger was fed up enough to leave, so you didn't mention it to anyone," Jim stated.

"Yeah, that's about it I would say," the old man concluded.

"But you are hinting that it is possible, that Ed Marson could have hit Roger with the post hole digger, and maybe shoved him into the river," the sheriff continued.

"You're wrong. You're all wrong," Grace lamented. "Ed would never kill anyone. You're saying that Ed killed Roger."

"I didn't say it, but if that's the conclusion you come to, so be it. Now girl, get up and git me some supper. I been workin' all day, not sittin' in a chair like you. An' I s'pose you let that worthless boy of yours go across the road agin. I saw him run over there. You think I don't know what goes on, but I do. I gotta get the chores done, but I'll be back in thirty minutes and I want supper on the table," and he stormed out of the room.

Everyone was silent for a minute or so. Jim was the first to break it. Well, this puts a whole new light on the situation. Guess I'll be going. I can see that I have a lot of work ahead of me," and he rose from his chair.

"Sheriff," said Grace, using his title. "Will you take this money and put it in the bank for me? If it is left here dad will take it."

"I can't put it in the bank for you, but I can lock it up in the safe in an envelope with your name on it. That should be pretty secure. I think you should get it into a bank account as soon as you can though."

"Yes, I will," she answered, "but if you could take it now, then I know I will have it when I need it."

"You will need some money to pay Anders for making the casket, and also to the person who digs the grave," advised Rev. Blakeley.

"Oh, yes," she answered. "How much do you think that will be?"

"I'm not sure, but $50.00 should be enough."

"Take that much money then Reverend, and the sheriff can take what's left."

Jim counted out fifty dollars and gave it to Rev. Blakeley, then collected the rest, put it back in the billfold, and soon left. As his car was heard leaving the yard, Rev. Blakeley rose also.

"This has been a rather upsetting afternoon for you Grace, and I don't want to add to your misery, but we do need to plan a service for Roger for perhaps Wednesday at the latest. Anders Anderson is making a casket, and it should be ready by tomorrow night, maybe even tonight, but that wouldn't be until about midnight even if he worked all evening on it."

"You do whatever you think is best Reverend. I don't think many people will come to the service anyway because they'll all be too busy harvesting. And it's just as well they can have that excuse, because not that many people liked Roger. And I can't blame them either. He never was nice to anyone. He always thought he was better than everyone." She paused. "My dad's right. All he ever wanted to do was to get enough money to leave this place. It's all I wanted to do too. I've hated this farm." Her voice was dead and unemotional.

"When I was a girl my mother was sick all the time. My father insisted that she have a baby boy, so she kept on havin' babies, but they all died. She did die when the last baby was

219

born, but she wouldn't have had to. He made her work all the time when she was expectin', and she was so thin. The best time I had was the two years I lived with my aunt in the county seat, then when my mother died I had to come home. I had to work and take my mother's place. I had to work in the fields and also do all the housework, the same as my mother." Grace continued almost as if she were in a trance.

"He wouldn't let me out of his sight. He kept thinkin' that I'd run away or somethin'. I didn't even get to go to Grabney or to church. I found out later that some of my friends at school had written me, but I never got their letters. My aunt, my mother's sister, came out to see me once, but they had a terrible argument and she realized that she was no match for him.

"Then Roger come along. We never knew where he came from. He talked about having lived in the Dakotas and Minnesota, but he never got any mail from anyone as far as I know. He preached about God and I knew how much I missed going to church. I felt that we were more Holy with him around sayin' prayers and talkin' about religion. He took charge of the farm and Dad didn't get on me any more because he didn't have to work so hard. Roger did the work that I had been made to do. I thought he was wonderful. It was my dad who suggested that we get married, but I think that Roger was thinkin' of that all along. I really loved him, and was happy when I was expectin' Joshua so soon. Roger kept me at home almost the same as Dad, but I didn't mind so much because I was a wife and gonna be a mother, and I could spend all my time in the house." Her eyes roamed toward the parlor door.

"It was sometime after Joshua was born that Roger began askin' me to see if Dad would sign the place over to him. I could see that he was doin' most of the work. He was like havin' a hired hand for free. I began to feel that it was our place, Roger's and mine, so I asked Dad about it. At first he didn't say much, 'cept that some day it would belong to Roger and me.

"Then I had the second baby and hadn't seen my aunt for so long, and was beginnin' to feel tied down to the place. That's when I went to the county seat. Roger and Dad both refused to let me go, and I couldn't understand why, so I ups and walks to town and gets on the train. I took some money that Roger had in a drawer to buy my ticket. I guess you know that we both got the flu and the baby died. Nothing was ever the same after that. Roger said it was God's will that the baby died because I had to be punished for what I did in disobeyin' my husband and my father. I used to think that was true, but I think Roger was punished as much as I was, because he really wanted that little boy. It was after that that Roger kept all his money with him." At this point she looked at Anna and Rev. Blakeley and focused on them.

"Roger started talking to Dad about deedin' over the place. We did talk about sellin' it and leavin' for some city, but that was mostly dream talk. We never would have sold it while Dad was alive, at least I wouldn't have. When Dad wouldn't sign, then Roger began to get really mean. He was more strict than ever with religion, and strict with Joshua. Dad never stood up to him. I tried but couldn't."

She furrowed her brows and shook her head slowly. "I was surprised when Jim said Roger had so much money on him. I knew that he had saved some from last year. He never let Dad or me know how much we got for the hogs or the corn. But I had to let Jim take the money, not only so Dad wouldn't get it, but so I wouldn't take it and catch the first train to my aunt's place. Well, now you know. I've talked too much, but it was nothin' you prob'ly didn't know, or guessed at. And Dad's goin' to be in for supper soon," and she heaved a huge sigh.

Anna and Rev. Blakeley had listened in silence, realizing that this was the catharsis Grace needed. He was the first to stir. "Grace," he said quietly. "Why don't you let me plan the funeral for Wednesday evening after supper. Everyone will be finished with work by that time, and I think you'll find that a great many people will want to come."

"I don't even know if I want to come," she admitted. "I don't feel I know anyone any more. I think I would be embarrassed to face everyone, that is if anyone would come."

"I know that I will be there Grace," said Anna, "and I feel sure that Milly and her family will too."

She turned her head to look at this young friend. "Thank you Anna. Do you think you could come in our buggy with me and the children? I just don't feel I would want to come alone."

"Of course," Anna answered. "What time do you think it will be Reverend?"

"Let's say seven o'clock. Most people eat about six, since they have to come in from the field by five, then do the milking. Well, let's make it about 7:30. That'll give them plenty of time. I'll pass the word around, and Anna can tell Milly and Inger." Taking out his notebook he wrote in it, "Wednesday, Nov. 8th, Roger Kloster funeral 7:30." I guess that's all Grace. If there's anything else you think of, you can call me. Don't worry about the casket or anything. We'll take care of that." Anna got up to leave also. She realized she hadn't taken off her coat the entire time she was there.

"Thank you both so much," Grace said getting out of the chair, holding Elaine in her arms, and still looking as if she were in a daze.

"I'll stop by tomorrow to see how you are Grace," added Anna, and she and Rev. Blakeley let themselves out.

She walked with him to his car. Before he got in he turned and said to her. "Anna, would you mind playing for the funeral service? You see I'm not sure that I can get anyone else."

"But do you think I'm good enough. Some of the hymns are so difficult."

"We'll choose the easy ones," he comforted her with a pat on the shoulder. "Can you come by the parsonage tomorrow after school so we can plan the service?"

"Yes, if that means that you would let me practice on your piano," she said with a smile.

"That's a bargain I can easily live with," he said with relief. "And I'll see if my good wife can make an apple pie."

Chapter Twenty-seven

As Anna walked to the Blakeley's Tuesday afternoon several things were on her mind. She felt pleased that school had gone as well that day as it had the day before. She had stopped at Grace's to see how things were, and arranged to bring Joshua over a little early on Wednesday evening so Grace could dress him in his best clothes. Milly had phoned Inger about the funeral and they had agreed to go. Olle and Sylvia Larson would attend also, since they were close neighbors and felt they should, and Erica would probably go to Milly's with Mabel and care for the children. If Joshua were still staying with Milly, then he could walk over to his place with Anna when she went to ride with Grace. Hopefully all would work out as planned.

The one thing which bothered her was the ranting that Bill Evans had done about Ed Marson having an argument with Roger down by the river, and the insinuation that Ed had been the one to kill Roger. Even Grace had dismissed the idea, but it was an accusation that could not be easily forgotten. If only she had seen Ed walking back to town, but then maybe that wouldn't prove anything either. The most likely theory is that Bill had heard someone arguing with Roger, and since he didn't like Ed, assumed it was he.

She went to the back door of the house this time. She could see Thelma Blakeley in the kitchen, and sure enough as the door was opened she could smell freshly baked apple pie. "Come in, come in," was the warm greeting from this gracious woman. "I was under orders to bake an apple pie for you," she continued, "but I think Tom just used that as an excuse to get some for himself," and she smiled a knowing smile to Anna.

"Now Mother, you know that's just poppycock," Rev. Blakeley said as he came in from the parlor. "Here let me take your coat. Sit down Anna. We have a few things to go over before tomorrow night." He hung up her coat and seated himself across from her at the table. "I suppose Milly has filled you up with coffee and cookies so you'll be too full for the pie."

"Not this time," Anna laughed. "I came away without a single sip of coffee. I wanted to save my appetite for what you promised me over here. Hardly ate any lunch either," she joked.

"Well, let's cut into that pie Mother. Here I'll pour the coffee," and he filled three cups while Mrs. Blakeley passed out the pie. "I brought the hymnal so we could discuss what songs to have. Why don't we start out with *What a Friend We Have in Jesus*. You played that last Sunday for the Sunday School."

"That's fine," replied Anna. "I think it would be appropriate too." She was relieved that there was no mention of Ed. Perhaps the situation had been cleared up.

"We should have one more hymn to end the service. Why don't you look over the index and choose one that you would feel comfortable playing," and he handed the hymnal to her.

"This is going to be a difficult service Tom," advised Mrs. Blakeley, "especially since Roger was never a part of the congregation. Grace hasn't come since her mother died, except when she had Elaine baptized. They weren't even married here. I don't know how many people will show up."

"Milly and Peter will be there," added Anna. "Also Inger and Floyd, and the Larsons said they would come. I will come with Grace and the children. With you, Mrs. Blakeley, that makes eight, not counting Grace. And I'm sure Anders and Hilma Anderson will come. That makes ten."

"We may have a few more, but I guess that will have to do. I'll try to keep the service short because we'll want to lower the body into the grave after the service and it'll be getting late."

"How can you find anyone to dig the grave with everyone so busy with harvest?" said Anna looking up from the hymnal.

"I was lucky there. This morning I went over to talk to Matt Crawford to ask him if he knew anyone who could dig the grave, and before I got home he had located a couple of roustabouts who had ridden in on the morning freight looking for work. He sent them over, and I told them five dollars each for digging the grave and covering it. They agreed so I gave them a shovel each, and as far as I know they are working at it now. I'll pay them when the job is finished. That's a big load off my mind. I offered the job to Thelma here," he said winking, "but she said she wouldn't do it for five dollars."

"I said I would do it if he came with me, but he was the one who refused," she countered.

"I'm glad you stayed home, I'd rather have the apple pie," added Anna as she put a piece in her mouth." She turned the pages of the hymnal and nodded her head. "Here is one which I think would be good, *My Faith Looks Up to Thee.*"

"Excellent," came the minister's approval. "I know you can play a pump organ, because you have one at school."

"Yes, that's no problem. A few times I also played one in the church at home. You know I'm still surprised that so many families around here have them. At home most people buy a piano, but in the country they seem to get organs."

"I think that's because most of the music they play is church music," said Mrs. Blakeley. "In town they probably play more popular music."

"Would it be all right if I went into the parlor and practiced these songs a time or two?" asked Anna. "I could practice at school but I would have to wait until tomorrow."

"Of course. That's what I intended you to do," said the Reverend. "While you're doing that I'll go check on my grave diggers. They could probably do with a piece of pie and some coffee when they're finished Mother."

"Yes, I expected that," she said. "Invite them to come in then, and I'll have it ready. I imagine they want to talk to Matt again and see if he can line up some work for them."

"Does Matt Crawford line up work for people who come in town?" asked Anna.

"Well, he pretty much knows what goes on around here, not without the help of Liza," she said with a smile, "and these fellows have probably been here before and know the ropes.

I'm sure Matt will find them something to do other than grave digging." She started clearing the plates and cups while Anna went into the parlor and Rev. Blakeley left to check on his hired help.

It was cold in the parlor so she put on her coat, and spent about half an hour at the keyboard, making sure that she could play the two songs without making any mistakes. Her confidence had grown considerably since she first played for the Sunday School a little over a month ago. When she was finished she went back into the kitchen, where Rev. Blakeley had just returned from talking to his workers.

"They've got about two hours more. That ground is harder than I thought."

"They are probably timing it so they finish just about supper time," his wife added. "I think there is a method to their slowness."

"Well, Mother, it wouldn't be the first time that we've fed a few extras. You may be right."

"Take off your coat again, and sit down so we can go over the rest of the service," said Rev. Blakeley. Anna had just sat down when there was a knock at the door, and then it was opened by a very pale looking Ed Marson.

"Ed smelled the pie," joked the Reverend. "Well come on in. Don't stand there with the door open." He paused and stared at the young man. "Say, is something the matter? You don't look good at all."

Ed came in and closed the door. "I've got to talk to you, got to talk to someone. I can't talk to my folks. They're too upset. Can I come in?"

"Come in boy. Of course you can come in. Sit down." The minister's demeanor became serious. "What's the matter?"

"Perhaps it's time for me to go," suggested Anna as she rose from her chair.

"No, please don't go," Ed mumbled as he shut the door. "You might be able to help too. Well, I dunno if you can or not, but you live close to the Klosters and I saw you that day." He sat down in the chair closest to the door and pulled it up to the table.

"Now tell us what the problem is, and we'll see if we can help." The calm voice of the minister was accustomed to counseling his parishioners.

The young man began slowly. "Well, you see it was this afternoon when I was workin' in the store and Jim Wilson comes in. Everyone stopped talkin' and looks at him. He says 'Hello' an' tries to make like it's just an ordinary visit, then says he'd like to talk to me so he walks over to where I'm workin'. Well I was over stackin' sacks of flour. He tells me it's about somethin' personal, so we go in the back room. The few folks in the store were wonderin' what was goin' on, I could tell by their looks, and I was too. We all knew about Roger. I thought maybe Jim was talkin' to everyone in town, tryin' to piece things together. Well, that wasn't quite it," and he buried his face in his hands.

"If you mean what old man Evans said about you, he's just crazy. Anna and I were there when he ranted and raved. Jim isn't going to take any stock in that," said Rev. Blakeley.

"The problem is, that part of what the old man said is true," Ed continued. "I did wait in the field after I gave the posthole digger to Roger, because I wanted to see if he was goin' to keep hittin' her. I saw her. She looked terrible, kneelin' on the floor to him and cryin' for him to forgive her and stop hittin' her. I wanted to kill him, I was so mad, but I didn't kill him. After I saw him leave the house I went through the rows of the corn which go back to your place here, and then went on home. I know I didn't get home until late, but I was thinkin' and walkin' pretty slow."

"Wait a minute now," came the calm voice of the minister. "Let's start at the beginning. I'm sure Jim doesn't think that you killed Roger. He's not going to believe that crazy old man, but he's got find out who did, so you're right, he's probably asking questions of a lot of people. He also questioned Anna. Isn't that right Anna?"

"Yes, he came to the Jensen's and asked me about going over to the Kloster's before I went to town to pick up my package at the Post Office. I told him I heard them fighting but I didn't go in. I turned back to the path and went to town."

"I didn't know that you heard them fightin' too," said Ed. "I thought you was just on your way to town."

She continued, "Well, when I met you I was so upset at what I heard, and so surprised at seeing anyone on the path, that I'm afraid I didn't say much. And when you said you were going to the Kloster's, I simply couldn't say a word, because I knew that you might hear the fight too. And then I thought that it might be over and things would be normal, and so it would be better if I didn't say anything."

"I thought you was rather quiet," Ed said, "but then I was in a hurry so I didn't really think too much about it. I was anxious to deliver the posthole digger and get back home. I didn't want to see Roger at all and was hopin' that he would be in the barn."

"So after you met Anna, you continued to the Klosters, where you heard the argument between Roger and Grace," Rev. Blakeley continued.

"It was more than an argument. It was a terrible fight, only he was the one doin' the fightin'. He has to be the meanest man I ever heard of." At this the young man clenched his fists.

"All right we have that straight. And after you left the house you hid in the field. Could you see the kitchen?"

"Oh sure. I could see the porch, and that's how I knew that Roger came out. But I didn't see ol' Bill Evans watchin' me. An' he should know I went home."

"Well, maybe he doesn't know that for sure," said the minister.

Ed looked up angrily, "You mean you think I killed Roger too!"

"Calm down son. I don't think anything of the kind. What I am saying is that it was dark, isn't that right?"

"Yeah, it was gettin' dark anyway."

"And Bill Evans eyesight probably isn't so good as it used to be."

"Yes," and Ed nodded.

"So he may have seen someone going to where Roger was, and thought it was you, or maybe he just wanted to think it was you."

"But why would he say it was me when he wasn't sure!" Ed blurted out angrily.

"You recall that you and he never did get along, and since he saw you watching the house, he just put two and two together and came up with five. What Jim will be wondering is if you like Grace well enough to kill Roger after you have seen him beat up on her?"

Ed looked up startled. "I couldn't kill anybody. I just couldn't. An' there's nothing between Grace and me any more, maybe there never was. Of course we knew each other in Grabney, 'cause we went to grade school together. Well, when we started high school, I was boardin' with Mrs. Plummer, and Grace was stayin' with her aunt. When you go away to high school you can be sort of alone, and Grace always thought of things that were fun to do. I guess we were—well—like sweethearts, but we were pretty young, and we never became serious, not really serious."

"Our son Mike boarded with Mrs. Plummer also," said Mrs. Blakeley, mostly for Anna's benefit. "Everyone was jealous of Ed because Grace was so cute, and she sure seemed to latch onto him."

"Yeah, I guess she kinda did," he acknowledged. Then turning more serious he continued, "Even after her mother died, and her dad made her quit school, we'd sometimes see each other, but we had to sneak around. He didn't like me, and—well—my folks didn't like her neither. Her ol' man never let her go off the place, not even to the store. And after Roger came she changed. She was just a different person. That last night that I saw her, and Roger and her ol' man found us, we hadn't even planned to meet. In fact I was walkin' home from bringin' some things to Anderson's, and she spies me and runs down to the path. She says she has somethin' to tell me so we get off the path 'cause she doesn't want anyone tellin' her ol' man that they saw us together.

"I didn't want to talk to her 'cause she was different somehow and I didn't really like her any more. I hadn't seen her for a long time. But she said it was real important and she had to tell me. What she told me was that she 'n Roger was gettin' married. She was so proud and acted stuck-up. Then her dad came and yelled at us. Roger was standin' a ways up in the field so's he could see us. Grace started screamin' at her dad an' he dragged her off. He accused us of doin' all sorts of things, and he was yellin' too. He said I was never to set foot on their place again or he would kill me. I was so scared of him that a couple of days later I cleared out of town. And the way she acted toward me, so uppity-like, made me feel sick. When my mom wrote that she was expectin' a baby and that things seemed to have calmed down, I came back.

"So I couldn't believe how she looked the other day when I saw her, and him so mean. I knew he was strange, but I never thought he would beat her. She looked so small and skinny like a sick animal. I don't know for sure what I would have done if he hadn't quit hitting her, but I know for sure I never would have killed him. I guess I would have been too scared to do that." He looked up suddenly realizing that Anna, a comparative stranger, had heard the whole story.

"Ed, what did Jim Wilson say to you?" asked Rev. Blakeley.

"He asked me some questions and I told him just what I told you now. He said that there certainly was not enough evidence to arrest me, but not to leave town. He talked about arresting me!"

"That's just legal talk," said the older man. "If you say you didn't do it, then of course we believe you. Last night when I came home and told Thelma what Evans had said, she agreed with me that you aren't the killing type. Isn't that right Mother?"

"Yes, we've known you since you were a little boy. You would never be capable of doing anything like that."

"Thanks for listenin' to me," he said as he rose to go. "I feel better now, like someone's on my side. My folks are real worried. If you could I would appreciate it if you could come over and talk to them tonight."

"Of course I will. Not sure what I can do, but I'll be over after supper," said Rev. Blakeley.

"I'll see you later then," he said as he opened the door to leave. "So long," and he left the room and closed the door behind him.

Anna got up to go also. "I can't believe that he could possibly have killed Roger."

"Of course he didn't," Rev. Blakeley said. "Ed isn't the type to do such a thing. He's always been shy and quite reserved."

"I would say that he wouldn't have the gumption to do it. Remember when he and Mike always palled around together? Mike was the go-getter and Ed the follower. After high school Mike takes off for Des Moines and gets a job, but Ed stays home. Even with Grace, she was the one who decided things. I don't think he would have taken up with her if she hadn't started it. After all they were only in their first two years of high school, just kids. She was the boss and she knew it, and he followed her around like a puppy."

"That's right Mother! In fact we couldn't believe it when he left town after the argument when Bill Evans found them in the field. But you heard him say, he was scared to death of the old man, and later we find out that he's staying with some of his mother's folks. Sure he didn't write to his parents for a while, but then Ed was never one to write. They said they didn't know where he was, but they knew all the time. Maybe they were all so scared that they thought that if he wrote his family, Liza would spread the word where he was and Bill Evans would find out and come after him. Well, who knows? But one thing I do know, is that Ed is no murderer."

"I'm going to have to be going," said Anna. "It's already dark, but at least there's a moon so I can see my way. Milly will probably be wondering where I am, but we didn't get to talk over the rest of the service."

"Oh, I'll keep it simple. There's really nothing to talk over. Thanks for coming by, and for saying you will play the piano. I didn't even bother to ask Florence Simms. She would turn me down anyway, and you can bet your bottom dollar that on Sunday she will complain because I didn't ask her. See if I'm not right," and he laughed.

"I'll see you tomorrow night a little before 7:30 then. Good-bye." And Anna headed home.

On Wednesday evening, Anna and Joshua arrived at Grace's a little before seven. She looked much better than she had the day before. Both she and Elaine were dressed and ready to go.

"I've put your clothes in my bedroom Joshua," she said as they arrived. "From now on you can sleep with me. You don't have to go upstairs."

The child nodded his head in approval, and soon was changed.

Bill Evans had hitched up the horse to the buggy, and in a few minutes they were off for the church. Milly and Peter had probably been waiting for them to leave, because shortly after, they heard the clatter of Belle's hooves.

They were the first to arrive at the churchyard, and made their way into the building which was lit with coal oil lamps, and warmed by the big wood stove in the back of the room. Rev. Blakeley greeted them as they entered, and suggested they sit in the front row. The coffin was resting on chairs in the front of the room. Naturally under the circumstances, it remained closed. Anna knew that Peter, Anders and Walter had brought it there about an hour ago. Luckily Milly never found out that it had been stored in her ice house.

Anna sat with Grace and the children until she would be called to play the organ. In about fifteen minutes Rev. Blakeley came to the front of the room, and the service began. As she turned to go to the organ she noticed there were more people there than she expected. Walter, she knew would come, but George and Lars were also there. Perhaps they wanted to see the final ending to the episode into which they had inadvertently stumbled. The Schmidts, who lived next to Jensen's and across from the Larson's came also. Esther Pearson and her husband were there. Esther had known Grace in school. Even Charley and Bill Wheeler were there. Matt and Liza sat near the back. Yes, she had forgotten. They were both basically good people, and staunch community supporters. There must have been nearly twenty people, twenty good people to come out to the evening funeral service for a man who had been civil to none of them. It was for Grace that they came.

The service was not long. They sang the first hymn and Rev. Blakeley read two psalms, the 23rd and the 100th. His remarks about Roger were not lengthy, as he knew very little about the man. He mentioned that Roger had been a Christian, and while his religion may have been different, it was not for them to criticize, but to understand, and now to support Grace and the children in their thoughts and deeds.

After the closing hymn everyone followed the pall bearers, Peter, Floyd, Walter, Anders, Olle Larson, and Frank Schmidt who carried the casket. They walked over to the cemetery, and Roger was laid to rest.

Grace remained almost in a trance during the entire time. She said very little to anyone, and people were kind enough to understand and not try to make conversation. Anna wondered if she would be all right after she got home, but she took the reins and almost with a sigh of relief, drove the distance back to her house.

"It's over," she said as they got out of the buggy. "It's really over. Thank you Anna for coming with us. I'll be fine now. Dad will unhitch the horse, and we'll go in and go to bed. I think that I could sleep for a week."

For the first time, Joshua spoke. "Was Dad really in that box?"

"Yes, Joshua, he was," Grace answered.

"You mean he's not coming back at all?"

"That's right. He's with the Lord now Joshua. You know he always talked about being with the Lord."

"But they put the box in the ground. And he's inside the box in the ground," the child continued.

"Yes," she answered, and seemed able to take control of the situation. "Come in Joshua. We'll talk about it in the house while we're getting ready for bed." And to Anna she gave her thanks for all Anna had done, and she opened the kitchen door and they went inside, while Anna made her way across the road to the Jensen's.

Chapter Twenty-eight

Anna was enjoying having the little children at school. They loved playing singing games as *The Farmer in the Dell* and *Go in and out the Window*. Mabel and Erica were superb assistants. On Thursday they helped the children learn two plays, *Little Red Riding Hood* and *The Three Bears*. Mabel rehearsed one while Erica rehearsed the other. The children chose the plays and fortunately there were the right number of parts for everyone. As Friday would be the last day of school they were planning to bring bits and pieces for costumes from home, and scheduled a performance for two o'clock, hoping that some of the mothers could attend.

As she walked home with Sarah, Mabel and Erica she was delighted at their youthful chatter about school and the fun they were having. She had almost forgotten about the Klosters and their problems until she saw their place. She decided to wait until she had visited with Milly before going over to see how Grace was. They saw the wagon in the yard and knew that Milly and Peter had unloaded another load and were no doubt in the house. Sarah ran up the steps to tell her parents all about the day's activities.

They opened the kitchen door to the usual smell of coffee. Milly and Peter were sitting and having a quick cup before going back into the field. "Here's your big school girl," said Anna. "You'd be surprised at what we've been doing."

"Yes," Sarah stated proudly. "We're doing a play and I get to be the mother bear, and, and we're going to do it tomorrow, and, and can you come Mother?" she added quickly.

"Well, I don't know about that. We'll have to check with your father."

"What time is this play?" he inquired.

"Two o'clock," said Anna. "I know this may be inconvenient. I think that most mothers will have to stay home and work."

"Can I go?" asked Davey who was playing on the other side of the room, but not missing out on a word of the conversation.

"I think you all can go," announced Peter, "even Lucy. Your mother has worked hard enough this week, and deserves a little time off."

"But Peter," Milly protested.

"We're coming along fine with the corn. It looks like I'll have the harvesting done in another week and everything finished by Thanksgiving. We shouldn't have snow before then, so I should make out all right. Yes, you go ahead. I'm sure that there will be other wives coming too, just happy to have an excuse to leave the chores."

"All right then," confirmed Milly. "We'll leave here about 1:30. Really Anna, I'm not sure I have been so much help to Peter. We do part of a row, and then I come in to see how Davey and Lucy are doing, and maybe start dinner. By the time I get back he has nearly finished the row and is ready to come in and unload the wagon."

"And get my cup of coffee. Don't forget that. I don't know what I would have done without you Milly," Peter said fondly. "No one can beat you for hard work. You deserve a week's vacation, and I'm only sorry that you can't have one."

"Oh, go on with you," she protested. "I don't do any more than anyone else."

"From what I have seen, you do a great deal more," Anna added. "And by the way I'm going to call Liza and see if a package has arrived for me."

"She phoned yust as I came in," Milly added quickly. "She said that one came for you in the afternoon mail."

"Oh, good!" Anna said enthusiastically. "I'll walk down and get it now, and look in on Grace on my way."

"What's in it?" asked Sarah.

"Sarah, you shouldn't ask questions like that," remonstrated her mother.

"Well, Sarah," said Anna with a gleam in her eye. "It just could be something for this Saturday. Let's see, what's happening this Saturday?"

"It's my birthday," Sarah happily announced.

"And Armistice Day," said her mother.

"Do people here celebrate Armistice Day?" asked Anna.

"No they don't," answered Peter. "We don't do anything special, but Milly and I remember it because it was the end of the war. Rev. Blakeley will mention it in church."

"And for Sarah to be born on the day that peace was declared is special," said Milly. "She was born almost at eleven o'clock, the time that the peace started, but we didn't hear about the peace until almost a week later. When we found out we were so proud that our Sarah was born on that day. That's why we think of it, but I guess most farm families don't."

"I think that farmers have too much to do about this time of year, that all they can think of is getting the crops in, and speaking of that, I'd better see to my own crops." With that Peter was out the door and on his way to the field again.

"And on Saturday," Milly continued excitedly, "we will have a birthday cake for Sarah. In Swedish it is called a fodelsekaka. Then all afternoon we will have coffee and cake and cookies and people can come and wish Sarah a happy birthday. Oh look at you Sarah," said Milly as she patted her daughter's head. "You are so tired. Go up to your bed and take a little rest."

"I'm not tired," the child exclaimed.

"Then yust a little rest, a little rest, that is all," said Milly as she took Sarah by the hand and led her upstairs. "Then when Lucy wakes up, you can get up too."

"Would you like to walk to town with me Davey?" asked Anna, who felt that the boy might like some exercise after being fairly cooped up all day.

"Oh, yes," he quickly replied.

"Then go upstairs and ask your mother."

In less than five minutes both were on their way out. "I want to stop at the Klosters before we go to town, but it won't take long. Perhaps Joshua will be there and you can talk to him." Davey thought this was a great idea and ran down the roadway. Soon they were knocking on the Kloster's kitchen

237

door. Anna knocked a second time, and still no answer. Finally she opened it a crack and called, "Hello Grace. It's Anna and Davey. Are you home?"

Grace came out of the bedroom slowly. Joshua was with her. Elaine was probably napping. "Oh, it's you Anna. I'm glad to see you. Hello Davey. I've told Joshua not to answer the door. I don't feel like talkin' to anyone, except people like you Anna," she quickly added.

"I understand Grace," replied Anna. "I came to see how you are, and if there's anything I can do. I'm on my way to Grabney to the Post Office."

"Oh, we're fine. I'm still not feelin' too well."

"That's to be expected. You've had a terrible shock. You should take it easy for at least a week or two."

"Sometimes I feel like I should be out helpin' Dad. He's workin' like a madman. Won't even come in for coffee. Works from dawn to dark, and often after dark. He gets mad so easy too. This morning I heard him swearin' at the horses and beatin' them with the reins. I guess they didn't move fast enough, or maybe too fast. I don't know what to do."

"Can't he hire someone to help him? I know that the men who were digging the grave were looking for work," Anna said.

"Not my dad," and she shook her head. "He refuses to hire anyone. Insists on doing it all himself. He won't listen to reason, and there's nothin' I can do. I think he's behavin' this way so I will come out and work, but I don't feel well enough to work. And I know if I did come out, he'd yell at me too. I've had that happen before, too many times."

"Can I get anything at the store for you? I brought Davey, and he's good for carrying something," Anna continued.

"I don't like to trouble you, you've done so much."

"It's no trouble at all," Anna replied firmly.

"Well, we're out of bread. If you could get two loaves, and I could use some cheese." She thought a moment before continuing. "It would be nice to have some sausage because we're out of meat. Rev. Blakeley came by today with nearly thirty dollars. He said that Anders didn't charge much to make the casket, so he returned what he had left from the fifty dollars, so I have some money."

"That's wonderful. I'll be happy to get these things for you?"

"Maybe Joshua could go with you. Would you like to go to Grabney with them Joshua?"

The child was almost stupefied at this question, and finally answered, "Yes. Oh, yes."

"He hasn't been to Grabney for a long time," said Grace mentally reflecting on the past. "And he's been cooped up all day and it would do him good to get out. Dad's also mad 'cause I won't let Joshua work with him, but Dad gets so mean. It's too much for a boy."

"I agree with you Grace, and we'd be happy to have Joshua come with us." Anna thought that this was a splendid idea, since the child had seldom had a chance to get out anywhere except to school. Now he and Davey could walk to town together.

"Just a minute. I have a muslin bag that my mother made for carryin' home groceries," and she rummaged through a kitchen cupboard until she found it. Looking at it sadly, she told them, "I remember walkin' to town with my mother. She always carried this bag. She said it was easier than carryin' a paper sack. We haven't used it for years. I don't know when was the last time I walked to town. And anyway, I'm not too sure I'd be welcome at the store." She looked quite downcast and stared at the floor. "There's just too much has happened lately. First my thinkin' Roger's left us, then findin' out he's dead, an' the funeral, an' then, oh I can't stop thinkin' of it all." She slowly walked to the rocking chair and slumped into it.

Anna thought she was going to cry, "Yes, it's been terrible for you, but you'll come through it all right."

"Sometimes, I don't know," came her answer. "Everything has changed now."

"Well, for a start you have two wonderful children, and keeping busy is a good way to get over something like this. That's what my mother said when my father died, and she had to keep busy to support us. Some day when you feel like it, why don't you walk to town with me. It might do you good.

Anyway, Joshua let's get your coat on. We need to hurry so we can get home before dark." He quickly put on his coat, and took the muslin bag from his mother. Grace gave Anna the money and they were out the door and on their way to Grabney.

The air had become colder since school was out, and they hurried along the path which led to the river. Anna was worried for fear Joshua would not want to walk that way, and he did start running when they came to where the path met the river pathway, the place where Roger had been digging the post holes. Davey quickly caught up with him and they slowed down. She could hear Bill Evans working a row fairly near her, and suddenly they were eye to eye. He looked haggard, gave her a sneer and continued, grabbing the back of the wagon from time to time as he puffed and struggled to tear each ear from the stalk and throw it into the wagon. Perhaps that was why Joshua had run, to avoid his grandfather.

At the Post Office she told the boys to wait outside while she went in. Liza Crawford was obviously eager for news. "How're things goin' out your way Anna?" she inquired.

"Just fine Liza," Anna answered. "I'm here to get the package my mother sent."

"Here it is," and she handed Anna a small parcel. "Might as well take the mail too. There's a letter for Peter."

"Thanks," replied Anna, and she turned to go.

"How's Grace doin'?" came the expected question. "Can't say as we liked Roger, but Grace's lived here all her life, an' Matt and I feel sorry for her. We used to know her as a little girl. What she and her mother had to put up with I can't begin to tell you."

"Yes. I've heard about it, but then I think Grace will make out all right," answered Anna. "In fact Joshua is here with Davey and me. I'm so pleased that he could walk to the store with us. Grace needed some things, so he was sent to carry them home. I am worried about one thing though, and so is Grace?"

"Oh, what's that?" and her curiosity was piqued.

"Bill Evans is working terribly hard. I saw him on our way here and he looks haggard. Grace worries that she should be out helping him, but Dr. Bailey told her to stay inside and take care of herself."

"Bill Evans is a stubborn ol' coot," Liza confided. "And Grace shouldn't go out at all. Doc Bailey's right. And I'll bet my bottom dollar that Bill won't hire anybody to help him. He'd rather die harvestin' that dratted corn than pay someone else to do it for him."

"You're right Liza," said Anna as she reached the door. "And the sad thing is that there's nothing that any of us can do about it. Thank you for the package and the mail," she said surprised that Liza hadn't asked her what was in the parcel. "By the way, the package is an apron my mother made for Sarah for her birthday, which is Saturday." Having imparted this piece of information, she left for the store with Davey and Joshua, knowing that at least she had contributed something to Liza's day.

"Hello Mr. Marson," said Anna as they entered the store. "You remember Grace's boy, don't you?"

"Been a long time since I seen you. Joshua ain't it?" the man inquired.

"Yes," the boy answered solemnly.

Anna caught sight of Vi Marson dashing up the steps to their living quarters. "Grace needs some bread, two loaves if you have it?" she asked.

"As I recall she likes white bread, and I have two loaves. Anything else?"

"Yes some cheese, and some sausage," Anna continued. "Joshua has a bag to put them in." Joshua handed the bag to Elmer.

He paused and looked at it for a few seconds. "I ain't seen that bag for a long time. I remember that your granny made it and she and your mom used to walk to town to buy groceries. Your granny was a lovely lady Joshua. It's good to see her bag again." Elmer was quick to get the items. "Now I'm puttin' the cheese and sausage in the bottom, 'cause they're heavier, and the bread on top. Don't be shiftin' them around or you'll squash the bread. Got that now?"

Joshua took the bag and nodded.

Anna paid for them, and asked Davey to choose which kind of candy Sarah would like for her party. He chose gum drops, so Anna bought a bag of them, giving some to each boy, and then told them to go on ahead. Anna and Elmer were then alone.

"I'm sorry that Vi ran upstairs," said Elmer. "She feels so bad about when the sheriff came here the other day. She ran up when she saw Joshua. It's not the boy's fault. Poor kid."

"I was over at the Blakeley's when Ed came over on Tuesday. Tell Vi not to worry. I'm sure things will turn out all right. No one believes that Ed had anything to do with it."

"He never should have got mixed up with that girl in the first place. Ma and I knowed that she was trouble but Ed wouldn't listen. Now look at what's happened. I blame myself. I should'a took the posthole digger over there myself."

"You can't blame yourself," came Anna's reply. "And tell Ed not to worry."

"He's upstairs with Ma now. He don't want to see no one. Can't blame him neither. Well here comes Joe Pearson."

She took this as a signal to make her exit. "Good-bye Elmer. And be sure and tell Vi hello from me."

"I'll do that. Hello Joe, what'll it be today?"

Anna hurried to catch up with the boys. It was getting dark and she was anxious to get home. When they arrived at Grace's she handed back the purse and inspected the bag of food to make sure the bread was still in good shape. Satisfied, she decided to broach a new subject. "Tomorrow at school the little children will be putting on a play. We're inviting the mothers. It'll be at two o'clock. If you and the children would like to come we would love to have you."

"Oh, I don't think so Anna," said Grace.

"Well then, Sarah's birthday is Saturday. Maybe you and the children would like to stop by in the afternoon for coffee and cake."

"Thanks Anna. I just don't know," replied Grace in a lifeless tone. Then seeing Joshua look up at her with a pleading expression on his face she added, "I'll think about it."

"We'll be going, then. But do think about it. Good-bye to all of you."

"Joshua didn't say too much," said Davey as they crossed the road. "But he told me that he didn't like to stay in the house all day. I told him that I didn't either."

"Well, it will soon be over, and then you and he can both be back in school."

As Friday afternoon approached, Anna felt quite apprehensive. At two o'clock she was most surprised to see Milly, Davey and Lucy accompanied by Joshua and Elaine. It seems that Milly had gone over there in the morning and invited them to walk with her. Grace still didn't feel she wanted to venture out, but relented and let the children come. In the next few minutes Hilma Anderson arrived, and after that several more mothers. Each one had brought some cookies. It was to be a real party.

The plays went well, with the usual bits of improvisation, plus extra coaching given in stage whispers from Mabel and Erica. Harvey Johnson was the wolf and his younger brother Algot the hunter. When it came time for the hunter to fight the wolf, they nearly had a real fight until Elsa, who was the grandmother, came out and told them to stop. *The Three Bears* also went well, with Sarah a proud Mother Bear. Cookies were served and everyone had a good time. As they left the mothers thanked Anna for giving the children such a special week, and for giving them some freedom. As she sat down at her desk to get ready for the next week, Anna was pleased that she had taken on this extra chore. It had worked out well.

Saturday afternoon the house was full of excitement. Milly had baked the standard birthday cake, or fodelsekaka. It was made of a bread dough, cut into strips and put in a large rectangular baking pan, (with the strips making a design), brushed with milk, and sprinkled with sugar and cinnamon. Milly had also made plenty of cookies and of course had coffee. Anna contributed the gum drops. There was milk for the children. If it had been summer she might have bought lemons and made lemonade.

Everyone was dressed in their best, except Peter who was still working on the corn. Walter had driven Inger over. Her ankle was much better, but definitely not completely healed, so she reluctantly sat in the rocking chair and let herself be waited on. Mabel came with her, but the men would be over later. They gave a present to Sarah, who shyly said her thanks.

"Open it now," said her aunt. "Might as well get it over with. Come on now! Hurry up!"

Sarah slowly undid the brown wrapping paper, tied with string. Inside was a little box which she opened carefully to reveal a shiny silver teaspoon. "It's a spoon. Is it just for me?"

"Of course it's just for you," came Inger's answer. "And each birthday I'll give you another one or maybe a fork or a knife, and by the time you are ready to get married you'll have almost a whole set."

"Do I get to eat with it now?" Sarah asked.

"No, you get to put it away and save it," answered her mother. "That way when you get married you will have beautiful new silver. Oh, Inger it is lovely, and such a pretty pattern."

"Well I hope she will like the pattern. I thought it was nice, and Mabel liked it too," came Inger's comment. "In fact it's almost like the one that Mabel has. We didn't want to get them the same — too confusing for family dinner parties in sorting out the silver afterwards."

"What do you tell your Aunt Inger, Sarah?" Milly asked the child.

"Thank you," came the answer, and she put it carefully on the table, still staring at it.

"Put it back in the box, with the lid on the bottom, so everyone can see it," Inger directed. "Oh, Anna, will you show her how to do it?" Anna immediately did as she was instructed and the spoon was put back on the table.

"Here, I'll cut the first piece for you Inger," said Milly as she put her knife into the cake and took out a corner piece which she put on a plate and gave to her sister. The festivities had begun.

Anna went upstairs and brought her gift for Sarah. The child carefully opened it, and was puzzled at its contents until Anna told her that it was an apron for her, and under it was one to match for her doll. She was delighted and had to put it on, then ran to get her doll and do the same. "When did you have time to make that Anna?" asked Milly.

"You can see that I didn't make it because it is sewed by machine. I asked my mother to do it. She had written and asked if there was anything that she could do for me. I told her

Sarah's size, and I can see that it just fits." Anna was as pleased as Sarah.

Davey gave Sarah a pencil, and told her not to lose it. Before long they were all eating cake and cookies, when Grace and her two children appeared at the door. "Come in! Come in!" said Milly as she welcomed them. "I am so glad you came. Let me take your coats. Davey you put the coats on my bed," and she handed Grace's coat to him, while she helped take Elaine's and Joshua's. "Sit down and have some cake and cookies, and let me pour you a cup of coffee."

"I brought a little present for Sarah," Grace said in a self-conscious fashion. "I didn't have any paper to wrap it in," and she held out her gift to the child.

"Oh, you shouldn't have done that," Milly exclaimed. "You have enough to worry about without having to worry about presents."

Sarah took the gift which was a pretty handkerchief. She held it up for everyone to see.

"It was one that my mother had, but she never used it. It's still like new. I thought that it would be nice to give it to Sarah," Grace explained.

"Oh, that makes it even more special," said Milly. "Sarah you will have to take good care of that pretty hankie."

"Yes, I will. I will put it in my drawer right now."

"Wait until later, Sarah," advised her mother. "Daddy and Uncle Floyd would like to see it. Put it on the table next to the spoon."

Erica and Sylvia Larson were the next to arrive. They brought Sarah some dried flowers which they had grown in their garden. "That is yust like in Sweden," Milly exclaimed.

"In Sweden I always remember that people got flowers on their birthday."

"Do you know how old you are?" Erica asked Sarah.

"Four", said the smiling child as she held up four fingers.

"And we brought you four flowers, one for each year. Can you count them?"

As she counted the flowers, everyone counted silently with her, and smiled proudly at her after she finished doing it correctly.

It was a grand afternoon. Coffee cups were never left empty and there seemed to be an endless supply of cookies. The children were allowed to play in the parlor, (if it had been an adult birthday they would have had their coffee in there). Peter, Floyd, Walter and George came later and added to the hilarity. It was at that time that Milly gave Sarah the present from her and Peter. Sarah looked wide-eyed at what her mother brought into the room. It was a pretty dress that Milly had made. "You are growing so fast that you need a new dress for Sunday," was her mother's comment. She held it up to the child, and it fit perfectly, with ample room to last through the winter and spring.

Chapter Twenty-nine

For the second Sunday in a row it was a congregation of women and children as the men and older boys stayed home to continue with the harvesting. Many school districts had two weeks off for fall harvest, but the folks in Grabney felt it wasn't necessary as most of the extra help came from older students and they had two weeks off from the high school in the county seat.

It was now common knowledge that Roger's body had been found and that the funeral had been held Wednesday night. Mrs. Simms let everyone know that of course she was too exhausted from cooking for the harvest crew to possibly play for the service, not realizing that so few people attended that she needn't have bothered with an explanation. Others commented that they would never go to a service for "that dreadful man". "So much for Christian charity," Anna thought as they climbed into the buggy and headed for home.

They waved to Peter as they came into the yard. "When he knows it's time for dinner he always manages to be close to the house," and Milly laughed at the thought. She had put the meal in the oven to cook while they were at church so it was ready, and it didn't take long to get the table set.

Soon they could hear Peter's footsteps as he came up the stairs, then the scraping of mud off his boots on the boot-scraper on the wide top step. "Just let me wash some of this dirt off," he exclaimed as he entered the kitchen, "and I'll be ready to eat. Don't know why, but I'm starving." At the sink he lathered his hands and arms well with the homemade soap, rinsed them, splashed water on his face and neck, and dried off on a towel Milly had waiting for him. "Sure is good to come in for a decent meal. It's times like this that I know why I married Milly," he joked as he winked at her.

"A working man needs good food I always say," commented his practical wife.

"It seems that you cook two dinners a day Milly," added Anna. "I know that most farm families have their main meal at noon, and only a supper at night."

"Huh!" she exclaimed. "Some people don't know how to feed their folks right. We may call it supper at night, but we never leave the table hungry."

"That's for darn sure," added Peter.

"Why I could tell you of some folks around here who have a scanty supper at night, but not us. I don't believe in it," she firmly announced. "Inger doesn't either."

Anna reminisced, "I knew of one girl who taught in eastern Iowa and she said that the family where she lived had their dinner at noon, while she had only bread and cheese, or maybe a peanut butter and jelly sandwich at school. Then at night they would eat leftovers or something light. She didn't get enough to eat, but wouldn't say so. She even lost weight."

"That's terrible," Milly said. "Everyone needs three good meals a day, especially Peter. And I don't see any fat on him. I'm the one who has the fat," and she giggled.

"Not too fat for me," smiled Peter. "You're just right." They laughed as they sat down at the table. Grace was said, plates were filled and the dinner began.

"I suppose church was filled with talk about Roger and the funeral," commented Peter.

"Yes, but let's not spoil a Sunday dinner by talking about him," Milly nervously replied. "I don't even want to think about it. Poor George and Lars, finding the body. Oh, quick! Let's talk about something else, something pleasant. Who can think of something fun?"

"I know something that would be fun," Davey interjected. "Dad, can we play in the ice house sometime? Can we, please?"

"In the ice house?" questioned his mother. "That's not a place to play. Besides you are in your good clothes, and it's Sunday. And Sarah is wearing her new dress."

"But we could change clothes," he suggested.

"And come in all dirty, I suppose," his father added. "No, Davey, one dirty person in the family is enough for a Sunday. Besides I want to look it over, maybe clean it out a little more before I let anyone go in, just to make sure I did it right. I don't want anyone in there yet."

"I already looked in there and I think it looks fine," he added.

"When did you do that?" asked his father, who had gone to great lengths to make sure Milly and the children were unaware that Roger's body had been stored in the ice house. (Anna glanced at him and guessed at his thoughts.) Fortunately it was behind the barn so it wasn't visible from the house. Milly must have been busy in the house when the men came to examine the body and when the coffin was brought. She had made the comment to Anna that she supposed all the men congregated at their place because it wasn't pleasant to stay at the Kloster's with a dead body there. Anna had purposely kept her occupied when it was carried out to the church. Perhaps Milly knew and was not admitting to it. Anyway Peter wanted to look the place over before anyone of the family went into it, just to make sure there were no signs of what it had contained during part of the past week.

"Dad! Are you listening to me?" Davey asked.

"Sure Davey," and Peter roused himself to attention.

"Well, I went into the ice house one day when Lucy was having her nap."

Before Peter could say anything, Milly added, "I think it's too dark for a playhouse."

"We could have a candle," suggested Davey.

"No! No! Candles might start a fire. And no ice house for a playhouse. That is an ice house and it is to be used for only that." With these words from Milly the discussion ended much to the relief of both Peter and Anna. "So now, what else can we talk about."

"I have something to talk about," added Anna. "I have saved almost enough S & H Green Trading Stamps for my Kodak Brownie camera, and tomorrow I am going to walk to Grabney after school, and buy something at the store that will give me enough stamps to fill my book. What do you think of that?"

"Oh Anna, that is wonderful," said Milly excitedly. "I think we could buy some things at the store, so you could have those stamps. Oh yes, I could use some sugar, and maybe some flour, and . . ."

She was interrupted by Peter who replied with a wink, "And you think that Anna can carry things like that home?"

"Oh, I forgot, they are too heavy. But maybe I could get something else. Or Anna could take the buggy. Or better yet, I would like to go to the store too. Could we take the buggy Peter? It would be so much fun. We could all go."

"Now just slow down Milly," he laughed. "Of course you can take the buggy. I can manage fine with one horse for awhile. But Anna, don't let her buy out the whole store. Just because we got the money from selling the hogs doesn't mean that she has to spend it, not in one afternoon anyway."

"I already know what I want to buy," stated Anna with a smile. "So Milly won't have to get any flour or sugar for me."

"Can we all go to the store?" Sarah inquired.

"Sure thing," said her father. "And I guess I'd better give Elmer a call to tell him to get the Green Stamps ready."

After school on Monday they piled into the buggy and headed for the store. As they pulled out of the yard they looked over at the farm across the way and could see Bill Evans harvesting in a frenzy. He looked exhausted. He had done about half of his crop with the fence still not mended so he couldn't turn the cattle in that field. Milly shook her head at the sight. "Sylvia Larson told me that one of her boys had volunteered to help, but Evans said he couldn't afford to pay anyone and he certainly wouldn't accept charity."

"It seems the man is half crazy," added Anna. "And I'm sure that he isn't easy to live with. I feel sorry for Grace and Joshua."

"If he would only be reasonable, he would use some of the money he got for the hogs and pay someone to help him. That way he could get in his crop. As it is now, he may lose half of it. Then where will he be?" Milly shook her head in disgust as she headed up the road.

At the store Davey jumped out and tied Ginger up to the railing. Sarah was next, then Anna. Milly handed Lucy to Anna before she climbed down. The children saw that Elmer was at the gas pump filling up a car and so dashed over there to see this amazing new contraption at work. Anna and Milly with Lucy made their way into the store. Vi was behind the counter, but Ed was nowhere to be seen. Anna was glad to see Vi back in the store again, hoping that she would feel she needn't hide from everyone.

"Hello Vi," she said.

"Oh, it's you Anna, and Milly. Seems with the new gas pump I have to spend more and more time in the store. What can I do for you?"

"Well," Milly spoke up quickly," Anna wants to fill up her Green Trading Stamp book so she can get a Kodak Brownie camera."

"Oh a camera," said Vi as her face lit up. "How many more stamps do you need."

"I think I have calculated it right," said Anna." If I buy two of your china teacups and saucers I should have enough. I want them as Christmas presents for my mother and sister. I know it's early to buy Christmas gifts, but this way I will have the camera before Christmas, and I can take pictures of Milly and the family and take them home and show my relatives."

"Oh Anna," Milly blushed. "You don't want a photo of me. Oh my goodness!"

The door opened and Elmer Marson entered, with Davey and Sarah tagging after him. "Well now, let me get this money in the till, and I'll be ready to help one of you ladies," he said as he ambled behind the counter. "Well Mother, which one do you want me to help?"

"Anna wants a Kodak Brownie with her Green Stamps," Vi informed him, "and she wants to buy two cups and saucers so she can fill up her book."

"I guess you better help her then, Mother, and I'll wait on these two youngsters here."

"Not me," said Sarah. "It's my mother who buys the things."

"Gosh, guess I made a mistake," Elmer teasingly acknowledged. "Well then Milly, what is it today?" Milly started giving her order while Vi and Anna walked over to the front window where the cups were displayed.

"I saw two that I like," Anna said as she reached to point out the pieces that she wanted.

"Not those," said Vi following Anna and shaking her head. "They are too dusty. I have some in boxes in the back room that are fresh. Let's go back there." Anna followed Vi as they wound their way through the store around shelves and tables into the store room, where they found Ed sorting through stock which had come in on the afternoon train. He nodded to them, but kept on with his work.

"Where's the china dishes Ed?"

"I put them up on the shelf over there," he pointed with his head, " so's they wouldn't get broke. We got so much stock in here that it'll take me all night to go through it. I don't know what it'll be like when we get the shoes from Jarvis."

"Are you going to start selling shoes?' Anna asked in surprise.

"We sure are," Ed replied. "Dad said that Jack is setting up a shop in the back of one of the dry goods stores in the county seat, and he wants to start one here."

"You mean in your store?"

"That's right."

"How can he run two stores? Is he going to stay in Grabney?" Anna looked at both Ed and Vi for an answer.

Ed sat down on a packing case. "I guess Ma gets to run our shoe store. You see Jack figures that if he sets up a place for his shoes here, then he won't have to traipse all around the country. I don't blame him."

"Well he 'n Dad got to talkin' the other day," Vi added, "and that's what they figured out. Once Dad got the gas pump, he's been hot to expand. I hope he knows what he's doin'. He said he's goin' to put up some shelves for the shoes in the front of the store, get a coupla' seats for people to sit on to try on the shoes, and if what we have in stock don't fit, we can call Jack and get the right size out on the next train. He says he'll keep a big stock in the county seat, enough to fill most orders. I'll be happy to help the ladies try on shoes, but I ain't helpin' no men what with their dirty feet."

Ed smiled at this. "Yup, Ma said she's goin' to put her foot down when it comes to tryin' on shoes." He laughed at his own joke, as did the other two, but somehow Anna sensed that this was a forced laughter. She was pleased to see him in a somewhat jovial mood, although his conversation seemed stilted. The last time she saw him was Tuesday at the Blakeley's and at that time he was desperately frightened. Perhaps there was no longer any suspicion of his having anything to do with Roger Kloster's death. Anyway it must have been a terrible shock to him to be singled out by the sheriff. It would probably take a long time before he got over it. She tried to think of something to keep up her end of the conversation.

"When you call this a general store, you really mean it," she said. "It seems to me you have a little bit of everything."

"What Dad doesn't seem to realize, is that it's going to mean a lot more work for all of us," Vi said. "But here now, let's go find those tea cups," and she made her way to the shelves Ed had indicated. "What kind did you want Anna?"

"I liked the one with roses, and another one with violets."

"You want the red or yellow roses?"

"The yellow roses if you have one."

Vi stood on a stool and poked around among the boxes.

"Here, I think I've found what you want," and she handed two boxes to Anna. "Let's open them up and see if they're right."

The women checked the contents, and they met with Anna's satisfaction. "Just perfect," Anna replied. "Now I was also wondering if you had any more cake plates. I don't want one now, maybe later. I saw one in the window a month or so ago, and it was so pretty."

"Oh that was hand painted by a lady in Brewster. She does beautiful work. I know she'd be happy to paint one for you. We told her we'd put one up in the window so she could take orders."

"How would I get hold of her?" asked Anna. "As I said, I don't want it now, but maybe later on. I was kind of thinking of it as a Christmas present for Milly."

253

"Milly would love that," Vi continued. "I can't think of anything she would like more. The woman who does the painting is Olga Clemson. She's Bertha's mother. You might of met Bertha at the dance."

Suddenly it dawned on Anna that Bertha was the young lady that Ed had brought to the dance. "I remember seeing Bertha, but I don't think that I met her."

"If you decide what you want, let me know. Ed can take the order over for you."

"That's Ma, always makin' plans for me," Ed remarked as he came from behind a stack of boxes. "Sure, Bertha's mother will be happy to paint another plate. You should see her house. The whole place is full of hand painted china. Let me know and I'll be glad to take her another order."

"Thanks Ed. I'll think about it. Let's take these cups and saucers out front. I think Milly will wonder what happened to us. She probably has her order all filled."

As Vi and Anna walked up to the counter they could see that Milly had indeed collected all the things she wanted. She and the children were standing visiting with Elmer. "Now let's see," he commented. "I'd write up this order if I could find my spectacles."

The children giggled and Davey said, "They're on the top of your head."

"Well, whata ya know," Elmer remarked as he put his right hand up to find them. "Sure enough they are. I keep thinkin' I'm losin' 'em, but they's most always on top a my head," and he laughed and winked at the children who joined in the fun. "A feller can't lose his specs in my business. Well, now I'll just get this written up an' then we'll load up the wagon and you can be on yer way."

After Anna had paid Vi for the cups and saucers, she carefully licked the green stamps and stuck them into her book. The children watched with fascination. "While you're getting things into the wagon I'll run over to the Post Office and mail in my order," she announced.

"See if there's any mail for us," called Milly as Anna went out the door.

"I'll get it if Floyd hasn't beat me to it," she called back. She hurried across the road, up the steps, and into the building where she saw Thelma Blakeley opening her box.

"Hello Anna," called Liza. "You here to collect the mail?"

"Hello Liza. Hello Mrs. Blakeley. I'm here to get the mail, but also to mail in my Green Trading Stamps book so I can get a Kodak Brownie camera. Can you weigh this Liza to see how much postage I need?" and she handed the thick brown envelope to the Postmistress.

"Just a coupla extra stamps will do it," said Liza as she took the parcel off the scale, and quickly the transaction was completed.

"I noticed you were over at the store," commented Mrs. Blakeley. "How are things going over there?"

"They seem fine," answered Anna.

"I hope that Vi is back at the counter. She seemed to take it so hard when the sheriff talked to Ed. I feel sorry for her, poor soul."

"She's back helping in the store for sure," replied Anna. "With the gas pump out front Elmer spends part of his time there, so she's needed in the store. She seemed to be almost like her old self."

"I hope so. Maybe we can now forget about the Klosters and their problems," said Mrs. Blakeley as she turned to go.

"There's somethin' that keeps botherin' me," Liza said with a thoughtful hesitation, unusual for her. Both women turned in her direction. "Well, what I mean is, I remember seein' Ed carry the posthole digger out of the store and head across the bridge."

"Yes," said Mrs. Blakeley rather matter of factly, as of course Liza would be the one to see anyone going anywhere.

"But I heard that he said he come back through your yard."

"Yes, he said that he stayed to make sure that Roger was not going to hurt Grace any more, and then he cut through the field to our place and went on home," Mrs. Blakeley continued.

"Well, I remember that it was gettin' dark, about supper time, and I remembered that I had to take in the clothes. You see I didn't get the wash finished until late on Monday, so's I hung the clothes out on Tuesday, bein' a nice day an' all.

Well I go out the front door here an' see that hired hand of the Pearsons jus' comin' out of the store. He never comes to town 'cept to buy tobacco, but he asked me if he could pick up their mail. So I goes back inside and gets it for him, and tell him he better hurry so's to make it in time for supper since he's got about three miles to walk."

"What does this have to do with Ed?" asked Anna.

"I'm comin to that," Liza continued. "Well I go around the depot to get to the back yard, sort of interested in seein' how fast that young man high tailed it for home, an' I see him makin' good time. I get busy with the clothes, and then I look up and see someone hurryin' down the river path. I thought maybe he was comin' back 'cause he forgot somethin', but it wasn't the Pearson's man. It was Ed."

"How do you know it was Ed?" asked Mrs. Blakeley. "As I was carryin' in the clothes I saw him continue down the path, cross the bridge and go into the store. An' then I knew of course it was Ed. He was jus' comin' home for supper, and hurryin' so Vi wouldn't be madder'n a hornet 'cause he was late. So I didn't give it another thought, until yesterday at church. That's when I heard that he said he had cut through your place."

"Maybe he cut down to the path from the picnic ground," Mrs. Blakeley contemplated.

"Could be," Liza answered, "but I'm sure that he didn't come from the picnic ground, 'cause if he had then he would have made a short cut across the field, and he didn't do that. Anyways I've known Ed since he was a little shaver an' he wouldn't do nothin' wrong. But why would he say somethin' was true when it wasn't?"

"I think he was so upset about what happened at the Kloster's that he couldn't think straight," Anna added. "He may have thought he went all the way to the Blakeley's."

"Oh dear!" Mrs. Blakeley sighed. "I suppose I'll have to tell my husband about this. Maybe it's important and maybe not. Anyway, he'll know what to do, but it scares me. It doesn't look too good for Ed. Someone else could have seen him coming down the path, like that hired hand of the Pearsons. I guess there's more to be done before this is cleared up. I can't believe that Ed had anything to do with the murder but I'm sure

Bill Evans will never rest until someone is found guilty, and the pity is that someone is guilty. It's obvious that Roger didn't kill himself."

"What about the Pearson's hired man?" asked Anna. "Could he have done it?"

"Him!" Liza sneered. "I don't want to say nothin' bad about him, but he don't have enough nerve. He walks around bein' half-scared all the time."

"Yes, I've met him. He's a very timid soul," added Mrs. Blakeley.

"That's a nice way to put it," laughed Liza. "I must say that you always have a nice way of putting things." The jangling ring of the phone startled them, and Liza went quickly to answer it. "Yes Bill," they heard her say. "You want me to contact the sheriff?————Speak slower, I can't understand you.————Yes, I'll do that.————I'll ring the county seat now and see if they can locate him.————What message do you want me to deliver?————You want him to come here right away.————You say you know who killed Roger?————————And you want him to do his duty and arrest————who?————Ed Marson!"

Chapter Thirty

Anna walked across the street to the store in shock. Milly and the children were laughing as Elmer helped them load their bundles into the wagon. She climbed in last and as the others were waving and calling to Elmer, Milly started up Ginger and headed for home. "You're mighty quiet Anna," Milly remarked half joking. "Cat got your tongue?"

"Uh, no Milly. I just heard some bad news." She looked and saw that the children were still waving and laughing so could not hear her. "When I was at the Post Office just now, Bill Evans asked Liza to put through a call to the sheriff. He said that he knows who killed Roger, and that is was Ed Marson."

"Oh that man is yust plain crazy," Milly commented. "I don't see how he can know such a thing."

"It still worries me," Anna commented. "I'll tell you more when we get home. The children have settled down now and I don't want them to hear."

"You watch Lucy and don't let her fall down the stairs Davey," Milly yelled at the children who had gone up to their rooms to play. "So now, let's sit down and have a cup of coffee. Good! I hear Peter. He probably saw us coming in."

"I see you got the wagon unloaded without my help," he joked as he came into the kitchen. "Floyd stopped by and said that the cornshellers are coming tomorrow. Lucky I've got a good enough crop to sell some. After they're through here they're going to Floyd's where they'll have a real job. Say, what's with you two? Here I am saying that we're going to make some money this year and you look like you lost your last nickel." He walked to the sink, cleaned up, and sat down at the table.

Milly poured the strong black coffee and put some cookies on a plate. "Anna heard some bad news Peter, about Bill Evans calling the sheriff. He says it was Ed Marson who killed Roger."

"I'm sure Jim Wilson won't take that seriously," was Peter's comment. "That old man has never liked Ed, and probably has some far-fetched idea he's trying to spring."

"I also learned from Liza that Ed didn't go through to the Blakeley's place as he claimed," Anna added. "Liza saw him coming down the river path."

"What does that old gossip know?" he chided. "And anyway it was nearly dark, and how could she see way across the river?"

"I think it's serious Peter," Milly commented.

"Maybe so. Anyway, we'll let Jim Wilson sort this out. So turn off your glum faces and let's celebrate. The crop is nearly in. What's left can go in the corn cribs and there's plenty to keep the hogs happy this winter. I'll start on the silage as soon as next week maybe, and I've finished with the south field so I'm turning the cows and hogs in there tomorrow."

"Well, then," Milly said decisively, "We'll yust have to wait and see what happens."

Twenty-four hours were to go by before they heard any news. It was during supper on Tuesday that there was a knock on the back door. Peter went to answer it and was surprised to see Jim Wilson. "Sorry to bother you during supper," he said as he removed his hat and came inside the room. "It seems that there has been a new development. I've been investigating it all day, and now I have to go back to the Evans' place and take down a statement from Bill. I need two witnesses and wondered Peter if you and Anna would be willing to help out. I thought Milly would just as soon stay home with the children." Her nod affirmed this.

"Of course Jim," Peter answered. "What about you Anna?"

"Yes, I'll come," she replied and wondered what she was getting herself into.

"Finish your supper first," he said.

"Oh, what about you? Have you had your supper?" Milly asked.

"Can't say as I have, but then don't worry about me. A cup of coffee will do."

"Nonsense," came Milly's stern reply. "You yust sit down there and I'll dish up a plate for you. There's plenty of food, and no one is going to leave my house hungry. Here's a cup. Peter pour him some coffee."

"That's mighty nice of you Milly," Jim said as he gratefully sat down in the chair offered him. "It has been a long time since I've eaten. This will also give me a chance to tell you what's been going on, and I must say I appreciate having a break from what I've had to go through this afternoon."

"Davey you and Sarah hurry and finish now and go upstairs," their Mother ordered. "You can work on your arithmetic Davey, and Sarah can play with her doll and get ready for bed." Soon Jim was digging gratefully into the hearty meal which Milly placed before him, and before long the children had left the table and were upstairs.

"I'm sure you're anxious to hear what's been happening," the sheriff volunteered. "I have to take seriously what Bill Evans has told me, because he may have a case. Oh, of course you don't know what he has told me," he apologized.

"If it's all right with you I'll try to talk and eat at the same time."

"Take your time Jim," Peter said. "We're in no rush."

"Well, I said I'd get back there as soon as I could, so I shouldn't delay too long. I guess you know that Bill had Liza Crawford call me yesterday. I understand Anna was in the Post Office when the call came in."

"Yes I was," said Anna, surprised that he knew this information.

"I arrived in Grabney about 11 o'clock this morning and first went to check with Liza. She seemed reluctant to talk to me, which was strange I must say, her being so talkative all the time. I soon learned the reason why when she explained that she saw Ed Marson walking down the path across the river, and not through the Blakeley place as he claimed."

"How could she see when it was almost dark, and anyway what does that mean?" Peter interjected.

"I checked out the story with Ed, and it's true. He said that he had gone down the river path, and not through to the Blakeley's. He claimed that he started to go through and then changed his mind." The sheriff seemed lost in thought.

"I don't understand why he didn't tell you that in the first place," Milly asked.

"Well, I think when he learned that Roger had been killed he was afraid to say that he had gone back to check on the man," Jim said with some hesitation. "After he heard that Roger was killed, he seemed to think that if he mentioned going down to see Roger, that he would be blamed for the murder. As it turns out, if he's innocent things look worse for him than if he told the truth in the first place."

"What do you mean, 'If he is innocent?' " Anna asked. "And what about the Pearson's hired man?"

"Oh you mean Harley Cobb," the sheriff replied. "Liza said that Harley probably saw Ed walk along the river path. Anyway Ed can't remember seeing anyone on the path. But I did check with the Pearsons and Harley's off to his brother's place near Webster City. I guess he's pretty dependable, so we can check with him if we need to."

"Then it doesn't look too good for Ed," Peter surmised.

"At this point it doesn't," Jim continued, "especially after what Bill Evans told me. And strange enough, what Bill says seems to make sense. Another thing is that Bill wasn't ranting and raving this afternoon, but seemed quite calm. If he was upset and unreasonable I would think he was making it all up." Jim shook his head thoughtfully. "I shouldn't say anything more. I've probably told you too much as it is. We'll have to wait until we get the official statement. Well, now as I'm finished with my supper, and I see you folks are too, let's go across the road and get this thing out of the way."

Anna shivered as they made their way up to the Evans' house even though she was wearing her warm winter coat. Jim knocked on the door which was quickly opened by Bill.

"What took you so long?" he growled. "Thought you were comin' right back."

"May we come in Bill?" Jim asked.

"Sure! Come in!" he said more calmly. Peter closed the door behind them.

"You understand Bill that this is a formal statement you are about to make," the sheriff explained. "I am going to write down what you tell me, and you are to sign it swearing that it is the truth. Then the two witnesses, Peter and Anna will sign to affirm that. Is that clear?"

"Yes, that's clear," the old man stated and nodded his head.

"I have Peter Jensen here, you know him as your neighbor, as one of the witnesses which you agreed upon," the sheriff continued.

"Yes, Peter and I don't always think alike, but I think he's honest, and people respect him," Evans added.

"And the other witness is Miss Anna Swenson, the school teacher," Jim stated. 'You also agreed to have her." This came as a surprise to Anna.

"School teachers have to be honest, and they get respect," the old man nodded as he spoke.

"You understand that they may or may not agree with you, but they are signing this statement of yours because they agree that it is your true statement."

"Yes, yes, you explained all that to me before."

"I'm only explaining this again to make sure everyone in the room understands. All right, I have my pen and paper here. May we sit down at the table?"

"Sure you kin sit down, but watch where you sit. Grace's a filthy housekeeper. She an' the kids is hidin' in the bedroom."

Anna brushed food from a chair and sat down. The other two did the same. Bill stood.

"Do you want Grace to come out and hear your statement?" Jim asked.

"No!" was the reply. "She'll come out when she wants to."

"Now tell us exactly what happened the night of Tuesday, October 24th," the sheriff directed Bill Evans. "Why don't you begin when you first heard Roger and Grace fighting."

"You already know all this," and Bill became cantankerous. "Why can't I just tell you what happened down by the river?"

"I think it's better if I have the whole story. Please begin," and Jim put his pen on the paper to write.

"Well I heerd them arguin', and so Joshua and I went to the barn to do the milkin', 'cause it was milkin' time anyway. Is this what you want?"

"Yes that's fine. Please go on, and not too fast because I have to write it down and I want to write it correctly."

"Awright, we goes to the barn to milk, the kid an' me. I keep checkin' to see what's happenin', 'cause when they have a real fight, an' this was a real one, you never know what kin happen. Well, next I sees the teacher comin' across the road."

"Where are you when you see her?" Jim asks.

"I'm stayin' in the barn mostly, just near the door, so's I see the teacher go up to the porch, but I can tell that she hears the fightin'. Well anyone could hear it. I could hear them an' I was jus' outside the barn. Then she turns aroun' and goes down the path to the river. Nothin' seems to be happenin' so I goes back to finish the milkin'. Joshua is curious when I tells him that the teacher has come so he goes to the barn door. A little later he comes to tell me that Ed Marson has come with the posthole digger. He is all excited 'cause he knows that Roger has been needin' it. I tells Joshua to finish the last cow so I go and see what's goin' on. Roger opens the door, looks sort of surprised that someone is there, and takes the posthole digger from Ed and then slams the door in Ed's face. I expected Ed to go back down the river path, but I wanted to watch him anyway. You never know what that young man is goin' to do. I tell you I've had more trouble with him. I could tell you . . ."

At this he was interrupted by Jim, "Let's continue from where you saw Ed leave the porch."

"Awright! I sees him leave the porch, but he don't go down by the river, he goes over to the field where he can keep an eye on the porch, an' he waits there. He keeps waitin' an' I keep waitin'. Then Roger leaves the house with the posthole digger in his hand, and heads for the river. I see that when Roger leaves for the river, Ed waits a little and then starts to head toward the Blakeley place through the field. The kid is through with the milkin' by this time, so I tell him the coast is clear an' we feed the pigs and bring the rest into the house. Grace is lookin' terrible, and I don't want any whinin' from her so I leave and just on a hunch go to see if Ed really has gone to the Blakeley's."

"What time do you think this is?" the sheriff asks.

"How do I know what time it was," came the surly reply. "It was gettin' dark is all I know. Well I go to the south side of the house, and stand on the front porch, and looks out to see what I can see. An' I see someone movin' through the corn. I take the path so I don't make no noise, and follow him, and sure enough it's Ed. He comes to where the fence is down next to the river and stares at Roger for awhile. Yeah, really stares, then walks over to Roger an' they start to argue. Ed's talkin' about how mean Roger is, and Roger tells him it's none of his business, but they get louder and louder. Roger's a lot stronger than Ed, and he could have beat him up easy, but he tells Ed to be a nice little boy and go home. After that Roger walks off and leaves Ed. He goes down to the river, where there is that cutbank and it's real steep, and jus' stands there an' looks like he is thinkin'. Ed is real mad at bein' treated this way so he stands there at first and then sees the posthole digger. He takes it in both hands, walks real slow and quiet toward Roger and hits Roger a good one on the head. Roger drops right into the water. Ed walks back and puts the post hole digger where he found it, and then walks down the river path to Grabney."

Anna and Peter are horrified at this account. Jim continues writing until he is finished. The entire room is silent and the only sound is the scratching of the pen on the paper.

"Tell us what you did then," Jim asks.

"Well, I stand there real shocked. I can't believe it has happened, like it is dark an' my eyes is playin' tricks on me, but I can't see Roger, so I turn around and come back to the house. When I gets about half way back I hear the dinner bell, and so I keeps on goin' an' come in the house."

"Why didn't you tell us this before?" Jim asks.

"Well, like I tol' ya this afternoon, in one way I wasn't sure it had happened, and in another way I knew it was true. Roger always said 'God takes care of all things', an' so I thought that this was the way God had taken care a things. Roger couldn't steal the farm from me now. I thought that I would have the place to misself agin."

"Why did you decide to tell us now?" came Jim's second question.

"Cause I'm an' ol' man, an' it's not fair that someone else killed Roger jus' so I have to spen' all my time workin' and slavin'. An' then I thought that mebbe Ed killed Roger so's he an' Grace could get together agin. An' that made me real mad." He pounded his fist on the table. "Here I was bein' quiet, protectin' someone who was about to steal my land from me."

"Yes, I think we have enough Bill," said Jim as he finished writing. "Now I'm going to read it over to the three of you. If there is anything that you think I did not get correct, please let me know," and he carefully read the entire statement to them. Everyone listened in silence. He looked at Anna and Peter. "Are you ready to sign this?"

Both nodded, but made no audible sound.

"Bill, you will sign it first." The pen was given to Bill and he quickly scratched out his name with a gleeful satisfaction which was evident to the others.

"Now Anna and Peter if you will sign." Each was given the pen and signed above a line on which Jim had written the word *witness*. Jim was the last to sign, as the sheriff.

Grace and the children remained silent in the bedroom next to the kitchen. Only occasionally could a sound be heard and Grace's quick "Shhhhh", to keep them quiet. No doubt she was listening but wanted no part of the procedure.

"If there's nothing else then, we'll leave," Jim stated.

"But aren't you goin' to arrest him? I want him arrested!" Bill Evans began to shout. "You said there would be a warrant for his arrest. If you're the sheriff you'd better get him in jail fast. He did this an' he's got to be punished." Bill's tones got louder and louder.

"That's possibly the next step," added the sheriff.

"But I want it done tonight! I want to make sure that bastard's in jail. Now that he knows I've told on him, no tellin' what he'll do. He could be comin' after me. Or he'll leave town agin an' you'll never find him." Bill's face was flushed red and as he stood he looked like a caged animal. "Yer the sheriff so do yer job."

"Yes, he will be arrested, and it will probably be tonight. You have sworn a statement accusing him of murder and that is a serious thing. Anna and Peter shall we be going?" The two of them rose in almost a trance from their chairs and followed Jim out the door into the cold air of the evening, which shook them back to reality.

They walked down the steps and up to Jim's car. "But Ed's story is so different," Anna pleaded. "How can you arrest him on just the word of this strange old man?"

"Bill told me this same story this afternoon, so I had a talk with Ed which lasted several hours," Jim volunteered. "It seems that Ed did go down and have an argument with Roger. He finally broke down and admitted it. He could give me no reason for twice telling false accounts of that night. At this time it doesn't look too good for him. I'll have to arrest him tonight."

Chapter Thirty-one

No one in the Jensen household slept well that night. After they arrived home, Anna and Peter told Milly all that had happened. In shock and disbelief they tried to make sense out of the situation. It was terrible enough when they found that Roger had been killed, but everyone seemed to think it was some drifter that had done it. Roger wasn't well liked, but murder, well, that just wasn't something that people they knew did. It was unbelievable that Ed could have perpetrated it.

At breakfast the next morning the children were unaware that anything untoward had happened and chatted with their usual gaiety. The adults were somber.

"I wish we knew if Ed has been arrested," Milly whispered to Anna. "I yust can't take all this not knowing."

Anna nodded her head, aware that Davey's eyes were on his mother. "It's about time to get going to school Davey," she said looking at the boy, and hoping to distract him from what he might have heard. "I'd like to get there a little early today. Think you can hurry and go with me?"

"Sure, Miss Swenson," he answered, and in somewhat unmannerly fashion gobbled up the rest of his breakfast. His mother was so preoccupied with her thoughts that she didn't notice.

After Davey dashed upstairs, Peter, who had been aware of Milly's concern, now tried to calm her fears. "If you really want to know you could phone Liza, but then I wouldn't advise it. I'm sure we'll find out soon enough. I think it's quite likely that he was arrested. We'll have to accept it at that and get on with our work. There's nothing we can do."

"Oh, but Peter," came Milly's anguished cry.

"Anyway I've got the cornshellers coming again this morning, and they'll be here for dinner, so we both have our day's work cut out for us." With that remark he got up from the table and headed outside.

As Anna and Davey left the yard and headed up the road on their way to school, they could see Bill Evans on his way to the barn. It looked as if he had renewed energy. "Perhaps with this off his conscience he feels he has had a great weight lifted off his shoulders," thought Anna. He certainly seemed a different person, but still she couldn't believe that Ed killed Roger. She was sure the old man had seen someone else do it and blamed Ed because of his hatred for him, or perhaps he really thought it was Ed. It was all so confusing.

"I guess Joshua is going to be late again," said Davey waking her from her reverie.

She looked back at his house and replied, "Yes. I guess you're right. I don't see him coming." She was hoping that he would come to school, although had her doubts. In all her life, thinking and preparing for teaching, she had never thought that an event like this would happen.

At nine o'clock she rang the bell and as she pulled the rope she could see Joshua running up the road to make it on time. He had a lunch pail too, so perhaps things would settle down for a fairly normal day, but it was not to be. She greeted him with, "Good morning, Joshua," as he dashed into the building, but he didn't answer. He slammed his lunch pail down on the shelf and deliberately kicked the side of his desk as he took his seat. This was so unlike him, but Anna could understand that there must be a great deal of tension in his household, and it was taking its toll on the child.

As the morning wore on, he became more sullen. At last it was recess time. Anna dismissed the students, but Joshua remained in his seat. "It's recess," Davey leaned over to tell him in case he hadn't heard.

"I ain't talkin' to no one," Joshua replied curtly.

"What a crosspatch," said Annie Lindquist who sat directly behind him. "I think he got up on the wrong side of the bed this morning," and she and Victoria looked scornfully at Joshua as they got out of their seats.

"I didn't get out on the wrong side of the bed," he yelled. "There's only one side I can get out on."

As the children were bundling into their coats and hats, Anna quickly shooed them out of the room, leaving Joshua sitting alone. She felt that her presence at his house last night might have something to do with his behavior, so decided to try to talk to him.

She went to him and put her hand on his arm, but he pulled it away, saying "Don't touch me."

"Joshua, all I want to do is to help you," she pleaded. "Do you feel badly that I had to come to your house last night?"

He looked at her and slowly nodded his head. His large brown eyes seemed to be looking inward rather than outward. He was staring into space and his thoughts seemed a million miles away. He was very quiet so she left him alone, and hoped that the rest of the day would go better. As she looked at him she thought of something he said to her when she first knew him, and that was, "Still water runs deep." That was what his father had told him about the river and the fishing, and you can't see into the deep water to know what is down there. The same held true for him. She couldn't see into him to know what was behind those big brown eyes.

It had been a long day and Anna was glad to get home. Davey ran over to where the cornhuskers were working, and she trudged up the back steps to find Milly sitting at the kitchen table, a cup of coffee in her hands. "Davey's gone to watch the cornhuskers. Did you hear any more about Ed?" she asked anxiously.

"Oh my, it's been a terrible day," Milly replied with exhaustion in her voice. "Inger called right after you left and said that Walter and William Larson were on their way back from seeing Gus Olson, a kid their age who lives south of Grabney, when they saw Yim's car pulled up in front of the store. They were curious to see what was going on, and waited by the station. Soon Yim came out with Ed, and from what little they heard of the conversation they guessed that he had been arrested."

"It's what we expected," Anna sighed.

271

"Floyd had to go to the depot this afternoon to collect an order he had shipped, and talked with Matt and Liza, and they said it's true. Liza wanted to go over to comfort Vi. I think she probably wanted to find out more gossip. Anyway, Matt told her to stay away since she was the first one who questioned Ed's story, and Vi wouldn't welcome her one bit. I guess the Blakeleys have been there. Here let me pour you come coffee," and she quickly gave Anna a cup.

Anna had barely sat down when they heard a car enter the yard. "Well, now I wonder who that can be?"

Davey quickly answered her question as he threw open the kitchen door. "It's Jack Jarvis Mother. And he has a new car. And he's comin' to see us." The child dashed back outside.

"Oh no!" Milly exclaimed as she buried her face in her hands. "Of all people. He's probably the last person I want to see now."

"I'll see if we can get rid of him fast Milly," Anna consoled her. "With the Marsons starting to sell shoes he won't be taking any more orders, so I doubt if he intends to stay long."

"I hope not," Milly added.

"He must be doing all right to have bought a car. Maybe he's come to show it to us. It will be good for us to change to a pleasant subject."

"Yes, we'll have to be nice to him," Milly agreed.

Jack's steps could be heard and soon he was standing in the open kitchen door. "Afternoon ladies."

Anna looked up so see him politely enter and shut the door. He was about thirty-five years old she would guess, of medium build and a little on the stocky side. His jet black hair was parted in the middle and slicked back against his head. He was also wearing a suit, probably now that he had his car and didn't have to walk around the countryside. Thus his appearance made quite a contrast to that of the local farmer, and gave him somewhat the look of a dandy.

"Come in Yack," Milly welcomed him courteously. "Sit down and have a cup of coffee."

"Thanks Milly," he replied, "but I can't stay long. Just come by to tell you about my new stores, and how you can order shoes from now on."

"We heard that Elmer and Vi will be selling shoes for you," Anna quickly added.

"Yes," and he looked at the floor. "I feel terrible about what's happened to that family. I can't believe that Ed did it."

"Oh, none of us can, in fact we refuse to believe it," Milly interrupted, as she gave him some coffee "Here, sit down."

He pulled up a chair and seated himself at the table. "I've had such good luck lately, that I can't believe things like this are happening to people I know, and such nice people too. It was bad enough to think that a murder had happened in these parts, even though not many people liked Roger. But to think that Ed might have done it is something I don't even want to think about."

"No one does," added Anna. "But tell us about your stores and all your good luck. I would like to hear about something good for a change. We heard that you will be selling shoes in the front part of a dry goods store in the county seat."

"That's right. You know I've been peddlin' shoes for about fifteen years, walkin' all over the countryside, wearin' out more shoe leather than I care to think of. Anyways I began to be sellin' most of my shoes near the county seat, and doin' a pretty good business at that, so one day I asked Joe Purcell, who runs the dry goods store, if I could come to some arrangement and sell shoes in his store. Well, it has worked out just dandy. It's more than I can believe, and so I asked Elmer and Vi if they would like to do the same, and they agreed. Grabney is about the farthest out I go, so with a store here I should be able to keep up the business. Elmer and Vi have always let me meet most of my customers in their store anyway. I only walk to the closest houses. This way I won't have to be here myself. They can sell the shoes, and if they don't have the right size, I can send out a pair on the next train."

"It certainly sounds simple enough to me. I hope it all works out," said Anna.

"I sure hope it does too," Jack agreed, and he stood to go. "Actually I also had another reason for comin' to your place, not to just explain about the store." He looked nervously around him. "This is goin' to be a little difficult for me, so I want your advice."

273

"What's the matter?" asked Milly, perplexed at the sudden change in him.

"Well, you see I room and board with Grace's aunt, and she asked me to stop by and see how Grace was doin'. She gave me a letter for her too," and he felt in his inside coat pocket to make sure it was there. "I feel awkward, 'cause I never really knew Grace that well. She's havin' such a hard time, she probably doesn't want to see anyone. But with this letter, well I feel I gotta go over there. And then there's her old man. I don't want anything to do with him."

"Bill Evans is out harvesting, so you won't see him," said Anna. "And I think Grace would be happy to see you, especially if you were bringing her a letter from her aunt. She's very fond of her aunt."

"What do you think Milly?" he asked. "Would I be interferin'?"

"Of course not! Especially since you have a letter. Her aunt was her mother's sister, and since her mother died she has felt the aunt is like a mother to her. Yust get there before Bill comes in. No one wants to meet up with him."

"In that case I'll get goin'. Is it all right if I leave my car at your place? This way I can go and come quietly. If I drive the car Evans is bound to hear it and as you said, I don't want to meet up with him."

"That's a good idea," Milly agreed. "And let us know if things aren't going too good over there will you? I should of stopped there today myself, but with the cornhuskers and all I yust didn't feel up to it."

"I'll let you know if there's somethin' you can do. Thanks for the coffee. Glad to see both of you. If you're ever in the county seat be sure to stop by and see the store." With that he was out the door and off to Grace's.

"I didn't know that he boarded with Grace's aunt," said Anna. "I remember seeing him at the dance, but somehow I thought that he might be living with his folks, or maybe even have a family of his own."

"You can't spend all your time going around the countryside selling shoes and have time to settle down," said Milly. "Anyway, I'm glad he's doing well. He's always been a nice fellow."

Peter's heavy-footed tread could be heard coming up the steps, followed by lighter footsteps of Davey and Sarah.

"Jack Jarvis said he was going to leave his car here while he goes over to Joshua's house," Davey said excitedly. "He said when he came back we could climb into it. He might even give us a ride. Do you think he would dad?"

"I think that's highly possible," came his father's reply. "Why don't you change your clothes and then go out and wait for him."

"Can I have a ride too?" asked Sarah longingly. "Oh please!"

"Well that's entirely up to Jack, but I think that he would be willing to take the both of you," smiled Peter as he answered her question.

Much to everyone's surprise, it was at least forty-five minutes before Jack returned. He was his usual jovial self, so they knew that the visit had not been unpleasant.

"Get your coats on and hop in the car," he called to Milly and Anna who were on the porch, as he opened the door for the children who were already waiting. "Come on Milly and Anna, and take the baby with you. The children can sit in the front seat with me, and that leaves plenty of room for the adults in back. What about you Peter?"

"I probably better get to the milking," Peter responded.

"Oh, let the milking wait for awhile. We'll only be gone a few minutes."

Anna and Milly hurried to the new Model T with Lucy tucked inside her mother's coat. Peter climbed into the back seat with the women. "Where're we going?" he asked.

"Just for a short ride up to Floyd's."

"Up to Floyd's!" Peter exclaimed. "We'll never hear the end of this."

"Well, you see Grace has a favor to ask of him, and she wanted me to do the askin'. She's decided to take the children and leave the farm to live with her aunt, and was hopin' that Floyd could take them and her baggage to catch the afternoon train on Friday."

Chapter Thirty-two

The next day at school Joshua didn't mention their moving so Anna didn't bring up the subject. It seemed like such a sudden decision that she wondered if Jack had all his facts straight when he told them. However when she arrived home that day Inger was there and she knew that she would find out.

"Hello Anna," Inger greeted her. "I guess you've heard that Grace and family are leaving."

"Joshua didn't mention a thing about it at school so I wondered if it were really true," she replied.

"Yes, it's true enough. Grace asked me to come over this morning. Floyd brought me 'cause with this bum ankle of mine I'm still not too good at walking distances. Anyway, he drove in here so Evans wouldn't catch on that something was up. I walked across the road when he was out in the west field. You see Grace wants to get out of here without his knowing about it."

"That's not going to be too easy," Anna said with surprise.

"Well, Grace thinks she can do it. She has one trunk and a suitcase, which she has in her bedroom. She says she can pack all they want to take with them in a day. Her dad never goes into the room so she is sure she can keep it from him. Joshua's been told to not tell a soul, and he is so scared of his grandpa that I'm sure he'll obey."

"I hope she's doing the right thing," Milly chimed in.

"I think it's the best thing that she can do. Living with that old man is purgatory for them. With her aunt she can begin to have a decent life, and I told her so. She really wanted me to come so we could talk things over and I could help her decide if this was the best thing to do."

"You've helped her so many times Inger," added Milly, "like when her babies were born and any other time that she needed someone. You're probably like a mother to her."

"Well, I'm not that old," Inger laughed. "Maybe more like a big sister. Anyway, I hope I did her some good."

"So they're leaving Friday?" Anna questioned.

"Yes! Joshua is to go to school as usual, so the old man won't suspect anything. The train comes through town about five, so Floyd will be here about four o'clock, with Walter to help load up the trunk. They can spare a couple of hours from harvest, and anyway this week the cornshellers are there so there's plenty of work being done."

"Peter could have taken them to the train," volunteered Milly.

"Yes, he could have. But then the trunk is too heavy for one person to lift up, and besides Grace felt that since you were such close neighbors and her dad seems to trust Peter from what he said the other night at the signing of the warrant, that she would rather have someone else do it so Peter won't be blamed. Old man Evans doesn't scare Floyd one bit, and the old man knows it."

"So we're not supposed to know a thing about this?" Anna asked.

"That's right. So don't mention it in front of the children, especially Davey."

"I wondered why Jack took so long over at Grace's yesterday," Anna continued. "Do you think he knows of her plan?"

"Oh yes!" Inger continued. "He even offered her a part time job selling shoes in his store. Said he needed someone else to help when he was on the road. Right now the wife of the dry goods man is taking care of it, but that isn't working out too well. Grace is thrilled that she will have something to do. Joshua will be in school, and she is sure that her aunt will look after Elaine. Elaine was named after her you know, and I think she's only seen the child once when she came to visit, and that was just for a few hours, thanks to old Bill Evans."

"They covered a lot more territory than I imagined," Anna commented with surprise.

"It's the best thing for her," Inger continued, "and for the children too."

"My yes," echoed Milly. "She is so lucky to have this aunt."

"Now I can't guarantee as to how things will work out," Inger went on. "You know Grace is high strung and has a mind of her own. But no one can say that she didn't have a chance now. I just hope she makes the best of it and I told her so."

The ringing of the phone interrupted them. "Two long and a short that's for us," said Milly as she went to answer it. She held out the receiver. "It's for you Anna."

"For me!" Anna said in surprise. "I don't think I've ever gotten a phone call here before. Who is it?" She got up to accept the call.

"It's a man, but don't get all excited," Milly laughed. "It's Rev. Blakeley," and she handed her the receiver.

"Hello.———Yes———Saturday morning, about ten o'clock.———Yes I could do that.———You really want me?———Oh, thank you. I will be happy if I can be of some help.———I'll see you at ten o'clock on Saturday then.———
—Good-bye."

"That was short and sweet," commented Inger. "What's going on Saturday morning at ten o'clock?"

"Rev. Blakeley's driving in to the county seat to visit Ed and thought it would be advisable for me to come along. I don't know why, but I'm happy to go if I can be of any help. He didn't want to talk too long I guess because the longer a person talks the more receivers that are picked up."

"He's right there," Inger commented. "Well that sounds interesting. I wonder what he hopes to accomplish by going to see Ed, but then I guess he feels it's his duty as pastor to visit the young man."

"If he can give Ed some hope, then he will be of some help," added Milly. "Poor Ed. I hate to think of him sitting in yail," and she shuddered. "It's yust too terrible."

School went as usual on Friday. Joshua was in a particularly good mood and didn't give any indication that he knew what was going to happen later that afternoon. He did ask if he could take home his project, which was a set of bookends. Lars thought he should wait until they were finished, but Anna intervened and said that perhaps Joshua could work on them at home. This was an idea that all accepted.

Joshua and Davey ran home from school and Anna was not far behind them. She was most anxious to see what happened when Grace and her family left.

At precisely four o'clock Floyd and Walter drove up to Grace's house. Floyd turned the wagon around so it was headed out and then the two of them went inside. Anna and Milly went into Davey's room to look out the upstairs window so they could see what was going on. Davey was outside with his father, oblivious to the situation. Sarah was playing with Lucy in her room. The women spoke with muted voices.

"I think the old man is still out in the field," Milly whispered to Anna.

"Yes, I can see the horses and the wagon way over by the Blakeley's. The corn stalks are moving over there too. Lucky for everyone that Floyd arrived when he did. If they can only hurry they can be gone before Evans turns at the end of the row and heads toward the house."

"Here come Walter and Floyd out of the house with the trunk. Oh I hope they hurry before Evans turns around," Milly lamented. "The trunk looks so heavy." There was a loud bang as the trunk landed on the floor of the wagon. Both women shuddered for fear the sound carried to Evans, but they could see no indication that it did.

"Now Walter is going back for something else. It must be to get her suitcase." Soon Walter was carrying out the suitcase. He heaved it next to the trunk and jumped into the wagon next to his father. "But where are Grace and the children?" Anna wondered.

Joshua soon appeared and jumped up on the wagon next to Walter.

"Where are Grace and Elaine?" Milly fumed. They should be out on the wagon by now. Evans is half way up the row."

"No, he's not that far Milly," Anna decided as she scrutinized the scene closely. "But I wish they'd hurry. Floyd came at such a perfect time. Do you think he was watching and waited until Bill was away from the house?"

Milly nodded her head. "I'm sure that's right Anna. Floyd would be yust the person to think of that. They could have waited up near the Larson's. Oh good! Here come Grace and Elaine, finally." Grace handed Elaine up to Walter and as she was doing so, Joshua suddenly jumped down off the wagon and ran into the house. They could see Grace calling after him. She started to run after him, but Walter was faster. He jumped off the wagon and tore after the boy.

"What's going on?" Milly wondered out loud. "What is Yoshua doing? Doesn't he want to leave?"

Grace was still standing by the wagon, and Floyd was trying to convince her to get up. Evidently he was successful because soon she was seen climbing up and seating herself next to Elaine. All heads were turned toward the house. There was still no sign of Joshua and Walter, and Bill Evans was definitely heading back. The women were is a state of suspense.

"Oh, I can't stand it," Milly said. "Where are Joshua and Walter?"

Soon they both were seen running out of the house. Joshua was clutching something in his hands and holding it close to his chest. "It looks like he ran back for something, but what can it be?" Anna strained to look. "It's so far away that I can't see." As the boy climbed into the wagon he let Walter hold his precious possession, rather it was two things, and Anna knew immediately what they were. "It's the bookends he was making at school. I am sure of it," Anna said happily. "Now Walter is handing them back to Joshua, yes that's what they are. He wanted to take them home from school today even though they weren't finished. I am so glad he remembered to take them with him."

By this time the boys were seated on the floor of the wagon next to the trunk and Floyd slapped the reins on the horses rears and told them to, "Giddap," which they did with a jolt that shoved the boys next to the trunk, and caused Grace to grab Elaine. As the wagon pulled out of the yard, Bill Evans came to the end of the row, just in time to see a trunk in the back of a wagon leaving his farm.

Chapter Thirty-three

For some reason it mustn't have dawned on Bill Evans what had happened until he went into the house at supper time and found no one there. Then his fury knew no bounds as he recalled seeing the trunk in the back of the wagon, and knew that Grace and the children had left him. It wasn't so much that he minded their leaving, it was more that he had not dictated that they do so. He had Liza call the sheriff immediately to arrest Grace, but it was explained to him that Grace was a free citizen and could go where she chose. The Jensens learned this when Floyd and Inger came over after supper.

"I tell you I high-tailed it out of there fast as I could," Floyd recounted. "Once I saw the horses comin' up to the end of the row, I knew we better get out of there in a hurry. If it wasn't for Joshua we could've got out sooner, but I don't blame the little shaver for wantin' to take somethin' he made at school. He'll have little enough to remember the place by."

"Lucky for him," countered Inger. "There's not much that's good to remember."

"Guess that's so," Floyd thought out loud nodding his head. "Anyway it looks like once Bill found out what had happened he was screamin' things that would make the Devil blush," Floyd continued. "Jim Wilson phoned me to ask what was goin' on, if you could call it a phone call, talkin' through Liza on the county line. The old man couldn't believe he couldn't have Grace arrested. Shows how crazy he is."

"Does he know it was you who took her to the station?" asked Peter.

"He's probably guessed it. What I can't understand is why he didn't take off after us. I was ready for a real chase.

Could have been rather excitin' but his old nags could never keep up with my pair."

"Don't you talk crazy Floyd," Inger scolded. "All we need is two old fogies chasin' each other down the country roads."

"Just be careful who you're callin' an ol' fogie Mother," came the retort. "Puttin' me 'n Bill Evans in the same category is downright insultin'." This brought laughter from everyone.

Still smiling Anna asked, "What did he do after he went into the house and found that they had gone?"

"That's when he got so mad he called the sheriff, accordin' to Liza. Well, first he talks to Liza and he's guessed that they've gone to her aunt's place. Liza says all she told him was that they got on the five o'clock train. Then he asks who brought them to the train station, and she says she didn't see who, all she did was sell Grace the tickets."

"Lucky for you I'd say," mused Peter. "That guy's crazy enough to try to settle the score by burning down your barn or something like it."

"That's what I'm afraid of," added Inger. "I told the boys to watch out tonight. Never can tell what will happen."

"Now Mother, calm down," admonished Floyd. "That old coot'd never have the strength to walk up to our place. And by the time he got there, if he made it, he'd wonder why he came."

"Don't be so sure," Inger told him. "Anyway I think we'd better be getting on home. It's late and enough's happened for one day."

"If you say so," said Floyd as he got up from his chair, "providin' I can take a coupla Milly's cookies with me. We never get tasty things like this at home, just plain ol' food at our house," and he grabbed a handful of cookies.

"Well if that isn't the last straw," said Inger as she limped toward the door. "Goodnight everybody."

"Goodnight," echoed Floyd. "Next time I'd 'preciate it if you'd make the cookies with the frostin' on top Milly. These is good, but those're better, an' be sure to give Mother the recipe," and with a wink at her he shut the door and they went out into the night.

A little before ten o'clock the next morning, Rev. Blakeley's car could be heard coming into the yard. Milly quickly untied her apron, put it over the back of a chair and dashed to the door to greet him. "Come in for a cup of coffee. Anna will be down in a minute."

"Oh, good morning Milly. Don't mind if I do," came the cheery reply, "but it will have to be a quick one. Plenty to do this morning." He followed Milly into the kitchen.

"Let me hang up your coat," she offered.

"Oh, no time for that," he answered. "Just a quick cup of coffee will do and then we must be on our way. Good morning Anna," he greeted as she came down the stairs.

"Here's your coffee," said Milly as she handed a full cup to him, "and sit down now."

He took the chair closest to the door, gave a sigh, and drank his coffee. "I hear that plenty's gone on across the way in the last twenty-four hours."

"When you phoned I wanted to tell you," Anna told him, "but if I had mentioned it everyone would have known, and Grace might not have been able to get away."

"I understand completely," he said. "Best thing in the world for Grace and the children to get to her aunt's place. Her aunt is a very kind person. Lost her husband some time ago. Never had any children."

"I yust hope that everything works out for her," Milly added. "She hasn't had a very happy life."

"Yes, I think Grace has been forced to do many things she didn't want to do, and unfortunately has not always used the best judgment in others. Let's hope that under the influence of her aunt that she can do better." He stood up. "I see that you're ready to go Anna, so let's not keep the chariot waiting." Together they went out the door calling their goodbyes to Milly and the children.

It was a chilly winter day and Anna was glad that the Model T had a top and windows to keep out the cold. He cranked up the engine and they had no sooner settled themselves in the front seat and were driving out of the yard when they saw Bill Evans waiting for them at the road. He looked worn out, whether from work or anger it was difficult to tell.

"I want to talk to you Reverend," he shouted as he ran

toward the car, and Rev. Blakeley had little choice but to stop and listen to him. Anna was frightened.

"Morning Bill. What's on your mind?" the minister called out in as cheerful a voice as possible as he braked the car but left the engine running.

"You know good'n well what's on my mind," he yelled menacingly as he approached the car. "My Grace's done left me, without nary a word about it. Jus' run off. She has no right to leave here without my say so."

"Here, let me get out of the car so we can talk," said the Reverend as he opened the door and let himself out into the cold, carefully shutting it behind him. "Is there something I can do for you Bill?" he said in as pleasant a voice as possible. Anna sat frozen to her seat, fearful for what would happen next.

Bill looked mean, like he was pushing for a fight. He banged his fist on the front fender. "Well she just run off, takin' the kids with her, leavin' me to run this place by misself, an' that ain't fair after all I done for her. Didn't even tell me she was goin'. Sneaked off that is. That's what she always was, sneaky. I saw a wagon leavin' my yard yesterday, an' I knows it was them. She got some fool to fetch her to the train. She thinks I don't know what she's doin', but I do. She's followin' that no-good boyfriend of hers to the county seat. Oh, you should of heard her the night that I had the sheriff here and got him arrested. She was screamin' an' cryin' and kep' yellin' at me half the night. But I paid no attention. I went right to sleep cause I knowed I done the right thing."

"No wonder Joshua was irritable the next morning in school," Anna thought. "It must have been a nightmare at that house."

"Well, I called the sheriff right away, last night, to get her back, and you know what he tells me? He says that she's old enough to make her own decisions, an' I can't force her to return. Hah! Old enough to make her own decisions! When did she ever make her own decisions. Never, I tell you. She don't have the sense to make a decision. Someone always had to do it for her. So now she'll have nothin' and that serves her right, the lazy bitch, oh 'scuse me Reverend. But she was lazy 'n no good. Wouldn't even work the harvest with me this fall after Roger got killed. She an' I could of done it together the way we used to when she was a girl, but no the doctor wouldn't let her work 'cause she was too sick. Huh! It made me sick just to look at her."

"Is there something you want me to do for you Bill?" asked Rev. Blakeley, and it was obvious to Anna that he wanted to end this diatribe.

"You! Well yes. When you see her, an' I know you go to the county seat, tell her I don't want her back no more, nor her kids neither. That boy can't do a lick a work, not like I did when I was his age. Worthless! That's what he is. Just like his mother. And Elaine! Cries all the time. Can't get no peace anywheres 'cause she's always whinin' 'n cryin'."

"Well, then, I guess you're better off without them," came the minister's quick evaluation.

"Yeah! I been thinkin'. I wouldna been so mad if they only tol' me, but they sneaked off. But I get the last laugh, 'cause that boy's gonna hang, an' then where'll she be. She'll have nothin'. Nothin'! That's the way God pays his debts, but she don't know it yet."

"I guess we should be leaving," said Rev. Blakeley as he opened the door to his car. "I'm glad that you can manage all right. If there's anything I can to for you let me know," and he slid into the driver's seat.

"Gotta get this harvest done, an' then I'll be sittin' pretty," came the answer. "Folks thought I couldn't do it by misself, but jus' look at what I done, an' with no help neither. An' you tell Grace that I don't need her no more, an' I wouldn' take her back if she came a beggin' on her knees. Tell her that. Yeah, you tell her that."

"I'll be sure and do that," the minister called out as he drove away. "Well, that was something we didn't need this morning," he said to Anna.

"I thought he was asking for a fight," she replied. "You are so good at calming people down."

"Well, most of it is just listening to them and letting them let out all the steam. And then they also realize that I'm not one for a fight anyway, and am more or less a neutral listener. Anyway, the way I see it, he has a lot more work to do before he finishes his harvest."

"One of the Larson boys offered to help him, but he refused," she added.

"Yes I heard about that. Stubborn old coot! I really don't know what's going to happen to him either. I don't see how he can get the harvest in before it snows, and then he has his stock, the hogs and a few milk cows."

"Grace is lucky to be away from here. I hope her aunt has a nicer place than this one."

"We might just meet her," the minister added. "Yes, her place is quite attractive, a nice house in a pleasant neighborhood, with a lawn and big elm trees next to the street. But if we do happen to run into Grace I'm not going to tell her that I saw her father this morning."

"Do you think Grace really left so she could be near Ed?" Anna asked.

"Not on your life," he replied. "Bill said Grace wasn't able to make a decision, but she's plenty able to do her own deciding when she has a chance. She knows what she wants."

"I couldn't believe it when he said that Ed would hang. That's horrible," she groaned.

"Well, he has a vivid imagination. Don't let what he says worry you. I still think that Ed is not guilty, but at this juncture we don't know how to prove it. Anyway, let's forget about Bill Evans, and talk about something more pleasant. How's school going?" With this remark the topic of conversation changed, and they had a good visit.

As they approached the county seat Anna could see that it was a pretty town of perhaps three or four hundred people. There were many comfortable homes on the main street which was lined with plenty of trees for shade in the summer. "Grace's aunt lives a couple of blocks that way," pointed Rev. Blakeley as they crossed an intersection. "The courthouse and jail are straight ahead, and I think we should go there first. I'm anxious to see Ed and learn what's happening. Oh, by the way, on the south side of the street is the dry goods store where Jack Jarvis is selling his shoes." Anna looked around as he pointed out various points of interest. Soon they had pulled up in front of a two story brick building. "Well, here we are. Let's get out."

They left the car and Anna followed Rev. Blakeley around to the back where there was a sign on a door that indicated it was the sheriff's office. It was obvious that he was no stranger to this building. "Hello Bert," he said as he opened the door. "We've come to see Ed Marson. This is Anna Swenson, the Grabney school teacher."

"How 'do Miss Swenson," came the deputy's response with what Anna thought was a slight smirk on his face.

"How do you do," was how Anna replied in a rather formal tone, not wanting to call him by his first name and not knowing his last.

"He's got a visitor in there now," Bert's continued," but she ain't goin' to be too long I guess. Why doncha sit down and wait."

"That will be fine Bert. Thanks. We'll do that," said the minister, and they walked over to the few wooden chairs lined against the wall and seated themselves. The room was fairly small with a desk just inside the door which belonged to the sheriff, and used by his deputy when he was not on duty. A hallway led off the room into an area of two jail cells. Anna could see a few of the bars of one cell through the doorway. They could also hear muffled voices, one a man's and the other a woman's.

"Don't suppose you've ever been in a jail before," said Rev. Blakeley.

"No I haven't," said Anna.

"Well this is it. They're pretty much all the same. Say Bert," he said, raising his voice slightly. "Any chance to see Jim today?"

"Don't think so," came the answer. "He's tryin' to catch up with his farm work. You folks have given him more trouble than he's seen for many a month. If you want him you can call him though."

"No that's not necessary. I'll catch him some other time." Turning to Anna he said, "Say you're mighty serious."

Anna had been listening intently trying to see if she could identify the woman's voice. Could it be Grace's? "Oh I was trying to see if that was Grace's voice in there," she said quietly.

"If I were a betting man I would bet the earth that it's not," smiled the minister. "I think it's more likely that it belongs to Bertha Clemson. Ed has been squiring her around off and on for a couple of years. She works as a clerk in the courthouse and I'm sure that with Ed here she's a regular visitor."

"I saw her at the dance in Brewster."

"Yes, her home is there, but she boards in town during the week because of her job. She usually goes home on weekends, but with Ed here I'm sure she's not going to leave."

"Her mother paints china. Isn't that right?" asked Anna.

"And does a beautiful job. The whole family is pretty talented."

The voices quieted down in the other room and soon Bertha was seen entering from the hallway. She was a perky young woman, but looked as if she were trying to keep up her spirits and put on a good face.

"Well, if it isn't Bertha," said Rev. Blakeley as he stood to greet her. "Good to see you," and he grabbed her hand to shake it. "I'm sure you're the best medicine that Ed could have."

"Oh, hello Rev. Blakeley," she answered quietly. "I just don't know." She looked close to tears.

"Come over here, there's someone I want you to meet," and he pulled her over to Anna. "This is Anna Swenson, the teacher in Grabney. You may have seen her at the dance. Anna, this is Bertha Clemson."

Somewhat formal greetings were exchanged with Bertha looking at Anna wondering what circumstances brought her here. Rev. Blakeley sensed this and quickly responded with, "Anna and I are here to do a little detective work on our own," and he laughed. "Well, you see neither of us believe that Ed is guilty, and so with Jim so busy on his farm, we decided we'd better get in here and talk to the young man ourselves." At this Bertha gave a small hint of a smile. "Also Anna saw Ed deliver the posthole digger on that fatal day, and she lives across the road from the Kloster farm. Anyway, nothing ventured, nothing gained."

"Oh, I'm so worried about Ed," Bertha quietly admitted. "I couldn't stand it if something happened to him. It's just not fair. I know Ed, and he didn't do it."

"Keep your chin up child. I know Jim will do his best to find out all the answers," and he gave her a loving pat on the shoulder. "Guess it's our turn now. That right Bert?"

"That's right. Usually it's just one at a time but I guess I can trust you Reverend. You know the way."

"Good-bye Bertha," said the minister. "And as I said, keep your chin up. Things will get better."

"Good-bye," said Anna, and quickly added as if to change the subject. "Oh, I understand your mother is the one who does the lovely china painting. Do you think she could do a cake plate for me to give Milly Jensen for Christmas? You know Milly don't you?"

"Oh, of course. She's the most lively one at the dances," and this brought a smile to Bertha's face. "Mother would love to paint a plate for her. What do you want on it?"

"I'll let your mother decide," Anna replied not able to think of paintings and plates at all. "Whatever she does will be fine. Oh, I guess Rev. Blakeley has gone in to see Ed, so I'd better go. Good-bye Bertha. I'm really happy to have met you," and the two women parted.

She took a deep breath, gave a sigh, and turned to go through the door. She had never been in a jail before, and it gave her a feeling of fear. She willed her courage not to leave her and hoped that she could face Ed with some composure.

Chapter Thirty-four

Her heart went thud as she entered the jail room and saw Ed sitting dejectedly on a cot in the first cell. The gray bars seemed so menacing. There was Ed behind them, like pictures she had seen of animals in a zoo.

"You're nice to come see me every day," she heard him say to Rev. Blakeley. She was surprised to learn that the minister had come before today. "But as much as we talk about it I can't think of anything that will do me any good. There's so much against me. Sometimes I wonder if I did kill Roger. There were plenty of times when I wish I could have."

"Let's not have any talk like that! Anyway I brought someone else to see you. Here's Anna Swenson. Thought she might be able to help us to a little detecting."

The young man looked up to see her. "Hello Anna. Thanks for comin' but I'm afraid there's not much anyone can do for me."

"Hello Ed," she managed to say. Vainly trying to think of something else she added, "You have lots of people on your side. No one thinks you did it."

"There's one person who says he knows I did, and I'm sure plenty of other folks feel the same. After all it's his word against mine. I say I didn't do it and he says I did, and Kloster is dead. So what does it look like."

"No! Anna's right Ed," Rev. Blakeley added. "And I think that Jim Wilson feels you're innocent. Anyway he is determined to make a fair case out of this. And you have Bertha visiting you as many times a day as she can. She's certainly on your side."

"I wish she wouldn't come," he said despondently. "I'm not good enough for her. What's she wastin' her time around

293

me for? I'm gonna tell her not to come again. Just all of you forget about me."

"Now don't talk like that. Your folks are planning to come in and see you tomorrow. It's going to be hard on them, so try to keep a stiff upper lip, for their sakes."

"I'll try," Ed added. "It's goin' to be hard to see them," and he slumped down on the cot.

"Now that we've got all the hard part out of our system," the Rev. said, "let's concentrate on what we can do to get you out of here, the legal way of course," he added with a forced smile. "Now Liza said that Harley Cobb probably saw you on the path to Grabney, and you say you don't remember seeing him. Are you sure?"

"Yes, I'm sure. I didn't see anyone on the path. Even though I was still upset, the path is not that wide and I know I would've seen him."

"Would you recognize Harley?" came another question.

"Yes, I know him. He never came to the store often, just to buy tobacco, but I waited on him a coupla times. I knew he worked at the Pearsons. Besides I told you I saw no one on the trail when I walked back to town."

There was a decided pause and Anna felt obligated to enter the conversation. "When you left Roger, what was he doing?"

Ed looked up. "He had just said somethin' like, 'Be a nice little boy and go home,' or somethin' like that, meanin' that I wasn't man enough to stand up to him." He stopped and shrugged his shoulders. "At first when I got there I had started arguin' with him and yellin' at him, tellin' him how mean he was to Grace, and how everyone around here knew it, how people don't even treat animals like that. Maybe he still thought I had a crush on Grace, but I got over her years ago. No one deserves to be treated the way he treated her and I just couldn't let him get by with what he had done without sayin' something about it. I know he's done it before and no one even stopped him. Most of the time no one knew because they kept so close to themselves."

"We all suspected," said Rev. Blakeley, "but then as you say they kept so close to themselves that no one had any proof."

"And I suppose Grace never complained to anyone," added Anna.

"I think that was because of her pride," Ed continued. "Well after I got through tellin' Roger off, he just looked at me like I was some stupid kid. Then he tells me to go home and completely ignores me and walks away toward the river. I know he never thought much of me, and I knew I wasn't up to fightin' him, so I turned tail and went home. Just like that! I did just what he said I should do. I went home. I would've never won in a fight with him, but I should've stayed and tried. Even if he killed me, it's no worse than what I'll get now."

"Let's not have any more talk like that Ed," Rev. Blakeley quickly spoke up.

Then Anna suddenly had an inspiration, "If you left him walking toward the river, then maybe someone was down by the river, where no one saw him, and came up and killed him. Remember there were lots of people who didn't like Roger Kloster."

"But enough to kill him?" asked Ed. "Anyway Bill said that I took up the post hole digger and bashed him in the head and killed him. Someone who was down by the river would have been seen by Roger as he came up to the path."

"Not necessarily," countered the minister. "He could have been a little downstream, heard you arguing, waited until you left and maybe went around Roger and then grabbed the posthole digger when Roger wasn't looking. Roger falls into the river, perhaps after a kick or two to shove him over the edge of the bank, and the person sneaks off."

"But Bill says he saw me do it," Ed reminded them.

"But I remember it was getting dark," Anna quickly added. "I know that I was hurrying to get to the store and get back again before it got dark. And Bill Evans doesn't see too well. He could have thought it was you because he heard you arguing. He probably wouldn't think of anyone else coming up from the river."

"That sounds like a good explanation to me Anna," said Rev. Blakeley. "So now, what we have to do is to find out who that other person was."

"If there was another person," Ed said skeptically.

"If Harley Cobb was walking back to the Pearsons he might have seen someone else," Rev. Blakeley said. "Maybe what we need to do is to find Harley Cobb. We know his brother lives near Webster City and that's where he was supposed to be headed."

"Finding Harley Cobb won't do any good," Ed added. "If I didn't see him, then we weren't on the path at the same time. He must of been there earlier."

"Could Harley have killed Roger?" Anna asked.

"That I doubt very much," the minister added. "Harley's a timid soul, as I think I have said before. No, Harley might have seen something, but he wouldn't be the one to kill anyone. One look from Roger and he would have run for cover. But to get back to the timing. Liza says that he was going about the same time as you were, and that you should have met each other."

"Oh what does Liza know!" Ed added disgustedly remembering that she was the one who started this whole investigation. "Just 'cause she saw someone headin' down the river path, she thinks she has it all figured out. We all know how mixed up she gets sometimes, tryin' to tell one story on someone and gettin' it confused with somethin' else that happened."

"You do have a point there," the minister said thinking back to other events. "I've known it to occur more than once. It's possible that when Harley walked home to the Pearsons he saw Roger working and kept on going, not giving it a second thought."

"I still think someone should talk to him though," Anna added.

"Yes, you're right and I'm sure the sheriff will do it," Rev. Blakeley nodded. "He's a pretty fair man. I've known him a long time and he'll do his best to get at the truth. I'll talk to him first thing next week."

Just then Bert popped his head around the edge of the doorway. "'Fraid I'm gonna have to ask you folks to leave. You see I have to feed him his lunch."

"Oh, yes, of course Bert. Well come on Anna, we'll be on our way. And Ed, if you think of anything that might help, be sure to let me know."

"Sure Reverend. But I've already thought of everythin' that I can. Anyway thanks for comin'. You too Anna."

"Good-bye Ed," was all that she could think of to say, and she left the room with the minister coming a few moments later.

The trip home was rather somber. Neither one felt like talking, and when one of them did think of something that might help Ed, it was only to recall that they were hitting another dead end. They both hoped that when Rev. Blakeley talked to Jim on Monday that he would hear some good news.

Sunday and Monday both passed without a word. As Anna came into the house on Tuesday, Milly said she had had a call from Rev. Blakeley, but it was not good news. He had caught up with Jim Wilson, who had been hunting Harley Cobb. He even went to Webster City but his brother didn't have any idea where he was. He checked with the Pearsons again to make sure they hadn't heard of his whereabouts, but the last they had heard was that he was heading for his brother's place. This made Jim even more anxious to find him. Harley was not one to simply disappear.

After supper, with the children tucked in bed, the three adults sat down to their usual evening rest. Suddenly the sound of a car could be heard pulling into the yard. "Well," said Peter puffing on his pipe and putting down the newspaper. "We have company Mother, and it's either the sheriff or the Reverend, 'cause I don't think Floyd has up and bought himself a car yet."

Milly was not one to wait and see who it was, so she hurried to the door, and dashed into the entryway, and then through the outer door out into the cold. "Oh sheriff it's you. Come in. Come in. Do you have any good news?"

"Afraid not Milly," the man replied with a look of exhaustion on his face.

"Have you had any supper?" she inquired.

"The answer's the same, afraid not," he said with a grin.

"Well you yust sit right down here and I'll fix something for you," and the sheriff took off his coat and gratefully sat down at the table.

"I knew this would be a good place to come," he winked at Milly who was busy at the stove dishing up the leftovers on a plate. Then looking at Anna who was seated at the table embroidering a bib for Lucy's birthday, he said, "How's life treating you Anna? Sorry I missed you Saturday when you came in to see Ed."

Looking up she answered, "We're all a little jumpy. I wish there was something we could do for Ed. But let me get you a cup of coffee," and she went to the stove where the pot was still hot and poured him a cup.

"Yes, I wish there was something too," he answered. "Things don't look too good for him. I've been talking to Charley Wheeler tonight for the second time."

"Charley Wheeler?" came Peter's astonished comment, as he got up from the rocking chair and sat down at the table. "You think Charlie Wheeler has something to do with it?"

"No, not Charley," he answered. "But when I was going around talking to all the families in the area I stopped at the Wheelers, and Charley swears that he talked to Harley Cobb and that Harley said he was going to a place called Morris."

"Where's that?" Peter exclaimed. "I've never heard of it."

"Charley said he was going to Minnesota, so I looked it up and found a town called Morris, Minnesota."

"What would Harley go all the way up there for?"

"I suppose he thought he could get a job there," the sheriff continued. "Anyway, who knows? You know how hard it is to talk to Charley, and then with his mother butting in, and with Bill adding his two cents worth, and saying that Charley was all wet, and Bill not being too reliable either. Well tonight I thought I'd go back there and see if I could make any more sense out of it, and you can see what it did to me," and he laughed.

"Here you eat this and you'll feel better," said Milly as she handed him a plate full of food.

"Thanks Milly. It shore looks good to a hungry stomach," and he ate with gusto. "This is the second time lately that you've fed me, and I really appreciate it."

"Is there any way that we can help you?" Peter asked.

"Well, actually there is," the sheriff admitted. "I can't help but think that Charley has some information that would be useful, but I simply can't talk to him. Not only is he a little backward, but he gets all tongue-tied and turns shy on me. Actually I phoned the sheriff in Morris to see if anyone there had heard of a Harley Cobb, but just as I thought, nothing. It's almost impossible to find someone that far away. There are so many farms he could be working on."

"Why is finding Harley Cobb so important?" asked Peter.

In between bites, the sheriff continued. "Well, he is the only other person that we know of who can shed some light on this whole dreadful business. I can't really believe that Harley had anything to do with it, but why has he disappeared? His brother claims that Harley is a good sort and they were expecting him, but then this isn't the first time that he didn't turn up when he was supposed to."

"Joe Pearson always liked him too," added Peter.

"Oh yes," Jim replied. "Joe said he's a dependable hand, and since Joe was nearly through with the harvest, it was all right with him if Harley left. He had some idea that Harley had promised his brother to help out with their place. Harley isn't much for talking anyway, and is fairly independent. As Joe said, when they have him they have him, and when they don't, they don't."

"There's only one person I know who can get Charley to make sense and that's Floyd," Milly chimed in. "You get Floyd to talk to him and you'll find out what he has to say."

"Milly's right," Peter added. "Floyd just seems to have the right touch with Charley. If you think that Charlie has some valuable information, let Floyd find out what it is."

"It's sure worth a try," replied the sheriff. "It may be nothing at all, but I can't leave any stone unturned, and in the back of my mind I just have a hunch that Charlie can tell us something."

"You don't think anything terrible has happened to Harley Cobb do you?" asked Anna.

"I hope not, but I'm not sure of that either. Right now I'm not sure of anything, except that Milly cooks about the best supper of anyone around here. Anyway, I've taken up enough of your time, so I'll get going. It's a long drive home. Peter if you could get Floyd to talk to Charlie, let me know what he says," and Jim got up from the table to leave. "So long, and thanks Milly. I sure appreciate the food."

"You yust come here any time you please," she stated proudly.

"I just might do that," he answered and with hearty good-byes exchanged, he left.

"I don't think it's too late to phone Floyd, do you Mother?" Peter asked.

"Well, no, but you're not thinking of having him talk to Charlie tonight are you?"

"No, no. I thought I would let him know what Jim said, and Floyd can figure out the best way to talk to Charlie." He phoned the Parkers, and explained the situation to Floyd. It was arranged that Floyd and Inger would come down after supper the next day and learn a little more about the information that was needed.

As Anna walked up the stairs to her room she hoped that this would lead somewhere. She knew the next day at school would be a long one while she tried to think of what help poor Charlie Wheeler could be in this mystifying situation.

Chapter Thirty-five

"It's been only two weeks since Roger Kloster's funeral," Anna commented to Milly and Peter as they sat in the kitchen waiting for Inger and Floyd to arrive."

"And if today's Wednesday the 22nd of November, which it is," Peter added, "Ed has been in jail for eight days."

"That's too long," Milly said. "It yust isn't fair that Ed has been in yail for that long. Isn't the sheriff going to do anything about it? Oh, I wish Inger and Floyd would get here. Maybe Floyd can find out something from Charley." She quickly stood up upon hearing a wagon pull into the yard, rushed to the door, and soon welcomed her sister and brother-in-law, who took chairs at the table.

"Now what's all this about me talkin' to Charley and solvin' this whole case," Floyd said as he made himself comfortable and took the cup of coffee which Milly handed him.

"This is no joke Dad," said Inger. "Don't try to make something funny which is dead serious."

"Now Mother, just calm down, and I'd be obliged if your didn't mention the word *dead*," came his reply with a pat of his hand on her arm. "I know this is serious, but seein' all these long faces around here, I was tryin' my best to bring a little life to the sitshiashun. What 'xactly does the sheriff want me to do Peter?"

Milly added quickly. "You know you are they only one who can talk to Charley and get him to make sense,"

"Well, I'm not so sure about that," Floyd answered her.

"Charley's not so difficult to talk to. He's sort of a slow thinker, but I talk to him all the time."

"I've often thought you and Charley had something in common," Inger retorted.

"Now Mother, that was unkind." Suppressed laughter was evident in his listeners. "I know Charley has his drawbacks, but he's real easy to talk to once you get to know him."

Peter came in with "That's probably the crux of the matter. You're the only one of us who has taken the time to get to know him. And he likes you because of it, and so he doesn't clam up around you because he knows you like him."

"It's not so difficult to like him. He's a pretty nice feller. An' it's not so difficult for me to talk to him 'cause he lives right across the road. But why are we talkin' so much about Charley, and who can talk to him an' all that?"

Peter began to explain. "You see Floyd, Jim Wilson has been all around the countryside asking questions about anything that would relate to Roger's murder."

"Yes, I know that. He's been to our place and talked to all of us. It's a wonder he gets any work done on his farm at all."

"Well, when he went to the Wheelers he talked to the old lady and Bill and Charley. The old lady and Bill didn't seem to know much about what he was asking, but Charley said he'd seen Harley Cobb. That got Jim interested and when he started asking questions Charley got confused, and Bill and the old lady started butting in. Then Charley clammed up completely as always and let them carry on, when they didn't know anything about Harley Cobb."

"That sounds typical," Floyd shook his head. "When them two get a jawin' no one can stop them. It's no wonder Charley is a bit retirin'. Then what happened Peter?"

"Jim gave up that time and came back last night, hoping to get Charley to himself, but the same thing happened. All he could make out from what he said, and he had gotten that information the time before, was that Harley went to Morris, Minnesota to get a job. Jim had already contacted the sheriff there and no one had heard of Harley."

"That don't mean nothin'," Floyd said. "That's a big area to hunt for one guy, with all them farms, like huntin' for a needle in a haystack. If Jim has the information that Harley went to Minnesota, I don't see what more I can find out."

"Jim seems to think that there was something else Charley knew. Charley seemed almost angry when they wouldn't let him talk, as if he had something else to say, but couldn't get it out."

"Well," Floyd nodded his head. "I do know that the only times I have been able to talk to him was when we was alone, or at least away from the rest of his family." He paused. "Got any more coffee Milly, and what about them cookies?" At this request Milly bustled around filling cups, and loading up the cookie plate again. "Oh, don't bother puttin' them things on a plate Milly, just save yerself the trouble and pass the cookie jar."

"Floyd can find the bottom of a cookie jar faster'n anyone I know, even faster'n the boys," added Inger.

"Now Mother, you're makin' me sound bad. An' here I am tryin' to make Milly feel good by eatin' her cookies," he said as he took another one. "Didn't make any doughnuts today did you Milly? I shore love yer doughnuts. I'm really partial to them."

"Oh Floyd," she laughed. "You are impossible!"

"Anyways, I wasn't tryin' to make light of a serious sitshiashun. I guess what we better do is find out a way for me to talk to Charley and find out what he knows about Harley Cobb. Is that was Jim wants?"

"I guess that's it," said Peter. "I'm not sure what he wants, and as I gather neither is he. But he feels that Charley knows something that might help. Actually he's not even sure if Harley Cobb can shed any light on the case, but he's the only other one that we know of who was near the area when Roger got bashed on the head."

"You'd better find a way to talk to Charley when his folks aren't around," added Inger. "And that's going to be difficult."

"I was figurin' on that," came her husband's reply. "Let's see. When I talk to him it's usually when I just happen to see him workin' around the place, but I can't count on that. And I can't think of a good reason to bring him over to our place. Maybe I could get him to come here, but why would he want to come here?"

"To look at the ice house," said Milly enthusiastically. "Peter built such a beautiful ice house."

"Don't rub it in Milly. I haven't even gotten started on ours, and now the ground is so hard that I'll have a devil of a time diggin' it." He winked at her and smiled. "But that is a good idea. Charley just might like to see your ice house. I'll see if I can get him over tomorrow afternoon, before milkin'. Then we can talk to him."

"You can do the talking Floyd," Peter advised. "We'll just be the listeners."

"Well, all right. I'll do the talkin'. I guess that's one job I can handle."

At this remark, Inger gave Anna and Milly a smile and nodded her head. She was in perfect agreement with Floyd. Talking was a job he could handle. She stood up and limped slightly as she put on her coat. "All right Floyd. Since we've settled this, it's time to go home and let these folks go to bed."

"You're right Mother. I'm feelin' a little weary myself. See you folks tomorrow then, at least I hope I can get Charley to come here. Shucks I don't know why I didn't think of it before."

"What's that Floyd?" asked Peter.

"Well, why try to lure Charley down to see a ice house, when tellin' him he could come and see the pretty schoolmarm would get him here faster."

Anna blushed and everyone laughed.

"Well, anyways, we'll try to be here tomorrow." He put on his coat and hat. "Come on Mother. It seems I'm always waitin' on that woman," and with laughter and good-byes they were out the door.

Floyd was good to his word. At about 4:30 he and Charley pulled up in the wagon. Peter was on hand to meet them. Anna saw them pull up, so went out to where they were. She wanted to be in on this discussion. Milly decided to stay in the house with the children and keep them out of the way. Charley was in his mid forties, with a stocky build, of medium height. He appeared friendly but shy.

"Say Peter," came Floyd's opening comment. "Charley here is interested in seein' your ice house, ain't that right

Charley?" The man nodded his head enthusiastically. "Oh, by the way Charley, this here's the new schoolmarm this fall, name's Anna Swenson."

"Hello Charley," Anna greeted. He responded with another nod of the head.

"Now let's go in this contrapshun and see what it's all about," and Floyd led the way. "You see Charley my missus wants me to build one too, so I gotta look around real careful. Milly says that Peter built this one perfect." They stood stooped in the center of the dugout, and took it all in. "Of course now the ground is so hard now I pro'bly will have the devil of a time diggin' it. It's a big job."

"Yeah," said Charley nodding his head.

"Let's go outside and you can see how it looks from there," continued Floyd, realizing that they had seen enough of the small, dank quarters, and they followed him out into the cold, fresh air. "Guess I'll have to find me someone to help dig it out. Don't know anyone do you?"

Charley shook his head.

"Gosh amighty," continued Floyd. "Wasn't there someone used to be around these parts, what was his name, Harley was it?"

"Yeah," and Charley smiled. "You mean Harley Cobb."

"That's right Charley," Floyd went on. "Wonder if he's around to help me."

"Nope. He went up to Morris'," and Charley smiled.

"Where's that?"

"Up north, in a what's that name?" Charley asked.

"Minnesota?"

"Yeah, that's right."

"Why'd he go there?" Floyd continued.

"He said he's gonna work on the Morris place, but I dunno," and Charley smiled again. "Well he was goin' by, walkin' there, an I seen him, an' so I stop him to talk. An' he says, 'Let's have a smoke,' an' I say 'Fine', an' he pulls out his bag of Bull Durham. An' he gets out the paper, an' puts the tobaccy on real neat, and rolls it an' licks it and it looks real good. An' he gives it to me. 'That's real nice.' I say. An' he makes one for hisself and we sit down right by the road and smoke." Charley stops talking as he remembers this pleasant incident.

"That was real nice of him Charley," Floyd comments, hoping to get him to say more.

"Yeah, real nice."

"You say he was walkin' all the way to Morris?

"Yeah."

"Isn't that pretty far?"

"Yeah, far enough."

"What kind of a place is this where he was goin' to work?" and Floyd continued the questions.

"Oh, Morris lives just over in that place you said."

"Minnesota?"

"Yeah"

"Is that a farm he was goin' to work on?"

"Well, yeah, mebbe," and Charley smiled again. "Harley tol' me he thinks the Morris girl is real purty," and he smiled again, "but don't tell no one I tol' you. Harley didn't want no one to know."

"So I get it, he was goin' to the Morris farm to see their girl."

"Yeah," and with this remark came a sheepish grin.

"Well, if you see him again, you tell him I'd sure like him to help me dig my ice house. Will you do that Charley?"

"Sure Floyd," Charley answered, and then looked around him quite puzzled. "But I was wonderin'. Why are you buildin' a house for ice?"

"Well, I'll explain that on the way home Charley. Come along now we'd better get back so's you can milk the cows."

"Yeah, Floyd." And the two of them climbed into the wagon. Right before they drove off Floyd looked at Peter and said, "I guess you know all you need to know."

"Right Floyd. Thanks. And thanks for coming Charley." The young man gave a happy grin and waved as they left the farmyard.

"Well let's hurry in the house and I'll call Jim," said Peter. "Now we know that Morris is the name of a farm family. They probably live just across the border if Harley expected to walk there. He might have hoped to hitch a ride with someone. It's a pretty fair distance to walk. It sounded as if he'd been there before, and if he had a girl in mind, no wonder he didn't tell anyone where he was going.

"Floyd really got him to talk," Anna commented. "From what I had heard about him I didn't think he could put two words together."

"Charley's all right. He's just got too much competition in the family." Peter paused. "On second thought, I think I'll ride into town and call the sheriff myself. Let the milking wait a little. I won't be long, and this is something that can't wait.

They waited two days to hear from Jim Wilson. It was now Friday afternoon. Anna, Milly and Peter were in the kitchen having afternoon coffee, when the phone rang.

"Oh, maybe it's Yim Wilson," said Milly as she jumped up to answer it. "Hello————Oh Floyd it's you" and her voice trailed off. "No I'm not disappointed————Oh, you talked to Yim————He's with you now," and she became excited.

"What does he say?————Oh————And you say he'll stop by here on his way home————Thanks for calling," and she hung up the phone.

She turned to face the other two. "Floyd says Yim went up to Morris' and Harley isn't there. Anyway Yim's going to stop by here before he goes home."

"If he went up there hoping to make time with their young daughter, I can imagine that the farmer ran him off," laughed Peter. "I think I hear Jim's car in the driveway now," and he got up to go meet him.

Milly poured another cup of coffee which she brought to the table as Jim entered the room. "Here's a cup of coffee Yim. Sit down and make yourself at home."

"Don't mind if I do," came the reply. "I've had a rather frustrating time lately," and he took off his coat and hat and settled into the chair offered him."

"Floyd told Milly that you couldn't find Harley. Is that right?" Peter asked him.

"I wish it weren't, but I'm afraid it is. It's a funny story though. Here I was hunting for him in the town of Morris, which was what I thought Charley was saying, and it turns out that he was going to the Morris farm, but of course you knew that."

"Yes, we had an interesting time when Floyd brought him down to look at our ice house," Peter said.

"Leave it to Floyd to think of an ingenious way to do something," and the sheriff laughed. "Anyway this morning I finally found this Morris farm, it's just across the state line by a couple of miles, and drove in to talk to them. They have several kids, one of them a pretty girl of about sixteen. I didn't see her as she was at school, but they showed me a picture of her."

"No wonder Harley was anxious to get up there," Peter added.

"You don't know the half of it," and Jim laughed again.

"You see Harley had helped them with some job or other last spring, and saw the girl. You know these fellows roam the countryside looking for work, and as Morris could use a hand at the time, he kept him on for a week or so. The girl was nice to Harley, even darned his socks one evening, and he took this to mean something, while she was just an innocent kid doing what she would do for her father or brothers. Well, he really got stuck on her, and when he left he promised he would be back and see her again. No one thought anything of it, not until Harley showed up on their doorstep last week. Morris thinks Harley is looking for work and so tells him that he doesn't have anything now, but being a nice family they see he is tired and invite him in for supper and tell him he can spend the night in the shed out by the barn."

"Sounds like the nice thing to do," adds Milly.

"Oh they are a nice family all right, no doubt about that," Jim continued. "But as the dinner progressed it was obvious that Harley was sweet on the girl and that this could cause a problem. They let him stay the night, and at breakfast the next morning Harley said something like he would like to stay, and finally admitted much to everyone's horror that he wanted to marry the daughter."

"Oh!" Milly screamed.

"What happened next Jim?"

"Morris was shaking his head as he told me, just like he couldn't believe what had happened. I guess Harley's a little thick between the ears, because he couldn't understand why the girl and he couldn't go off together. Guess he had thought about it so much that in his mind it became a reality. Well Morris practically had to shove him off the place with a shotgun. He said he felt terrible about it, because Harley's a nice chap, but he had to make it clear that under no circumstances was Harley to come back, ever again! So Harley took off with his tail between his legs, and now has completely disappeared. That was several days ago. I even checked with his brother in Webster City and they haven't seen hide nor hair of him."

"That leaves us just about where we were before Floyd talked with Charley," Peter said as he shook his head. "I wonder where he could've gone?"

"Well, who knows," answered Jim. "Anyway I did want to talk to him for another reason in addition to his being on the river path at the same time Ed was, because he left the Pearsons so soon after Roger's body was found, but now it appears that he left because he thought he could make time with this girl. At least it seems like it's as simple as that. I suppose he's looking for work somewhere, but it's nearly impossible to find him."

"Now what do we do?" asked Peter.

"Well, your guess is as good as mine. I keep telling the judge that I don't want to go to trial because I'm collecting evidence, but I can postpone this only so long. By the way how's Bill Evans doing? I see he's still working on his harvest."

"Oh, don't even talk about that man," Milly shuddered as she said it and threw up her hands."

"He's a strange one all right. With his daughter gone at least all he has to worry about is himself."

"As if he ever worried about her," Milly continued. "Why the way he treated her was disgraceful."

"You're right Milly," Jim replied. "And the real disgraceful thing is that he signed a warrant that could mean a long prison sentence for Ed Marson, or even worse, if we can't prove he's wrong, and something keeps nagging at me that he is wrong." He got up to go, putting on his coat and hat.

"Thanks for the coffee and cookies Milly. Guess I'd better get on home. Try as I might, I just can't seem to get anywhere on this case," and he shook his head as he headed for the door.

Chapter Thirty six

Sunday night Anna was seated at the table going over her lessons for the next day. Peter was at the other end with pencil and paper figuring our the receipts of the farm. Milly was between them, also at the table, mending Davey's socks.

"Fine thing on a Sunday night, all of us working," Milly laughed.

"Can't think of a better time to do it," Peter replied. "Can't really call this work anyway when the receipts are so good."

"What about you Anna," Milly asked. "Did you ever think that you would be working on Sunday. I suppose your Mother always kept the Sabbath."

"We went to church and had a Sunday dinner, but when you're earning your living sewing, every minute counts. We often tried to do something special on Sunday, but usually never got around to it. Anyway, looking over the lessons for tomorrow isn't really work."

They were interrupted by the sound of horse's hooves coming into the yard. All of them looked up with questioning expressions on their faces, and Peter got up and went to the door. "Who could be coming at this time of night?"

In a minute or so Floyd could be heard making his way to the back door. "What brings you out at this time of night?" asked Peter.

"Well, I'll tell you somethin', you folks have really got me in a pickle," he exclaimed as he took off his hat and coat and sat down. "Now jus' when I thought I was doin' everyone a favor, I find that now I done and got myself in a real jam." Floyd had a most serious look on his face.

"What's the matter?" Peter asked anxiously, afraid that something seriously was wrong.

"Now you jus' recall when I willin'ly got Charley to come down here an' look at the ice house so's I could ask him questions about Harley. Now remember you asked me?"

All three nodded their heads accompanied by three puzzled expressions. He obviously had their attention.

"Well now, just about a hour ago, Charley comes over to my place, an' stands aroun' for goodness how long, an' then suddenly says he found Harley who can dig my ice house. An' he looks as proud as a peacock."

"What!" Peter exclaimed. "He found Harley! How?"

"Well, it seems that after Harley got kicked off the Morris place, he didn't know where to go, so he thinks of Charley an' that nice smoke they had together, an' he knows that the Wheelers have a nice bunk house. So this afternoon I guess he was hidin' in the field until he sees Charley alone in the yard, an' then goes up to him an' asks him if he can stay in their bunk house for a few days. Well, Charley is really tickled about this, 'cause he tells Harley that he has a job for him, so here is Charley pleased as punch comin' over to my house, sayin' he has found Harley to help me out and dig my ice house. Actchally it's pro'bly one of the first times that Charley has ever felt he has done somethin' important."

"You mean Harley is at the Wheeler's now?" Peter asked.

"That's right," came Floyd's answer. "An' first thing in the mornin' he's goin' to start diggin my ice house."

"Are you sure he's there? Did you talk to him?" Anna asked.

"You're darn right I'm sure. I go back over to Wheeler's with Charley and talk to Harley, and sure enough Harley is tickled pink to have a job. So's now I'm stuck with hirin' him to do the work while I have two great big louts who could easily dig for me. An' all this time Inger is laughin' her fool head off. Now she gets her ice house."

"Good!" said Milly firmly.

"Wait a minute, but did you call Jim?" Peter asked.

"Yep," came the answer. "That's why I have the horse. I rode over to the station and talked to him. He's comin' first thing in the mornin'. Now, an' this here's the question I'm puttin' up to you folks, 'cause I think you got good judgment."

At this statement the other three looked rather suspiciously at Floyd. "Don't you think the county should pay for my ice house, since I did a favor for the law, pro'bly saved them a pile of money huntin' down this Harley." The laughter that followed filled the room. "Well, I guess I couldn't' 'spect you folks to agree with me," and he laughed with them.

"Are you really going to let him dig your ice house for you?" asked Milly.

"Well now, of course. Can't say I wanted to dig it myself, and the boys is none to keen on it neither. An' since Inger is determined to have one, guess I'll keep ol' Harley on 'til he finishes the job. I may get Walter and George to help him out. Once they get below the first six inches of ground it'll be fairly easy diggin'. Of course now Inger'll have another mouth to feed, but that suits her fine. An' the Wheelers say that Harley can sleep in their bunk house."

"Looks like you did a good job Floyd, but don't let Harley get interested in Mabel," and Peter let out a hearty chuckle.

"Don't you worry none about that. I got me a buggy whip that'll do better than a shotgun. Anyways, I better get goin'. Jus' thought I'd spread the news," and he left them without even asking for coffee or cookies.

School had barely started the next morning when Anna heard Jim's Chevy go up the road and into Floyd's yard. She waited to hear what time he would leave. About an hour later she thought she heard him go and was most anxious to learn what had happened, but knew that she would have to wait until she got home from school to find out anything. As the day wore on the sky darkened with black clouds. Peter had said it might snow, and she and the students kept glancing out of the windows to see if this were true. About one o'clock a light snow started to fall, and by the time she dismissed the students it was a few inches deep. Nothing to worry about, they all had heavy shoes and she had worn her overshoes for some time now, so they would make it home safely.

Anna left with Davey, not wanting to stay any longer than she had to, and anxious to learn what Harley had told Jim. As they passed the Evans' farm to turn into their own yard, they could see Bill still trying to finish the harvest. He was nearly done. It was a tremendous job for an old man.

They shook the snow off their shoes, Anna took off her overshoes, left their coats in the entryway, and entered the warm, welcoming kitchen. Peter and Milly were there as well as Sarah and Lucy.

"What happened this morning?" Anna asked anxiously.

"Oh, Anna," Milly rushed to explain. "You'll never believe it. The sheriff talked to Harley and then took him to the county seat.'

"What for? Did they arrest him too?" she asked with incredulity.

"No, no. Floyd was down here and told us the whole story, yust sit down and I'll tell you."

Reluctantly Anna took a chair and waited for Milly to continue. "Harley said that he saw Ed on the path by the river, and that Ed was going back home."

"But why didn't Ed see Harley?" Anna asked in frustration.

"Oh, you tell her Peter," Milly continued. "I will get it all mixed up."

"What Milly's trying to tell you is that Harley was walking back to the Pearsons when he had to stop in the bushes, so he gets off the path. You know the willows are pretty thick along some parts of the river. Well, so he sees Ed coming, and stays in the bushes until Ed gets by, then continues walking home."

"Oh, I see," said Anna, thinking that this was not such a big discovery.

"But that's not the important part Peter," Milly lamented.

"Now Milly, I'm coming to that. Harley continues walking and sees Roger standing by the river as Harley said, 'Lookin' like Abe Lincoln all skinny and tall and dark.' He said Roger was just standing there, looking toward the river, and turned to look at Harley when he passed, but then ignored him and continued to stare at the river."

"But then that means that Roger was alive when Ed left him," Anna said excitedly."

"Precisely," Peter continued. "And Jim thinks that Harley is a credible witness."

"But then, who killed Roger?" she asked.

"That's what we don't know. But to try to learn that, Jim brought Harley to the county seat, and with the snow like it is, no doubt he will keep him there tonight. It's possible that if Harley really thinks about it, he'll remember seeing someone else. Anyway, we'll have to wait until tomorrow to find out."

"But this means that Ed is free!"

"It seems to, but Jim said he would have to talk it over with the authorities and let them decide, and we probably won't know until tomorrow. With this snow, Jim won't be able to drive through it to bring Harley back here, so he'll probably have to come on the train. Anyway, all this is only conjecture, so we'll just have to wait and see."

"What about Vi and Elmer?" Anna asked. "Do they know all of this?"

"I'm sure Jim talked to them when he went through Grabney and gave them some hope. Anyway we'll find out tomorrow. So now let's have a cup of coffee and then I'll go out and do the milking."

Anna looked out of her window the next morning. The snow lay about a foot deep on the ground. She could hear Milly in the kitchen, and felt the warmth coming through the register in the floor. After she dressed she closed it so the heat would not be wasted, and hurried down the steps. Peter had just come in from milking and was going downstairs to do the separating. "There sure is a racket over at Bill Evans' place," he said as he started down. "He must be late because you can hear the cows bellowing way over here."

"With the snow he's probably behind schedule," Anna commented. "And that reminds me, I think I'll leave for school a little early. It'll take longer to walk there, and besides I have a few chores to finish before nine o'clock. Do you want to leave early with me Davey?" she asked as he came down the stairs.

"Oh, sure!" he said with a gleam in his eyes that meant snowballs. "I can eat breakfast real fast."

"You don't have to hurry too much, I'm just starting myself. I think if we leave a little before eight o'clock, that will be time enough."

Peter had finished the separating, and came and sat down to the table. They were interrupted by the phone ringing three long rings.

"That's for Inger and Floyd," Milly said in alarm. "Who would be calling them at this time of morning? I yust have to know. It must be something important." She walked over to the phone and put her hand over the mouthpiece before picking up the receiver.

"Milly!" Peter said in disgust. She shook her head for him to shush. "You all criticize Liza for listening in on conversations, and now you do it yourself."

She shook her head disgustedly, and hung up the phone. "Well it's my own sister's phone and with so much going on I wanted to know if there was any more trouble. It was only Charley Wheeler wondering when Harley was coming back to their place."

"Charley! On the phone!" and Peter laughed. "I'd never heard of him talking on the phone before. Are you sure Milly?"

"Of course I'm sure," she answered firmly, and then smiled at the thought. "I guess Floyd has really started something now. Imagine Charley Wheeler calling up someone and talking on the phone."

Breakfast over, and Anna and Davey headed out the door. "I'll walk part way with you," Peter said, and he put on his hat and coat and they were on their way.

Coming down to the road they could hear Bill Evans' cows still bellowing. "I don't understand it," Peter commented. "It's not like Bill to let his cattle go like that. Think I'll stop by and see if something's the matter."

"Can I come too Dad?" Davey asked.

"Sure. You're plenty early. We'll just be a minute Anna," he called as they walked into the yard. He suddenly stopped, and called back to her again. "I don't see any tracks in the yard. He must have left his stock in the barn last night, but from the looks of things no one has been around this morning, and I don't think it has snowed since about midnight."

Anna had slowly followed them, not wanting to stand waiting in the road by herself, and also curious as to the reason for this. "Peter, I don't think he's been out this morning," she yelled to him. "The snow on the steps is still fresh also."

"By golly, you're right. Maybe the old man's sick," said Peter as he ran for the house. "He's been workin' too hard lately. Let me go inside and see," and he pushed past her into the kitchen. "Bill! Bill Evans!" he shouted. "Are you all right?" No answer was forthcoming, so he hurriedly went through the rooms in the house, continuing his call.

Anna could see the place was a complete mess, and she thought of how she and Inger and the Larson boys had worked so hard to clean it up. Even when Grace was there it wasn't too good, and she remembered brushing food off the chair that Tuesday night before she sat down. The smell was almost un- bearable.

"Can't find him anywhere," Peter said hurriedly. "Let's go out to the barn. Maybe he had an accident out there," and they ran across the freshly fallen snow as quickly as they could.

"Hey Dad, where's his team?" Davey called from the barn. "The cows are in the stalls, but there aren't any horses."

Peter was bewildered. "Are you sure Davey? He wouldn't leave his team out all night, not in this weather. Here let me look," and Peter dashed into the barn.

"See, I was right Dad. There aren't any horses here, just the cows."

"And we have some pretty unhappy cows," replied his father. "Davey, you run home and ask your mother to call Uncle Floyd and get him over here as fast as he can. Then she can call the Larsons too. You stay home and wait for Miss Swenson to get you before you go to school."

As Davey dashed off, happy to be on an important er- rand, Peter said to Anna. "This doesn't look good at all. I wonder if the old man just went out of his mind and drove off, but that doesn't seem likely. He did the milking last night, or the cows would have been bellowing half the night and we would have heard them. Our bedroom's on the front of the house and I must say that we have heard things coming from this place more than once. Anyway I can see the snow was trampled after it started to fall, but no one has been out in the yard since yesterday evening. We can get help soon to milk the cows. I think we should walk around and see if we can find something else." Slowly they made their way back toward the house.

At that point they heard what they thought was a horse whinny. They stood quietly, listening to see if they could hear it again. "Let's get away from the house. I can't tell if that's the phone from Milly calling or if it is a horse," said Peter, and they walked out toward the barn. They heard it again. "Well, it wasn't close by, but it sounded like it was coming from over by the fence. That's about the only part that's still not harvested, that field next to the church grounds." He took off at a fairly steady pace, heard the whinny again and knew he was headed in the right direction.

Anna waited what seemed like forever. She could feel her heart throbbing in her chest. She stamped her feet to get the circulation going as she realized they were getting cold, so decided to walk around a little herself. She might as well follow Peter she thought, but took a slightly different route. He had run at an angle through the dried and snowy cornstalks, and she, wanting to get as little snow on herself as possible, walked in the yard area where it was cleared, to look down each row to determine if she could see the horses. Finally she thought she saw them, by the fence, so she began walking where it seemed obvious the wagon had been the night before. There was fresh snow on top, but it was trampled underneath. She was looking ahead hoping to see Peter get to the horses, and not paying any attention to where she was walking. She hadn't gone too far when she suddenly stumbled and looked down at her feet. There, half covered in snow, was Bill Evans.

She stood there almost numb, not believing what she saw, and then she heard a horse gallop into the yard. She turned. It was Walter. He got off his horse and tied it up at the barn. "Anna is that you down there?" he called out to her.

"Yes, it is," she answered feebly.

"What seems to be the problem?" he said as he walked toward her. "Aunt Milly called Mom and didn't seem to know except Davey said to get here fast 'cause Bill's cows were bellowin' up a storm so I jumped on my horse. Dad is comin' behind me, and I passed Jonah Larson runnin' down the road." When he got to her he stopped. She was looking at the corpse, and didn't need to tell him any more.

"Oh my God! I can't believe it. That's Bill?"

She nodded her head. "I guess so."

"What happened?"

"I don't know," Anna said, feeling a little weak in the knees.

"Where's Peter?"

"Down there," she pointed. "He found the team. He's going to bring them back."

"The teams' been out all night?"

"It looks that way," she spoke quietly.

"Well, nothin' I can do with Bill, but we better get the team in and get them rubbed down. No tellin' what can happen to them," and he dashed off to help Peter.

Anna remained frozen to the spot. Jonah and Floyd arrived at about the same time. They heard Walter talking to her, and as Walter took off they arrived where she was standing. "Sure is some commotion that's goin' on here today, and what're you doin' here an' not at school." Floyd jovially asked Anna.

With her face getting whiter by the minute she pointed to the corpse. "It's Bill. I think I'd better go sit down."

Floyd took a good look at the body, and then at her and realized she was about to faint. Here, Jonah, you take Anna over to where she can set a spell, an' I'll take over here. This has been too much of a shock to her this mornin'."

"Come on into the barn," Jonah said kindly. "There's somethin' for you to sit on there and we'll get you out of the cold."

She was so grateful to get away from this scene, but when she started to walk her legs wouldn't move as she wanted them to and she became very dizzy. The next thing she knew, she was lying on a pile of hay in the barn. She opened her eyes, and felt so foolish when she realized that she had fainted. Jonah was beside her, quite relieved that she was all right.

"I'm sorry the cows are bellowing so," he said. "I'm afraid that this isn't a very good place to have any quiet, but

I'm glad you're all right. You are all right, aren't you?"

"Oh yes," she answered, weakly. "I've got to get up. I've got to get to school."

He put a restraining hand on her. "No, don't get up yet. School won't start for another half hour at least, and I think the students won't mind if it's delayed a little today. You'll find they'll be out in the yard snowballing."

She was going to ask him how she got there, and then realized that he had carried her. This made her feel even more embarrassed. "Oh, I'm so sorry I fainted and that you had to, well, I mean . . ."

"Don't worry about anything," he said. "You've had a terrible shock. I know what it's like to faint. The first time I saw my dad butchering I passed out cold. My mother was in the house and saw me and came out running and sure gave my dad heck for letting me watch. It took me a long time before I got over that feeling when I saw someone butcher meat." He saw her smile. "I don't know what I'm talking about that for, I should think of something pleasant."

She tried to get up. "I really should get up, but I still feel a little wobbly."

"Try sitting up for a while, maybe that would be all right," and he helped her to sit up and put a mound of hay behind her back.

"You're Jonah, aren't you? I thought you were away working?"

"Well my job petered out, and anyway I'm still trying to complete my correspondence courses. I guess I took on too much this semester, so Mom said to say home and study."

"What are you studying?" she asked with interest.

"Agriculture. The way I'm going it'll take me another year or so to get my two year certificate. You see, I want to be a farmer, but I want to learn some of the new methods. Dad's a little old fashioned and doesn't think it's important, but I always liked going to school, and I'm learning things that will be useful."

"That's wonderful," said Anna, trying to make herself heard over the bellowing of the cows.

"Listen, if you feel better, I'll help you over to the Jensen's and then you can rest a bit before you go to school. A

320

good cup of coffee might help too."

"Yes, I think that's a good idea," she said as he helped her up.

As they were leaving the barn, Peter and Walter appeared with the team. Floyd was close behind them.

"Looks like Bill tried to work last night in the snow and maybe had a heart attack," Peter commented. "He made it just so far, and the team, used to keeping on going, just kept on going after he fell, and then were stopped at the fence. Anyway, got to get them in the barn and get them rubbed down and get some blankets on them."

"William and Dad should be here soon," volunteered Jonah. "They can do the milking. I'm going to take Anna across the road to your house Peter and get Milly to give her a cup of coffee. She's had a terrible shock this morning."

"I'm so sorry about that Anna," Peter said solicitously. "I never expected anything as bad as this. Are you sure you're all right?"

"Oh, yes, I'm fine," she said with more hope than conviction.

"Well, you let Jonah take you over home. Get Milly to call Rev. Blakeley, will you?" He assumed her answer was in the positive, because he continued giving directions. "The Reverend can call the Doc and decide what to do with the body. No point in moving him inside anywhere, because he's frozen now, and we don't want him to thaw out. Oh here come William and Olle."

"Hey Jonah!" yelled Floyd. "After you get a cup of coffee in Anna, take my rig and drive her to school, an' then stop by and pick up the Reverend. I was right. We weren't never intended to have cars. Come a little snow and they ain't worth a . . . well, they ain't worth nothin." Leave it to Floyd. With this remark they all found something to laugh at.

Chapter Thirty-seven

After Anna had sat and collected herself at the Jensen's, and had a cup of coffee, Jonah drove her and Davey to school. The children were unaware of what had occurred at the Evans' place and thought that she was later than usual due to the snow. All Davey knew was that Bill had not milked his cows when they left and needed some help with that chore. If George had any inkling of what had happened, he gave no sign of it. Anna tried to avoid thinking of her experience and concentrate on teaching. At the end of the day she was pleased that she had somehow gotten through it much better than she expected.

After school Davey waited for her as she finished some lessons and together they slogged through the snow and arrived home about four o'clock.

"Oh Anna, guess what has happened today," said Milly, all smiles as they entered the kitchen.

"What do you mean Milly," answered Anna, all too aware of what had happened that morning.

Milly saw the puzzled look on her face and quickly added, "No, no. I don't mean this morning. I mean guess who came in on the noon train from the county seat?" Anna still didn't comment. "It was Harley and Ed. Ed Marson has been freed. He came home today. Isn't that wonderful?"

"Oh yes, Milly. That is wonderful," said Anna as she sank into a chair. "Oh, I can't believe it. To think that getting Harley here made all the difference. Wasn't it wonderful that Floyd could get Charley to talk. Oh, I'm so tired Milly. Could I have some coffee?"

"Oh, yes, of course. Poor Anna. I didn't think of all the problems you had this morning. What a terrible thing to happen. Davey you go upstairs and change your clothes, and Sa-

rah you take Lucy to my room and play with your doll. How
did you ever manage to teach today? "

"It worked out better than I expected," she replied as
she took a sip of coffee. "But I was so embarrassed to faint
over at the Evans' place. And then when I came to I was lying
on a pile of hay in the barn. Jonah had carried me there. How
could I do such a stupid thing as to faint?"

"Well if I had been the one to find Bill Evans' body I
would have screamed and made a terrible scene," said Milly.

"And Peter said he will never forgive himself for leaving you when he went to find the horses. He said he should
have known better."

"But how was he to know?" Anna asked rhetorically.
"Anyway, that part is over now."

"Oh, I think you were so brave to go on and teach
school. When you left here I didn't know all that had happened
or I would never have let you go. I thought you were yust cold
and needed some coffee to warm up. It wasn't until Peter came
back that I learned exactly what happened. Then I felt terrible
for you. I am so glad that Yonah brought you to school. He is
such a nice young man, and so intelligent too. All the teachers
who had him said he was one of the smartest students they
have had."

"Yes, Jonah was very kind, but I still feel so embarrassed to think that I collapsed and he had to carry me all the
way to the barn," and she paused and shuddered as if to clear
her mind. "But tell me, what has happened since this morning?"

"Peter knows more than I do, and he should be in by
now because it's four o'clock." They waited and talked more
and before too long Peter came in.

"What a day!" he exclaimed as he dropped into a chair.
"I hope we never see another one like it. Oh Anna, I'm sure
that goes for you too. I'm so sorry that you had to be the one
to find Bill."

"Don't worry about that," she answered. "No one knew
he would be there. Anyway, it's all over now. Tell me what has
happened since I left."

"Let's see now, when you left Walter and I were just bringing in the team. We got them in the barn and he and William got to work rubbing them down, giving them some feed and water and putting blankets on them. I think they'll probably be all right. Horses can stand to be out in bad weather, depending upon their age and condition, but it won't hurt to keep a watch on them. Oh yes, Floyd and Olle did the milking. They gave it all to the hogs and fed them too. The cows had feed in their stalls. I hadn't gotten a good look at Bill's body, so I went to see what it was like. He probably had a heart attack, fell down, and died fairly soon. With the weather so cold the body froze, at least this is what the Doc thought when he came a few hours later. He said it was possible he was conscious for a while and tried to get up but couldn't, but the way the body was lying it looked as if he went fast and didn't suffer."

"I think he worked himself into the grave," Anna commented. "The way he was flogging himself to get the crops in, it's a wonder he lasted as long as he did."

"You're right Anna," Milly added.

"When we went to school in the morning I would see him out there yelling and lashing out at the horses, and the same thing when we came home in the afternoon. But, Peter, did Rev. Blakeley get there?"

"Yes, Jonah drove over to his place after he left you at school, and good soul that he is he came back in the wagon. He called the doctor on Bill's phone, and so by afternoon it was decided to get Anders Anderson to build a casket and in the meantime lay the body on a board and put it in the house. It's cold enough in there to keep it. We took some sheets off the bed and wrapped it up. I guess that's all of the gruesome part of it."

"What about Grace? Who will tell her, and when will the funeral be?"

"Let's see now, Dr. Bailey said he will be going into the county seat to see a patient and he would tell Grace. Rev. Blakeley said if it is all right with Grace we can have the funeral on Saturday afternoon. That way she will have a few days to take this all in. If she wanted she could arrive in Grabney on the noon train from the west, and take the 5:10 back. We could have the funeral at two o'clock. Rev. Blakeley planned to write a letter to Grace and send it with the doctor."

"Who is going to look after the farm?" came another question from Anna.

"That seems to be made to order. Olle Larson has always had his eye on that land since it is next to his, and is a good parcel. With two sons he could use more acreage. Except for the small area sold off for the parsonage and park, it's two homestead sites. Since Jonah has always wanted a farm, he said he'd take care of the livestock until he talks to Grace. Olle's place is free and clear so he could afford to buy it, but I think Jonah wants to buy it himself. Anyway, we don't know yet if Grace wants to sell it."

"I think it's mighty nice of Yonah to offer to take care of it until he hears from Grace," added Milly. "She's lucky her animals don't starve since she's gone and really doesn't care about them."

"Well, knowing Jonah, he would never let that happen. I don't think any of us would for that matter. But this just seems made to order for him. He's always wanted a farm, and land is not that available. Anyway, this is all pie in the sky for now. Who knows what Grace will do?"

"Who does indeed," said Anna. "We'll just have to wait and see."

"And in the meantime you heard the good news about Ed coming home, I'm sure," added Peter.

"Yes," replied Anna. "And now I want to see how fast Harley gets Inger's ice house made."

"I think first Harley and Walter will be digging the grave," announced Peter. "Rev. Blakeley asked if we knew who could do it, and Floyd volunteered them. I believe I heard William say he would work also."

"I just remembered," said Anna. "Since we have proof that Ed did not kill Roger, who did? We can't ask Bill Evans to go over it again. Did the sheriff talk to Harley about it?"

"I understand that he did, but he hasn't been around to let us know what he found out. Anyway, first things first. Let's bury Bill and since Ed is in the clear that's all we have to worry about now. Milly says she's heard the phone ringing all afternoon with calls to the store, and I'm sure they're celebrating with a big dinner. The rest is the sheriff's problem, and if Roger had some other enemies that we don't know about, let Jim find them.

Thursday the 30th of November was the official day to celebrate Thanksgiving. There was no school holiday, and no real celebration, but Milly who had heard that the Pilgrims had turkey, did the next best thing and stuffed one of her biggest hens for dinner and they all gave thanks that Ed was home.

By Saturday the snow had melted enough so that people could get out and about a little easier. Some even ventured to drive their cars, although one person had to be towed out of a ditch by a team. Floyd said that he thought he'd make his fortune this winter by doing this.

Grace and Joshua came in on the noon train. Elaine remained in town with Grace's aunt. They went to the Blakeley home for lunch. Mrs. Blakeley invited Anna to come also, since she had been Joshua's teacher, and it was thought that she would be able to help Joshua through any difficult time he might have. This was the second funeral in his family in less than a month, and it might be hard on him. Anna was flattered to be asked.

Anna walked to the Blakeley's and arrived about noon. She was helping her hostess set the table when they heard the train arrive. Soon Grace and Joshua were at the front door and greeted by the Reverend, "Come in! Come in!" They could hear his hearty voice. "Mother and Miss Swenson are in the kitchen. Take off your coats and let's go in there."

Soon the three of them came through the door. Grace looked tired as could be expected. Joshua was rather pale.

"I'm glad to see you Joshua," Anna said as she went over to him. "We miss you at school." The child looked at her but didn't reply. "And I hope you are feeling all right Grace, and I hope that you have a wonderful new life in town."

"It's much better," said Grace. "This, losin' Dad was a shock, but I should have expected it. He was drivin' himself to death. But I can't say I'm sorry to be livin' in town. It's such a relief to be away from here. I really didn't have any idea of how awful it was for me."

"It's the best thing you could do to go live with your aunt," Mrs. Blakeley added. "I think you'll find that you are a new person in a few months."

"I hope so," she replied. "Anyway, in the short time I've been there I've gotten to feelin' better. My aunt's a good cook, and I'll be gettin' fat I'm afraid."

"Hardly a chance of that," came Rev. Blakeley's remark. "I've always known you as a skinny little thing," and he laughed. "By the way, Joshua, how's your new school?"

"It's all right, but we don't have the fun of making things on Friday afternoon like Miss Swenson had us do."

"I'm glad you liked that Joshua," Anna replied.

"And I got the bookends that I was makin'. I've almost finished them too. Jack is helpin' me and said when I got them finished we could buy some books to put between them."

"That's wonderful. You mean Jack Jarvis?" asked Anna.

"Yes," answered Grace. "He boards with Aunt Elaine, and he's taken an interest in Joshua."

The lunch conversation continued much the same until Grace brought up the question to Rev. Blakeley about what he thought she should do with the farm. She knew that Jonah was taking care of the animals. He told her that Jonah very much wanted to buy it.

"I really couldn't keep it," she stated. "It means nothing but unhappiness to me. The sooner I get rid of it the better, but I know that land is scarce and I want to get a fair price."

"Land is pretty much the same price when it's available," said the minister, "and I think you could find someone in the county seat who could draw up a contract for you. There are a couple of people that I've heard of who would charge you a flat fee and not a commission."

"Yes, Jack told me something about that. He also said that I should sell the land, and he thinks that Jonah should have it. He always liked the Larsons He said Jonah would improve the farm and make it his own, and not just farm it and live somewhere else. I know I don't like the place, but my mother always had such hopes of bein' happy, and she never was. I just want someone to live there who'll be happy, and take all the evil out of what's gone on there."

"Well, in that case let's talk to Jonah this afternoon. He'll be at the service."

"Speaking of services, Dad," Mrs. Blakeley reminded him, "It's after 1:30 and we'd better get a move on or we'll be late.

The church service was about thirty minutes long. Anna played the organ. It was similar to the one held for Roger, although there were more people attending. Anna and Peter brought Davey, who wanted to come to see Joshua. Mabel took care of Sarah and Lucy.

Afterward they went to the graveside. The minister said a few words and read another verse from the Bible. Joshua was standing between Anna and his mother, who was next to Rev. Blakeley. The rest of the crowd surrounded the grave.

"Is Grandpa in that box the same as Dad was?" asked Joshua.

"That's right," answered Grace. "This is the way we bury people when they die." She was solemn, but her eyes were dry.

"Do people die because God is punishing them?" the child asked.

"Why do you ask that?" his mother questioned. The entire group was silent, listening to the conversation. It was sad to think of a child losing both a father and a grandfather in such a short period of time, and they felt sympathy for him.

Joshua was unaware that so much attention was being paid to him, and he continued talking. "Dad said that God punishes people who do wrong. I think that's why Grandpa died."

"Yes, I remember your father did say that," answered Grace, rather anxious to terminate the conversation, "but that's not why Grandpa died."

"Yes it is!" he stated quite firmly. "God punished Grandpa for killin' Dad."

"What do you mean?" his mother asked.

"Well the day after Miss Swenson and Davey's dad came over, you know the night when you cried so much?"

Grace gasped that he was telling this to the world, and was moving to quiet him when he continued. "Well, I was leavin' for school, and Grandpa was a little late with the milkin' an' he

329

was in the barn. I heard him laughin' an' I couldn't believe it after all the arguin' you did with him that night. An he told the cows that he killed Dad."

"Oh, Joshua, I don't understand what you are talkin' about," his mother said. "Just hush!"

"Joshua," said Rev. Blakeley stepping over to him. "Tell me what you heard your Grandpa say."

Joshua looked up at him and replied, "Grandpa said somethin' like, 'Well I did it Bossy, I did it. I killed him and now Ed's goin' to hang for it.' An then he said that everyone thought he was stupid, but he showed 'em. An he said that Ed was no good. An' then the worst part is that he gave Bossy a slap on the rear an tol' her to move over or he'd hit her like he hit Dad with the posthole digger. An' he laughed and laughed." Then turning toward his mother he said, "He can't hurt me now can he? Now that I told you."

Chapter Thirty-eight

In the next week the crew worked on Inger's ice house, women were starting to do their Christmas baking, the men were making the farms ready for winter, and the people of Grabney breathed a little easier now that the terrible ordeal which had fallen on their community was settled. That first snowfall was also almost a memory. The ground was hard and frozen, and snow could still be seen, but it had been trampled enough so that getting around was no problem. Much to Floyd's disgust, even the cars were moving. However, expecting more snow, more families got out their sleighs, which had usually been stored in the back of the barn.

On Wednesday Liza called to tell Anna that her Kodak Brownie had arrived, and so directly after she came home from school, she set off again for the Post Office. She walked quickly, hurrying by the spot where Roger had gone into the river. There was a thin skin of ice around the edges and she wondered how long it would be before Peter could cut some for the ice house. He had mentioned that January or February were the best months for that since it took several weeks of cold weather before the ice was thick enough. She passed the parsonage and waved to Mrs. Blakeley who was looking out of the kitchen window. It was slippery walking across the bridge, but she managed not to fall and headed for the Post Office.

"Afternoon Anna," called Liza as she looked up from behind the counter where she was getting the mail ready to go out on the 5:10. "I've got your Brownie right here," and she reached behind the counter and handed the package to her. "Elmer's got the film for it if you don't have any. I knew you were gettin' it and so I asked him if he had some."

"Thanks Liza. I didn't realize it would be here so soon or I would have thought more about getting the film. I'll go over to the store. I'd like to see them anyway. How are they doing?"

"Just fine as far as I can make out," came her reply. "An' you know what I think," and she leaned half way across the counter as if this were some conspiracy. "I think Ed's got himself a girl. I saw Bertha Clemson over there last Sunday. She come in on the noon train and left again on the 5:10. I s'pose if there hadn't been so much snow around Ed'd drove to town to of got her. You know they've been seein' each other off 'n on for a coupla years."

"Yes I had heard that. I'm so happy for him."

"You'd like her Anna. Comes from a nice family up Brewster way. Hope you can meet her sometime. You don't know her do you?" came the inquisitive question.

Anna was not about to divulge her visit to the county jail and meeting Bertha there, and so replied that no she didn't know her. To change the subject she asked, "Is there any other mail?"

"I woulda give it to you if there was," Liza replied. Seeing Anna start to leave and wanting to talk some more she said, "Let me see some of yer photos when you git 'em. I'm real int'rested."

"I will," Anna answered as she went out the door and closed it firmly behind her. She made her way across the street. Elmer didn't seem to be doing any business at the gas pump today, so no doubt he was in the store. She hoped to see Vi also. As she came up the steps the door opened. She expected to see someone leaving, but instead it was Ed, standing there smiling at her.

"Hello Anna."

"Hello Ed," she said smiling at him as she entered the store. She looked around and they seemed to be the only two there. "It's good to see you back."

"You don't know how good it is," he replied. "I can't believe that everything turned out so good. Even Ma is almost her old self again. And I want to thank you for helpin' so much."

Surprised at this she answered, "I don't think I was much help at all. I wish I could have been."

"Well from what I hear, you were, and thanks for comin' to see me. I know I wasn't in the best mood that day, but I sure feel better now."

"I was happy to come," and to change the subject she added, "It's the first ride I've had in Rev. Blakeley's car, and the first time I'd been to the county seat."

"How's he at drivin'? I heard that once he's on the road he really lets 'er go," and they both laughed. "Oh, say, Ma wants to see ya. Bertha was here Sunday and brought a cake plate that you might like. This'd be a good time to get it, since it's for Milly 'n she's not here with you." He went over to the stairs. "Hey Ma! Anna's here. What about that cake plate that Bertha brought?"

Anna realized that Vi must have been listening at the top of the steps because she replied immediately, "I'll be right down with it."

Soon she was bustling down the steps carrying a package. She put it on the counter and opened it. "Here now! What do ya think of that? Pretty nice isn't it?"

"Oh, it's beautiful," replied Anna. "I had no idea she would have one ready so quickly."

"Oh I think she has a few on hand," came Vi's reply. "Bertha said if you don't like this one then she'll take it back and bring another."

"Oh I love this one. Now to get it into the house without Milly seeing it. But I think I can manage. I want to buy some film for my new Kodak Brownie. Liza said you had some. That'll give me enough parcels so I can get up to my room without her guessing. And I also want to get a can of Peter's favorite pipe tobacco for him."

"That's Dad's department," Vi admitted. "Say Dad, get on out here will ya. I've got to get upstairs an' finish dinner. Ed can help you with the film, but Dad knows more about what kind of tobacco people like."

"You go back upstairs Ma," said Ed. "Don't want that dinner to burn." And Vi trundled off up the steps.

Elmer appeared from the back room. "Gettin' so dark back there a body can't see," he confessed. "Anyway, what can I get for you Anna? Don't tell me Ed and Ma couldn't fill your order."

"I want a tin of pipe tobacco for Peter, for Christmas that is. I know it's early, but I usually come to the store with them, and this time I'm alone, so I can get it. I also need film for my new Brownie camera."

Quickly Elmer reached up and got what he thought would be a little more special than the kind Peter usually bought. Anna was pleased, so as he wrapped the plate, the film and the tobacco, they continued the pleasant visit. Anna paid him, and soon was on her way thinking how wonderful it was that life had now returned to normal and they could enjoy the holidays without the specter of doom hanging over them.

Each day now when Anna and Davey came into the house after school a new and delicious odor awaited them. Christmas baking was being done on a grand scale. Inger had accumulated more cooking irons and tins than Milly, so there was an almost daily exchange of these items. Rosettes, krumkake, sandbakkelse, abelskiver and spritz were made with them and carefully stored for the week or two of celebration. Lefse, fattigman and yulekake were other treats that Milly was preparing. She had saved her butter and egg money for items as raisins, nuts and extra sugar. This was a special time indeed and a festival that everyone looked forward to. Anna had never seen the like of it. "I want to have most of the baking done by the end of next week, because the week before Christmas I will have to clean the house," she announced. Little did Anna realize what Milly meant by cleaning. Anna thought the house was spotless, but this cleaning was a scrubbing of floors, furniture and anything scrubbable.

On Tuesday evening, December 12th Milly and Anna were busy getting ready for Lucia. Milly didn't have a written recipe for Lucia buns and as Anna had promised to help Sarah make them, Milly was constantly standing by to make sure they were done correctly.

Milly had made a crown of small willow branches, with various leaves poked into it, including some evergreen leaves. Neither she nor Anna knew the names of them, but it didn't matter, they made a beautiful crown. They decided to let Sarah carry a candle instead of having some in the crown. Both

Milly and Anna knew that a lighted candle on a little girl's head would be courting disaster.

"If I could have only made a better one," Milly said. "Then maybe it would have been strong enough to hold some candles, but never mind. We will have our first Lucia, and I am so proud." To make a robe-type dress for Sarah, Milly took a 100 pound flour sack which was mostly white and cut out a neck and armholes. It served the purpose beautifully.

Sarah was asleep when the buns came out of the oven, so Anna put them aside, and hoped she would wake up early enough to bring off this whole event. Peter had promised to stay in bed until they finished and then do the milking. That night he banked the fire and put coffee water on the stove. It would probably still be hot in the morning.

Anna woke from a sound sleep as she heard someone in the kitchen. She looked at her watch. It was 4:30. Looking through the register she could barely make out Milly's figure. Of course, she was adding plenty of corn cobs to make a hot fire as she was making coffee so it would be ready for the Lucia party.

At five o'clock Anna got up, dressed, and quietly went to Sarah's room. The child was so sleepy, but they splashed cold water on her face and once she realized that this was Lucia day she became fairly perky. Anna dressed Sarah in the Lucia gown, which being without sleeves was a little chilly, but they soon were downstairs into the warm kitchen. The coffee being made, thanks to Milly, Anna poured two cups full, added cream and sugar, and put them on a small tray. She also put on it a small plate of the Lucia buns and gave Sarah a lighted candle to hold. Sarah took the candle in her left hand, and knocked on the door of her parents' bedroom before they entered. Anna held the tray, although Sarah occasionally gripped it with her free hand.

Milly and Peter pretended to be asleep. Anna had to coax Sarah to wish them a happy Lucia, at which point they awakened, sat up in bed next to pillows propped against the head of the bed, and thanked her for such a lovely treat. Milly was thrilled to tears, Anna got a cup of coffee for herself, Sarah ate a Lucia bun, and Lucy slept through the entire affair.

That afternoon there was a party for Lucy for her first birthday. Inger's family came, as well as Sylvia and Erica Larson and Mrs. Schmidt. Lucy wore the bib that Anna gave her and was in general unaware of all the attention she was receiving. She spent most of the time banging her spoon against the tray of her high chair and laughing at all the commotion she was making. Milly served some of the precious Christmas cookies. Anna took them all outside while she took several photos. It was a wonderful beginning for the Christmas season. More snow began to fall that night.

The following Sunday, December 17th, they drove to church in the sleigh, cramming everyone in. The horses were stabled in the church barn with blankets thrown over them, and fed the hay which had been in the sleigh. When they entered the church they saw it had been decorated. In the windows were homemade candles of fat which were to be lighted for the service. Someone had decorated the front wall with green boughs. For the next Sunday, December 24th, the decorations would be even more special as a farmer had promised to find an evergreen tree. There weren't too many evergreens in this part of the state.

Anna, Milly and the children went downstairs for Sunday School. Even though the stove had been lit quite early, it was so cold that they kept on their coats. The piano keys were like ice, and for once Anna played with her gloves on. It didn't help the playing, but as she said later, it saved her from frostbite. Everyone was in a cheery mood, and they sang many more songs than usual, the songs being Christmas carols.

By the time they arrived upstairs the candles had been lit, and it was beautiful. More Christmas carols were sung, followed by a thoughtful sermon. Anna wished she could be here for the service the next Sunday. She felt such a part of this community.

This was the time of year when it was hard on the minister. He had to get out his horses and his sleigh, so that he could go on to Brewster and Langton. Walter and William hitched up the team so they would be ready when he had finished a quick lunch. Jonah insisted on going with him, saying that the weather was none too good, and while Rev. Blakeley protested, his protest was a mild one, and Mrs. Blakeley happily invited him in to lunch, relieved that her husband would not have to be out alone.

At school Anna and the children were busy this week before Christmas preparing a Christmas program that all the families were invited to attend. First the younger children wrote letters to Santa Claus, and everyone brought home an invitation to the event, which was to be held Friday afternoon at two o'clock. Victoria Pearson's father was able to find a tree which they decorated with red and green paper chains and popcorn. They also strung paper chains from one corner of the room to the other. Anna had gotten some clay from the county and so each child made a candle holder as a gift for his or her parents and brought ten cents from home to buy a candle. Anna also purchased a small present for each child with Vi Marson helping her select the gifts. Elmer Marson had a Santa Claus suit and so promised to do his usual turn at being Santa Claus. Then there was the preparation of the songs and the Christmas play. It was exhausting but exciting.

Milly was also busy, cleaning house with a vengeance. The only time she seemed to rest was after school when they sat down for a cup of coffee and some cake or cookies. On Wednesday they heard Peter stamping his feet more than usual on the back porch, and then stopping in the entryway a rather long time. "What's going on?" asked Milly as she opened the kitchen door.

"I know it's a little early, but I found us a Christmas tree. Just happened to be down near the river and found this gooseberry bush. It's pretty big, and I think it will do fine. We can pop some popcorn and string it up like we did last year."

"Oh! It's wonderful," cooed Milly. "There aren't any evergreen trees around here, and I so want a Christmas tree."

"Well, this may be more of a Christmas bush, but anyway we'll decorate it and it'll look fine. I'll get a bucket and fill it with sand, to make it higher. Then it should be at least four feet."

"I have some paper and colored crayons," said Anna. "Tonight the children and I will make some Christmas ornaments to hang on the tree. We are already making some at school so Davey will know how."

"That would be so nice. And Peter if you could bring in some clean straw, we could make some decorations," Milly suggested. "It will be yust like at home. Oh I don't mean home, I mean Sweden," and she waved her hands in front of her face and shook her head to clear out the cobwebby images of Christmas time in the old country. "We can all sit around the table and make straw stars and horses and oh yes angels and so many things. Have you made them before Anna?"

"No I haven't. I've seen them, but they look so difficult to make."

"Oh no, they're easy," Milly responded. "I'll call Inger and she and Mabel can come down tomorrow after school and we can make them then," and she quickly went to the phone, rang three long rings, and before too long the matter was settled.

"Guess I'd better start looking for some good clean straw first thing tomorrow morning," said Peter," or I won't be a very popular person around here. Anyway, it'll get me out of the house and the housecleaning."

Thus Wednesday evening Anna and the children made paper decorations for the tree. She even cut out strings of little paper dolls to put in the pot of sand at the foot of the tree, as well as some for the branches.

Thursday at school they had the final rehearsal for the program as well as giving the room a good cleaning. In the evening Inger and Mabel came and everyone worked on making straw decorations. Milly was especially good at it, and had some bits of red material that she cut into ribbons so she could tie it on the straw figures, so they could hang them up. The adults worked on horses and angels, Mabel was particularly good at stars, while Sarah and Davey were more inventive and were not sure what to call their creations, except "decorations". Mabel promised to bring those she made to put on the tree at school if she could take them home after the program.

Friday afternoon was the big day at school. The room was filled nearly to overflowing with the families. The program went superbly. It ended with Santa Claus passing out presents and everyone singing Christmas carols and eating the cookies and little cakes which were brought from home. As the families walked home through the snow Anna could hear them singing. She went back to her desk to blow out the candles and realized that several students had left gifts for her.

Friday evening they popped corn and strung it in long strips to hang on the tree. After dinner Friday they decorated the tree. "I know it's a little early. We usually put up the tree on Christmas Eve, but I wanted you to see it Anna, so we will have an early Christmas Eve tonight." It was wonderful fun. They opened up the parlor. Milly put candles in each window and lighted them, and the tree was set in the corner between the windows. "We don't have room for any candles on the tree, but we don't need them," she decided. "Now let's have some coffee and cake in the parlor."

"While you're doing that," Anna said, "I'm going to go upstairs and get some things I have." She decided that this was the best time to bring down the gifts she had for the family. As she reentered the parlor all eyes were on her. She carefully placed the wrapped gifts under the tree. She had tried to make them look decorative by making designs on the brown paper, and it was effective. "I'm going to put this one on the table," she told them. "It's breakable so don't touch it. This way Lucy won't be able to get at it, since she's crawling around all over now."

"Oh Anna, you shouldn't have done that," Milly said with mild admonishment, which of course was the proper thing to do. "Now here's the coffee and cookies, and I have hot chocolate for you children as a special treat."

"Feel like I should put on my Sunday clothes, sitting in the parlor and all," laughed Peter.

"You do have a lovely parlor Milly," remarked Anna. "This is one of the nicest times I have ever had at Christmas."

"But you'll be going home. And then you'll have a wonderful time," Milly added.

"Yes, I will, but then I feel now that you are my family too. And I love to be with you. You have all been so wonderful to me, taking me in, a complete stranger," and Anna was becoming a little emotional.

"We have been so happy to have you here," added Milly.

"And don't forget, Mother will get a new ice box because of the money you're paying her," Davey chimed in.

"Oh Davey!" said his mother, horrified. And they all laughed, and it was a wonderful way to end an evening.

The next day Anna packed her valise and was ready by eleven o'clock to have Peter drive her to the station. She looked at her room and remembered the first time she saw it with the pink rose flowered wallpaper, the birdseye maple dresser and the brass bed with the golden wedding ring quilt. It had been her room for four months. The trunk she would leave there for she didn't need to pack it home just for the short vacation. And it would be her room when she returned. She was fortunate that she would have a week off from school as they started on time in the fall and didn't have to make up any days.

She went downstairs. Milly had a package for her, and from the size of it she guessed that it was full of wonderful Christmas cookies and cakes. "Thank you so much Milly, for everything," she said almost tearfully. "You have been like a sister to me."

"Well, you won't be gone long, and we'll leave the tree up until you get back, so we can celebrate again. We always leave it up about two weeks."

Anna went into the entryway to put on her hat, coat and overshoes. Davey and Sarah were there doing the same.

"I told the children they could go too. I hope that's all right," said Milly.

"Oh, yes, I was hoping they could come and see me off," Anna added. "Well, I see your father now, so let's get going."

"I'll take your suitcase," said Davey as he struggled to get it down the stairs to the amusement of Anna and Milly.

"Good-bye Milly," Anna said, and reached over to give her a fond embrace which was warmly welcomed and reciprocated. "And do have a very merry Christmas."

"You too, Anna. And we'll see you in Yanuary. Oh dear! That's next year isn't it?" and they laughed again.

The ride to the train station was uneventful. They got there early and she bought her ticket. "I remember the first day you was here," Matt said as he handed her the ticket. "Remember Floyd an' Jimmy Burns, an' that big trunk a yours.

Glad to see you don't have it this time," and he chuckled at the thought of it.

Anna remembered also; seeing Floyd for the first time and wondering what she had gotten herself into. "Well, good-bye Matt. Have a nice Christmas, the same to Liza. I'll be back soon, and I promise I won't have another trunk."

They waited a while for the train. At first they could hear the whistle, then the sound of the engine, and the feel of the ground shaking.

"I wish I could go on a train," said Davey.

"Me too," said Sarah.

"Sometime maybe you can. Wouldn't that be fun," Anna added as the train chugged to a screeching stop. "Here's where I leave you." She shook hands with Peter, and gave each of the children a hug, then climbed on the first step. Peter handed her the valise, and she managed to put it on the top step, without damaging the cookies parcel which was in the other hand . Her purse was on her arm.

"Good-bye," she called as the porter put up the step and the train started off. She could hear their "good-byes" and see them waving for some distance until they disappeared.

The ride to Fort Dodge was very different from the ride she had taken in August. She found a seat next to a window, across from a middle-aged couple. She looked out. Snow covered the ground. It was cold outside. She could see only a few animals. It was a cloudy afternoon and occasionally she could glimpse a warm rectangle of light shining from a window, undoubtedly a kitchen window where preparations for the holiday were being made. Everyone was getting ready for Christmas. The train was fairly crowded, and a feeling of anticipated excitement filled the air. Her thoughts drifted to Grabney and Milly and Peter and the children and the Blakeleys and so many others. In four short months they had become such an important part of her life.

Coming out of her reverie she realized they were nearly to Fort Dodge. The train slowed then the brakes screeched. "Fort Dodge," bawled the conductor. Several people were getting off and she waited until the aisle was clear before she left.

She came down the steps hauling her valise in her right hand, and carrying the precious package of cookies in her left, with her purse still over her left arm. She heard a voice call, "Anna! Anna!" It was Elsa, dodging through passengers, running to meet her. She rushed up to Anna and threw her arms around her. "Oh Anna, it's so good to see you again. How have you been? Oh you look good."

Soon she saw her mother. Mrs. Swenson was walking quickly, careful not to brush up to anyone. "Oh Anna, you're home at last. I couldn't see you so I thought you might have missed the train. You were so long getting off. Here Elsa you take her valise."

"Anna how was it in Grabney? We loved getting your letters. Were they really nice people? Tell us all about it," Elsa chirped on merrily.

"Never mind Elsa," came Mrs. Swenson's voice. "Anna will have plenty of time to tell us later. Now Anna, did you buy a return ticket? Oh, you really wrinkled your coat sitting in the train. Let's hurry now. Uncle Lars is waiting for us. Oh, yes, he got reports that you were a good teacher. I'm glad of that. I just hope it wasn't too tiresome for you." And Anna knew she was home.

About the Author

Marianne Gutteridge was the daughter of an Iowa school teacher and a Montana rancher. Though she moved to Seattle as a child, she spent many extended vacations in Iowa and Montana during the 1930's where she became fascinated with the life-styles, language and customs of the people who lived there. She remembers using kerosene lanterns and getting their water from the well outside the house. Her mother said that this was no different from when she started teaching many years earlier.

After receiving her B.A. and her M.A. in English from the University of Washington, she became a teacher and started writing autobiographical material. She started a family history through nightly phone calls she had with her mother. Stillwater Runs Deep is the result of that research.

She is currently Production Manager and Choreographer for the Seattle Gilbert and Sullivan Society. She has three grown children and five grandchildren and resides with her husband, Gordon.

Order Form

To order additional copies of:

Stillwater Runs Deep

please send $14.95 plus $3.00
Shipping & Handling,
Washington residents please include 8.2% sales tax. Make
check or money order payable to:

Peanut Butter Publishing
226 2nd Ave W.
Seattle, WA 98119
(206) 281-5965

If you prefer to use VISA or Mastercard, please fill in your
card's number and expiration date. Please circle appropriate
card.

☐ ☐ ☐ ☐ ☐ ☐ ☐ ☐ ☐ ☐ ☐ ☐ ☐ ☐ ☐ ☐ ☐ ☐

Signature_____

exp. date_____
_____Copies @ $14.95 ea._____
$3.00 Shipping & Handling_____
Washington State residents add 8.2%_____
Total enclosed_____

Name_____
Address_____
City, State, Zip_____

Please list additional copies to be sent to other addresses on a
separate sheet.